The Editors

CHARLES E. MODLIN is Professor of English Emeritus at Virginia Polytechnic Institute and State University. He is the editor of *The Egg and Other Stories, Sherwood Anderson's Love Letters to Eleanor Copenhaver Anderson,* and *Sherwood Anderson: Selected Letters* and co-editor of *Southern Odyssey: Selected Writings by Sherwood Anderson* and *Sherwood Anderson: Centennial Studies.* He is co-editor of the *Sherwood Anderson Review* and author of many articles related to Sherwood Anderson.

RAY LEWIS WHITE was Distinguished Professor of English at Illinois State University. He is the author of *Gore Vidal* and *"Winesburg, Ohio": An Exploration.* He edited many books, including *The Achievement of Sherwood Anderson, Sherwood Anderson's Memoirs, Sherwood Anderson/Gertrude Stein, Sherwood Anderson's Secret Love Letters,* and *Sherwood Anderson's Winesburg, Ohio.* His articles on various aspects of American literature have been widely published.

WINESBURG, OHIO

AUTHORITATIVE TEXT
BACKGROUNDS AND CONTEXTS
CRITICISM

W. W. NORTON & COMPANY, INC.
Also Publishes

THE NORTON ANTHOLOGY OF AFRICAN AMERICAN LITERATURE
edited by Henry Louis Gates Jr. and Nellie Y. McKay et al.

THE NORTON ANTHOLOGY OF AMERICAN LITERATURE
edited by Nina Baym et al.

THE NORTON ANTHOLOGY OF CHILDREN'S LITERATURE
edited by Jack Zipes et al.

THE NORTON ANTHOLOGY OF CONTEMPORARY FICTION
edited by R. V. Cassill and Joyce Carol Oates

THE NORTON ANTHOLOGY OF ENGLISH LITERATURE
edited by M. H. Abrams and Stephen Greenblatt et al.

THE NORTON ANTHOLOGY OF LITERATURE BY WOMEN
edited by Sandra M. Gilbert and Susan Gubar

THE NORTON ANTHOLOGY OF MODERN AND CONTEMPORARY POETRY
edited by Jahan Ramazani, Richard Ellmann, and Robert O'Clair

THE NORTON ANTHOLOGY OF POETRY
edited by Margaret Ferguson, Mary Jo Salter, and Jon Stallworthy

THE NORTON ANTHOLOGY OF SHORT FICTION
edited by R. V. Cassill and Richard Bausch

THE NORTON ANTHOLOGY OF THEORY AND CRITICISM
edited by Vincent B. Leitch et al.

THE NORTON ANTHOLOGY OF WORLD LITERATURE
edited by Sarah Lawall et al.

THE NORTON FACSIMILE OF THE FIRST FOLIO OF SHAKESPEARE
prepared by Charlton Hinman

THE NORTON INTRODUCTION TO LITERATURE
edited by Alison Booth, J. Paul Hunter, and Kelly J. Mays

THE NORTON INTRODUCTION TO THE SHORT NOVEL
edited by Jerome Beaty

THE NORTON READER
edited by Linda H. Peterson and John C. Brereton

THE NORTON SAMPLER
edited by Thomas Cooley

THE NORTON SHAKESPEARE, BASED ON THE OXFORD EDITION
edited by Stephen Greenblatt et al.

For a complete list of Norton Critical Editions, visit
www.wwnorton.com/college/english/nce_home.htm

A NORTON CRITICAL EDITION

Sherwood Anderson

WINESBURG, OHIO

AUTHORITATIVE TEXT

BACKGROUNDS AND CONTEXTS

CRITICISM

Edited by

CHARLES E. MODLIN
VIRGINIA POLYTECHNIC INSTITUTE
AND STATE UNIVERSITY

and

RAY LEWIS WHITE
LATE OF
ILLINOIS STATE UNIVERSITY

W • W • NORTON & COMPANY • *New York* • *London*

This title is printed on permanent paper containing 30 percent
post-consumer waste recycled fiber.

Printed in the United States of America.

First Edition.

The text of this book is composed in Electra
with the display set in Bernhard Modern.
Composition by Binghamton Valley Composition.
Manufacturing by the Maple-Vail Book Manufacturing Group.

Library of Congress Cataloging-in-Publication Data

Anderson, Sherwood, 1876–1941
Winesburg, Ohio : an authoritative text, backgrounds and contexts,
criticism / Sherwood Anderson : edited by Charles E. Modlin and Ray
Lewis White.
p. cm. — (A Norton critical edition)
Includes bibliographical references.
1. Ohio—Social life and customs—Fiction. 2. City and town life—
Ohio—Fiction. 3. Anderson, Sherwood, 1876–1941. Winesburg, Ohio.
4. City and town life in literature. 5. Ohio—In literature.
I. Modlin, Charles E. II. White, Ray Lewis. III. Title.
PS3501.N4W578 1995
813'.52—dc20 95–10378

ISBN 0-393-96795-6 (paper)

W. W. Norton & Company, Inc., 500 Fifth Avenue, New York, N.Y. 10110
www.wwnorton.com

W. W. Norton & Company Ltd., Castle House, 75/76 Wells Street,
London W1T 3QT

2 3 4 5 6 7 8 9 0

Contents

Preface

Our intent in this Norton Critical Edition is to provide the reader with an accurate text of *Winesburg, Ohio* along with some of the best materials for understanding its origins, artistry, and place in American literary history. The map of Winesburg on p. 2 was drawn by Harald Toksvig for the first edition in 1919. The text is edited and annotated by Ray Lewis White from that edition. In "Backgrounds and Contexts" we have included selections from Anderson's letters and memoirs, which provide revealing glimpses into his writing of the stories and his own ideas about them, and a sampling of reviews (including a previously undiscovered one in the *New York Evening Post*) representing the mixed reactions to the book. In "Criticism" we have collected some of the most illuminating studies of *Winesburg* published in the last three decades. We have also included a chronology of Anderson's life, which lists his major publications, and a selected bibliography as a guide to further studies.

We are indebted to a host of Anderson scholars, especially David Anderson, Hilbert H. Campbell, Walter B. Rideout, Judy Jo Small, Welford D. Taylor, Kim Townsend, and Kenny J. Williams; also to Diana Haskell, Margaret Kulis and their staff at the Newberry Library, Jenny Bay, Patricia Powell, Marjorie Modlin, and our editor, Carol Bemis of W. W. Norton & Company.

Note on the Text

This Norton Critical Edition of *Winesburg, Ohio* is the first fully collated text of Sherwood Anderson's masterpiece to be published since the story cycle first appeared in print, on May 8, 1919. Having since 1915 written and (contrary to received opinion) *rewritten* his stories about Ohio village life in the 1890s, Anderson in 1918 submitted the probably untitled collection to B. W. Huebsch, a small-scale New York City publisher willing to encourage and accept unconventional and innovative fiction. Huebsch liked the author and the stories and, he claimed, himself entitled the work *Winesburg, Ohio*, with the subtitle (his or Anderson's) becoming *A Group of Tales of Ohio Small Town Life*.

Because no production materials such as the publisher's typescript or galley or page proofs have survived the editing and publishing process that Anderson's tales underwent in the Huebsch offices, the 1919 first edition of *Winesburg, Ohio* must serve as the basis for this bibliographically sound text. From this 1919 text the editor must determine the author's intentions for his words, a determination based on collation of the (rarely found) first printing (that of May 8, 1919) with the six (even more rarely found) reprintings of this text from the same plates through 1931 published by Huebsch and by his successor in 1925, the Viking Press. Collation reveals only a very few emendations made to the printing plates as the years passed, changes including removal of an obtrusive preposition and correction of some verb-agreement errors. In sum, no actual rewriting by Anderson took place after his book first appeared. Thus the present text of *Winesburg, Ohio* is the seventh (1931) reprinting of the 1919 first edition, a text supplemented by occasional editorial corrections of grammar, punctuation, and contradictory spelling.

Minimal annotation is needed, for Anderson's story cycle is practically hermetic, a world almost separate from the political, economic, military, industrial, and even literary contexts of its setting in the Ohio of the 1890s or the environment of its creator in the Chicago of the 1910s. Thus basic notes are required to identify such persons as William McKinley, Mark Hanna, Charles Lamb, and Benvenuto Cellini; such an entity as the Epworth League; and (rarely) such customs and artifacts as may be unfamiliar to the present-day reader.

RAY LEWIS WHITE

The Text of WINESBURG, OHIO

A Group of Tales of Ohio Small Town Life

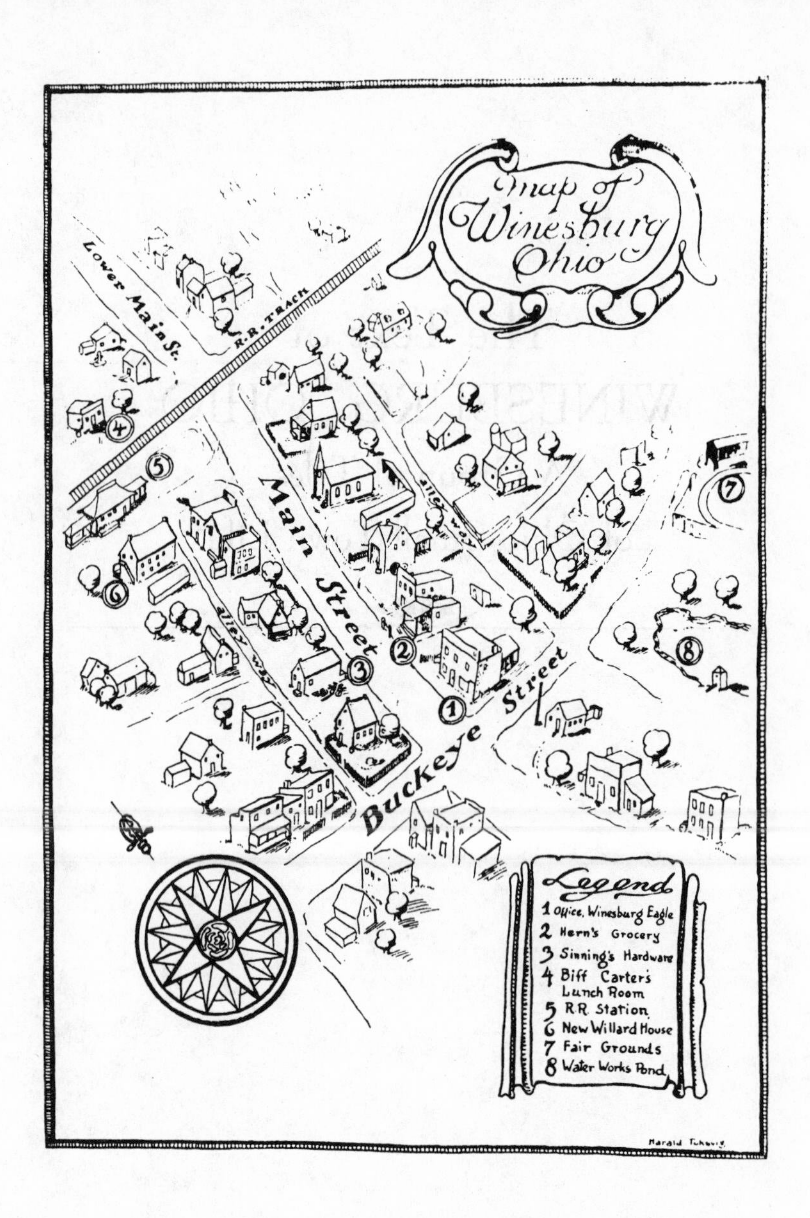
Map of Winesburg Ohio
Lower Main St.
R.R. TRACK
Main Street
alley way
alley way
Buckeye Street
Legend
1 Office, Winesburg Eagle
2 Hern's Grocery
3 Sinning's Hardware
4 Biff Carter's Lunch Room
5 R.R. Station
6 New Willard House
7 Fair Grounds
8 Water Works Pond
Harald Toksvig

The Tales and the Persons

The Book of the Grotesque

The writer, an old man with a white mustache, had some difficulty in getting into bed. The windows of the house in which he lived were high and he wanted to look at the trees when he awoke in the morning. A carpenter came to fix the bed so that it would be on a level with the window.

Quite a fuss was made about the matter. The carpenter, who had been a soldier in the Civil War, came into the writer's room and sat down to talk of building a platform for the purpose of raising the bed. The writer had cigars lying about and the carpenter smoked.

For a time the two men talked of the raising of the bed and then they talked of other things. The soldier got on the subject of the war. The writer, in fact, led him to that subject. The carpenter had once been a prisoner in Andersonville prison and had lost a brother.[1] The brother had died of starvation, and whenever the carpenter got upon that subject he cried. He, like the old writer, had a white mustache, and when he cried he puckered up his lips and the mustache bobbed up and down. The weeping old man with the cigar in his mouth was ludicrous. The plan the writer had for the raising of his bed was forgotten and later the carpenter did it in his own way and the writer, who was past sixty, had to help himself with a chair when he went to bed at night.

In his bed the writer rolled over on his side and lay quite still. For years he had been beset with notions concerning his heart. He was a hard smoker and his heart fluttered. The idea had got into his mind that he would some time die unexpectedly and always when he got into bed he thought of that. It did not alarm him. The effect in fact was quite a special thing and not easily explained. It made him more alive, there in bed, than at any other time. Perfectly still he lay and his body was old and not of much use any more, but something inside him was altogether young. He was like a pregnant woman, only that the thing inside him was not a baby but a youth. No, it wasn't a youth, it was a woman, young, and wearing a coat of mail like a knight. It is absurd, you see, to try to tell what was inside the old writer as he lay on his high bed and listened to the fluttering of his heart. The thing to get at is what the writer, or the young thing within the writer, was thinking about.

The old writer, like all of the people in the world, had got, during his long life, a great many notions in his head. He had once been quite handsome and a number of women had been in love with him. And then, of course, he had known people, many people, known them in a

1. During the American Civil War (1861–65), Confederate military forces imprisoned thousands of Union soldiers near Andersonville, Georgia. In 1864–65, over 13,000 of these prisoners died from starvation and brutality; upon the war's end, the camp commander was hanged by the Union powers.

peculiarly intimate way that was different from the way in which you and I know people. At least that is what the writer thought and the thought pleased him. Why quarrel with an old man concerning his thoughts?

In the bed the writer had a dream that was not a dream. As he grew somewhat sleepy but was still conscious, figures began to appear before his eyes. He imagined the young indescribable thing within himself was driving a long procession of figures before his eyes.

You see the interest in all this lies in the figures that went before the eyes of the writer. They were all grotesques. All of the men and women the writer had ever known had become grotesques.[2]

The grotesques were not all horrible. Some were amusing, some almost beautiful, and one, a woman all drawn out of shape, hurt the old man by her grotesqueness. When she passed he made a noise like a small dog whimpering. Had you come into the room you might have supposed the old man had unpleasant dreams or perhaps indigestion.

For an hour the procession of grotesques passed before the eyes of the old man, and then, although it was a painful thing to do, he crept out of bed and began to write. Some one of the grotesques had made a deep impression on his mind and he wanted to describe it.

At his desk the writer worked for an hour. In the end he wrote a book which he called "The Book of the Grotesque."[3] It was never published, but I saw it once and it made an indelible impression on my mind. The book had one central thought that is very strange and has always remained with me. By remembering it I have been able to understand many people and things that I was never able to understand before. The thought was involved but a simple statement of it would be something like this:

That in the beginning when the world was young there were a great many thoughts but no such thing as a truth. Man made the truths himself and each truth was a composite of a great many vague thoughts. All about in the world were the truths and they were all beautiful.

The old man had listed hundreds of the truths in his book. I will not try to tell you of all of them. There was the truth of virginity and the truth of passion, the truth of wealth and of poverty, of thrift and of profligacy, of carefulness and abandon. Hundreds and hundreds were the truths and they were all beautiful.

And then the people came along. Each as he appeared snatched up one of the truths and some who were quite strong snatched up a dozen of them.

It was the truths that made the people grotesques. The old man had

2. *Grotesque* derives from *grotto*, because on the walls of grottos (or caves) ancient artists sometimes drew human figures that were distorted, exaggerated, or ugly, at least by later standards of beauty.
3. No such writer or book ever existed to impress Anderson, who invents them here to serve as the implied inspiration for his theory of human character and imaginative writing.

quite an elaborate theory concerning the matter. It was his notion that the moment one of the people took one of the truths to himself, called it his truth, and tried to live his life by it, he became a grotesque and the truth he embraced became a falsehood.

You can see for yourself how the old man, who had spent all of his life writing and was filled with words, would write hundreds of pages concerning this matter. The subject would become so big in his mind that he himself would be in danger of becoming a grotesque. He didn't, I suppose, for the same reason that he never published the book. It was the young thing inside him that saved the old man.

Concerning the old carpenter who fixed the bed for the writer, I only mentioned him because he, like many of what are called very common people, became the nearest thing to what is understandable and lovable of all the grotesques in the writer's book.

Winesburg, Ohio

Hands

Upon the half decayed veranda of a small frame house that stood near the edge of a ravine near the town of Winesburg, Ohio, a fat little old man walked nervously up and down. Across a long field that had been seeded for clover but that had produced only a dense crop of yellow mustard weeds, he could see the public highway along which went a wagon filled with berry pickers returning from the fields. The berry pickers, youths and maidens, laughed and shouted boisterously. A boy clad in a blue shirt leaped from the wagon and attempted to drag after him one of the maidens who screamed and protested shrilly. The feet of the boy in the road kicked up a cloud of dust that floated across the face of the departing sun. Over the long field came a thin girlish voice. "Oh, you Wing Biddlebaum, comb your hair, it's falling into your eyes," commanded the voice to the man, who was bald and whose nervous little hands fiddled about the bare white forehead as though arranging a mass of tangled locks.

Wing Biddlebaum, forever frightened and beset by a ghostly band of doubts, did not think of himself as in any way a part of the life of the town where he had lived for twenty years. Among all the people of Winesburg but one had come close to him. With George Willard, son of Tom Willard, the proprietor of the New Willard House, he had formed something like a friendship. George Willard was the reporter on the *Winesburg Eagle* and sometimes in the evenings he walked out along the highway to Wing Biddlebaum's house. Now as the old man walked up and down on the veranda, his hands moving nervously about, he was hoping that George Willard would come and spend the evening with him. After the wagon containing the berry pickers had passed, he went across the field through the tall mustard weeds and climbing a rail fence peered anxiously along the road to the town. For a moment he stood thus, rubbing his hands together and looking up and down the road, and then, fear overcoming him, ran back to walk again upon the porch on his own house.

In the presence of George Willard, Wing Biddlebaum, who for twenty years had been the town mystery, lost something of his timidity, and his shadowy personality, submerged in a sea of doubts, came forth to look at the world. With the young reporter at his side, he ventured in the light of day into Main Street or strode up and down on the rickety front porch of his own house, talking excitedly. The voice that had been low and trembling became shrill and loud. The bent figure straightened. With a kind of wriggle, like a fish returned to the brook by the fisherman, Biddlebaum the silent began to talk, striving to put into words the ideas that had been accumulated by his mind during long years of silence.

Wing Biddlebaum talked much with his hands. The slender expressive fingers, forever active, forever striving to conceal themselves in his pockets or behind his back, came forth and became the piston rods of his machinery of expression.

The story of Wing Biddlebaum is a story of hands. Their restless activity, like unto the beating of the wings of an imprisoned bird, had given him his name. Some obscure poet of the town had thought of it. The hands alarmed their owner. He wanted to keep them hidden away and looked with amazement at the quiet inexpressive hands of other men who worked beside him in the fields, or passed, driving sleepy teams on country roads.

When he talked to George Willard, Wing Biddlebaum closed his fists and beat with them upon a table or on the walls of his house. The action made him more comfortable. If the desire to talk came to him when the two were walking in the fields, he sought out a stump or the top board of a fence and with his hands pounding busily talked with renewed ease.

The story of Wing Biddlebaum's hands is worth a book in itself. Sympathetically set forth it would tap many strange, beautiful qualities in obscure men. It is a job for a poet. In Winesburg the hands had attracted attention merely because of their activity. With them Wing Biddlebaum had picked as high as a hundred and forty quarts of strawberries in a day. They became his distinguishing feature, the source of his fame. Also they made more grotesque an already grotesque and elusive individuality. Winesburg was proud of the hands of Wing Biddlebaum in the same spirit in which it was proud of Banker White's new stone house and Wesley Moyer's bay stallion, Tony Tip, that had won the two-fifteen trot at the fall races in Cleveland.

As for George Willard, he had many times wanted to ask about the hands. At times an almost overwhelming curiosity had taken hold of him. He felt that there must be a reason for their strange activity and their inclination to keep hidden away and only a growing respect for Wing Biddlebaum kept him from blurting out the questions that were often in his mind.

Once he had been on the point of asking. The two were walking in the fields on a summer afternoon and had stopped to sit upon a grassy bank. All afternoon Wing Biddlebaum had talked as one inspired. By a fence he had stopped and beating like a giant woodpecker upon the top board had shouted at George Willard, condemning his tendency to be too much influenced by the people about him. "You are destroying yourself," he cried. "You have the inclination to be alone and to dream and you are afraid of dreams. You want to be like others in town here. You hear them talk and you try to imitate them."

On the grassy bank Wing Biddlebaum had tried again to drive his point home. His voice became soft and reminiscent, and with a sigh of contentment he launched into a long rambling talk, speaking as one lost in a dream.

Out of the dream Wing Biddlebaum made a picture for George Willard. In the picture men lived again in a kind of pastoral golden age. Across a green open country came clean-limbed young men, some afoot, some mounted upon horses. In crowds the young men came to gather about the feet of an old man who sat beneath a tree in a tiny garden and who talked to them.[1]

Wing Biddlebaum became wholly inspired. For once he forgot the hands. Slowly they stole forth and lay upon George Willard's shoulders. Something new and bold came into the voice that talked. "You must try to forget all you have learned," said the old man. "You must begin to dream. From this time on you must shut your ears to the roaring of the voices."

Pausing in his speech, Wing Biddlebaum looked long and earnestly at George Willard. His eyes glowed. Again he raised the hands to caress the boy and then a look of horror swept over his face.

With a convulsive movement of his body, Wing Biddlebaum sprang to his feet and thrust his hands deep into his trousers pockets. Tears came to his eyes. "I must be getting along home. I can talk no more with you," he said nervously.

Without looking back, the old man had hurried down the hillside and across a meadow, leaving George Willard perplexed and frightened upon the grassy slope. With a shiver of dread the boy arose and went along the road toward town. "I'll not ask him about his hands," he thought, touched by the memory of the terror he had seen in the man's eyes. "There's something wrong, but I don't want to know what it is. His hands have something to do with his fear of me and of everyone."

And George Willard was right. Let us look briefly into the story of the hands. Perhaps our talking of them will arouse the poet who will tell the hidden wonder story of the influence for which the hands were but fluttering pennants of promise.

In his youth Wing Biddlebaum had been a school teacher in a town

1. The unnamed teacher of young men whom Biddlebaum describes is probably either Socrates (470?–399 B.C.), the Greek philosopher who suffered death for questioning the bases of Athenian society, or Plato (427?–347 B.C.), student of Socrates who established the idea of a college or a university through teaching young Greek men in a grove of trees in Athens.

in Pennsylvania. He was not then known as Wing Biddlebaum, but went by the less euphonic name of Adolph Myers. As Adolph Myers he was much loved by the boys of his school.

Adolph Myers was meant by nature to be a teacher of youth. He was one of those rare, little-understood men who rule by a power so gentle that it passes as a lovable weakness. In their feeling for the boys under their charge such men are not unlike the finer sort of women in their love of men.

And yet that is but crudely stated. It needs the poet there. With the boys of his school, Adolph Myers had walked in the evening or had sat talking until dusk upon the schoolhouse steps lost in a kind of dream. Here and there went his hands, caressing the shoulders of the boys, playing about the tousled heads. As he talked his voice became soft and musical. There was a caress in that also. In a way the voice and the hands, the stroking of the shoulders and the touching of the hair was a part of the school-master's effort to carry a dream into the young minds. By the caress that was in his fingers he expressed himself. He was one of those men in whom the force that creates life is diffused, not centralized. Under the caress of his hands doubt and disbelief went out of the minds of the boys and they began also to dream.

And then the tragedy. A half-witted boy of the school became enamored of the young master. In his bed at night he imagined unspeakable things and in the morning went forth to tell his dreams as facts. Strange, hideous accusations fell from his loose-hung lips. Through the Pennsylvania town went a shiver. Hidden, shadowy doubts that had been in men's minds concerning Adolph Myers were galvanized into beliefs.

The tragedy did not linger. Trembling lads were jerked out of bed and questioned. "He put his arms about me," said one. "His fingers were always playing in my hair," said another.

One afternoon a man of the town, Henry Bradford, who kept a saloon, came to the schoolhouse door. Calling Adolph Myers into the school yard he began to beat him with his fists. As his hard knuckles beat down into the frightened face of the schoolmaster, his wrath became more and more terrible. Screaming with dismay, the children ran here and there like disturbed insects. "I'll teach you to put your hands on my boy, you beast," roared the saloon keeper, who, tired of beating the master, had begun to kick him about the yard.

Adolph Myers was driven from the Pennsylvania town in the night. With lanterns in their hands a dozen men came to the door of the house where he lived alone and commanded that he dress and come forth. It was raining and one of the men had a rope in his hands. They had intended to hang the schoolmaster, but something in his figure, so small, white, and pitiful, touched their hearts and they let him escape. As he ran away into the darkness they repented of their weakness and ran after him, swearing and throwing sticks and great balls of soft mud at the figure that screamed and ran faster and faster into the darkness.

For twenty years Adolph Myers had lived alone in Winesburg. He was but forty but looked sixty-five. The name of Biddlebaum he got from a box of goods seen at a freight station as he hurried through an eastern Ohio town. He had an aunt in Winesburg, a black-toothed old woman who raised chickens, and with her he lived until she died. He had been ill for a year after the experience in Pennsylvania, and after his recovery worked as a day laborer in the fields, going timidly about and striving to conceal his hands. Although he did not understand what had happened he felt that the hands must be to blame. Again and again the fathers of the boys had talked of the hands. "Keep your hands to yourself," the saloon keeper had roared, dancing with fury in the schoolhouse yard.

Upon the veranda of his house by the ravine, Wing Biddlebaum continued to walk up and down until the sun had disappeared and the road beyond the field was lost in the grey shadows. Going into his house he cut slices of bread and spread honey upon them. When the rumble of the evening train that took away the express cars loaded with the day's harvest of berries had passed and restored the silence of the summer night, he went again to walk upon the veranda. In the darkness he could not see the hands and they became quiet. Although he still hungered for the presence of the boy, who was the medium through which he expressed his love of man, the hunger became again a part of his loneliness and his waiting. Lighting a lamp, Wing Biddlebaum washed the few dishes soiled by his simple meal and, setting up a folding cot by the screen door that led to the porch, prepared to undress for the night. A few stray white bread crumbs lay on the cleanly washed floor by the table; putting the lamp upon a low stool he began to pick up the crumbs, carrying them to his mouth one by one with unbelievable rapidity. In the dense blotch of light beneath the table, the kneeling figure looked like a priest engaged in some service of his church. The nervous expressive fingers, flashing in and out of the light, might well have been mistaken for the fingers of the devotee going swiftly through decade after decade of his rosary.

Paper Pills

He was an old man with a white beard and huge nose and hands. Long before the time during which we will know him, he was a doctor and drove a jaded white horse from house to house through the streets of Winesburg. Later he married a girl who had money. She had been left a large fertile farm when her father died. The girl was quiet, tall, and dark, and to many people she seemed very beautiful. Everyone in

Winesburg wondered why she married the doctor. Within a year after the marriage she died.

The knuckles of the doctor's hands were extraordinarily large. When the hands were closed they looked like clusters of unpainted wooden balls as large as walnuts fastened together by steel rods. He smoked a cob pipe and after his wife's death sat all day in his empty office close by a window that was covered with cobwebs. He never opened the window. Once on a hot day in August he tried but found it stuck fast and after that he forgot all about it.

Winesburg had forgotten the old man, but in Doctor Reefy there were the seeds of something very fine. Alone in his musty office in the Heffner Block[1] above the Paris Dry Goods Company's Store, he worked ceaselessly, building up something that he himself destroyed. Little pyramids of truth he erected and after erecting knocked them down again that he might have the truths to erect other pyramids.

Doctor Reefy was a tall man who had worn one suit of clothes for ten years. It was frayed at the sleeves and little holes had appeared at the knees and elbows. In the office he wore also a linen duster with huge pockets into which he continually stuffed scraps of paper. After some weeks the scraps of paper became little hard round balls, and when the pockets were filled he dumped them out upon the floor. For ten years he had but one friend, another old man named John Spaniard who owned a tree nursery. Sometimes, in a playful mood, old Doctor Reefy took from his pockets a handful of the paper balls and threw them at the nursery man. "That is to confound you, you blithering old sentimentalist," he cried, shaking with laughter.

The story of Doctor Reefy and his courtship of the tall dark girl who became his wife and left her money to him is a very curious story. It is delicious, like the twisted little apples that grow in the orchards of Winesburg. In the fall one walks in the orchards and the ground is hard with frost underfoot. The apples have been taken from the trees by the pickers. They have been put in barrels and shipped to the cities where they will be eaten in apartments that are filled with books, magazines, furniture, and people. On the trees are only a few gnarled apples that the pickers have rejected. They look like the knuckles of Doctor Reefy's hands. One nibbles at them and they are delicious. Into a little round place at the side of the apple has been gathered all of its sweetness. One runs from tree to tree over the frosted ground picking the gnarled, twisted apples and filling his pockets with them. Only the few know the sweetness of the twisted apples.

The girl and Doctor Reefy began their courtship on a summer afternoon. He was forty-five then and already he had begun the practice of filling his pockets with the scraps of paper that became hard balls and

1. *Block* referred to a long building two or three stories high, with spaces to be rented to offices or retail stores.

were thrown away. The habit had been formed as he sat in his buggy behind the jaded grey horse and went slowly along country roads. On the papers were written thoughts, ends of thoughts, beginnings of thoughts.

One by one the mind of Doctor Reefy had made the thoughts. Out of many of them he formed a truth that arose gigantic in his mind. The truth clouded the world. It became terrible and then faded away and the little thoughts began again.

The tall dark girl came to see Doctor Reefy because she was in the family way and had become frightened. She was in that condition because of a series of circumstances also curious.

The death of her father and mother and the rich acres of land that had come down to her had set a train of suitors on her heels. For two years she saw suitors almost every evening. Except two they were all alike. They talked to her of passion and there was a strained eager quality in their voices and in their eyes when they looked at her. The two who were different were much unlike each other. One of them, a slender young man with white hands, the son of a jeweler in Winesburg, talked continually of virginity. When he was with her he was never off the subject. The other, a black-haired boy with large ears, said nothing at all but always managed to get her into the darkness where he began to kiss her.

For a time the tall dark girl thought she would marry the jeweler's son. For hours she sat in silence listening as he talked to her and then she began to be afraid of something. Beneath his talk of virginity she began to think there was a lust greater than in all the others. At times it seemed to her that as he talked he was holding her body in his hands. She imagined him turning it slowly about in the white hands and staring at it. At night she dreamed that he had bitten into her body and that his jaws were dripping. She had the dream three times, then she became in the family way to the one who said nothing at all but who in the moment of his passion actually did bite her shoulder so that for days the marks of his teeth showed.

After the tall dark girl came to know Doctor Reefy it seemed to her that she never wanted to leave him again. She went into his office one morning and without her saying anything he seemed to know what had happened to her.

In the office of the doctor there was a woman, the wife of the man who kept the bookstore in Winesburg. Like all old-fashioned country practitioners, Doctor Reefy pulled teeth, and the woman who waited held a handkerchief to her teeth and groaned. Her husband was with her and when the tooth was taken out they both screamed and blood ran down on the woman's white dress. The tall dark girl did not pay any attention. When the woman and the man had gone the doctor smiled. "I will take you driving into the country with me," he said.

For several weeks the tall dark girl and the doctor were together almost every day. The condition that had brought her to him passed in an illness, but she was like one who has discovered the sweetness of the twisted apples, she could not get her mind fixed again upon the round perfect fruit that is eaten in the city apartments. In the fall after the beginning of her acquaintanceship with him she married Doctor Reefy and in the following spring she died. During the winter he read to her all of the odds and ends of thoughts he had scribbled on the bits of paper. After he had read them he laughed and stuffed them away in his pockets to become round hard balls.

Mother

Elizabeth Willard, the mother of George Willard, was tall and gaunt and her face was marked with smallpox scars. Although she was but forty-five, some obscure disease had taken the fire out of her figure. Listlessly she went about the disorderly old hotel looking at the faded wall-paper and the ragged carpets and, when she was able to be about, doing the work of a chambermaid among beds soiled by the slumbers of fat traveling men. Her husband, Tom Willard, a slender, graceful man with square shoulders, a quick military step, and a black mustache, trained to turn sharply up at the ends, tried to put the wife out of his mind. The presence of the tall ghostly figure, moving slowly through the halls, he took as a reproach to himself. When he thought of her he grew angry and swore. The hotel was unprofitable and forever on the edge of failure and he wished himself out of it. He thought of the old house and the woman who lived there with him as things defeated and done for. The hotel in which he had begun life so hopefully was now a mere ghost of what a hotel should be. As he went spruce and business-like through the streets of Winesburg, he sometimes stopped and turned quickly about as though fearing that the spirit of the hotel and of the woman would follow him even into the streets. "Damn such a life, damn it!" he sputtered aimlessly.

Tom Willard had a passion for village politics and for years had been the leading Democrat in a strongly Republican community. Some day, he told himself, the tide of things political will turn in my favor and the years of ineffectual service count big in the bestowal of rewards. He dreamed of going to Congress and even of becoming governor. Once when a younger member of the party arose at a political conference and began to boast of his faithful service, Tom Willard grew white with fury. "Shut up, you," he roared, glaring about. "What do you know of service? What are you but a boy? Look at what I've done here! I was a Democrat here in Winesburg when it was a crime to be a Democrat. In the old days they fairly hunted us with guns."

Between Elizabeth and her one son George there was a deep unexpressed bond of sympathy, based on a girlhood dream that had long ago died. In the son's presence she was timid and reserved, but sometimes while he hurried about town intent upon his duties as a reporter, she went into his room and closing the door knelt by a little desk, made of a kitchen table, that sat near a window. In the room by the desk she went through a ceremony that was half a prayer, half a demand, addressed to the skies. In the boyish figure she yearned to see something half forgotten that had once been a part of herself recreated. The prayer concerned that. "Even though I die, I will in some way keep defeat from you," she cried, and so deep was her determination that her whole body shook. Her eyes glowed and she clenched her fists. "If I am dead and see him becoming a meaningless drab figure like myself, I will come back," she declared. "I ask God now to give me that privilege. I demand it. I will pay for it. God may beat me with his fists. I will take any blow that may befall if but this my boy be allowed to express something for us both." Pausing uncertainly, the woman stared about the boy's room. "And do not let him become smart and successful either," she added vaguely.

The communion between George Willard and his mother was outwardly a formal thing without meaning. When she was ill and sat by the window in her room he sometimes went in the evening to make her a visit. They sat by a window that looked over the roof of a small frame building into Main Street. By turning their heads they could see, through another window, along an alleyway that ran behind the Main Street stores and into the back door of Abner Groff's bakery. Sometimes as they sat thus a picture of village life presented itself to them. At the back door of his shop appeared Abner Groff with a stick or an empty milk bottle in his hand. For a long time there was a feud between the baker and a grey cat that belonged to Sylvester West, the druggist. The boy and his mother saw the cat creep into the door of the bakery and presently emerge followed by the baker who swore and waved his arms about. The baker's eyes were small and red and his black hair and beard were filled with flour dust. Sometimes he was so angry that, although the cat had disappeared, he hurled sticks, bits of broken glass, and even some of the tools of his trade about. Once he broke a window at the back of Sinnings' Hardware Store. In the alley the grey cat crouched behind barrels filled with torn paper and broken bottles above which flew a black swarm of flies. Once when she was alone, and after watching a prolonged and ineffectual outburst on the part of the baker, Elizabeth Willard put her head down on her long white hands and wept. After that she did not look along the alleyway any more, but tried to forget the contest between the bearded man and the cat. It seemed like a rehearsal of her own life, terrible in its vividness.

In the evening when the son sat in the room with his mother, the silence made them both feel awkward. Darkness came on and the evening train came in at the station. In the street below feet tramped up and down upon a board sidewalk. In the station yard, after the evening train had gone, there was a heavy silence. Perhaps Skinner Leason, the express agent, moved a truck[1] the length of the station platform. Over on Main Street sounded a man's voice, laughing. The door of the express office banged. George Willard arose and crossing the room fumbled for the doorknob. Sometimes he knocked against a chair, making it scrape along the floor. By the window sat the sick woman, perfectly still, listless. Her long hands, white and bloodless, could be seen drooping over the ends of the arms of the chair. "I think you had better be out among the boys. You are too much indoors," she said, striving to relieve the embarrassment of the departure. "I thought I would take a walk," replied George Willard, who felt awkward and confused.

One evening in July, when the transient guests who made the New Willard House their temporary homes had become scarce, and the hallways, lighted only by kerosene lamps turned low, were plunged in gloom, Elizabeth Willard had an adventure. She had been ill in bed for several days and her son had not come to visit her. She was alarmed. The feeble blaze of life that remained in her body was blown into a flame by her anxiety and she crept out of bed, dressed and hurried along the hallway toward her son's room, shaking with exaggerated fears. As she went along she steadied herself with her hand, slipped along the papered walls of the hall and breathed with difficulty. The air whistled through her teeth. As she hurried forward she thought how foolish she was. "He is concerned with boyish affairs," she told herself. "Perhaps he has now begun to walk about in the evening with girls."

Elizabeth Willard had a dread of being seen by guests in the hotel that had once belonged to her father and the ownership of which still stood recorded in her name in the county courthouse. The hotel was continually losing patronage because of its shabbiness and she thought of herself as also shabby. Her own room was in an obscure corner and when she felt able to work she voluntarily worked among the beds, preferring the labor that could be done when the guests were abroad seeking trade among the merchants of Winesburg.

By the door of her son's room the mother knelt upon the floor and listened for some sound from within. When she heard the boy moving about and talking in low tones a smile came to her lips. George Willard had a habit of talking aloud to himself and to hear him doing so had always given his mother a peculiar pleasure. The habit in him, she felt, strengthened the secret bond that existed between them. A thousand times she had whispered to herself of the matter. "He is groping about, trying to find himself," she thought. "He is not a dull clod, all words

1. Before the automobile age, a *truck* was a large, heavy-wheeled container used for moving goods by hand.

and smartness. Within him there is a secret something that is striving to grow. It is the thing I let be killed in myself."

In the darkness in the hallway by the door the sick woman arose and started again toward her own room. She was afraid that the door would open and the boy come upon her. When she had reached a safe distance and was about to turn a corner into a second hallway she stopped and bracing herself with her hands waited, thinking to shake off a trembling fit of weakness that had come upon her. The presence of the boy in the room had made her happy. In her bed, during the long hours alone, the little fears that had visited her had become giants. Now they were all gone. "When I get back to my room I shall sleep," she murmured gratefully.

But Elizabeth Willard was not to return to her bed and to sleep. As she stood trembling in the darkness the door of her son's room opened and the boy's father, Tom Willard, stepped out. In the light that streamed out at the door he stood with the knob in his hand and talked. What he said infuriated the woman.

Tom Willard was ambitious for his son. He had always thought of himself as a successful man, although nothing he had ever done had turned out successfully. However, when he was out of sight of the New Willard House and had no fear of coming upon his wife, he swaggered and began to dramatize himself as one of the chief men of the town. He wanted his son to succeed. He it was who had secured for the boy the position on the *Winesburg Eagle*. Now, with a ring of earnestness in his voice, he was advising concerning some course of conduct. "I tell you what, George, you've got to wake up," he said sharply. "Will Henderson has spoken to me three times concerning the matter. He says you go along for hours not hearing when you are spoken to and acting like a gawky girl. What ails you?" Tom Willard laughed good-naturedly. "Well, I guess you'll get over it," he said. "I told Will that. You're not a fool and you're not a woman. You're Tom Willard's son and you'll wake up. I'm not afraid. What you say clears things up. If being a newspaper man had put the notion of becoming a writer into your mind that's all right. Only I guess you'll have to wake up to do that too, eh?"

Tom Willard went briskly along the hallway and down a flight of stairs to the office. The woman in the darkness could hear him laughing and talking with a guest who was striving to wear away a dull evening by dozing in a chair by the office door. She returned to the door of her son's room. The weakness had passed from her body as by a miracle and she stepped boldly along. A thousand ideas raced through her head. When she heard the scraping of a chair and the sound of a pen scratching upon paper, she again turned and went back along the hallway to her own room.

A definite determination had come into the mind of the defeated wife of the Winesburg hotel keeper. The determination was the result of long years of quiet and rather ineffectual thinking. "Now," she told herself, "I will act. There is something threatening my boy and I will ward it off." The fact that the conversation between Tom Willard and his son had been rather quiet and natural, as though an understanding existed between them, maddened her. Although for years she had hated her husband, her hatred had always before been a quite impersonal thing. He had been merely a part of something else that she hated. Now, and by the few words at the door, he had become the thing personified. In the darkness of her own room she clenched her fists and glared about. Going to a cloth bag that hung on a nail by the wall she took out a long pair of sewing scissors and held them in her hand like a dagger. "I will stab him," she said aloud. "He has chosen to be the voice of evil and I will kill him. When I have killed him something will snap within myself and I will die also. It will be a release for all of us."

In her girlhood and before her marriage with Tom Willard, Elizabeth had borne a somewhat shaky reputation in Winesburg. For years she had been what is called "stage-struck" and had paraded through the streets with traveling men guests at her father's hotel, wearing loud clothes and urging them to tell her of life in the cities out of which they had come. Once she startled the town by putting on men's clothes and riding a bicycle down Main Street.

In her own mind the tall dark girl had been in those days much confused. A great restlessness was in her and it expressed itself in two ways. First there was an uneasy desire for change, for some big definite movement to her life. It was this feeling that had turned her mind to the stage. She dreamed of joining some company and wandering over the world, seeing always new faces and giving something out of herself to all people. Sometimes at night she was quite beside herself with the thought, but when she tried to talk of the matter to the members of the theatrical companies that came to Winesburg and stopped at her father's hotel, she got nowhere. They did not seem to know what she meant, or if she did get something of her passion expressed, they only laughed. "It's not like that," they said. "It's as dull and uninteresting as this here. Nothing comes of it."

With the traveling men when she walked about with them, and later with Tom Willard, it was quite different. Always they seemed to understand and sympathize with her. On the side streets of the village, in the darkness under the trees, they took hold of her hand and she thought that something unexpressed in herself came forth and became a part of an unexpressed something in them.

And then there was the second expression of her restlessness. When that came she felt for a time released and happy. She did not blame the men who walked with her and later she did not blame Tom Willard. It was always the same, beginning with kisses and ending, after strange wild emotions, with peace and then sobbing repentance. When she sobbed she put her hand upon the face of the man and had always the same thought. Even though he were large and bearded she thought he had become suddenly a little boy. She wondered why he did not sob also.

In her room, tucked away in a corner of the old Willard House, Elizabeth Willard lighted a lamp and put it on a dressing table that stood by the door. A thought had come into her mind and she went to a closet and brought out a small square box and set it on the table. The box contained material for make-up and had been left with other things by a theatrical company that had once been stranded in Winesburg. Elizabeth Willard had decided that she would be beautiful. Her hair was still black and there was a great mass of it braided and coiled about her head. The scene that was to take place in the office below began to grow in her mind. No ghostly worn-out figure should confront Tom Willard, but something quite unexpected and startling. Tall and with dusky cheeks and hair that fell in a mass from her shoulders, a figure should come striding down the stairway before the startled loungers in the hotel office. The figure would be silent—it would be swift and terrible. As a tigress whose cub had been threatened would she appear, coming out of the shadows, stealing noiselessly along and holding the long wicked scissors in her hand.

With a little broken sob in her throat, Elizabeth Willard blew out the light that stood upon the table and stood weak and trembling in the darkness. The strength that had been as a miracle in her body left and she half reeled across the floor, clutching at the back of the chair in which she had spent so many long days staring out over the tin roofs into the main street of Winesburg. In the hallway there was the sound of footsteps and George Willard came in at the door. Sitting in a chair beside his mother he began to talk. "I'm going to get out of here," he said. "I don't know where I shall go or what I shall do but I am going away."

The woman in the chair waited and trembled. An impulse came to her. "I suppose you had better wake up," she said. "You think that? You will go to the city and make money, eh? It will be better for you, you think, to be a business man, to be brisk and smart and alive?" She waited and trembled.

The son shook his head. "I suppose I can't make you understand, but oh, I wish I could," he said earnestly. "I can't even talk to father about it. I don't try. There isn't any use. I don't know what I shall do. I just want to go away and look at people and think."

Silence fell upon the room where the boy and woman sat together. Again, as on the other evenings, they were embarrassed. After a time the boy tried again to talk. "I suppose it won't be for a year or two but I've been thinking about it," he said, rising and going toward the door.

"Something father said makes it sure that I shall have to go away." He fumbled with the door knob. In the room the silence became unbearable to the woman. She wanted to cry out with joy because of the words that had come from the lips of her son, but the expression of joy had become impossible to her. "I think you had better go out among the boys. You are too much indoors," she said. "I thought I would go for a little walk," replied the son stepping awkwardly out of the room and closing the door.

The Philosopher

Doctor Parcival was a large man with a drooping mouth covered by a yellow mustache. He always wore a dirty white waistcoat out of the pockets of which protruded a number of the kind of black cigars known as stogies. His teeth were black and irregular and there was something strange about his eyes. The lid of the left eye twitched; it fell down and snapped up; it was exactly as though the lid of the eye were a window shade and someone stood inside the doctor's head playing with the cord.

Doctor Parcival had a liking for the boy, George Willard. It began when George had been working for a year on the *Winesburg Eagle* and the acquaintanceship was entirely a matter of the doctor's own making.

In the late afternoon Will Henderson, owner and editor of the *Eagle*, went over to Tom Willy's saloon. Along an alleyway he went and slipping in at the back door of the saloon began drinking a drink made of a combination of sloe gin and soda water. Will Henderson was a sensualist and had reached the age of forty-five. He imagined the gin renewed the youth in him. Like most sensualists he enjoyed talking of women, and for an hour he lingered about gossiping with Tom Willy. The saloon keeper was a short, broad-shouldered man with peculiarly marked hands. That flaming kind of birthmark that sometimes paints with red the faces of men and women had touched with red Tom Willy's fingers and the backs of his hands. As he stood by the bar talking to Will Henderson he rubbed the hands together. As he grew more and more excited the red of his fingers deepened. It was as though the hands had been dipped in blood that had dried and faded.

As Will Henderson stood at the bar looking at the red hands and talking of women, his assistant, George Willard, sat in the office of the *Winesburg Eagle* and listened to the talk of Doctor Parcival.

Doctor Parcival appeared immediately after Will Henderson had disappeared. One might have supposed that the doctor had been watching from his office window and had seen the editor going along the alleyway. Coming in at the front door and finding himself a chair, he lighted one of the stogies and crossing his legs began to talk. He seemed intent upon convincing the boy of the advisability of adopting a line of conduct that he was himself unable to define.

"If you have your eyes open you will see that although I call myself a doctor I have mighty few patients," he began. "There is a reason for that. It is not an accident and it is not because I do not know as much of medicine as anyone here. I do not want patients. The reason, you see, does not appear on the surface. It lies in fact in my character, which has, if you think about it, many strange turns. Why I want to talk to you of the matter I don't know. I might keep still and get more credit in your eyes. I have a desire to make you admire me, that's a fact. I don't know why. That's why I talk. It's very amusing, eh?"

Sometimes the doctor launched into long tales concerning himself. To the boy the tales were very real and full of meaning. He began to admire the fat unclean-looking man and, in the afternoon when Will Henderson had gone, looked forward with keen interest to the doctor's coming.

Doctor Parcival had been in Winesburg about five years. He came from Chicago and when he arrived was drunk and got into a fight with Albert Longworth, the baggageman. The fight concerned a trunk and ended by the doctor's being escorted to the village lockup. When he was released he rented a room above a shoe-repairing shop at the lower end of Main Street and put out the sign that announced himself as a doctor. Although he had but few patients and these of the poorer sort who were unable to pay, he seemed to have plenty of money for his needs. He slept in the office that was unspeakably dirty and dined at Biff Carter's lunch room in a small frame building opposite the railroad station. In the summer the lunch room was filled with flies and Biff Carter's white apron was more dirty than his floor. Doctor Parcival did not mind. Into the lunch room he stalked and deposited twenty cents upon the counter. "Feed me what you wish for that," he said laughing. "Use up food that you wouldn't otherwise sell. It makes no difference to me. I am a man of distinction, you see. Why should I concern myself with what I eat."

The tales that Doctor Parcival told George Willard began nowhere and ended nowhere. Sometimes the boy thought they must all be inventions, a pack of lies. And then again he was convinced that they contained the very essence of truth.

"I was a reporter like you here," Doctor Parcival began. "It was in a town in Iowa—or was it in Illinois? I don't remember and anyway it makes no difference. Perhaps I am trying to conceal my identity and don't want to be very definite. Have you ever thought it strange that I have money for my needs although I do nothing? I may have stolen a great sum of money or been involved in a murder before I came here. There is food for thought in that, eh? If you were a really smart newspaper reporter you would look me up. In Chicago there was a Doctor

Cronin who was murdered.[1] Have you heard of that? Some men murdered him and put him in a trunk. In the early morning they hauled the trunk across the city. It sat on the back of an express wagon and they were on the seat as unconcerned as anything. Along they went through quiet streets where everyone was asleep. The sun was just coming up over the lake. Funny, eh—just to think of them smoking pipes and chattering as they drove along as unconcerned as I am now. Perhaps I was one of those men. That would be a strange turn of things, now wouldn't it, eh?" Again Doctor Parcival began his tale: "Well, anyway there I was, a reporter on a paper just as you are here, running about and getting little items to print. My mother was poor. She took in washing. Her dream was to make me a Presbyterian minister and I was studying with that end in view.

"My father had been insane for a number of years. He was in an asylum over at Dayton, Ohio. There you see I have let it slip out! All of this took place in Ohio, right here in Ohio. There is a clew if you ever get the notion of looking me up.

"I was going to tell you of my brother. That's the object of all this. That's what I'm getting at. My brother was a railroad painter and had a job on the Big Four. You know that road runs through Ohio here. With other men he lived in a box car and away they went from town to town painting the railroad property—switches, crossing gates, bridges, and stations.

"The Big Four paints its stations a nasty orange color. How I hated that color! My brother was always covered with it. On pay days he used to get drunk and come home wearing his paint-covered clothes and bringing his money with him. He did not give it to mother but laid it in a pile on our kitchen table.

"About the house he went in the clothes covered with the nasty orange colored paint. I can see the picture. My mother, who was small and had red, sad-looking eyes, would come into the house from a little shed at the back. That's where she spent her time over the washtub scrubbing people's dirty clothes. In she would come and stand by the table, rubbing her eyes with her apron that was covered with soapsuds.

" 'Don't touch it! Don't you dare touch that money,' my brother roared, and then he himself took five or ten dollars and went tramping off to the saloons. When he had spent what he had taken he came back for more. He never gave my mother any money at all but stayed about until he had spent it all, a little at a time. Then he went back to his job with the painting crew on the railroad. After he had gone things began to arrive at our house, groceries and such things. Sometimes there would be a dress for mother or a pair of shoes for me.

1. Dr. Patrick Cronin of Chicago, associated with one of the Irish immigrant clans or secret societies, was killed in May 1889 by members of a rival clan; one suspect in his murder escaped from Chicago before trial could be held.

"Strange, eh? My mother loved my brother much more than she did me, although he never said a kind word to either of us and always raved up and down threatening us if we dared so much as touch the money that sometimes lay on the table three days.

"We got along pretty well. I studied to be a minister and prayed. I was a regular ass about saying prayers. You should have heard me. When my father died I prayed all night, just as I did sometimes when my brother was in town drinking and going about buying the things for us. In the evening after supper I knelt by the table where the money lay and prayed for hours. When no one was looking I stole a dollar or two and put it in my pocket. That makes me laugh now but then it was terrible. It was on my mind all the time. I got six dollars a week from my job on the paper and always took it straight home to mother. The few dollars I stole from my brother's pile I spent on myself, you know, for trifles, candy and cigarettes and such things.

"When my father died at the asylum over at Dayton, I went over there. I borrowed some money from the man for whom I worked and went on the train at night. It was raining. In the asylum they treated me as though I were a king.

"The men who had jobs in the asylum had found out I was a newspaper reporter. That made them afraid. There had been some negligence, some carelessness, you see, when father was ill. They thought perhaps I would write it up in the paper and make a fuss. I never intended to do anything of the kind.

"Anyway, in I went to the room where my father lay dead and blessed the dead body. I wonder what put that notion into my head. Wouldn't my brother, the painter, have laughed, though. There I stood over the dead body and spread out my hands. The superintendent of the asylum and some of his helpers came in and stood about looking sheepish. It was very amusing. I spread out my hands and said, 'Let peace brood over this carcass.' That's what I said."

Jumping to his feet and breaking off the tale, Doctor Parcival began to walk up and down in the office of the *Winesburg Eagle* where George Willard sat listening. He was awkward and, as the office was small, continually knocked against things. "What a fool I am to be talking," he said. "That is not my object in coming here and forcing my acquaintanceship upon you. I have something else in mind. You are a reporter just as I was once and you have attracted my attention. You may end by becoming just such another fool. I want to warn you and keep on warning you. That's why I seek you out."

Doctor Parcival began talking of George Willard's attitude toward men. It seemed to the boy that the man had but one object in view, to make everyone seem despicable. "I want to fill you with hatred and contempt so that you will be a superior being," he declared. "Look at my brother. There was a fellow, eh? He despised everyone, you see.

You have no idea with what contempt he looked upon mother and me. And was he not our superior? You know he was. You have not seen him and yet I have made you feel that. I have given you a sense of it. He is dead. Once when he was drunk he lay down on the tracks and the car in which he lived with the other painters ran over him."

• • • • • • • •

One day in August Doctor Parcival had an adventure in Winesburg. For a month George Willard had been going each morning to spend an hour in the doctor's office. The visits came about through a desire on the part of the doctor to read to the boy from the pages of a book he was in the process of writing. To write the book Doctor Parcival declared was the object of his coming to Winesburg to live.

On the morning in August before the coming of the boy, an incident had happened in the doctor's office. There had been an accident on Main Street. A team of horses had been frightened by a train and had run away. A little girl, the daughter of a farmer, had been thrown from a buggy and killed.

On Main Street everyone had become excited and a cry for doctors had gone up. All three of the active practitioners of the town had come quickly but had found the child dead. From the crowd someone had run to the office of Doctor Parcival who had bluntly refused to go down out of his office to the dead child. The useless cruelty of his refusal had passed unnoticed. Indeed, the man who had come up the stairway to summon him had hurried away without hearing the refusal.

All of this, Doctor Parcival did not know and when George Willard came to his office he found the man shaking with terror. "What I have done will arouse the people of this town," he declared excitedly. "Do I not know human nature? Do I not know what will happen? Word of my refusal will be whispered about. Presently men will get together in groups and talk of it. They will come here. We will quarrel and there will be talk of hanging. Then they will come again bearing a rope in their hands."

Doctor Parcival shook with fright. "I have a presentiment," he declared emphatically. "It may be that what I am talking about will not occur this morning. It may be put off until to-night but I will be hanged. Everyone will get excited. I will be hanged to a lamp-post on Main Street."

Going to the door of his dirty little office, Doctor Parcival looked timidly down the stairway leading to the street. When he returned the fright that had been in his eyes was beginning to be replaced by doubt. Coming on tip-toe across the room he tapped George Willard on the shoulder. "If not now, sometime," he whispered, shaking his head. "In the end I will be crucified, uselessly crucified."

Doctor Parcival began to plead with George Willard. "You must pay attention to me," he urged. "If something happens perhaps you will be able to write the book that I may never get written. The idea is very simple, so simple that if you are not careful you will forget it. It is this—that everyone in the world is Christ and they are all crucified. That's what I want to say. Don't you forget that. Whatever happens, don't you dare let yourself forget."

Nobody Knows

Looking cautiously about, George Willard arose from his desk in the office of the *Winesburg Eagle* and went hurriedly out at the back door. The night was warm and cloudy and although it was not yet eight o'clock, the alleyway back of the *Eagle* office was pitch dark. A team of horses tied to a post somewhere in the darkness stamped on the hard-baked ground. A cat sprang from under George Willard's feet and ran away into the night. The young man was nervous. All day he had gone about his work like one dazed by a blow. In the alleyway he trembled as though with fright.

In the darkness George Willard walked along the alleyway, going carefully and cautiously. The back doors of the Winesburg stores were open and he could see men sitting about under the store lamps. In Myerbaum's Notion Store Mrs. Willy the saloon keeper's wife stood by the counter with a basket on her arm. Sid Green the clerk was waiting on her. He leaned over the counter and talked earnestly.

George Willard crouched and then jumped through the path of light that came out at the door. He began to run forward in the darkness. Behind Ed Griffith's saloon old Jerry Bird the town drunkard lay asleep on the ground. The runner stumbled over the sprawling legs. He laughed brokenly.

George Willard had set forth upon an adventure. All day he had been trying to make up his mind to go through with the adventure and now he was acting. In the office of the *Winesburg Eagle* he had been sitting since six o'clock trying to think.

There had been no decision. He had just jumped to his feet, hurried past Will Henderson who was reading proof in the print shop and started to run along the alleyway.

Through street after street went George Willard, avoiding the people who passed. He crossed and recrossed the road. When he passed a street lamp he pulled his hat down over his face. He did not dare think. In his mind there was a fear but it was a new kind of fear. He was afraid the adventure on which he had set out would be spoiled, that he would lose courage and turn back.

George Willard found Louise Trunnion in the kitchen of her father's house.[1] She was washing dishes by the light of a kerosene lamp. There she stood behind the screen door in the little shed-like kitchen at the back of the house. George Willard stopped by a picket fence and tried to control the shaking of his body. Only a narrow potato patch separated him from the adventure. Five minutes passed before he felt sure enough of himself to call to her. "Louise! Oh Louise!" he called. The cry stuck in his throat. His voice became a hoarse whisper.

Louise Trunnion came out across the potato patch holding the dish cloth in her hand. "How do you know I want to go out with you," she said sulkily. "What makes you so sure?"

George Willard did not answer. In silence the two stood in the darkness with the fence between them. "You go on along," she said. "Pa's in there. I'll come along. You wait by Williams' barn."

The young newspaper reporter had received a letter from Louise Trunnion. It had come that morning to the office of the *Winesburg Eagle*. The letter was brief. "I'm yours if you want me," it said. He thought it annoying that in the darkness by the fence she had pretended there was nothing between them. "She has a nerve! Well, gracious sakes, she has a nerve," he muttered as he went along the street and passed a row of vacant lots where corn grew. The corn was shoulder high and had been planted right down to the sidewalk.

When Louise Trunnion came out of the front door of her house she still wore the gingham dress in which she had been washing dishes. There was no hat on her head. The boy could see her standing with the doorknob in her hand talking to someone within, no doubt to old Jake Trunnion, her father. Old Jake was half deaf and she shouted. The door closed and everything was dark and silent in the little side street. George Willard trembled more violently than ever.

In the shadows by Williams' barn George and Louise stood, not daring to talk. She was not particularly comely and there was a black smudge on the side of her nose. George thought she must have rubbed her nose with her finger after she had been handling some of the kitchen pots.

The young man began to laugh nervously. "It's warm," he said. He wanted to touch her with his hand. "I'm not very bold," he thought. Just to touch the folds of the soiled gingham dress would, he decided, be an exquisite pleasure. She began to quibble. "You think you're better than I am. Don't tell me, I guess I know," she said drawing closer to him.

A flood of words burst from George Willard. He remembered the look that had lurked in the girl's eyes when they had met on the streets and thought of the note she had written. Doubt left him. The whispered tales concerning her that had gone about town gave him confidence.

1. Louise Tru*nn*ion, resident of the poorer district of Winesburg, is not related to the dignitary for whom Tru*n*ion Pike, a major Winesburg thoroughfare, is named.

He became wholly the male, bold and aggressive. In his heart there was no sympathy for her. "Ah, come on, it'll be all right. There won't be anyone know anything. How can they know?" he urged.

They began to walk along a narrow brick sidewalk between the cracks of which tall weeds grew. Some of the bricks were missing and the sidewalk was rough and irregular. He took hold of her hand that was also rough and thought it delightfully small. "I can't go far," she said and her voice was quiet, unperturbed.

They crossed a bridge that ran over a tiny stream and passed another vacant lot in which corn grew. The street ended. In the path at the side of the road they were compelled to walk one behind the other. Will Overton's berry field lay beside the road and there was a pile of boards. "Will is going to build a shed to store berry crates here," said George and they sat down upon the boards.

. . . .

When George Willard got back into Main Street it was past ten o'clock and had begun to rain. Three times he walked up and down the length of Main Street. Sylvester West's Drug Store was still open and he went in and bought a cigar. When Shorty Crandall the clerk came out at the door with him he was pleased. For five minutes the two stood in the shelter of the store awning and talked. George Willard felt satisfied. He had wanted more than anything else to talk to some man. Around a corner toward the New Willard House he went whistling softly.

On the sidewalk at the side of Winney's Dry Goods Store where there was a high board fence covered with circus pictures, he stopped whistling and stood perfectly still in the darkness, attentive, listening as though for a voice calling his name. Then again he laughed nervously. "She hasn't got anything on me. Nobody knows," he muttered doggedly and went on his way.

Godliness

A TALE IN FOUR PARTS

Part One

There were always three or four old people sitting on the front porch of the house or puttering about the garden of the Bentley farm. Three of the old people were women and sisters to Jesse. They were a colorless, soft-voiced lot. Then there was a silent old man with thin white hair who was Jesse's uncle.

The farmhouse was built of wood, a board outer-covering over a framework of logs. It was in reality not one house but a cluster of houses joined together in a rather haphazard manner. Inside, the place was full of surprises. One went up steps from the living room into the dining room and there were always steps to be ascended or descended in passing from one room to another. At meal times the place was like a beehive. At one moment all was quiet, then doors began to open, feet clattered on stairs, a murmur of soft voices arose and people appeared from a dozen obscure corners.

Beside the old people, already mentioned, many others lived in the Bentley house. There were four hired men, a woman named Aunt Callie Beebe, who was in charge of the housekeeping, a dull-witted girl named Eliza Stoughton, who made beds and helped with the milking, a boy who worked in the stables, and Jesse Bentley himself, the owner and overlord of it all.

By the time the American Civil War had been over for twenty years, that part of Northern Ohio where the Bentley farms lay had begun to emerge from pioneer life. Jesse then owned machinery for harvesting grain. He had built modern barns and most of his land was drained with carefully laid tile drain, but in order to understand the man we will have to go back to an earlier day.

The Bentley family had been in Northern Ohio for several generations before Jesse's time. They came from New York State and took up land when the country was new and land could be had at a low price. For a long time they, in common with all the other Middle Western people, were very poor. The land they had settled upon was heavily wooded and covered with fallen logs and underbrush. After the long hard labor of clearing these away and cutting the timber, there were still the stumps to be reckoned with. Plows run through the fields caught on hidden roots, stones lay all about, on the low places water gathered, and the young corn turned yellow, sickened and died.

When Jesse Bentley's father and brothers had come into their ownership of the place, much of the harder part of the work of clearing had been done, but they clung to old traditions and worked like driven animals. They lived as practically all of the farming people of the time lived. In the spring and through most of the winter the highways leading into the town of Winesburg were a sea of mud. The four young men of the family worked hard all day in the fields, they ate heavily of coarse, greasy food, and at night slept like tired beasts on beds of straw. Into their lives came little that was not coarse and brutal and outwardly they were themselves coarse and brutal. On Saturday afternoons they hitched a team of horses to a three-seated wagon and went off to town. In town they stood about the stoves in the stores talking to other farmers or to the store keepers. They were dressed in overalls and in the winter wore heavy coats that were flecked with mud. Their hands as they stretched them out to the heat of the stoves were cracked and red. It was difficult for them to talk and so they for the most part kept silent. When they had bought meat, flour, sugar, and salt, they went into one of the Winesburg saloons and drank beer. Under the influence of drink the naturally strong lusts of their natures, kept suppressed by the heroic labor of breaking up new ground, were released. A kind of crude and animal-like poetic fervor took possession of them. On the road home they stood up on the wagon seats and shouted at the stars. Sometimes they fought long and bitterly and at other times they broke forth into songs. Once Enoch Bentley, the older one of the boys, struck his father, old Tom Bentley, with the butt of a teamster's whip, and the old man seemed likely to die. For days Enoch lay hid in the straw in the loft of the stable ready to flee if the result of his momentary passion turned out to be murder. He was kept alive with food brought by his mother who also kept him informed of the injured man's condition. When all turned out well he emerged from his hiding place and went back to the work of clearing land as though nothing had happened.

• • • • • • • •

The Civil War brought a sharp turn to the fortunes of the Bentleys and was responsible for the rise of the youngest son, Jesse. Enoch, Edward, Harry, and Will Bentley all enlisted and before the long war ended they were all killed. For a time after they went away to the South, old Tom tried to run the place, but he was not successful. When the last of the four had been killed he sent word to Jesse that he would have to come home.

Then the mother, who had not been well for a year, died suddenly, and the father became altogether discouraged. He talked of selling the farm and moving into town. All day he went about shaking his head and muttering. The work in the fields was neglected and weeds grew high in the corn. Old Tom hired men but he did not use them intelligently. When they had gone away to the fields in the morning he wandered into the woods and sat down on a log. Sometimes he forgot to come home at night and one of the daughters had to go in search of him.

When Jesse Bentley came home to the farm and began to take charge of things he was a slight, sensitive-looking man of twenty-two. At eighteen he had left home to go to school to become a scholar and eventually to become a minister of the Presbyterian Church. All through his boyhood he had been what in our country was called an "odd sheep" and had not got on with his brothers. Of all the family only his mother had understood him and she was now dead. When he came home to take charge of the farm, that had at that time grown to more than six hundred acres, everyone on the farms about and in the nearby town of Winesburg smiled at the idea of his trying to handle the work that had been done by his four strong brothers.

There was indeed good cause to smile. By the standards of his day Jesse did not look like a man at all. He was small and very slender and womanish of body and, true to the traditions of young ministers, wore a long black coat and a narrow black string tie. The neighbors were amused when they saw him, after the years away, and they were even more amused when they saw the woman he had married in the city.

As a matter of fact, Jesse's wife did soon go under. That was perhaps Jesse's fault. A farm in Northern Ohio in the hard years after the Civil War was no place for a delicate woman, and Katherine Bentley was delicate. Jesse was hard with her as he was with everybody about him in those days. She tried to do such work as all the neighbor women about her did and he let her go on without interference. She helped to do the milking and did part of the housework; she made the beds for the men and prepared their food. For a year she worked every day from sunrise until late at night and then after giving birth to a child she died.

As for Jesse Bentley—although he was a delicately built man there was something within him that could not easily be killed. He had brown curly hair and grey eyes that were at times hard and direct, at times wavering and uncertain. Not only was he slender but he was also short of stature. His mouth was like the mouth of a sensitive and very determined child. Jesse Bentley was a fanatic. He was a man born out of his time and place and for this he suffered and made others suffer. Never did he succeed in getting what he wanted out of life and he did not know what he wanted. Within a very short time after he came home to the Bentley farm he made everyone there a little afraid of him, and his wife, who should have been close to him as his mother had been, was afraid also. At the end of two weeks after his coming, old Tom Bentley made over to him the entire ownership of the place and retired into the background. Everyone retired into the background. In spite of his youth and inexperience, Jesse had the trick of mastering the souls of his people. He was so in earnest in everything he did and said that no one understood him. He made everyone on the farm work as they had never worked before and yet there was no joy in the work. If things went well they went well for Jesse and never for the people who were his dependents. Like a thousand other strong men who have come into the world here in America in these later times, Jesse was but half strong. He could master others but he could not master himself. The running of the farm as it had never been run before was easy for him. When he came home from Cleveland where he had been in school, he shut himself off from all of his people and began to make plans. He thought about the farm night and day and that made him successful. Other men on the farms about him worked too hard and were too tired to think, but to think of the farm and to be everlastingly making plans for its success was a relief to Jesse. It partially satisfied something in his passionate nature. Immediately after he came home he had a wing built on to the old house and in a large room facing the west he had windows that looked into the barnyard and other windows that looked off across the fields. By the window he sat down to think. Hour after hour and day after day he sat and looked over the land and thought out his new place in life. The passionate burning thing in his nature flamed up and his eyes became hard. He wanted to make the farm produce as no farm in his state had ever produced before and then he wanted something else. It was the indefinable hunger within that made his eyes waver and that kept him always more and more silent before people. He would have given much to achieve peace and in him was a fear that peace was the thing he could not achieve.

All over his body Jesse Bentley was alive. In his small frame was gathered the force of a long line of strong men. He had always been extraordinarily alive when he was a small boy on the farm and later when he was a young man in school. In the school he had studied and thought of God and the Bible with his whole mind and heart. As time passed and he grew to know people better, he began to think of himself as an extraordinary man, one set apart from his fellows. He wanted terribly to make his life a thing of great importance, and as he looked about at his fellow men and saw how like clods they lived it seemed to him that he could not bear to become also such a clod. Although in his absorption in himself and in his own destiny he was blind to the fact that his young wife was doing a strong woman's work even after she had become large with child and that she was killing herself in his service, he did not intend to be unkind to her. When his father, who was old and twisted with toil, made over to him the ownership of the farm and seemed content to creep away to a corner and wait for death, he shrugged his shoulders and dismissed the old man from his mind.

In the room by the window overlooking the land that had come down to him sat Jesse thinking of his own affairs. In the stables he could hear the tramping of his horses and the restless movement of his cattle. Away in the fields he could see other cattle wandering over green hills. The voices of men, his men who worked for him, came in to him through the window. From the milk house there was the steady thump, thump of a churn being manipulated by the half-witted girl, Eliza Stoughton. Jesse's mind went back to the men of Old Testament days who had also owned lands and herds. He remembered how God had come down out of the skies and talked to these men and he wanted God to notice and to talk to him also. A kind of feverish boyish eagerness to in some way achieve in his own life the flavor of significance that had hung over these men took possession of him. Being a prayerful man he spoke of the matter aloud to God and the sound of his own words strengthened and fed his eagerness.

"I am a new kind of man come into possession of these fields," he declared. "Look upon me, O God, and look Thou also upon my neighbors and all the men who have gone before me here! O God, create in me another Jesse, like that one of old, to rule over men and to be the father of sons who shall be rulers!" Jesse grew excited as he talked aloud and jumping to his feet walked up and down in the room. In fancy he saw himself living in old times and among old peoples. The land that lay stretched out before him became of vast significance, a place peopled by his fancy with a new race of men sprung from himself. It seemed to him that in his day as in those other and older days, kingdoms might be created and new impulses given to the lives of men by the power of God speaking through a chosen servant. He longed to be such a servant. "It is God's work I have come to the land to do," he declared in a loud voice and his short figure straightened and he thought that something like a halo of Godly approval hung over him.

• • • • • • • •

It will perhaps be somewhat difficult for the men and women of a later day to understand Jesse Bentley. In the last fifty years a vast change has taken place in the lives of our people. A revolution has in fact taken place. The coming of industrialism, attended by all the roar and rattle of affairs, the shrill cries of millions of new voices that have come among us from over seas, the going and coming of trains, the growth of cities, the building of the interurban car lines that weave in and out of towns and past farmhouses, and now in these later days the coming of the automobiles has worked a tremendous change in the lives and in the habits of thought of our people of Mid-America. Books, badly imagined and written though they may be in the hurry of our times, are in every household, magazines circulate by the millions of copies, newspapers are everywhere. In our day a farmer standing by the stove in the store in his village has his mind filled to overflowing with the words of other men. The newspapers and the magazines have pumped him full. Much of the old brutal ignorance that had in it also a kind of beautiful childlike innocence is gone forever. The farmer by the stove is brother to the men of the cities, and if you listen you will find him talking as glibly and as senselessly as the best city man of us all.

In Jesse Bentley's time and in the country districts of the whole Middle West in the years after the Civil War it was not so. Men labored too hard and were too tired to read. In them was no desire for words printed upon paper. As they worked in the fields, vague, half-formed thoughts took possession of them. They believed in God and in God's power to control their lives. In the little Protestant churches they gathered on Sunday to hear of God and his works. The churches were the center of the social and intellectual life of the times. The figure of God was big in the hearts of men.

And so, having been born an imaginative child and having within him a great intellectual eagerness, Jesse Bentley had turned wholeheartedly toward God. When the war took his brothers away, he saw the hand of God in that. When his father became ill and could no longer attend to the running of the farm, he took that also as a sign from God. In the city, when the word came to him, he walked about at night through the streets thinking of the matter and when he had come home and had got the work on the farm well under way, he went again at night to walk through the forests and over the low hills and to think of God.

As he walked the importance of his own figure in some divine plan grew in his mind. He grew avaricious and was impatient that the farm contained only six hundred acres. Kneeling in a fence corner at the edge of some meadow, he sent his voice abroad into the silence and looking up he saw the stars shining down at him.

One evening, some months after his father's death, and when his wife Katherine was expecting at any moment to be laid abed of childbirth, Jesse left his house and went for a long walk. The Bentley farm was situated in a tiny valley watered by Wine Creek, and Jesse walked along the banks of the stream to the end of his own land and on through the fields of his neighbors. As he walked the valley broadened and then narrowed again. Great open stretches of field and wood lay before him. The moon came out from behind clouds, and, climbing a low hill, he sat down to think.

Jesse thought that as the true servant of God the entire stretch of country through which he had walked should have come into his possession. He thought of his dead brothers and blamed them that they had not worked harder and achieved more. Before him in the moonlight the tiny stream ran down over stones, and he began to think of the men of old times who like himself had owned flocks and lands.

A fantastic impulse, half fear, half greediness took possession of Jesse Bentley. He remembered how in the old Bible story the Lord had appeared to that other Jesse and told him to send his son David to where Saul and the men of Israel were fighting the Philistines in the Valley of Elah.[1] Into Jesse's mind came the conviction that all of the Ohio farmers who owned land in the valley of Wine Creek were Philistines and enemies of God. "Suppose," he whispered to himself, "there should come from among them one who, like Goliath the Philistine of Gath, could defeat me and take from me my possessions." In fancy he felt the sickening dread that he thought must have lain heavy on the heart of Saul before the coming of David. Jumping to his feet, he began to run through the night. As he ran he called to God. His voice carried far over the low hills. "Jehovah of Hosts," he cried, "send to me this night out of the womb of Katherine, a son. Let thy grace alight upon me. Send me a son to be called David who shall help me to pluck at last all of

1. Saul, the first king of Old Testament Israel, was summoned by the prophet Samuel to battle the enemy Philistines in the Valley of Elah for control of central Israel (see 1 Samuel 9–29). Jesse sent his youngest son, David, who would much later become king of Israel, to lead Israelite forces under Saul to conquer the enemy Philistines.

these lands out of the hands of the Philistines and turn them to Thy service and to the building of Thy kingdom on earth."

Godliness

Part Two

David Hardy of Winesburg, Ohio was the grandson of Jesse Bentley, the owner of Bentley farms. When he was twelve years old he went to the old Bentley place to live. His mother, Louise Bentley, the girl who came into the world on that night when Jesse ran through the fields crying to God that he be given a son, had grown to womanhood on the farm and had married young John Hardy of Winesburg who became a banker. Louise and her husband did not live happily together and everyone agreed that she was to blame. She was a small woman with sharp grey eyes and black hair. From childhood she had been inclined to fits of temper and when not angry she was often morose and silent. In Winesburg it was said that she drank. Her husband, the banker, who was a careful, shrewd man, tried hard to make her happy. When he began to make money he bought for her a large brick house on Elm Street in Winesburg and he was the first man in that town to keep a manservant to drive his wife's carriage.

But Louise could not be made happy. She flew into half insane fits of temper during which she was sometimes silent, sometimes noisy and quarrelsome. She swore and cried out in her anger. She got a knife from the kitchen and threatened her husband's life. Once she deliberately set fire to the house, and often she hid herself away for days in her own room and would see no one. Her life, lived as a half recluse, gave rise to all sorts of stories concerning her. It was said that she took drugs and that she hid herself away from people because she was often so under the influence of drink that her condition could not be concealed. Sometimes on summer afternoons she came out of the house and got into her carriage. Dismissing the driver she took the reins in her own hands and drove off at top speed through the streets. If a pedestrian got in her way she drove straight ahead and the frightened citizen had to escape as best he could. To the people of the town it seemed as though she wanted to run them down. When she had driven through several streets, tearing around corners and beating the horses with the whip, she drove off into the country. On the country roads after she had gotten out of sight of the houses she let the horses slow down to a walk and her wild, reckless mood passed. She became thoughtful and muttered words. Sometimes tears came into her eyes. And then when she came back into town she again drove furiously through the quiet streets. But for the influence of her husband and the respect he inspired in people's minds she would have been arrested more than once by the town marshal.

Young David Hardy grew up in the house with this woman and as can well be imagined there was not much joy in his childhood. He was too young then to have opinions of his own about people, but at times it was difficult for him not to have very definite opinions about the woman who was his mother. David was always a quiet orderly boy and for a long time was thought by the people of Winesburg to be something of a dullard. His eyes were brown and as a child he had a habit of looking at things and people a long time without appearing to see what he was looking at. When he heard his mother spoken of harshly or when he overheard her berating his father, he was frightened and ran away to hide. Sometimes he could not find a hiding place and that confused him. Turning his face toward a tree or if he were indoors toward the wall, he closed his eyes and tried not to think of anything. He had a habit of talking aloud to himself, and early in life a spirit of quiet sadness often took possession of him.

On the occasions when David went to visit his grandfather on the Bentley farm, he was altogether contented and happy. Often he wished that he would never have to go back to town and once when he had come home from the farm after a long visit, something happened that had a lasting effect on his mind.

David had come back into town with one of the hired men. The man was in a hurry to go about his own affairs and left the boy at the head of the street in which the Hardy house stood. It was early dusk of a fall evening and the sky was overcast with clouds. Something happened to David. He could not bear to go into the house where his mother and father lived, and on an impulse he decided to run away from home. He intended to go back to the farm and to his grandfather, but lost his way and for hours he wandered weeping and frightened on country roads. It started to rain and lightning flashed in the sky. The boy's imagination was excited and he fancied that he could see and hear strange things in the darkness. Into his mind came the conviction that he was walking and running in some terrible void where no one had ever been before. The darkness about him seemed limitless. The sound of the wind blowing in trees was terrifying. When a team of horses approached along the road in which he walked he was frightened and climbed a fence. Through a field he ran until he came into another road and getting upon his knees felt of the soft ground with his fingers. But for the figure of his grandfather, whom he was afraid he would never find in the darkness, he thought the world must be altogether empty. When his cries were heard by a farmer who was walking home from town and he was brought back to his father's house, he was so tired and excited that he did not know what was happening to him.

By chance David's father knew that he had disappeared. On the street he had met the farm hand from the Bentley place and knew of his son's return to town. When the boy did not come home an alarm was set up and John Hardy with several men of the town went to search the country. The report that David had been kidnapped ran about through the streets of Winesburg. When he came home there were no lights in the house, but his mother appeared and clutched him eagerly in her arms. David thought she had suddenly become another woman. He could not believe that so delightful a thing had happened. With her own hands Louise Hardy bathed his tired young body and cooked him food. She would not let him go to bed but, when he had put on his nightgown, blew out the lights and sat down in a chair to hold him in her arms. For an hour the woman sat in the darkness and held her boy. All the time she kept talking in a low voice. David could not understand what had so changed her. Her habitually dissatisfied face had become, he thought, the most peaceful and lovely thing he had ever seen. When he began to weep she held him more and more tightly. On and on went her voice. It was not harsh or shrill as when she talked to her husband, but was like rain falling on trees. Presently men began coming to the door to report that he had not been found, but she made him hide and be silent until she had sent them away. He thought it must be a game his mother and the men of the town were playing with him and laughed joyously. Into his mind came the thought that his having been lost and frightened in the darkness was an altogether unimportant matter. He thought that he would have been willing to go through the frightful experience a thousand times to be sure of finding at the end of the long black road a thing so lovely as his mother had suddenly become.

• • • • • • •

During the last years of young David's boyhood he saw his mother but seldom and she became for him just a woman with whom he had once lived. Still he could not get her figure out of his mind and as he grew older it became more definite. When he was twelve years old he went to the Bentley farm to live. Old Jesse came into town and fairly demanded that he be given charge of the boy. The old man was excited and determined on having his own way. He talked to John Hardy in the office of the Winesburg Savings Bank and then the two men went to the house on Elm Street to talk with Louise. They both expected her to make trouble but were mistaken. She was very quiet and when Jesse had explained his mission and had gone on at some length about the advantages to come through having the boy out of doors and in the quiet atmosphere of the old farmhouse, she nodded her head in approval. "It is an atmosphere not corrupted by my presence," she said sharply. Her shoulders shook and she seemed about to fly into a fit of temper. "It is a place for a man child, although it was never a place for me," she went on. "You never wanted me there and of course the air of your house did me no good. It was like poison in my blood but it will be different with him."

Louise turned and went out of the room, leaving the two men to sit in embarrassed silence. As very often happened she later stayed in her room for days. Even when the boy's clothes were packed and he was taken away she did not appear. The loss of her son made a sharp break in her life and she seemed less inclined to quarrel with her husband. John Hardy thought it had all turned out very well indeed.

And so young David went to live in the Bentley farmhouse with Jesse. Two of the old farmer's sisters were alive and still lived in the house. They were afraid of Jesse and rarely spoke when he was about. One of the women who had been noted for her flaming red hair when she was younger was a born mother and became the boy's caretaker. Every night when he had gone to bed she went into his room and sat on the floor until he fell asleep. When he became drowsy she became bold and whispered things that he later thought he must have dreamed.

Her soft low voice called him endearing names and he dreamed that his mother had come to him and that she had changed so that she was always as she had been that time after he ran away. He also grew bold and reaching out his hand stroked the face of the woman on the floor so that she was ecstatically happy. Everyone in the old house became happy after the boy went there. The hard insistent thing in Jesse Bentley that had kept the people in the house silent and timid and that had never been dispelled by the presence of the girl Louise was apparently swept away by the coming of the boy. It was as though God had relented and sent a son to the man.

The man who had proclaimed himself the only true servant of God in all the valley of Wine Creek, and who had wanted God to send him a sign of approval by way of a son out of the womb of Katherine, began to think that at last his prayers had been answered. Although he was at that time only fifty-five years old he looked seventy and was worn out with much thinking and scheming. The effort he had made to extend his land holdings had been successful and there were few farms in the valley that did not belong to him, but until David came he was a bitterly disappointed man.

There were two influences at work in Jesse Bentley and all his life his mind had been a battleground for these influences. First there was the old thing in him. He wanted to be a man of God and a leader among men of God. His walking in the fields and through the forests at night had brought him close to nature and there were forces in the passionately religious man that ran out to the forces in nature. The disappointment that had come to him when a daughter and not a son had been born to Katherine had fallen upon him like a blow struck by some unseen hand and the blow had somewhat softened his egotism. He still believed that God might at any moment make himself manifest out of the winds or the clouds, but he no longer demanded such recognition. Instead he prayed for it. Sometimes he was altogether doubtful and thought God had deserted the world. He regretted the fate that had not let him live in a simpler and sweeter time when at the beckoning of some strange cloud in the sky men left their lands and houses and went forth into the wilderness to create new races. While he worked night and day to make his farms more productive and to extend his holdings of land, he regretted that he could not use his own restless energy in the building of temples, the slaying of unbelievers and in general in the work of glorifying God's name on earth.

That is what Jesse hungered for and then also he hungered for something else. He had grown into maturity in America in the years after the Civil War and he, like all men of his time, had been touched by the deep influences that were at work in the country during those years when modern industrialism was being born. He began to buy machines that would permit him to do the work of the farms while employing fewer men and he sometimes thought that if he were a younger man he would give up farming altogether and start a factory in Winesburg for the making of machinery. Jesse formed the habit of reading newspapers and magazines. He invented a machine for the making of fence out of wire. Faintly he realized that the atmosphere of old times and places that he had always cultivated in his own mind was strange and foreign to the thing that was growing up in the minds of others. The beginning of the most materialistic age in the history of the world, when wars would be fought without patriotism, when men would forget God and only pay attention to moral standards, when the will to power would replace the will to serve and beauty would be well-nigh forgotten in the terrible headlong rush of mankind toward the acquiring of possessions, was telling its story to Jesse the man of God as it was to the men about him. The greedy thing in him wanted to make money faster than it could be made by tilling the land. More than once he went into Winesburg to talk with his son-in-law John Hardy about it. "You are a banker and you will have chances I never had," he said and his eyes shone. "I am thinking about it all the time. Big things are going to be done in the country and there will be more money to be made than I ever dreamed of. You get into it. I wish I were younger and had your chance." Jesse Bentley walked up and down in the bank office and grew more and more excited as he talked. At one time in his life he had been threatened with paralysis and his left side remained somewhat weakened. As he talked his left eyelid twitched. Later when he drove back home and when night came on and the stars came out it was harder to get back the old feeling of a close and personal God who lived in the sky overhead and who might at any moment reach out his hand, touch him on the shoulder, and appoint for him some heroic task to be done. Jesse's mind was fixed upon the things read in newspapers and magazines, on fortunes to be made almost without effort by shrewd men who bought and sold. For him the coming of the boy David did much to bring back with renewed force the old faith and it seemed to him that God had at last looked with favor upon him.

As for the boy on the farm, life began to reveal itself to him in a thousand new and delightful ways. The kindly attitude of all about him expanded his quiet nature and he lost the half timid, hesitating manner he had always had with his people. At night when he went to bed after a long day of adventures in the stables, in the fields, or driving about from farm to farm with his grandfather he wanted to embrace everyone in the house. If Sherley Bentley, the woman who came each night to sit on the floor by his bedside, did not appear at once, he went to the head of the stairs and shouted, his young voice ringing through the narrow halls where for so long there had been a tradition of silence. In the morning when he awoke and lay still in bed, the sounds that came in to him through the windows filled him with delight. He thought with a shudder of the life in the house in Winesburg and of his mother's angry voice that had always made him tremble. There in the country all sounds were pleasant sounds. When he awoke at dawn the barnyard back of the house also awoke. In the house people stirred about. Eliza Stoughton the half-witted girl was poked in the ribs by a farm hand and giggled noisily, in some distant field a cow bawled and was answered by the cattle in the stables, and one of the farm hands spoke sharply to the horse he was grooming by the stable door. David leaped out of bed and ran to a window. All of the people stirring about excited his mind, and he wondered what his mother was doing in the house in town.

From the windows of his own room he could not see directly into the barnyard where the farm hands had now all assembled to do the morning chores, but he could hear the voices of the men and the neighing of the horses. When one of the men laughed, he laughed also. Leaning out at the open window, he looked into an orchard where a fat sow wandered about with a litter of tiny pigs at her heels. Every morning he counted the pigs. "Four, five, six, seven," he said slowly, wetting his finger and making straight up and down marks on the window ledge. David ran to put on his trousers and shirt. A feverish desire to get out of doors took possession of him. Every morning he made such a noise coming down stairs that Aunt Callie, the housekeeper, declared he was trying to tear the house down. When he had run through the long old house, shutting doors behind him with a bang, he came into the barnyard and looked about with an amazed air of expectancy. It seemed to him that in such a place tremendous things might have happened during the night. The farm hands looked at him and laughed. Henry Strader, an old man who had been on the farm since Jesse came into possession and who before David's time had never been known to make a joke, made the same joke every morning. It amused David so that he laughed and clapped his hands. "See, come here and look," cried the old man, "Grandfather Jesse's white mare has torn the black stocking she wears on her foot."

Day after day through the long summer, Jesse Bentley drove from farm to farm up and down the valley of Wine Creek, and his grandson went with him. They rode in a comfortable old phaeton drawn by the white horse. The old man scratched his thin white beard and talked to himself of his plans for increasing the productiveness of the fields they visited and of God's part in the plans all men made. Sometimes he looked at David and smiled happily and then for a long time he appeared to forget the boy's existence. More and more every day now his mind turned back again to the dreams that had filled his mind when he had first come out of the city to live on the land. One afternoon he startled David by letting his dreams take entire possession of him. With the boy as a witness, he went through a ceremony and brought about an accident that nearly destroyed the companionship that was growing up between them.

Jesse and his grandson were driving in a distant part of the valley some miles from home. A forest came down to the road and through the forest Wine Creek wriggled its way over stones toward a distant river. All the afternoon Jesse had been in a meditative mood and now he began to talk. His mind went back to the night when he had been frightened by thoughts of a giant that might come to rob and plunder him of his possessions, and again as on that night when he had run through the fields crying for a son, he became excited to the edge of insanity. Stopping the horse he got out of the buggy and asked David to get out also. The two climbed over a fence and walked along the bank of the stream. The boy paid no attention to the muttering of his grandfather, but ran along beside him and wondered what was going to happen. When a rabbit jumped up and ran away through the woods, he clapped his hands and danced with delight. He looked at the tall trees and was sorry that he was not a little animal to climb high in the air without being frightened. Stooping, he picked up a small stone and threw it over the head of his grandfather into a clump of bushes. "Wake up, little animal. Go and climb to the top of the trees," he shouted in a shrill voice.

Jesse Bentley went along under the trees with his head bowed and with his mind in a ferment. His earnestness affected the boy who presently became silent and a little alarmed. Into the old man's mind had come the notion that now he could bring from God a word or a sign out of the sky, that the presence of the boy and man on their knees in some lonely spot in the forest would make the miracle he had been waiting for almost inevitable. "It was in just such a place as this that other David tended the sheep when his father came and told him to go down unto Saul," he muttered.

Taking the boy rather roughly by the shoulder, he climbed over a fallen log and when he had come to an open place among the trees, he dropped upon his knees and began to pray in a loud voice.

A kind of terror he had never known before took possession of David. Crouching beneath a tree he watched the man on the ground before him and his own knees began to tremble. It seemed to him that he was in the presence, not only of his grandfather but of someone else, someone who might hurt him, someone who was not kindly but dangerous and brutal. He began to cry and reaching down picked up a small stick which he held tightly gripped in his fingers. When Jesse Bentley, absorbed in his own idea, suddenly arose and advanced toward him, his terror grew until his whole body shook. In the woods an intense silence seemed to lie over everything and suddenly out of the silence came the old man's harsh and insistent voice. Gripping the boy's shoulders, Jesse turned his face to the sky and shouted. The whole left side of his face twitched and his hand on the boy's shoulder twitched also. "Make a sign to me, God," he cried, "here I stand with the boy David. Come down to me out of the sky and make Thy presence known to me."

With a cry of fear, David turned and shaking himself loose from the hands that held him, ran away through the forest. He did not believe that the man who turned up his face and in a harsh voice shouted at the sky, was his grandfather at all. The man did not look like his grandfather. The conviction that something strange and terrible had happened, that by some miracle a new and dangerous person had come into the body of the kindly old man took possession of him. On and on he ran down the hillside sobbing as he ran. When he fell over the roots of a tree and in falling struck his head, he arose and tried to run on again. His head hurt so that presently he fell down and lay still, but it was only after Jesse had carried him to the buggy and he awoke to find the old man's hand stroking his head tenderly, that the terror left him. "Take me away. There is a terrible man back there in the woods," he declared firmly, while Jesse looked away over the tops of the trees and again his lips cried out to God. "What have I done that Thou doest not approve of me," he whispered softly, saying the words over and over as he drove rapidly along the road with the boy's cut and bleeding head held tenderly against his shoulder.

Godliness

Part Three

SURRENDER

The story of Louise Bentley, who became Mrs. John Hardy and lived with her husband in a brick house on Elm Street in Winesburg, is a story of misunderstanding.

Before such women as Louise can be understood and their lives made livable, much will have to be done. Thoughtful books will have to be written and thoughtful lives lived by people about them.

Born of a delicate and overworked mother, and an impulsive, hard, imaginative father, who did not look with favor upon her coming into the world, Louise was from childhood a neurotic, one of the race of over-sensitive women that in later days industrialism was to bring in such great numbers into the world.

During her early years she lived on the Bentley farm, a silent, moody child, wanting love more than anything else in the world and not getting it. When she was fifteen she went to live in Winesburg with the family of Albert Hardy who had a store for the sale of buggies and wagons, and who was a member of the town board of education.

Louise went into town to be a student in the Winesburg High School and she went to live at the Hardys' because Albert Hardy and her father were friends.

Hardy, the vehicle merchant of Winesburg, like thousands of other men of his times, was an enthusiast on the subject of education. He had made his own way in the world without learning got from books, but he was convinced that had he but known books things would have gone better with him. To everyone who came into his shop he talked of the matter, and in his own household he drove his family distracted by his constant harping on the subject.

He had two daughters and one son, John Hardy, and more than once the daughters threatened to leave school altogether. As a matter of principle they did just enough work in their classes to avoid punishment. "I hate books and I hate anyone who likes books," Harriet, the younger of the two girls, declared passionately.

In Winesburg as on the farm Louise was not happy. For years she had dreamed of the time when she could go forth into the world, and she looked upon the move into the Hardy household as a great step in the direction of freedom. Always when she had thought of the matter, it had seemed to her that in town all must be gaiety and life, that there men and women must live happily and freely, giving and taking friendship and affection as one takes the feel of a wind on the cheek. After the silence and the cheerlessness of life in the Bentley house, she dreamed of stepping forth into an atmosphere that was warm and pulsating with life and reality. And in the Hardy household Louise might have got something of the thing for which she so hungered but for a mistake she made when she had just come to town.

Louise won the disfavor of the two Hardy girls, Mary and Harriet, by her application to her studies in school. She did not come to the house until the day when school was to begin and knew nothing of the feeling they had in the matter. She was timid and during the first month made no acquaintances. Every Friday afternoon one of the hired men from the farm drove into Winesburg and took her home for the week-end, so that she did not spend the Saturday holiday with the town people. Because she was embarrassed and lonely she worked constantly at her studies. To Mary and Harriet, it seemed as though she tried to make trouble for them by her proficiency. In her eagerness to appear well Louise wanted to answer every question put to the class by the teacher. She jumped up and down and her eyes flashed. Then when she had answered some question the others in the class had been unable to answer, she smiled happily. "See, I have done it for you," her eyes seemed to say. "You need not bother about the matter. I will answer all questions. For the whole class it will be easy while I am here."

In the evening after supper in the Hardy house, Albert Hardy began to praise Louise. One of the teachers had spoken highly of her and he was delighted. "Well, again I have heard of it," he began, looking hard at his daughters and then turning to smile at Louise. "Another of the teachers has told me of the good work Louise is doing. Everyone in Winesburg is telling me how smart she is. I am ashamed that they do not speak so of my own girls." Arising, the merchant marched about the room and lighted his evening cigar.

The two girls looked at each other and shook their heads wearily. Seeing their indifference the father became angry. "I tell you it is something for you two to be thinking about," he cried, glaring at them. "There is a big change coming here in America and in learning is the only hope of the coming generations. Louise is the daughter of a rich man but she is not ashamed to study. It should make you ashamed to see what she does."

The merchant took his hat from a rack by the door and prepared to depart for the evening. At the door he stopped and glared back. So fierce was his manner that Louise was frightened and ran upstairs to her own room. The daughters began to speak of their own affairs. "Pay attention to me," roared the merchant. "Your minds are lazy. Your indifference to education is affecting your characters. You will amount to nothing. Now mark what I say—Louise will be so far ahead of you that you will never catch up."

The distracted man went out of the house and into the street shaking with wrath. He went along muttering words and swearing, but when he got into Main Street his anger passed. He stopped to talk of the weather or the crops with some other merchant or with a farmer who had come into town and forgot his daughters altogether or, if he thought of them, only shrugged his shoulders. "Oh, well, girls will be girls," he muttered philosophically.

In the house when Louise came down into the room where the two girls sat, they would have nothing to do with her. One evening after she had been there for more than six weeks and was heartbroken because of the continued air of coldness with which she was always greeted, she burst into tears. "Shut up your crying and go back to your own room and to your books," Mary Hardy said sharply.

• • • • • • •

The room occupied by Louise was on the second floor of the Hardy house, and her window looked out upon an orchard. There was a stove in the room and every evening young John Hardy carried up an armful of wood and put it in a box that stood by the wall. During the second month after she came to the house, Louise gave up all hope of getting on a friendly footing with the Hardy girls and went to her own room as soon as the evening meal was at an end.

Her mind began to play with thoughts of making friends with John Hardy. When he came into the room with the wood in his arms, she pretended to be busy with her studies but watched him eagerly. When he had put the wood in the box and turned to go out, she put down her head and blushed. She tried to make talk but could say nothing, and after he had gone she was angry at herself for her stupidity.

The mind of the country girl became filled with the idea of drawing close to the young man. She thought that in him might be found the quality she had all her life been seeking in people. It seemed to her that between herself and all the other people in the world, a wall had been built up and that she was living just on the edge of some warm inner circle of life that must be quite open and understandable to others. She became obsessed with the thought that it wanted but a courageous act on her part to make all of her association with people something quite different, and that it was possible by such an act to pass into a new life as one opens a door and goes into a room. Day and night she thought of the matter, but although the thing she wanted so earnestly was something very warm and close it had as yet no conscious connection with sex. It had not become that definite, and her mind had only alighted upon the person of John Hardy because he was at hand and unlike his sisters had not been unfriendly to her.

The Hardy sisters, Mary and Harriet, were both older than Louise. In a certain kind of knowledge of the world they were years older. They lived as all of the young women of Middle Western towns lived. In those days young women did not go out of our towns to eastern colleges and ideas in regard to social classes had hardly begun to exist. A daughter of a laborer was in much the same social position as a daughter of a farmer or a merchant, and there were no leisure classes. A girl was "nice" or she was "not nice." If a nice girl, she had a young man who came to her house to see her on Sunday and on Wednesday evenings. Sometimes she went with her young man to a dance or a church social. At other times she received him at the house and was given the use of the parlor for that purpose. No one intruded upon her. For hours the two sat behind closed doors. Sometimes the lights were turned low and the young man and woman embraced. Cheeks became hot and hair disarranged. After a year or two, if the impulse within them became strong and insistent enough, they married.

One evening during her first winter in Winesburg, Louise had an adventure that gave a new impulse to her desire to break down the wall that she thought stood between her and John Hardy. It was Wednesday and immediately after the evening meal Albert Hardy put on his hat and went away. Young John brought the wood and put it in the box in Louise's room. "You do work hard, don't you?" he said awkwardly, and then before she could answer he also went away.

Louise heard him go out of the house and had a mad desire to run after him. Opening her window she leaned out and called softly. "John, dear John, come back, don't go away." The night was cloudy and she could not see far into the darkness, but as she waited she fancied she could hear a soft little noise as of someone going on tiptoes through the trees in the orchard. She was frightened and closed the window quickly. For an hour she moved about the room trembling with excitement and when she could not longer bear the waiting, she crept into the hall and down the stairs into a closet-like room that opened off the parlor.

Louise had decided that she would perform the courageous act that had for weeks been in her mind. She was convinced that John Hardy had concealed himself in the orchard beneath her window and she was determined to find him and tell him that she wanted him to come close to her, to hold her in his arms, to tell her of his thoughts and dreams and to listen while she told him her thoughts and dreams. "In the darkness it will be easier to say things," she whispered to herself, as she stood in the little room groping for the door.

And then suddenly Louise realized that she was not alone in the house. In the parlor on the other side of the door a man's voice spoke softly and the door opened. Louise just had time to conceal herself in a little opening beneath the stairway when Mary Hardy, accompanied by her young man, came into the little dark room.

For an hour Louise sat on the floor in the darkness and listened. Without words Mary Hardy, with the aid of the man who had come to spend the evening with her, brought to the country girl a knowledge of men and women. Putting her head down until she was curled into a little ball she lay perfectly still. It seemed to her that by some strange impulse of the gods, a great gift had been brought to Mary Hardy and she could not understand the older woman's determined protest.

The young man took Mary Hardy into his arms and kissed her. When she struggled and laughed, he but held her the more tightly. For an hour the contest between them went on and then they went back into the parlor and Louise escaped up the stairs. "I hope you were quiet out there. You must not disturb the little mouse at her studies," she heard Harriet saying to her sister as she stood by her own door in the hallway above.

Louise wrote a note to John Hardy and late that night when all in the house were asleep, she crept downstairs and slipped it under his door. She was afraid that if she did not do the thing at once her courage would fail. In the note she tried to be quite definite about what she wanted. "I want someone to love me and I want to love someone," she wrote. "If you are the one for me I want you to come into the orchard at night and make a noise under my window. It will be easy for me to crawl down over the shed and come to you. I am thinking about it all the time, so if you are to come at all you must come soon."

For a long time Louise did not know what would be the outcome of her bold attempt to secure for herself a lover. In a way she still did not know whether or not she wanted him to come. Sometimes it seemed to her that to be held tightly and kissed was the whole secret of life, and then a new impulse came and she was terribly afraid. The age-old woman's desire to be possessed had taken possession of her, but so vague was her notion of life that it seemed to her just the touch of John Hardy's hand upon her own hand would satisfy. She wondered if he would understand that. At the table next day while Albert Hardy talked and the two girls whispered and laughed, she did not look at John but at the table and as soon as possible escaped. In the evening she went out of the house until she was sure he had taken the wood to her room and gone away. When after several evenings of intense listening she heard no call from the darkness in the orchard, she was half beside herself with grief and decided that for her there was no way to break through the wall that had shut her off from the joy of life.

And then on a Monday evening two or three weeks after the writing of the note, John Hardy came for her. Louise had so entirely given up the thought of his coming that for a long time she did not hear the call that came up from the orchard. On the Friday evening before, as she was being driven back to the farm for the week-end by one of the hired men, she had on an impulse done a thing that had startled her, and as John Hardy stood in the darkness below and called her name softly and insistently, she walked about in her room and wondered what new impulse had led her to commit so ridiculous an act.

The farm hand, a young fellow with black curly hair, had come for her somewhat late on that Friday evening and they drove home in the darkness. Louise, whose mind was filled with thoughts of John Hardy, tried to make talk but the country boy was embarrassed and would say nothing. Her mind began to review the loneliness of her childhood and she remembered with a pang the sharp new loneliness that had just come to her. "I hate everyone," she cried suddenly, and then broke forth into a tirade that frightened her escort. "I hate father and old man

Hardy, too," she declared vehemently. "I get my lessons there in the school in town but I hate that also."

Louise frightened the farm hand still more by turning and putting her cheek down upon his shoulder. Vaguely she hoped that he like that young man who had stood in the darkness with Mary would put his arms about her and kiss her, but the country boy was only alarmed. He struck the horse with the whip and began to whistle. "The road is rough, eh?" he said loudly. Louise was so angry that reaching up she snatched his hat from his head and threw it into the road. When he jumped out of the buggy and went to get it, she drove off and left him to walk the rest of the way back to the farm.

Louise Bentley took John Hardy to be her lover. That was not what she wanted but it was so the young man had interpreted her approach to him, and so anxious was she to achieve something else that she made no resistance. When after a few months they were both afraid that she was about to become a mother, they went one evening to the county seat and were married. For a few months they lived in the Hardy house and then took a house of their own. All during the first year Louise tried to make her husband understand the vague and intangible hunger that had led to the writing of the note and that was still unsatisfied. Again and again she crept into his arms and tried to talk of it, but always without success. Filled with his own notions of love between men and women, he did not listen but began to kiss her upon the lips. That confused her so that in the end she did not want to be kissed. She did not know what she wanted.

When the alarm that had tricked them into marriage proved to be groundless, she was angry and said bitter, hurtful things. Later when her son David was born, she could not nurse him and did not know whether she wanted him or not. Sometimes she stayed in the room with him all day, walking about and occasionally creeping close to touch him tenderly with her hands, and then other days came when she did not want to see or be near the tiny bit of humanity that had come into the house. When John Hardy reproached her for her cruelty, she laughed. "It is a man child and will get what it wants anyway," she said sharply. "Had it been a woman child there is nothing in the world I would not have done for it."

Godliness

PART FOUR

Terror

When David Hardy was a tall boy of fifteen, he, like his mother, had an adventure that changed the whole current of his life and sent him out of his quiet corner into the world. The shell of the circumstances of his life was broken and he was compelled to start forth. He left Winesburg and no one there ever saw him again. After his disappearance, his mother and grandfather both died and his father became very rich. He spent much money in trying to locate his son, but that is no part of this story.

It was in the late fall of an unusual year on the Bentley farms. Everywhere the crops had been heavy. That spring, Jesse had bought part of a long strip of black swamp land that lay in the valley of Wine Creek. He got the land at a low price but had spent a large sum of money to improve it. Great ditches had to be dug and thousands of tile laid. Neighboring farmers shook their heads over the expense. Some of them laughed and hoped that Jesse would lose heavily by the venture, but the old man went silently on with the work and said nothing.

When the land was drained he planted it to cabbages and onions, and again the neighbors laughed. The crop was, however, enormous and brought high prices. In the one year Jesse made enough money to pay for all the cost of preparing the land and had a surplus that enabled him to buy two more farms. He was exultant and could not conceal his delight. For the first time in all the history of his ownership of the farms, he went among his men with a smiling face.

Jesse bought a great many new machines for cutting down the cost of labor and all of the remaining acres in the strip of black fertile swamp land. One day he went into Winesburg and bought a bicycle and a new suit of clothes for David and he gave his two sisters money with which to go to a religious convention at Cleveland, Ohio.

In the fall of that year when the frost came and the trees in the forests along Wine Creek were golden brown, David spent every moment when he did not have to attend school, out in the open. Alone or with other boys he went every afternoon into the woods to gather nuts. The other boys of the countryside, most of them sons of laborers on the Bentley farms, had guns with which they went hunting rabbits and squirrels, but David did not go with them. He made himself a sling with rubber bands and a forked stick and went off by himself to gather nuts. As he went about thoughts came to him. He realized that he was almost a man and wondered what he would do in life, but before they came to anything, the thoughts passed and he was a boy again. One day he killed a squirrel that sat on one of the lower branches of a tree and chattered at him. Home he ran with the squirrel in his hand. One of the Bentley sisters cooked the little animal and he ate it with great gusto. The skin he tacked on a board and suspended the board by a string from his bedroom window.

That gave his mind a new turn. After that he never went into the woods without carrying the sling in his pocket and he spent hours shooting at imaginary animals concealed among the brown leaves in the trees.

Thoughts of his coming manhood passed and he was content to be a boy with a boy's impulses.

One Saturday morning when he was about to set off for the woods with the sling in his pocket and a bag for nuts on his shoulder, his grandfather stopped him. In the eyes of the old man was the strained serious look that always a little frightened David. At such times Jesse Bentley's eyes did not look straight ahead but wavered and seemed to be looking at nothing. Something like an invisible curtain appeared to have come between the man and all the rest of the world. "I want you to come with me," he said briefly, and his eyes looked over the boy's head into the sky. "We have something important to do to-day. You may bring the bag for nuts if you wish. It does not matter and anyway we will be going into the woods."

Jesse and David set out from the Bentley farmhouse in the old phaeton[1] that was drawn by the white horse. When they had gone along in silence for a long way they stopped at the edge of a field where a flock of sheep were grazing. Among the sheep was a lamb that had been born out of season, and this David and his grandfather caught and tied so tightly that it looked like a little white ball. When they drove on again Jesse let David hold the lamb in his arms. "I saw it yesterday and it put me in mind of what I have long wanted to do," he said, and again he looked away over the head of the boy with the wavering, uncertain stare in his eyes.

After the feeling of exaltation that had come to the farmer as a result of his successful year, another mood had taken possession of him. For a long time he had been going about feeling very humble and prayerful. Again he walked alone at night thinking of God and as he walked he again connected his own figure with the figures of old days. Under the stars he knelt on the wet grass and raised up his voice in prayer. Now he had decided that like the men whose stories filled the pages of the Bible, he would make a sacrifice to God. "I have been given these abundant crops and God has also sent me a boy who is called David," he whispered to himself. "Perhaps I should have done this thing long ago." He was sorry the idea had not come into his mind in the days before his daughter Louise had been born and thought that surely now when he had erected a pile of burning sticks in some lonely place in the woods and had offered the body of a lamb as a burnt offering, God would appear to him and give him a message.

More and more as he thought of the matter, he thought also of David and his passionate self love was partially forgotten. "It is time for the boy to begin thinking of going out into the world and the message will be one concerning him," he decided. "God will make a pathway for him. He will tell me what place David is to take in life and when he shall set

1. A light-duty, horse-drawn, four-wheeled carriage, usually topless and fitted with two forward-facing seats.

out on his journey. It is right that the boy should be there. If I am fortunate and an angel of God should appear, David will see the beauty and glory of God made manifest to man. It will make a true man of God of him also."

In silence Jesse and David drove along the road until they came to that place where Jesse had once before appealed to God and had frightened his grandson. The morning had been bright and cheerful, but a cold wind now began to blow and clouds hid the sun. When David saw the place to which they had come he began to tremble with fright, and when they stopped by the bridge where the creek came down from among the trees, he wanted to spring out of the phaeton and run away.

A dozen plans for escape ran through David's head, but when Jesse stopped the horse and climbed over the fence into the wood, he followed. "It is foolish to be afraid. Nothing will happen," he told himself as he went along with the lamb in his arms. There was something in the helplessness of the little animal, held so tightly in his arms that gave him courage. He could feel the rapid beating of the beast's heart and that made his own heart beat less rapidly. As he walked swiftly along behind his grandfather, he untied the string with which the four legs of the lamb were fastened together. "If anything happens we will run away together," he thought.

In the woods, after they had gone a long way from the road, Jesse stopped in an opening among the trees where a clearing, overgrown with small bushes, ran up from the creek. He was still silent but began at once to erect a heap of dry sticks which he presently set afire. The boy sat on the ground with the lamb in his arms. His imagination began to invest every movement of the old man with significance and he became every moment more afraid. "I must put the blood of the lamb on the head of the boy," Jesse muttered when the sticks had begun to blaze greedily, and taking a long knife from his pocket he turned and walked rapidly across the clearing toward David.[2]

Terror seized upon the soul of the boy. He was sick with it. For a moment he sat perfectly still and then his body stiffened and he sprang to his feet. His face became as white as the fleece of the lamb, that now finding itself suddenly released, ran down the hill. David ran also. Fear made his feet fly. Over the low bushes and logs he leaped frantically. As he ran he put his hand into his pocket and took out the branched stick from which the sling for shooting squirrels was suspended. When he came to the creek that was shallow and splashed down over the stones, he dashed into the water and turned to look back, and when he saw his grandfather still running toward him with the long knife held tightly in his hand he did not hesitate but reaching down, selected a stone and put

2. Abraham, patriarch of the Israelites, was willing to kill his only son, Isaac, to demonstrate his faith in God; Abraham's faith tested satisfactorily, God provided in time an animal to substitute for Isaac in the ceremony (see Genesis 22).

it in the sling. With all his strength he drew back the heavy rubber bands and the stone whistled through the air. It hit Jesse, who had entirely forgotten the boy and was pursuing the lamb, squarely in the head.[3] With a groan he pitched forward and fell almost at the boy's feet. When David saw that he lay still and that he was apparently dead, his fright increased immeasurably. It became an insane panic.

With a cry he turned and ran off through the woods weeping convulsively. "I don't care—I killed him, but I don't care," he sobbed. As he ran on and on he decided suddenly that he would never go back again to the Bentley farms or to the town of Winesburg. "I have killed the man of God and now I will myself be a man and go into the world," he said stoutly as he stopped running and walked rapidly down a road that followed the windings of Wine Creek as it ran through fields and forests into the west.

On the ground by the creek Jesse Bentley moved uneasily about. He groaned and opened his eyes. For a long time he lay perfectly still and looked at the sky. When at last he got to his feet, his mind was confused and he was not surprised by the boy's disappearance. By the roadside he sat down on a log and began to talk about God. That is all they ever got out of him. Whenever David's name was mentioned he looked vaguely at the sky and said that a messenger from God had taken the boy. "It happened because I was too greedy for glory," he declared, and would have no more to say in the matter.

A Man of Ideas

He lived with his mother, a grey, silent woman with a peculiar ashy complexion. The house in which they lived stood in a little grove of trees beyond where the main street of Winesburg crossed Wine Creek. His name was Joe Welling, and his father had been a man of some dignity in the community, a lawyer and a member of the state legislature at Columbus. Joe himself was small of body and in his character unlike anyone else in town. He was like a tiny little volcano that lies silent for days and then suddenly spouts fire. No, he wasn't like that—he was like a man who is subject to fits, one who walks among his fellow men inspiring fear because a fit may come upon him suddenly and blow him away into a strange uncanny physical state in which his eyes roll and his legs and arms jerk. He was like that, only that the visitation that descended upon Joe Welling was a mental and not a physical thing. He was beset by ideas and in the throes of one of his ideas was uncontrollable. Words rolled and tumbled from his mouth. A peculiar smile came

3. The Philistine giant Goliath, who had defeated the Israelite army, was killed by the boy David, who shot one rock from his sling into the forehead of the giant (see 1 Samuel 17). See n. 1, p. 35.

upon his lips. The edges of his teeth that were tipped with gold glistened in the light. Pouncing upon a bystander he began to talk. For the bystander there was no escape. The excited man breathed into his face, peered into his eyes, pounded upon his chest with a shaking forefinger, demanded, compelled attention.

In those days the Standard Oil Company did not deliver oil to the consumer in big wagons and motor trucks as it does now, but delivered instead to retail grocers, hardware stores and the like. Joe was the Standard Oil agent in Winesburg and in several towns up and down the railroad that went through Winesburg. He collected bills, booked orders, and did other things. His father, the legislator, had secured the job for him.

In and out of the stores of Winesburg went Joe Welling—silent, excessively polite, intent upon his business. Men watched him with eyes in which lurked amusement tempered by alarm. They were waiting for him to break forth, preparing to flee. Although the seizures that came upon him were harmless enough, they could not be laughed away. They were overwhelming. Astride an idea, Joe was overmastering. His personality became gigantic. It overrode the man to whom he talked, swept him away, swept all away, all who stood within sound of his voice.

In Sylvester West's Drug Store stood four men who were talking of horse racing. Wesley Moyer's stallion, Tony Tip, was to race at the June meeting at Tiffin, Ohio, and there was a rumor that he would meet the stiffest competition of his career. It was said that Pop Geers, the great racing driver, would himself be there.[1] A doubt of the success of Tony Tip hung heavy in the air of Winesburg.

Into the drug store came Joe Welling, brushing the screen door violently aside. With a strange absorbed light in his eyes he pounced upon Ed Thomas, he who knew Pop Geers and whose opinion of Tony Tip's chances was worth considering.

"The water is up in Wine Creek," cried Joe Welling with the air of Pheidippides bringing news of the victory of the Greeks in the struggle at Marathon.[2] His finger beat a tattoo upon Ed Thomas' broad chest. "By Trunion bridge it is within eleven and a half inches of the flooring," he went on, the words coming quickly and with a little whistling noise from between his teeth. An expression of helpless annoyance crept over the faces of the four.

"I have my facts correct. Depend upon that. I went to Sinnings' Hard-

1. Edward Franklin Geers (1851–1924), called "Pop," expert rider and trainer of racehorses, known to Anderson by reputation and through *Ed Geers' Experience with Trotters and Pacers* (1901).
2. Before the battle of the Athenians and the Persians on the Plains of Marathon in 490 B.C., Pheidippides, the Athenian messenger who had been sent racing on foot to Sparta to secure that city's help against the Persians, had not succeeded in bringing the Spartans in time to be of use to the greatly outnumbered Greek forces, who, through strategy and luck, defeated the enemy (with deaths of 6400 to 192). Anderson confuses Pheidippides with another runner—the bringer of news of victory home to Athens.

ware Store and got a rule. Then I went back and measured. I could hardly believe my own eyes. It hasn't rained you see for ten days. At first I didn't know what to think. Thoughts rushed through my head. I thought of subterranean passages and springs. Down under the ground went my mind, delving about. I sat on the floor of the bridge and rubbed my head. There wasn't a cloud in the sky, not one. Come out into the street and you'll see. There wasn't a cloud. There isn't a cloud now. Yes, there was a cloud. I don't want to keep back any facts. There was a cloud in the west down near the horizon, a cloud no bigger than a man's hand.

"Not that I think that has anything to do with it. There it is you see. You understand how puzzled I was.

"Then an idea came to me. I laughed. You'll laugh, too. Of course it rained over in Medina County. That's interesting, eh? If we had no trains, no mails, no telegraph, we would know that it rained over in Medina County. That's where Wine Creek comes from. Everyone knows that. Little old Wine Creek brought us the news. That's interesting. I laughed. I thought I'd tell you—it's interesting, eh?"

Joe Welling turned and went out at the door. Taking a book from his pocket, he stopped and ran a finger down one of the pages. Again he was absorbed in his duties as agent of the Standard Oil Company. "Hern's Grocery will be getting low on coal oil. I'll see them," he muttered, hurrying along the street, and bowing politely to the right and left at the people walking past.

When George Willard went to work for the *Winesburg Eagle* he was besieged by Joe Welling. Joe envied the boy. It seemed to him that he was meant by Nature to be a reporter on a newspaper. "It is what I should be doing, there is no doubt of that," he declared, stopping George Willard on the sidewalk before Daugherty's Feed Store. His eyes began to glisten and his forefinger to tremble. "Of course I make more money with the Standard Oil Company and I'm only telling you," he added. "I've got nothing against you, but I should have your place. I could do the work at odd moments. Here and there I would run finding out things you'll never see."

Becoming more excited Joe Welling crowded the young reporter against the front of the feed store. He appeared to be lost in thought, rolling his eyes about and running a thin nervous hand through his hair. A smile spread over his face and his gold teeth glittered. "You get out your note book," he commanded. "You carry a little pad of paper in your pocket, don't you? I knew you did. Well, you set this down. I thought of it the other day. Let's take decay. Now what is decay? It's fire. It burns up wood and other things. You never thought of that? Of course not. This sidewalk here and this feed store, the trees down the street there—they're all on fire. They're burning up. Decay you see is always going on. It don't stop. Water and paint can't stop it. If a thing is iron, then what? It rusts, you see. That's fire, too. The world is on fire. Start your pieces in the paper that way. Just say in big letters '*The World Is On Fire.*' That will make 'em look up. They'll say you're a smart one. I don't care. I don't envy you. I just snatched that idea out of the air. I would make a newspaper hum. You got to admit that."

Turning quickly, Joe Welling walked rapidly away. When he had taken several steps he stopped and looked back. "I'm going to stick to you," he said. "I'm going to make you a regular hummer. I should start a newspaper myself, that's what I should do. I'd be a marvel. Everybody knows that."

When George Willard had been for a year on the *Winesburg Eagle*, four things happened to Joe Welling. His mother died, he came to live at the New Willard House, he became involved in a love affair, and he organized the Winesburg Baseball Club.

Joe organized the baseball club because he wanted to be a coach and in that position he began to win the respect of his townsmen. "He is a wonder," they declared after Joe's team had whipped the team from Medina County. "He gets everybody working together. You just watch him."

Upon the baseball field Joe Welling stood by first base, his whole body quivering with excitement. In spite of themselves all of the players watched him closely. The opposing pitcher became confused.

"Now! Now! Now! Now!" shouted the excited man. "Watch me! Watch me! Watch my fingers! Watch my hands! Watch my feet! Watch my eyes! Let's work together here! Watch me! In me you see all the movements of the game! Work with me! Work with me! Watch me! Watch me! Watch me!"

With runners of the Winesburg team on bases, Joe Welling became as one inspired. Before they knew what had come over them, the base runners were watching the man, edging off the bases, advancing, retreating, held as by an invisible cord. The players of the opposing team also watched Joe. They were fascinated. For a moment they watched and then as though to break a spell that hung over them, they began hurling the ball wildly about, and amid a series of fierce animal-like cries from the coach, the runners of the Winesburg team scampered home.

Joe Welling's love affair set the town of Winesburg on edge. When it began everyone whispered and shook his head. When people tried to laugh, the laughter was forced and unnatural. Joe fell in love with Sarah King, a lean, sad-looking woman who lived with her father and brother in a brick house that stood opposite the gate leading to the Winesburg Cemetery.

The two Kings, Edward the father, and Tom the son, were not popular in Winesburg. They were called proud and dangerous. They had come to Winesburg from some place in the South and ran a cider mill on the Trunion Pike. Tom King was reported to have killed a man before he came to Winesburg. He was twenty-seven years old and rode about town on a grey pony. Also he had a long yellow mustache that dropped down over his teeth, and always carried a heavy, wicked-looking walking stick in his hand. Once he killed a dog with the stick. The dog belonged to Win Pawsey, the shoe merchant, and stood on the sidewalk wagging its tail. Tom King killed it with one blow. He was arrested and paid a fine of ten dollars.

Old Edward King was small of stature and when he passed people in the street laughed a queer unmirthful laugh. When he laughed he scratched his left elbow with his right hand. The sleeve of his coat was almost worn through from the habit. As he walked along the street, looking nervously about and laughing, he seemed more dangerous than his silent, fierce looking son.

When Sarah King began walking out in the evening with Joe Welling, people shook their heads in alarm. She was tall and pale and had dark rings under her eyes. The couple looked ridiculous together. Under the trees they walked and Joe talked. His passionate eager protestations of love, heard coming out of the darkness by the cemetery wall, or from the deep shadows of the trees on the hill that ran up to the Fair Grounds from Waterworks Pond, were repeated in the stores. Men stood by the bar in the New Willard House laughing and talking of Joe's courtship. After the laughter came silence. The Winesburg baseball team, under his management, was winning game after game, and the town had begun to respect him. Sensing a tragedy, they waited, laughing nervously.

Late on a Saturday afternoon the meeting between Joe Welling and the two Kings, the anticipation of which had set the town on edge, took place in Joe Welling's room in the New Willard House. George Willard was a witness to the meeting. It came about in this way:

When the young reporter went to his room after the evening meal he saw Tom King and his father sitting in the half darkness in Joe's room. The son had the heavy walking stick in his hand and sat near the door. Old Edward King walked nervously about, scratching his left elbow with his right hand. The hallways were empty and silent.

George Willard went to his own room and sat down at his desk. He tried to write but his hand trembled so that he could not hold the pen. He also walked nervously up and down. Like the rest of the town of Winesburg he was perplexed and knew not what to do.

It was seven-thirty and fast growing dark when Joe Welling came along the station platform toward the New Willard House. In his arms he held a bundle of weeds and grasses. In spite of the terror that made his body shake, George Willard was amused at the sight of the small spry figure holding the grasses and half running along the platform.

Shaking with fright and anxiety, the young reporter lurked in the hallway outside the door of the room in which Joe Welling talked to the two Kings. There had been an oath, the nervous giggle of old Edward King, and then silence. Now the voice of Joe Welling, sharp and clear, broke forth. George Willard began to laugh. He understood. As he had swept all men before him, so now Joe Welling was carrying the two men in the room off their feet with a tidal wave of words. The listener in the hall walked up and down, lost in amazement.

Inside the room Joe Welling had paid no attention to the grumbled threat of Tom King. Absorbed in an idea he closed the door and lighting a lamp, spread the handful of weeds and grasses upon the floor. "I've got something here," he announced solemnly. "I was going to tell George Willard about it, let him make a piece out of it for the paper. I'm glad you're here. I wish Sarah were here also. I've been going to come to your house and tell you of some of my ideas. They're interesting. Sarah wouldn't let me. She said we'd quarrel. That's foolish."

Running up and down before the two perplexed men, Joe Welling began to explain. "Don't you make a mistake now," he cried. "This is something big." His voice was shrill with excitement. "You just follow me, you'll be interested. I know you will. Suppose this—suppose all of the wheat, the corn, the oats, the peas, the potatoes, were all by some miracle swept away. Now here we are, you see, in this county. There is a high fence built all around us. We'll suppose that. No one can get over the fence and all the fruits of the earth are destroyed, nothing left but these wild things, these grasses. Would we be done for? I ask you that. Would we be done for?" Again Tom King growled and for a moment there was silence in the room. Then again Joe plunged into the exposition of his idea. "Things would go hard for a time. I admit that. I've got to admit that. No getting around it. We'd be hard put to it. More than one fat stomach would cave in. But they couldn't down us. I should say not."

Tom King laughed good naturedly and the shivery, nervous laugh of Edward King rang through the house. Joe Welling hurried on. "We'd begin, you see, to breed up new vegetables and fruits. Soon we'd regain all we had lost. Mind, I don't say the new things would be the same as the old. They wouldn't. Maybe they'd be better, maybe not so good. That's interesting, eh? You can think about that. It starts your mind working, now don't it?"

In the room there was silence and then again old Edward King laughed nervously. "Say, I wish Sarah was here," cried Joe Welling. "Let's go up to your house. I want to tell her of this."

There was a scraping of chairs in the room. It was then that George Willard retreated to his own room. Leaning out at the window he saw Joe Welling going along the street with the two Kings. Tom King was forced to take extraordinary long strides to keep pace with the little man. As he strode along, he leaned over, listening—absorbed, fascinated. Joe

Welling again talked excitedly. "Take milkweed now," he cried. "A lot might be done with milkweed, eh? It's almost unbelievable. I want you to think about it. I want you two to think about it. There would be a new vegetable kingdom you see. It's interesting, eh? It's an idea. Wait till you see Sarah, she'll get the idea. She'll be interested. Sarah is always interested in ideas. You can't be too smart for Sarah, now can you? Of course you can't. You know that."

Adventure

Alice Hindman, a woman of twenty-seven when George Willard was a mere boy, had lived in Winesburg all her life. She clerked in Winney's Dry Goods Store and lived with her mother who had married a second husband.

Alice's step-father was a carriage painter, and given to drink. His story is an odd one. It will be worth telling some day.

At twenty-seven Alice was tall and somewhat slight. Her head was large and overshadowed her body. Her shoulders were a little stooped and her hair and eyes brown. She was very quiet but beneath a placid exterior a continual ferment went on.

When she was a girl of sixteen and before she began to work in the store, Alice had an affair with a young man. The young man, named Ned Currie, was older than Alice. He, like George Willard, was employed on the *Winesburg Eagle* and for a long time he went to see Alice almost every evening. Together the two walked under the trees through the streets of the town and talked of what they would do with their lives. Alice was then a very pretty girl and Ned Currie took her into his arms and kissed her. He became excited and said things he did not intend to say and Alice, betrayed by her desire to have something beautiful come into her rather narrow life, also grew excited. She also talked. The outer crust of her life, all of her natural diffidence and reserve, was torn away and she gave herself over to the emotions of love. When, late in the fall of her sixteenth year, Ned Currie went away to Cleveland where he hoped to get a place on a city newspaper and rise in the world, she wanted to go with him. With a trembling voice she told him what was in her mind. "I will work and you can work," she said. "I do not want to harness you to a needless expense that will prevent your making progress. Don't marry me now. We will get along without that and we can be together. Even though we live in the same house no one will say anything. In the city we will be unknown and people will pay no attention to us."

Ned Currie was puzzled by the determination and abandon of his sweetheart and was also deeply touched. He had wanted the girl to become his mistress but changed his mind. He wanted to protect and care for her. "You don't know what you're talking about," he said sharply; "you may be sure I'll let you do no such thing. As soon as I get a good job I'll come back. For the present you'll have to stay here. It's the only thing we can do."

On the evening before he left Winesburg to take up his new life in the city, Ned Currie went to call on Alice. They walked about through the streets for an hour and then got a rig from Wesley Moyer's livery and went for a drive in the country. The moon came up and they found themselves unable to talk. In his sadness the young man forgot the resolutions he had made regarding his conduct with the girl.

They got out of the buggy at a place where a long meadow ran down to the bank of Wine Creek and there in the dim light became lovers. When at midnight they returned to town they were both glad. It did not seem to them that anything that could happen in the future could blot out the wonder and beauty of the thing that had happened. "Now we will have to stick to each other, whatever happens we will have to do that," Ned Currie said as he left the girl at her father's door.

The young newspaper man did not succeed in getting a place on a Cleveland paper and went west to Chicago. For a time he was lonely and wrote to Alice almost every day. Then he was caught up by the life of the city; he began to make friends and found new interests in life. In Chicago he boarded at a house where there were several women. One of them attracted his attention and he forgot Alice in Winesburg. At the end of a year he had stopped writing letters, and only once in a long time, when he was lonely or when he went into one of the city parks and saw the moon shining on the grass as it had shone that night on the meadow by Wine Creek, did he think of her at all.

In Winesburg the girl who had been loved grew to be a woman. When she was twenty-two years old her father, who owned a harness repair shop, died suddenly. The harness maker was an old soldier, and after a few months his wife received a widow's pension. She used the first money she got to buy a loom and became a weaver of carpets, and Alice got a place in Winney's store. For a number of years nothing could have induced her to believe that Ned Currie would not in the end return to her.

She was glad to be employed because the daily round of toil in the store made the time of waiting seem less long and uninteresting. She began to save money, thinking that when she had saved two or three hundred dollars she would follow her lover to the city and try if her presence would not win back his affections.

Alice did not blame Ned Currie for what had happened in the moonlight in the field, but felt that she could never marry another man. To her the thought of giving to another what she still felt could belong only to Ned seemed monstrous. When other young men tried to attract her attention she would have nothing to do with them. "I am his wife and shall remain his wife whether he comes back or not," she whispered to herself, and for all of her willingness to support herself could not have understood the growing modern idea of a woman's owning herself and giving and taking for her own ends in life.

Alice worked in the dry goods store from eight in the morning until six at night and on three evenings a week went back to the store to stay from seven until nine. As time passed and she became more and more lonely she began to practice the devices common to lonely people. When at night she went upstairs into her own room she knelt on the floor to pray and in her prayers whispered things she wanted to say to her lover. She became attached to inanimate objects, and because it was her own, could not bear to have anyone touch the furniture of her room. The trick of saving money, begun for a purpose, was carried on after the scheme of going to the city to find Ned Currie had been given up. It became a fixed habit, and when she needed new clothes she did not get them. Sometimes on rainy afternoons in the store she got out her bank book and, letting it lie open before her, spent hours dreaming impossible dreams of saving money enough so that the interest would support both herself and her future husband.

"Ned always liked to travel about," she thought. "I'll give him the chance. Some day when we are married and I can save both his money and my own, we will be rich. Then we can travel together all over the world."

In the dry goods store weeks ran into months and months into years as Alice waited and dreamed of her lover's return. Her employer, a grey old man with false teeth and a thin grey mustache that drooped down over his mouth, was not given to conversation, and sometimes, on rainy days and in the winter when a storm raged in Main Street, long hours passed when no customers came in. Alice arranged and rearranged the stock. She stood near the front window where she could look down the deserted street and thought of the evenings when she had walked with Ned Currie and of what he had said. "We will have to stick to each other now." The words echoed and re-echoed through the mind of the maturing woman. Tears came into her eyes. Sometimes when her employer had gone out and she was alone in the store she put her head on the counter and wept. "Oh, Ned, I am waiting," she whispered over and over, and all the time the creeping fear that he would never come back grew stronger within her.

In the spring when the rains have passed and before the long hot days of summer have come, the country about Winesburg is delightful. The town lies in the midst of open fields, but beyond the fields are pleasant patches of woodlands. In the wooded places are many little cloistered nooks, quiet places where lovers go to sit on Sunday afternoons. Through the trees they look out across the fields and see farmers at work about the barns or people driving up and down on the roads. In the town bells ring and occasionally a train passes, looking like a toy thing in the distance.

For several years after Ned Currie went away Alice did not go into the wood with other young people on Sunday, but one day after he had been gone for two or three years and when her loneliness seemed unbearable, she put on her best dress and set out. Finding a little sheltered place from which she could see the town and a long stretch of the fields, she sat down. Fear of age and ineffectuality took possession of her. She could not sit still, and arose. As she stood looking out over the land something, perhaps the thought of never ceasing life as it expresses itself in the flow of the seasons, fixed her mind on the passing years. With a shiver of dread, she realized that for her the beauty and freshness of youth had passed. For the first time she felt that she had been cheated. She did not blame Ned Currie and did not know what to blame. Sadness swept over her. Dropping to her knees, she tried to pray, but instead of prayers words of protest came to her lips. "It is not going to come to me. I will never find happiness. Why do I tell myself lies?" she cried, and an odd sense of relief came with this, her first bold attempt to face the fear that had become a part of her everyday life.

In the year when Alice Hindman became twenty-five two things happened to disturb the dull uneventfulness of her days. Her mother married Bush Milton, the carriage painter of Winesburg, and she herself became a member of the Winesburg Methodist Church. Alice joined the church because she had become frightened by the loneliness of her position in life. Her mother's second marriage had emphasized her isolation. "I am becoming old and queer. If Ned comes he will not want me. In the city where he is living men are perpetually young. There is so much going on that they do not have time to grow old," she told herself with a grim little smile, and went resolutely about the business of becoming acquainted with people. Every Thursday evening when the store had closed she went to a prayer meeting in the basement of the church and on Sunday evening attended a meeting of an organization called The Epworth League.[1]

When Will Hurley, a middle-aged man who clerked in a drug store and who also belonged to the church, offered to walk home with her she did not protest. "Of course I will not let him make a practice of being with me, but if he comes to see me once in a long time there can be no harm in that," she told herself, still determined in her loyalty to Ned Currie.

Without realizing what was happening, Alice was trying feebly at first, but with growing determination, to get a new hold upon life. Beside the drug clerk she walked in silence, but sometimes in the darkness as they

1. A Methodist youth fellowship, named for the rectory in Lincolnshire, England, where a youthful John Wesley (1703–91), founder of Methodism, served as his father's aide. The League encouraged upright living, social service, and missionary activity.

went stolidly along she put out her hand and touched softly the folds of his coat. When he left her at the gate before her mother's house she did not go indoors, but stood for a moment by the door. She wanted to call to the drug clerk, to ask him to sit with her in the darkness on the porch before the house, but was afraid he would not understand. "It is not him that I want," she told herself; "I want to avoid being so much alone. If I am not careful I will grow unaccustomed to being with people."

• • • • • • •

During the early fall of her twenty-seventh year a passionate restlessness took possession of Alice. She could not bear to be in the company of the drug clerk, and when, in the evening, he came to walk with her she sent him away. Her mind became intensely active and when, weary from the long hours of standing behind the counter in the store, she went home and crawled into bed, she could not sleep. With staring eyes she looked into the darkness. Her imagination, like a child awakened from long sleep, played about the room. Deep within her there was something that would not be cheated by phantasies and that demanded some definite answer from life.

Alice took a pillow into her arms and held it tightly against her breasts. Getting out of bed, she arranged a blanket so that in the darkness it looked like a form lying between the sheets and, kneeling beside the bed, she caressed it, whispering words over and over, like a refrain. "Why doesn't something happen? Why am I left here alone?" she muttered. Although she sometimes thought of Ned Currie, she no longer depended on him. Her desire had grown vague. She did not want Ned Currie or any other man. She wanted to be loved, to have something answer the call that was growing louder and louder within her.

And then one night when it rained Alice had an adventure. It frightened and confused her. She had come home from the store at nine and found the house empty. Bush Milton had gone off to town and her mother to the house of a neighbor. Alice went upstairs to her room and undressed in the darkness. For a moment she stood by the window hearing the rain beat against the glass and then a strange desire took possession of her. Without stopping to think of what she intended to do, she ran downstairs through the dark house and out into the rain. As she stood on the little grass plot before the house and felt the cold rain on her body a mad desire to run naked through the streets took possession of her.

She thought that the rain would have some creative and wonderful effect on her body. Not for years had she felt so full of youth and courage. She wanted to leap and run, to cry out, to find some other lonely human and embrace him. On the brick sidewalk before the house a man stumbled homeward. Alice started to run. A wild, desperate mood took possession of her. "What do I care who it is. He is alone, and I will go to him," she thought; and then without stopping to consider the possible result of her madness, called softly. "Wait!" she cried. "Don't go away. Whoever you are, you must wait."

The man on the sidewalk stopped and stood listening. He was an old man and somewhat deaf. Putting his hand to his mouth, he shouted: "What? What say?" he called.

Alice dropped to the ground and lay trembling. She was so frightened at the thought of what she had done that when the man had gone on his way she did not dare get to her feet, but crawled on hands and knees through the grass to the house. When she got to her own room she bolted the door and drew her dressing table across the doorway. Her body shook as with a chill and her hands trembled so that she had difficulty getting into her nightdress. When she got into bed she buried her face in the pillow and wept broken-heartedly. "What is the matter with me? I will do something dreadful if I am not careful," she thought, and turning her face to the wall, began trying to force herself to face bravely the fact that many people must live and die alone, even in Winesburg.

Respectability

If you have lived in cities and have walked in the park on a summer afternoon, you have perhaps seen, blinking in a corner of his iron cage, a huge, grotesque kind of monkey, a creature with ugly, sagging, hairless skin below his eyes and a bright purple underbody. This monkey is a true monster. In the completeness of his ugliness he achieved a kind of perverted beauty. Children stopping before the cage are fascinated, men turn away with an air of disgust, and women linger for a moment, trying perhaps to remember which one of their male acquaintances the thing in some faint way resembles.

Had you been in the earlier years of your life a citizen of the village of Winesburg, Ohio, there would have been for you no mystery in regard to the beast in his cage. "It is like Wash Williams," you would have said. "As he sits in the corner there, the beast is exactly like old Wash sitting on the grass in the station yard on a summer evening after he has closed his office for the night."

Wash Williams, the telegraph operator of Winesburg, was the ugliest thing in town. His girth was immense, his neck thin, his legs feeble. He was dirty. Everything about him was unclean. Even the whites of his eyes looked soiled.

I go too fast. Not everything about Wash was unclean. He took care of his hands. His fingers were fat, but there was something sensitive and shapely in the hand that lay on the table by the instrument in the telegraph office. In his youth Wash Williams had been called the best telegraph operator in the state, and in spite of his degradement to the obscure office at Winesburg, he was still proud of his ability.

Wash Williams did not associate with the men of the town in which he lived. "I'll have nothing to do with them," he said, looking with bleary eyes at the men who walked along the station platform past the telegraph office. Up along Main Street he went in the evening to Ed Griffith's saloon, and after drinking unbelievable quantities of beer staggered off to his room in the New Willard House and to his bed for the night.

Wash Williams was a man of courage. A thing had happened to him that made him hate life, and he hated it whole-heartedly, with the abandon of a poet. First of all, he hated women. "Bitches," he called them. His feeling toward men was somewhat different. He pitied them. "Does not every man let his life be managed for him by some bitch or another?" he asked.

In Winesburg no attention was paid to Wash Williams and his hatred of his fellows. Once Mrs. White, the banker's wife, complained to the telegraph company, saying that the office in Winesburg was dirty and smelled abominably, but nothing came of her complaint. Here and there a man respected the operator. Instinctively the man felt in him a glowing resentment of something he had not the courage to resent. When Wash walked through the streets such a one had an instinct to pay him homage, to raise his hat or to bow before him. The superintendent who had supervision over the telegraph operators on the railroad that went through Winesburg felt that way. He had put Wash into the obscure office at Winesburg to avoid discharging him, and he meant to keep him there. When he received the letter of complaint from the banker's wife, he tore it up and laughed unpleasantly. For some reason he thought of his own wife as he tore up the letter.

Wash Williams once had a wife. When he was still a young man he married a woman at Dayton, Ohio. The woman was tall and slender and had blue eyes and yellow hair. Wash was himself a comely youth. He loved the woman with a love as absorbing as the hatred he later felt for all women.

In all of Winesburg there was but one person who knew the story of the thing that had made ugly the person and the character of Wash Williams. He once told the story to George Willard and the telling of the tale came about in this way:

George Willard went one evening to walk with Belle Carpenter, a trimmer of women's hats who worked in a millinery shop kept by Mrs. Nate McHugh. The young man was not in love with the woman, who, in fact, had a suitor who worked as bartender in Ed Griffith's saloon, but as they walked about under the trees they occasionally embraced. The night and their own thoughts had aroused something in them. As they were returning to Main Street they passed the little lawn beside the railroad station and saw Wash Williams apparently asleep on the grass beneath a tree. On the next evening the operator and George Willard walked out together. Down the railroad they went and sat on a pile of decaying railroad ties beside the tracks. It was then that the operator told the young reporter his story of hate.

Perhaps a dozen times George Willard and the strange, shapeless man who lived at his father's hotel had been on the point of talking. The young man looked at the hideous, leering face staring about the hotel dining room and was consumed with curiosity. Something he saw lurking in the staring eyes told him that the man who had nothing to say to others had nevertheless something to say to him. On the pile of railroad ties on the summer evening, he waited expectantly. When the operator remained silent and seemed to have changed his mind about talking, he tried to make conversation. "Were you ever married, Mr. Williams?" he began. "I suppose you were and your wife is dead, is that it?"

Wash Williams spat forth a succession of vile oaths. "Yes, she is dead," he agreed. "She is dead as all women are dead. She is a living-dead thing, walking in the sight of men and making the earth foul by her presence." Staring into the boy's eyes, the man became purple with rage. "Don't have fool notions in your head," he commanded. "My wife, she is dead; yes, surely. I tell you, all women are dead, my mother, your mother, that tall dark woman who works in the millinery store and with whom I saw you walking about yesterday—all of them, they are all dead. I tell you there is something rotten about them. I was married, sure. My wife was dead before she married me, she was a foul thing come out of a woman more foul. She was a thing sent to make life unbearable to me. I was a fool, do you see, as you are now, and so I married this woman. I would like to see men a little begin to understand women. They are sent to prevent men making the world worth while. It is a trick in Nature. Ugh! They are creeping, crawling, squirming things, they with their soft hands and their blue eyes. The sight of a woman sickens me. Why I don't kill every woman I see I don't know."

Half frightened and yet fascinated by the light burning in the eyes of the hideous old man, George Willard listened, afire with curiosity. Darkness came on and he leaned forward trying to see the face of the man who talked. When, in the gathering darkness, he could no longer see the purple, bloated face and the burning eyes, a curious fancy came to him. Wash Williams talked in low even tones that made his words seem the more terrible. In the darkness the young reporter found himself imagining that he sat on the railroad ties beside a comely young man with black hair and black shining eyes. There was something almost beautiful in the voice of Wash Williams, the hideous, telling his story of hate.

The telegraph operator of Winesburg, sitting in the darkness on the railroad ties, had become a poet. Hatred had raised him to that elevation. "It is because I saw you kissing the lips of that Belle Carpenter that I tell you my story," he said. "What happened to me may next happen to you. I want to put you on your guard. Already you may be having dreams in your head. I want to destroy them."

Wash Williams began telling the story of his married life with the tall blonde girl with blue eyes whom he had met when he was a young operator at Dayton, Ohio. Here and there his story was touched with moments of beauty intermingled with strings of vile curses. The operator had married the daughter of a dentist who was the youngest of three sisters. On his marriage day, because of his ability, he was promoted to a position as dispatcher at an increased salary and sent to an office at Columbus, Ohio. There he settled down with his young wife and began buying a house on the installment plan.

The young telegraph operator was madly in love. With a kind of religious fervor he had managed to go through the pitfalls of his youth and to remain virginal until after his marriage. He made for George Willard a picture of his life in the house at Columbus, Ohio, with the young wife. "In the garden back of our house we planted vegetables," he said, "you know, peas and corn and such things. We went to Columbus in early March and as soon as the days became warm I went to work in the garden. With a spade I turned up the black ground while she ran about laughing and pretending to be afraid of the worms I uncovered. Late in April came the planting. In the little paths among the seed beds she stood holding a paper bag in her hand. The bag was filled with seeds. A few at a time she handed me the seeds that I might thrust them into the warm, soft ground."

For a moment there was a catch in the voice of the man talking in the darkness. "I loved her," he said. "I don't claim not to be a fool. I love her yet. There in the dusk in the spring evening I crawled along the black ground to her feet and groveled before her. I kissed her shoes and the ankles above her shoes. When the hem of her garment touched my face I trembled. When after two years of that life I found she had managed to acquire three other lovers who came regularly to our house when I was away at work, I didn't want to touch them or her. I just sent her home to her mother and said nothing. There was nothing to say. I had four hundred dollars in the bank and I gave her that. I didn't ask her reasons. I didn't say anything. When she had gone I cried like a silly boy. Pretty soon I had a chance to sell the house and I sent that money to her."

Wash Williams and George Willard arose from the pile of railroad ties and walked along the tracks toward town. The operator finished his tale quickly, breathlessly.

"Her mother sent for me," he said. "She wrote me a letter and asked me to come to their house at Dayton. When I got there it was evening about this time."

Wash Williams' voice rose to a half scream. "I sat in the parlor of that house two hours. Her mother took me in there and left me. Their house was stylish. They were what is called respectable people. There were plush chairs and a couch in the room. I was trembling all over. I hated the men I thought had wronged her. I was sick of living alone and wanted her back. The longer I waited the more raw and tender I became. I thought that if she came in and just touched me with her hand I would perhaps faint away. I ached to forgive and forget."

Wash Williams stopped and stood staring at George Willard. The boy's body shook as from a chill. Again the man's voice became soft and low. "She came into the room naked," he went on. "Her mother did that. While I sat there she was taking the girl's clothes off, perhaps coaxing her to do it. First I heard voices at the door that led into a little hallway and then it opened softly. The girl was ashamed and stood perfectly still staring at the floor. The mother didn't come into the room. When she had pushed the girl in through the door she stood in the hallway waiting, hoping we would—well, you see—waiting."

George Willard and the telegraph operator came into the main street of Winesburg. The lights from the store windows lay bright and shining on the sidewalks. People moved about laughing and talking. The young reporter felt ill and weak. In imagination, he also became old and shapeless. "I didn't get the mother killed," said Wash Williams, staring up and down the street. "I struck her once with a chair and then the neighbors came in and took it away. She screamed so loud you see. I won't ever have a chance to kill her now. She died of a fever a month after that happened."

The Thinker

The house in which Seth Richmond of Winesburg lived with his mother had been at one time the show place of the town, but when young Seth lived there its glory had become somewhat dimmed. The huge brick house which Banker White had built on Buckeye Street had overshadowed it. The Richmond place was in a little valley far out at the end of Main Street. Farmers coming into town by a dusty road from the south passed by a grove of walnut trees, skirted the Fair Ground with its high board fence covered with advertisements, and trotted their horses down through the valley past the Richmond place into town. As much of the country north and south of Winesburg was devoted to fruit and berry raising, Seth saw wagon-loads of berry pickers—boys, girls, and women—going to the fields in the morning and returning covered with dust in the evening. The chattering crowd, with their rude jokes cried out from wagon to wagon, sometimes irritated him sharply. He regretted that he also could not laugh boisterously, shout meaningless jokes and make of himself a figure in the endless stream of moving, giggling activity that went up and down the road.

The Richmond house was built of limestone, and although it was said in the village to have become run down, had in reality grown more beautiful with every passing year. Already time had begun a little to color the stone, lending a golden richness to its surface and in the evening or on dark days touching the shaded places beneath the eaves with wavering patches of browns and blacks.

The house had been built by Seth's grandfather, a stone quarryman, and it, together with the stone quarries on Lake Erie eighteen miles to the north, had been left to his son, Clarence Richmond, Seth's father. Clarence Richmond, a quiet passionate man extraordinarily admired by his neighbors, had been killed in a street fight with the editor of a newspaper in Toledo, Ohio. The fight concerned the publication of Clarence Richmond's name coupled with that of a woman school teacher, and as the dead man had begun the row by firing upon the editor, the effort to punish the slayer was unsuccessful. After the quarryman's death it was found that much of the money left to him had been squandered in speculation and in insecure investments made though the influence of friends.

Left with but a small income, Virginia Richmond had settled down to a retired life in the village and to the raising of her son. Although she had been deeply moved by the death of the husband and father, she did not at all believe the stories concerning him that ran about after his death. To her mind, the sensitive, boyish man whom all had instinctively loved, was but an unfortunate, a being too fine for everyday life. "You'll be hearing all sorts of stories, but you are not to believe what you hear," she said to her son. "He was a good man, full of tenderness for everyone, and should not have tried to be a man of affairs. No matter how much I were to plan and dream of your future, I could not imagine anything better for you than that you turn out as good a man as your father."

Several years after the death of her husband, Virginia Richmond had become alarmed at the growing demands upon her income and had set herself to the task of increasing it. She had learned stenography and through the influence of her husband's friends got the position of court stenographer at the county seat. There she went by train each morning during the sessions of the court and when no court sat, spent her days working among the rosebushes in her garden. She was a tall, straight figure of a woman with a plain face and a great mass of brown hair.

In the relationship between Seth Richmond and his mother, there was a quality that even at eighteen had begun to color all of his traffic with men. An almost unhealthy respect for the youth kept the mother for the most part silent in his presence. When she did speak sharply to him he had only to look steadily into her eyes to see dawning there the puzzled look he had already noticed in the eyes of others when he looked at them.

The truth was that the son thought with remarkable clearness and the mother did not. She expected from all people certain conventional reactions to life. A boy was your son, you scolded him and he trembled and looked at the floor. When you had scolded enough he wept and all was forgiven. After the weeping and when he had gone to bed, you crept into his room and kissed him.

Virginia Richmond could not understand why her son did not do these things. After the severest reprimand, he did not tremble and look at the floor but instead looked steadily at her, causing uneasy doubts to invade her mind. As for creeping into his room—after Seth had passed his fifteenth year, she would have been half afraid to do anything of the kind.

Once when he was a boy of sixteen, Seth in company with two other boys, ran away from home. The three boys climbed into the open door of an empty freight car and rode some forty miles to a town where a fair was being held. One of the boys had a bottle filled with a combination of whiskey and blackberry wine, and the three sat with legs dangling out of the car door drinking from the bottle. Seth's two companions sang and waved their hands to idlers about the stations of the towns through which the train passed. They planned raids upon the baskets of farmers who had come with their families to the fair. "We will live like kings and won't have to spend a penny to see the fair and horse races," they declared boastfully.

After the disappearance of Seth, Virginia Richmond walked up and down the floor of her home filled with vague alarms. Although on the next day she discovered, through an inquiry made by the town marshal, on what adventure the boys had gone, she could not quiet herself. All through the night she lay awake hearing the clock tick and telling herself that Seth, like his father, would come to a sudden and violent end. So determined was she that the boy should this time feel the weight of her wrath that, although she would not allow the marshal to interfere with his adventure, she got out pencil and paper and wrote down a series of sharp, stinging reproofs she intended to pour out upon him. The reproofs she committed to memory, going about the garden and saying them aloud like an actor memorizing his part.

And when, at the end of the week, Seth returned, a little weary and with coal soot in his ears and about his eyes, she again found herself unable to reprove him. Walking into the house he hung his cap on a nail by the kitchen door and stood looking steadily at her. "I wanted to turn back within an hour after we had started," he explained. "I didn't know what to do. I knew you would be bothered, but I knew also that if

I didn't go on I would be ashamed of myself. I went through with the thing for my own good. It was uncomfortable, sleeping on wet straw, and two drunken negroes came and slept with us. When I stole a lunch basket out of a farmer's wagon I couldn't help thinking of his children going all day without food. I was sick of the whole affair, but I was determined to stick it out until the other boys were ready to come back."

"I'm glad you did stick it out," replied the mother, half resentfully, and kissing him upon the forehead pretended to busy herself with the work about the house.

On a summer evening Seth Richmond went to the New Willard House to visit his friend, George Willard. It had rained during the afternoon, but as he walked through Main Street, the sky had partially cleared and a golden glow lit up the west. Going around a corner, he turned in at the door of the hotel and began to climb the stairway leading up to his friend's room. In the hotel office the proprietor and two traveling men were engaged in a discussion of politics.

On the stairway Seth stopped and listened to the voices of the men below. They were excited and talked rapidly. Tom Willard was berating the traveling men. "I am a Democrat but your talk makes me sick," he said. "You don't understand McKinley. McKinley and Mark Hanna are friends.[1] It is impossible perhaps for your mind to grasp that. If anyone tells you that a friendship can be deeper and bigger and more worth while than dollars and cents, or even more worth while than state politics, you snicker and laugh."

The landlord was interrupted by one of the guests, a tall grey-mustached man who worked for a wholesale grocery house. "Do you think that I've lived in Cleveland all these years without knowing Mark Hanna?" he demanded. "Your talk is piffle. Hanna is after money and nothing else. This McKinley is his tool. He has McKinley bluffed and don't you forget it."

The young man on the stairs did not linger to hear the rest of the discussion, but went on up the stairway and into a little dark hall. Something in the voices of the men talking in the hotel office started a chain of thoughts in his mind. He was lonely and had begun to think that loneliness was a part of his character, something that would always stay with him. Stepping into a side hall he stood by a window that looked into an alleyway. At the back of his shop stood Abner Groff, the town baker. His tiny bloodshot eyes looked up and down the alleyway. In his shop someone called the baker who pretended not to hear. The baker had an empty milk bottle in his hand and an angry sullen look in his eyes.

1. Mark Hanna (1837–1904), Republican Ohio businessman, spent and worked hugely to have his friend William McKinley (1843–1901) elected Republican governor of Ohio (1892–96) and president (1897–1901).

In Winesburg, Seth Richmond was called the "deep one." "He's like his father," men said as he went through the streets. "He'll break out some of these days. You wait and see."

The talk of the town and the respect with which men and boys instinctively greeted him, as all men greet silent people, had affected Seth Richmond's outlook on life and on himself. He, like most boys, was deeper than boys are given credit for being, but he was not what the men of the town, and even his mother, thought him to be. No great underlying purpose lay back of his habitual silence, and he had no definite plan for his life. When the boys with whom he associated were noisy and quarrelsome, he stood quietly at one side. With calm eyes he watched the gesticulating lively figures of his companions. He wasn't particularly interested in what was going on, and sometimes wondered if he would ever be particularly interested in anything. Now, as he stood in the half-darkness by the window watching the baker, he wished that he himself might become thoroughly stirred by something, even by the fits of sullen anger for which Baker Groff was noted. "It would be better for me if I could become excited and wrangle about politics like windy old Tom Willard," he thought, as he left the window and went again along the hallway to the room occupied by his friend, George Willard.

George Willard was older than Seth Richmond, but in the rather odd friendship between the two, it was he who was forever courting and the younger boy who was being courted. The paper on which George worked had one policy. It strove to mention by name in each issue, as many as possible of the inhabitants of the village. Like an excited dog, George Willard ran here and there, noting on his pad of paper who had gone on business to the county seat or had returned from a visit to a neighboring village. All day he wrote little facts upon the pad. "A. P. Wringlet has received a shipment of straw hats. Ed Byerbaum and Tom Marshall were in Cleveland Friday. Uncle Tom Sinnings is building a new barn on his place on the Valley Road."

The idea that George Willard would some day become a writer had given him a place of distinction in Winesburg, and to Seth Richmond he talked continually of the matter. "It's the easiest of all lives to live," he declared, becoming excited and boastful. "Here and there you go and there is no one to boss you. Though you are in India or in the South Seas in a boat, you have but to write and there you are. Wait till I get my name up and then see what fun I shall have."

In George Willard's room, which had a window looking down into an alleyway and one that looked across railroad tracks to Biff Carter's Lunch Room facing the railroad station, Seth Richmond sat in a chair and looked at the floor. George Willard who had been sitting for an hour idly playing with a lead pencil, greeted him effusively. "I've been trying to write a love story," he explained, laughing nervously. Lighting a pipe he began walking up and down the room. "I know what I'm going to do. I'm going to fall in love. I've been sitting here and thinking it over and I'm going to do it."

As though embarrassed by his declaration, George went to a window and turning his back to his friend leaned out. "I know who I'm going to fall in love with," he said sharply. "It's Helen White. She is the only girl in town with any 'get-up' to her."

Struck with a new idea, young Willard turned and walked towards his visitor. "Look here," he said. "You know Helen White better than I do. I want you to tell her what I said. You just get to talking to her and say that I'm in love with her. See what she says to that. See how she takes it, and then you come and tell me."

Seth Richmond arose and went towards the door. The words of his comrade irritated him unbearably. "Well, good-bye," he said briefly.

George was amazed. Running forward he stood in the darkness trying to look into Seth's face. "What's the matter? What are you going to do? You stay here and let's talk," he urged.

A wave of resentment directed against his friend, the men of the town who were, he thought, perpetually talking of nothing, and most of all, against his own habit of silence, made Seth half desperate. "Aw, speak to her yourself," he burst forth and then going quickly through the door, slammed it sharply in his friend's face. "I'm going to find Helen White and talk to her, but not about him," he muttered.

Seth went down the stairway and out at the front door of the hotel muttering with wrath. Crossing a little dusty street and climbing a low iron railing, he went to sit upon the grass in the station yard. George Willard he thought a profound fool, and he wished that he had said so more vigorously. Although his acquaintanceship with Helen White, the banker's daughter, was outwardly but casual, she was often the subject of his thoughts and he felt that she was something private and personal to himself. "The busy fool with his love stories," he muttered, staring back over his shoulder at George Willard's room, "why does he never tire of his eternal talking."

It was berry harvest time in Winesburg and upon the station platform men and boys loaded the boxes of red, fragrant berries into two express cars that stood upon the siding. A June moon was in the sky, although in the west a storm threatened, and no street lamps were lighted. In the dim light the figures of the men standing upon the express truck and pitching the boxes in at the doors of the cars were but dimly discernible. Upon the iron railing that protected the station lawn sat other men. Pipes were lighted. Village jokes went back and forth. Away in the distance a train whistled and the men loading the boxes into the cars worked with renewed activity.

Seth arose from his place on the grass and went silently past the men perched upon the railing and into Main Street. He had come to a resolution. "I'll get out of here," he told himself. "What good am I here? I'm going to some city and go to work. I'll tell mother about it to-morrow."

Seth Richmond went slowly along Main Street, past Wacker's Cigar Store and the Town Hall, and into Buckeye Street. He was depressed by the thought that he was not a part of the life in his own town, but the depression did not cut deeply as he did not think of himself as at fault. In the heavy shadows of a big tree before Dr. Welling's house, he stopped and stood watching half-witted Turk Smollet, who was pushing a wheelbarrow in the road. The old man with his absurdly boyish mind had a dozen long boards on the wheelbarrow, and as he hurried along the road, balanced the load with extreme nicety. "Easy there, Turk! Steady now, old boy!" the old man shouted to himself, and laughed so that the load of boards rocked dangerously.

Seth knew Turk Smollet, the half dangerous old wood chopper whose peculiarities added so much of color to the life of the village. He knew that when Turk got into Main Street he would become the center of a whirlwind of cries and comments, that in truth the old man was going far out of his way in order to pass through Main Street and exhibit his skill in wheeling the boards. "If George Willard were here, he'd have something to say," thought Seth. "George belongs to this town. He'd shout at Turk and Turk would shout at him. They'd both be secretly pleased by what they had said. It's different with me. I don't belong. I'll not make a fuss about it, but I'm going to get out of here."

Seth stumbled forward through the half darkness, feeling himself an outcast in his own town. He began to pity himself, but a sense of the absurdity of his thoughts made him smile. In the end he decided that he was simply old beyond his years and not at all a subject for self-pity. "I'm made to go to work. I may be able to make a place for myself by steady working, and I might as well be at it," he decided.

Seth went to the house of Banker White and stood in the darkness by the front door. On the door hung a heavy brass knocker, an innovation introduced into the village by Helen White's mother, who had also organized a woman's club for the study of poetry. Seth raised the knocker and let it fall. Its heavy clatter sounded like a report from distant guns. "How awkward and foolish I am," he thought. "If Mrs. White comes to the door, I won't know what to say."

It was Helen White who came to the door and found Seth standing at the edge of the porch. Blushing with pleasure, she stepped forward, closing the door softly. "I'm going to get out of town. I don't know what I'll do, but I'm going to get out of here and go to work. I think I'll go to Columbus," he said. "Perhaps I'll get into the State University down there. Anyway, I'm going. I'll tell mother to-night." He hesitated and looked doubtfully about. "Perhaps you wouldn't mind coming to walk with me?"

Seth and Helen walked through the streets beneath the trees. Heavy clouds had drifted across the face of the moon, and before them in the deep twilight went a man with a short ladder upon his shoulder. Hurrying forward, the man stopped at the street crossing and, putting the ladder against the wooden lamp post, lighted the village lights so that their way was half lighted, half darkened, by the lamps and by the deepening shadows cast by the low-branched trees. In the tops of the trees the wind began to play, disturbing the sleeping birds so that they flew about calling plaintively. In the lighted space before one of the lamps, two bats wheeled and circled, pursuing the gathering swarm of night flies.

Since Seth had been a boy in knee trousers there had been a half expressed intimacy between him and the maiden who now for the first time walked beside him. For a time she had been beset with a madness for writing notes which she addressed to Seth. He had found them concealed in his books at school and one had been given him by a child met in the street, while several had been delivered through the village post office.

The notes had been written in a round, boyish hand and had reflected a mind inflamed by novel reading. Seth had not answered them, although he had been moved and flattered by some of the sentences scrawled in pencil upon the stationery of the banker's wife. Putting them into the pocket of his coat, he went through the street or stood by the fence in the school yard with something burning at his side. He thought it fine that he should be thus selected as the favorite of the richest and most attractive girl in town.

Helen and Seth stopped by a fence near where a low dark building faced the street. The building had once been a factory for the making of barrel staves but was now vacant. Across the street upon the porch of a house a man and woman talked of their childhood, their voices coming clearly across to the half-embarrassed youth and maiden. There was the sound of scraping chairs and the man and woman came down the gravel path to a wooden gate. Standing outside the gate, the man leaned over and kissed the woman. "For old times' sake," he said and, turning, walked rapidly away along the sidewalk.

"That's Belle Turner," whispered Helen, and put her hand boldly into Seth's hand. "I didn't know she had a fellow. I thought she was too old for that." Seth laughed uneasily. The hand of the girl was warm and a strange, dizzy feeling crept over him. Into his mind came a desire to tell her something he had been determined not to tell. "George Willard's in love with you," he said, and in spite of his agitation his voice was low and quiet. "He's writing a story, and he wants to be in love. He wants to know how it feels. He wanted me to tell you and see what you said."

Again Helen and Seth walked in silence. They came to the garden surrounding the old Richmond place and going through a gap in the hedge sat on a wooden bench beneath a bush.

On the street as he walked beside the girl new and daring thoughts had come into Seth Richmond's mind. He began to regret his decision to get out of town. "It would be something new and altogether delightful to remain and walk often through the streets with Helen White," he thought. In imagination he saw himself putting his arm about her waist and feeling her arms clasped tightly about his neck. One of those odd combinations of events and places made him connect the idea of love-making with this girl and a spot he had visited some days before. He had gone on an errand to the house of a farmer who lived on a hillside beyond the Fair Ground and had returned by a path through a field. At the foot of the hill below the farmer's house Seth had stopped beneath a sycamore tree and looked about him. A soft humming noise had greeted his ears. For a moment he had thought the tree must be the home of a swarm of bees.

And then, looking down, Seth had seen the bees everywhere all about him in the long grass. He stood in a mass of weeds that grew waist-high in the field that ran away from the hillside. The weeds were abloom with tiny purple blossoms and gave forth an overpowering fragrance. Upon the weeds the bees were gathered in armies, singing as they worked.

Seth imagined himself lying on a summer evening, buried deep among the weeds beneath the tree. Beside him, in the scene built in his fancy, lay Helen White, her hand lying in his hand. A peculiar reluctance kept him from kissing her lips, but he felt he might have done that if he wished. Instead, he lay perfectly still, looking at her and listening to the army of bees that sang the sustained masterful song of labor above his head.

On the bench in the garden Seth stirred uneasily. Releasing the hand of the girl, he thrust his hands into his trouser pockets. A desire to impress the mind of his companion with the importance of the resolution he had made came over him and he nodded his head toward the house. "Mother'll make a fuss, I suppose," he whispered. "She hasn't thought at all about what I'm going to do in life. She thinks I'm going to stay on here forever just being a boy."

Seth's voice became charged with boyish earnestness. "You see, I've got to strike out. I've got to get to work. It's what I'm good for."

Helen White was impressed. She nodded her head and a feeling of admiration swept over her. "This is as it should be," she thought. "This boy is not a boy at all, but a strong, purposeful man." Certain vague desires that had been invading her body were swept away and she sat up very straight on the bench. The thunder continued to rumble and flashes of heat lightning lit up the eastern sky. The garden that had been so mysterious and vast, a place that with Seth beside her might have become the background for strange and wonderful adventures, now seemed no more than an ordinary Winesburg back yard, quite definite and limited in its outlines.

"What will you do up there?" she whispered.

Seth turned half around on the bench, striving to see her face in the darkness. He thought her infinitely more sensible and straightforward than George Willard, and was glad he had come away from his friend. A feeling of impatience with the town that had been in his mind returned, and he tried to tell her of it. "Everyone talks and talks," he began. "I'm sick of it. I'll do something, get into some kind of work where talk don't count. Maybe I'll just be a mechanic in a shop. I don't know. I guess I don't care much. I just want to work and keep quiet. That's all I've got in my mind."

Seth arose from the bench and put out his hand. He did not want to bring the meeting to an end but could not think of anything more to say. "It's the last time we'll see each other," he whispered.

A wave of sentiment swept over Helen. Putting her hand upon Seth's shoulder, she started to draw his face down towards her own upturned face. The act was one of pure affection and cutting regret that some vague adventure that had been present in the spirit of the night would now never be realized. "I think I'd better be going along," she said, letting her hand fall heavily to her side. A thought came to her. "Don't you go with me; I want to be alone," she said. "You go and talk with your mother. You'd better do that now."

Seth hesitated and, as he stood waiting, the girl turned and ran away through the hedge. A desire to run after her came to him, but he only stood staring, perplexed and puzzled by her action as he had been perplexed and puzzled by all of the life of the town out of which she had come. Walking slowly toward the house, he stopped in the shadow of a large tree and looked at his mother sitting by a lighted window busily sewing. The feeling of loneliness that had visited him earlier in the evening returned and colored his thoughts of the adventure through which he had just passed. "Huh!" he exclaimed, turning and staring in the direction taken by Helen White. "That's how things'll turn out. She'll be like the rest. I suppose she'll begin now to look at me in a funny way." He looked at the ground and pondered this thought. "She'll be embarrassed and feel strange when I'm around," he whispered to himself. "That's how it'll be. That's how everything'll turn out. When it comes to loving some one, it won't never be me. It'll be some one else—some fool—some one who talks a lot—some one like that George Willard."

Tandy

Until she was seven years old she lived in an old unpainted house on an unused road that led off Trunion Pike. Her father gave her but little attention and her mother was dead. The father spent his time talking and thinking of religion. He proclaimed himself an agnostic and was so absorbed in destroying the ideas of God that had crept into the minds of his neighbors that he never saw God manifesting himself in the little child that, half forgotten, lived here and there on the bounty of her dead mother's relatives.

A stranger came to Winesburg and saw in the child what the father did not see. He was a tall, red-haired young man who was almost always drunk. Sometimes he sat in a chair before the New Willard House with Tom Hard, the father. As Tom talked, declaring there could be no God, the stranger smiled and winked at the bystanders. He and Tom became friends and were much together.

The stranger was the son of a rich merchant of Cleveland and had come to Winesburg on a mission. He wanted to cure himself of the habit of drink, and thought that by escaping from his city associates and living in a rural community he would have a better chance in the struggle with the appetite that was destroying him.

His sojourn in Winesburg was not a success. The dullness of the passing hours led to his drinking harder than ever. But he did succeed in doing something. He gave a name rich with meaning to Tom Hard's daughter.

One evening when he was recovering from a long debauch the stranger came reeling along the main street of the town. Tom Hard sat in a chair before the New Willard House with his daughter, then a child of five, on his knees. Beside him on the board sidewalk sat young George Willard. The stranger dropped into a chair beside them. His body shook and when he tried to talk his voice trembled.

It was late evening and darkness lay over the town and over the railroad that ran along the foot of a little incline before the hotel. Somewhere in the distance, off to the west, there was a prolonged blast from the whistle of a passenger engine. A dog that had been sleeping in the roadway arose and barked. The stranger began to babble and made a prophecy concerning the child that lay in the arms of the agnostic.

"I came here to quit drinking," he said, and tears began to run down his cheeks. He did not look at Tom Hard, but leaned forward and stared into the darkness as though seeing a vision. "I ran away to the country to be cured, but I am not cured. There is a reason." He turned to look at the child who sat up very straight on her father's knee and returned the look.

The stranger touched Tom Hard on the arm. "Drink is not the only thing to which I am addicted," he said. "There is something else. I am a lover and have not found my thing to love. That is a big point if you know enough to realize what I mean. It makes my destruction inevitable, you see. There are few who understand that."

The stranger became silent and seemed overcome with sadness, but another blast from the whistle of the passenger engine aroused him. "I have not lost faith. I proclaim that. I have only been brought to the place where I know my faith will not be realized," he declared hoarsely. He looked hard at the child and began to address her, paying no more attention to the father. "There is a woman coming," he said, and his voice was now sharp and earnest. "I have missed her, you see. She did not come in my time. You may be the woman. It would be like fate to let me stand in her presence once, on such an evening as this, when I have destroyed myself with drink and she is as yet only a child."

The shoulders of the stranger shook violently, and when he tried to roll a cigarette the paper fell from his trembling fingers. He grew angry and scolded. "They think it's easy to be a woman, to be loved, but I know better," he declared. Again he turned to the child. "I understand," he cried. "Perhaps of all men I alone understand."

His glance again wandered away to the darkened street. "I know about her, although she has never crossed my path," he said softly. "I know about her struggles and her defeats. It is because of her defeats that she is to me the lovely one. Out of her defeats has been born a new quality in woman. I have a name for it. I call it Tandy. I made up the name when I was a true dreamer and before my body became vile. It is the quality of being strong to be loved. It is something men need from women and that they do not get."

The stranger arose and stood before Tom Hard. His body rocked back and forth and he seemed about to fall, but instead he dropped to his knees on the sidewalk and raised the hands of the little girl to his drunken lips. He kissed them ecstatically. "Be Tandy, little one," he plead. "Dare to be strong and courageous. That is the road. Venture anything. Be brave enough to dare to be loved. Be something more than man or woman. Be Tandy."

The stranger arose and staggered off down the street. A day or two later he got aboard a train and returned to his home in Cleveland. On the summer evening, after the talk before the hotel, Tom Hard took the girl child to the house of a relative where she had been invited to spend the night. As he went along in the darkness under the trees he forgot the babbling voice of the stranger and his mind returned to the making of arguments by which he might destroy men's faith in God. He spoke his daughter's name and she began to weep.

"I don't want to be called that," she declared. "I want to be called Tandy—Tandy Hard." The child wept so bitterly that Tom Hard was touched and tried to comfort her. He stopped beneath a tree and, taking her into his arms, began to caress her. "Be good, now," he said sharply; but she would not be quieted. With childish abandon she gave herself over to grief, her voice breaking the evening stillness of the street. "I want to be Tandy. I want to be Tandy. I want to be Tandy Hard," she cried, shaking her head and sobbing as though her young strength were not enough to bear the vision the words of the drunkard had brought to her.

The Strength of God

The Reverend Curtis Hartman was pastor of the Presbyterian Church of Winesburg, and had been in that position ten years. He was forty years old, and by his nature very silent and reticent. To preach, standing in the pulpit before the people, was always a hardship for him and from Wednesday morning until Saturday evening he thought of nothing but the two sermons that must be preached on Sunday. Early on Sunday morning he went into a little room called a study in the bell tower of the church and prayed. In his prayers there was one note that always predominated. "Give me strength and courage for Thy work, O Lord!" he plead, kneeling on the bare floor and bowing his head in the presence of the task that lay before him.

The Reverend Hartman was a tall man with a brown beard. His wife, a stout, nervous woman, was the daughter of a manufacturer of underwear at Cleveland, Ohio. The minister himself was rather a favorite in the town. The elders of the church liked him because he was quiet and unpretentious and Mrs. White, the banker's wife, thought him scholarly and refined.

The Presbyterian Church held itself somewhat aloof from the other churches of Winesburg. It was larger and more imposing and its minister was better paid. He even had a carriage of his own and on summer evenings sometimes drove about town with his wife. Through Main Street and up and down Buckeye Street he went, bowing gravely to the people, while his wife, afire with secret pride, looked at him out of the corners of her eyes and worried lest the horse become frightened and run away.

For a good many years after he came to Winesburg things went well with Curtis Hartman. He was not one to arouse keen enthusiasm among the worshippers in his church but on the other hand he made no enemies. In reality he was much in earnest and sometimes suffered prolonged periods of remorse because he could not go crying the word of God in the highways and byways of the town. He wondered if the flame of the spirit really burned in him and dreamed of a day when a strong sweet new current of power would come like a great wind into his voice and his soul and the people would tremble before the spirit of God made manifest in him. "I am a poor stick and that will never really happen to me," he mused dejectedly and then a patient smile lit up his features. "Oh well, I suppose I'm doing well enough," he added philosophically.

The room in the bell tower of the church, where on Sunday mornings the minister prayed for an increase in him of the power of God, had but one window. It was long and narrow and swung outward on a hinge like a door. On the window, made of little leaded panes, was a design showing the Christ laying his hand upon the head of a child. One Sunday morning in the summer as he sat by his desk in the room with a large Bible opened before him, and the sheets of his sermon scattered about, the minister was shocked to see, in the upper room of the house next door, a woman lying in her bed and smoking a cigarette while she read a book. Curtis Hartman went on tiptoe to the window and closed it softly. He was horror stricken at the thought of a woman smoking and trembled also to think that his eyes, just raised from the pages of the book of God, had looked upon the bare shoulders and white throat of a woman. With his brain in a whirl he went down into the pulpit and preached a long sermon without once thinking of his gestures or his voice. The sermon attracted unusual attention because of its power and clearness. "I wonder if she is listening, if my voice is carrying a message into her soul," he thought and began to hope that on future Sunday mornings he might be able to say words that would touch and awaken the woman apparently far gone in secret sin.

The house next door to the Presbyterian Church, through the windows of which the minister had seen the sight that had so upset him, was occupied by two women. Aunt Elizabeth Swift,[1] a grey competent-looking widow with money in the Winesburg National Bank, lived there with her daughter Kate Swift, a school teacher. The school teacher was thirty years old and had a neat trim-looking figure. She had few friends and bore a reputation of having a sharp tongue. When he began to think about her, Curtis Hartman remembered that she had been to Europe and had lived for two years in New York City. "Perhaps after all her smoking means nothing," he thought. He began to remember that when he was a student in college and occasionally read novels, good, although somewhat worldly women, had smoked through the pages of a book that had once fallen into his hands. With a rush of new determination he worked on his sermons all through the week and forgot, in his zeal to reach the ears and the soul of this new listener, both his embarrassment in the pulpit and the necessity of prayer in the study on Sunday mornings.

Reverend Hartman's experience with women had been somewhat limited. He was the son of a wagon maker from Muncie, Indiana, and

1. Respected older women were often addressed honorifically as "aunt" by nonrelatives; Elizabeth Swift is thus "Aunt" to others but "Mother" to Kate.

had worked his way through college. The daughter of the underwear manufacturer had boarded in a house where he lived during his school days and he had married her after a formal and prolonged courtship, carried on for the most part by the girl herself. On his marriage day the underwear manufacturer had given his daughter five thousand dollars and he promised to leave her at least twice that amount in his will. The minister had thought himself fortunate in marriage and had never permitted himself to think of other women. He did not want to think of other women. What he wanted was to do the work of God quietly and earnestly.

In the soul of the minister a struggle awoke. From wanting to reach the ears of Kate Swift, and through his sermons to delve into her soul, he began to want also to look again at the figure lying white and quiet in the bed. On a Sunday morning when he could not sleep because of his thoughts he arose and went to walk in the streets. When he had gone along Main Street almost to the old Richmond place he stopped and picking up a stone rushed off to the room in the bell tower. With the stone he broke out a corner of the window and then locked the door and sat down at the desk before the open Bible to wait. When the shade of the window to Kate Swift's room was raised he could see, through the hole, directly into her bed, but she was not there. She also had arisen and had gone for a walk and the hand that raised the shade was the hand of Aunt Elizabeth Swift.

The minister almost wept with joy at this deliverance from the carnal desire to "peep" and went back to his own house praising God. In an ill moment he forgot, however, to stop the hole in the window. The piece of glass broken out at the corner of the window just nipped off the bare heel of the boy standing motionless and looking with rapt eyes into the face of the Christ.

Curtis Hartman forgot his sermon on that Sunday morning. He talked to his congregation and in his talk said that it was a mistake for people to think of their minister as a man set aside and intended by nature to lead a blameless life. "Out of my own experience I know that we, who are the ministers of God's word, are beset by the same temptations that assail you," he declared. "I have been tempted and have surrendered to temptation. It is only the hand of God, placed beneath my head, that has raised me up. As he has raised me so also will he raise you. Do not despair. In your hour of sin raise your eyes to the skies and you will be again and again saved."

Resolutely the minister put the thoughts of the woman in the bed out of his mind and began to be something like a lover in the presence of his wife. One evening when they drove out together he turned the horse out of Buckeye Street and in the darkness on Gospel Hill, above Waterworks Pond, put his arm about Sarah Hartman's waist. When he had eaten breakfast in the morning and was ready to retire to his study at the back of his house he went around the table and kissed his wife on the cheek. When thoughts of Kate Swift came into his head, he smiled and raised his eyes to the skies. "Intercede for me, Master," he muttered, "keep me in the narrow path intent on Thy work."

And now began the real struggle in the soul of the brown-bearded minister. By chance he discovered that Kate Swift was in the habit of lying in her bed in the evenings and reading a book. A lamp stood on a table by the side of the bed and the light streamed down upon her white shoulders and bare throat. On the evening when he made the discovery the minister sat at the desk in the study from nine until after eleven and when her light was put out stumbled out of the church to spend two more hours walking and praying in the streets. He did not want to kiss the shoulders and the throat of Kate Swift and had not allowed his mind to dwell on such thoughts. He did not know what he wanted. "I am God's child and he must save me from myself," he cried, in the darkness under the trees as he wandered in the streets. By a tree he stood and looked at the sky that was covered with hurrying clouds. He began to talk to God intimately and closely. "Please, Father, do not forget me. Give me power to go to-morrow and repair the hole in the window. Lift my eyes again to the skies. Stay with me, Thy servant, in his hour of need."

Up and down through the silent streets walked the minister and for days and weeks his soul was troubled. He could not understand the temptation that had come to him nor could he fathom the reason for its coming. In a way he began to blame God, saying to himself that he had tried to keep his feet in the true path and had not run about seeking sin. "Through my days as a young man and all through my life here I have gone quietly about my work," he declared. "Why now should I be tempted? What have I done that this burden should be laid on me?"

Three times during the early fall and winter of that year Curtis Hartman crept out of his house to the room in the bell tower to sit in the darkness looking at the figure of Kate Swift lying in her bed and later went to walk and pray in the streets. He could not understand himself. For weeks he would go along scarcely thinking of the school teacher and telling himself that he had conquered the carnal desire to look at her body. And then something would happen. As he sat in the study of his own house, hard at work on a sermon, he would become nervous and begin to walk up and down the room. "I will go out into the streets," he told himself and even as he let himself in at the church door he persistently denied to himself the cause of his being there. "I will not repair the hole in the window and I will train myself to come here at night and sit in the presence of this woman without raising my eyes. I will not be defeated in this thing. The Lord has devised this temptation as a test of my soul and I will grope my way out of darkness into the light of righteousness."

One night in January when it was bitter cold and snow lay deep on the streets of Winesburg Curtis Hartman paid his last visit to the room in the bell tower of the church. It was past nine o'clock when he left his own house and he set out so hurriedly that he forgot to put on his overshoes. In Main Street no one was abroad but Hop Higgins the night watchman and in the whole town no one was awake but the watchman and young George Willard, who sat in the office of the *Winesburg Eagle* trying to write a story. Along the street to the church went the minister, plowing through the drifts and thinking that this time he would utterly give way to sin. "I want to look at the woman and to think of kissing her shoulders and I am going to let myself think what I choose," he declared bitterly and tears came into his eyes. He began to think that he would get out of the ministry and try some other way of life. "I shall go to some city and get into business," he declared. "If my nature is such that I cannot resist sin, I shall give myself over to sin. At least I shall not be a hypocrite, preaching the word of God with my mind thinking of the shoulders and neck of a woman who does not belong to me."

It was cold in the room of the bell tower of the church on that January night and almost as soon as he came into the room Curtis Hartman knew that if he stayed he would be ill. His feet were wet from tramping in the snow and there was no fire. In the room in the house next door Kate Swift had not yet appeared. With grim determination the man sat down to wait. Sitting in the chair and gripping the edge of the desk on which lay the Bible he stared into the darkness thinking the blackest thoughts of his life. He thought of his wife and for the moment almost hated her. "She has always been ashamed of passion and has cheated me," he thought. "Man has a right to expect living passion and beauty in a woman. He has no right to forget that he is an animal and in me there is something that is Greek.[2] I will throw off the woman of my bosom and seek other women. I will besiege this school teacher. I will fly in the face of all men and if I am a creature of carnal lusts I will live then for my lusts."

The distracted man trembled from head to foot, partly from cold, partly from the struggle in which he was engaged. Hours passed and a fever assailed his body. His throat began to hurt and his teeth chattered. His feet on the study floor felt like two cakes of ice. Still he would not give up. "I will see this woman and will think the thoughts I have never dared to think," he told himself, gripping the edge of the desk and waiting.

2. The desperate Reverend Hartman decides that his life of denial and repression (Hebraic or Old Testament qualities) must give way to a new life of expression and fulfillment (classic Greek qualities).

Curtis Hartman came near dying from the effects of that night of waiting in the church, and also he found in the thing that happened what he took to be the way of life for him. On other evenings when he had waited he had not been able to see, through the little hole in the glass, any part of the school teacher's room except that occupied by her bed. In the darkness he had waited until the woman suddenly appeared sitting in the bed in her white night-robe. When the light was turned up she propped herself up among the pillows and read a book. Sometimes she smoked one of the cigarettes. Only her bare shoulders and throat were visible.

On the January night, after he had come near dying with cold and after his mind had two or three times actually slipped away into an odd land of fantasy so that he had by an exercise of will power to force himself back into consciousness, Kate Swift appeared. In the room next door a lamp was lighted and the waiting man stared into an empty bed. Then upon the bed before his eyes a naked woman threw herself. Lying face downward she wept and beat with her fists upon the pillow. With a final outburst of weeping she half arose, and in the presence of the man who had waited to look and to think thoughts the woman of sin began to pray. In the lamplight her figure, slim and strong, looked like the figure of the boy in the presence of the Christ on the leaded window.

Curtis Hartman never remembered how he got out of the church. With a cry he arose, dragging the heavy desk along the floor. The Bible fell, making a great clatter in the silence. When the light in the house next door went out he stumbled down the stairway and into the street. Along the street he went and ran in at the door of the *Winesburg Eagle*. To George Willard, who was tramping up and down in the office undergoing a struggle of his own, he began to talk half incoherently. "The ways of God are beyond human understanding," he cried, running in quickly and closing the door. He began to advance upon the young man, his eyes glowing and his voice ringing with fervor. "I have found the light," he cried. "After ten years in this town, God has manifested himself to me in the body of a woman." His voice dropped and he began to whisper. "I did not understand," he said. "What I took to be a trial of my soul was only a preparation for a new and more beautiful fervor of the spirit. God has appeared to me in the person of Kate Swift, the school teacher, kneeling naked on a bed. Do you know Kate Swift? Although she may not be aware of it, she is an instrument of God, bearing the message of truth."

Reverend Curtis Hartman turned and ran out of the office. At the door he stopped, and after looking up and down the deserted street, turned again to George Willard. "I am delivered. Have no fear." He held up a bleeding fist for the young man to see. "I smashed the glass of the window," he cried. "Now it will have to be wholly replaced. The strength of God was in me and I broke it with my fist."

The Teacher

Snow lay deep in the streets of Winesburg. It had begun to snow about ten o'clock in the morning and a wind sprang up and blew the snow in clouds along Main Street. The frozen mud roads that led into town were fairly smooth and in places ice covered the mud. "There will be good sleighing," said Will Henderson, standing by the bar in Ed Griffith's saloon. Out of the saloon he went and met Sylvester West the druggist stumbling along in the kind of heavy overshoes called arctics. "Snow will bring the people into town on Saturday," said the druggist. The two men stopped and discussed their affairs. Will Henderson, who had on a light overcoat and no overshoes, kicked the heel of his left foot with the toe of the right. "Snow will be good for the wheat," observed the druggist sagely.

Young George Willard, who had nothing to do, was glad because he did not feel like working that day. The weekly paper had been printed and taken to the post office on Wednesday evening and the snow began to fall on Thursday. At eight o'clock, after the morning train had passed, he put a pair of skates in his pocket and went up to Waterworks Pond but did not go skating. Past the pond and along a path that followed Wine Creek he went until he came to a grove of beech trees. There he built a fire against the side of a log and sat down at the end of the log to think. When the snow began to fall and the wind to blow he hurried about getting fuel for the fire.

The young reporter was thinking of Kate Swift who had once been his school teacher. On the evening before he had gone to her house to get a book she wanted him to read and had been alone with her for an hour. For the fourth or fifth time the woman had talked to him with great earnestness and he could not make out what she meant by her talk. He began to believe she might be in love with him and the thought was both pleasing and annoying.

Up from the log he sprang and began to pile sticks on the fire. Looking about to be sure he was alone he talked aloud pretending he was in the presence of the woman. "Oh, you're just letting on, you know you are," he declared. "I am going to find out about you. You wait and see."

The young man got up and went back along the path toward town leaving the fire blazing in the wood. As he went through the streets the skates clanked in his pocket. In his own room in the New Willard House he built a fire in the stove and lay down on top of the bed. He began to have lustful thoughts and pulling down the shade of the window closed his eyes and turned his face to the wall. He took a pillow into his arms and embraced it thinking first of the school teacher, who by her words had stirred something within him and later of Helen White, the slim daughter of the town banker, with whom he had been for a long time half in love.

By nine o'clock of that evening snow lay deep in the streets and the weather had become bitter cold. It was difficult to walk about. The stores were dark and the people had crawled away to their houses. The evening train from Cleveland was very late but nobody was interested in its arrival. By ten o'clock all but four of the eighteen hundred citizens of the town were in bed.

Hop Higgins, the night watchman, was partially awake. He was lame and carried a heavy stick. On dark nights he carried a lantern. Between nine and ten o'clock he went his rounds. Up and down Main Street he stumbled through the drifts trying the doors of the stores. Then he went into alleyways and tried the back doors. Finding all tight he hurried around the corner to the New Willard House and beat on the door. Through the rest of the night he intended to stay by the stove. "You go to bed. I'll keep the stove going," he said to the boy who slept on a cot in the hotel office.

Hop Higgins sat down by the stove and took off his shoes. When the boy had gone to sleep he began to think of his own affairs. He intended to paint his house in the spring and sat by the stove calculating the cost of paint and labor. That led him into other calculations. The night watchman was sixty years old and wanted to retire. He had been a soldier in the Civil War and drew a small pension. He hoped to find some new method of making a living and aspired to become a professional breeder of ferrets. Already he had four of the strangely shaped savage little creatures, that are used by sportsmen in the pursuit of rabbits, in the cellar of his house. "Now I have one male and three females," he mused. "If I am lucky by spring I shall have twelve or fifteen. In another year I shall be able to begin advertising ferrets for sale in the sporting papers."

The night watchman settled into his chair and his mind became a blank. He did not sleep. By years of practice he had trained himself to sit for hours through the long nights neither asleep nor awake. In the morning he was almost as refreshed as though he had slept.

With Hop Higgins safely stowed away in the chair behind the stove only three people were awake in Winesburg. George Willard was in the office of the *Eagle* pretending to be at work on the writing of a story but in reality continuing the mood of the morning by the fire in the wood. In the bell tower of the Presbyterian Church the Reverend Curtis Hartman was sitting in the darkness preparing himself for a revelation from God, and Kate Swift, the school teacher, was leaving her house for a walk in the storm.

It was past ten o'clock when Kate Swift set out and the walk was unpremeditated. It was as though the man and the boy, by thinking of her, had driven her forth into the wintry streets. Aunt Elizabeth Swift had gone to the county seat concerning some business in connection with mortgages in which she had money invested and would not be back until the next day. By a huge stove, called a base burner, in the living room of the house sat the daughter reading a book. Suddenly she sprang to her feet and, snatching a cloak from a rack by the front door, ran out of the house.

At the age of thirty Kate Swift was not known in Winesburg as a pretty woman. Her complexion was not good and her face was covered with blotches that indicated ill health. Alone in the night in the winter streets she was lovely. Her back was straight, her shoulders square and her features were as the features of a tiny goddess on a pedestal in a garden in the dim light of a summer evening.

During the afternoon the school teacher had been to see Dr. Welling concerning her health. The doctor had scolded her and had declared she was in danger of losing her hearing. It was foolish for Kate Swift to be abroad in the storm, foolish and perhaps dangerous.

The woman in the streets did not remember the words of the doctor and would not have turned back had she remembered. She was very cold but after walking for five minutes no longer minded the cold. First she went to the end of her own street and then across a pair of hay scales set in the ground before a feed barn and into Trunion Pike. Along Trunion Pike she went to Ned Winters' barn and turning east followed a street of low frame houses that led over Gospel Hill and into Sucker Road that ran down a shallow valley past Ike Smead's chicken farm to Waterworks Pond. As she went along, the bold, excited mood that had driven her out of doors passed and then returned again.

There was something biting and forbidding in the character of Kate Swift. Everyone felt it. In the schoolroom she was silent, cold, and stern, and yet in an odd way very close to her pupils. Once in a long while something seemed to have come over her and she was happy. All of the children in the schoolroom felt the effect of her happiness. For a time they did not work but sat back in their chairs and looked at her.

With hands clasped behind her back the school teacher walked up and down in the schoolroom and talked very rapidly. It did not seem to matter what subject came into her mind. Once she talked to the children of Charles Lamb[1] and made up strange intimate little stories concerning the life of the dead writer. The stories were told with the air of one who had lived in a house with Charles Lamb and knew all the secrets of his private life. The children were somewhat confused, thinking Charles Lamb must be someone who had once lived in Winesburg.

On another occasion the teacher talked to the children of Benvenuto

1. English Romantic essayist (1775–1834) whose personal and nostalgic writings as "Elia" endeared him to escapist readers.

Cellini.[2] That time they laughed. What a bragging, blustering, brave, lovable fellow she made of the old artist! Concerning him also she invented anecdotes. There was one of a German music teacher who had a room above Cellini's lodgings in the city of Milan that made the boys guffaw. Sugars McNutts, a fat boy with red cheeks, laughed so hard that he became dizzy and fell off his seat and Kate Swift laughed with him. Then suddenly she became again cold and stern.

On the winter night when she walked through the deserted snow-covered streets, a crisis had come into the life of the school teacher. Although no one in Winesburg would have suspected it, her life had been very adventurous. It was still adventurous. Day by day as she worked in the schoolroom or walked in the streets, grief, hope, and desire fought within her. Behind a cold exterior the most extraordinary events transpired in her mind. The people of the town thought of her as a confirmed old maid and because she spoke sharply and went her own way thought her lacking in all the human feeling that did so much to make and mar their own lives. In reality she was the most eagerly passionate soul among them, and more than once, in the five years since she had come back from her travels to settle in Winesburg and become a school teacher, had been compelled to go out of the house and walk half through the night fighting out some battle raging within. Once on a night when it rained she had stayed out six hours and when she came home had a quarrel with Aunt Elizabeth Swift. "I am glad you're not a man," said the mother sharply. "More than once I've waited for your father to come home, not knowing what new mess he had got into. I've had my share of uncertainty and you cannot blame me if I do not want to see the worst side of him reproduced in you."

• • • • • • • •

Kate Swift's mind was ablaze with thoughts of George Willard. In something he had written as a school boy she thought she had recognized the spark of genius and wanted to blow on the spark. One day in the summer she had gone to the *Eagle* office and finding the boy unoccupied had taken him out Main Street to the fair ground, where the two sat on a grassy bank and talked. The school teacher tried to bring home to the mind of the boy some conception of the difficulties he would have to face as a writer. "You will have to know life," she declared, and her voice trembled with earnestness. She took hold of George Willard's shoulders and turned him about so that she could look into his eyes. A passer-by might have thought them about to embrace. "If you are to become a writer you'll have to stop fooling with words," she explained.

2. Italian sculptor and metalsmith (1500–1571) who recounted his many adventures in his *Vita* (1558–62); Cellini was, however, more closely associated with Rome, Florence, and Paris than with Milan.

"It would be better to give up the notion of writing until you are better prepared. Now it's time to be living. I don't want to frighten you, but I would like to make you understand the import of what you think of attempting. You must not become a mere peddler of words. The thing to learn is to know what people are thinking about, not what they say."

On the evening before that stormy Thursday night, when the Reverend Curtis Hartman sat in the bell tower of the church waiting to look at her body, young Willard had gone to visit the teacher and to borrow a book. It was then the thing happened that confused and puzzled the boy. He had the book under his arm and was preparing to depart. Again Kate Swift talked with great earnestness. Night was coming on and the light in the room grew dim. As he turned to go she spoke his name softly and with an impulsive movement took hold of his hand. Because the reporter was rapidly becoming a man something of his man's appeal, combined with the winsomeness of the boy, stirred the heart of the lonely woman. A passionate desire to have him understand the import of life, to learn to interpret it truly and honestly, swept over her. Leaning forward, her lips brushed his cheek. At the same moment he for the first time became aware of the marked beauty of her features. They were both embarrassed, and to relieve her feeling she became harsh and domineering. "What's the use? It will be ten years before you begin to understand what I mean when I talk to you," she cried passionately.

• • • • • • •

On the night of the storm and while the minister sat in the church waiting for her, Kate Swift went to the office of the *Winesburg Eagle*, intending to have another talk with the boy. After the long walk in the snow she was cold, lonely, and tired. As she came through Main Street she saw the light from the print shop window shining on the snow and on an impulse opened the door and went in. For an hour she sat by the stove in the office talking of life. She talked with passionate earnestness. The impulse that had driven her out into the snow poured itself out into talk. She became inspired as she sometimes did in the presence of the children in school. A great eagerness to open the door of life to the boy, who had been her pupil and who she thought might possess a talent for the understanding of life, had possession of her. So strong was her passion that it became something physical. Again her hands took hold of his shoulders and she turned him about. In the dim light her eyes blazed. She arose and laughed, not sharply as was customary with her, but in a queer, hesitating way. "I must be going," she said. "In a moment, if I stay, I'll be wanting to kiss you."

In the newspaper office a confusion arose. Kate Swift turned and walked to the door. She was a teacher but she was also a woman. As she looked at George Willard, the passionate desire to be loved by a man, that had a thousand times before swept like a storm over her body, took possession of her. In the lamplight George Willard looked no longer a boy, but a man ready to play the part of a man.

The school teacher let George Willard take her into his arms. In the warm little office the air became suddenly heavy and the strength went out of her body. Leaning against a low counter by the door she waited. When he came and put a hand on her shoulder she turned and let her body fall heavily against him. For George Willard the confusion was immediately increased. For a moment he held the body of the woman tightly against his body and then it stiffened. Two sharp little fists began to beat on his face. When the school teacher had run away and left him alone, he walked up and down in the office swearing furiously.

It was into this confusion that the Reverend Curtis Hartman protruded himself. When he came in George Willard thought the town had gone mad. Shaking a bleeding fist in the air, the minister proclaimed the woman George had only a moment before held in his arms an instrument of God bearing a message of truth.

• • • • • • •

George blew out the lamp by the window and locking the door of the print shop went home. Through the hotel office, past Hop Higgins lost in his dream of the raising of ferrets, he went and up into his own room. The fire in the stove had gone out and he undressed in the cold. When he got into bed the sheets were like blankets of dry snow.

George Willard rolled about in the bed on which he had lain in the afternoon hugging the pillow and thinking thoughts of Kate Swift. The words of the minister, who he thought had gone suddenly insane, rang in his ears. His eyes stared about the room. The resentment, natural to the baffled male, passed and he tried to understand what had happened. He could not make it out. Over and over he turned the matter in his mind. Hours passed and he began to think it must be time for another day to come. At four o'clock he pulled the covers up about his neck and tried to sleep. When he became drowsy and closed his eyes, he raised a hand and with it groped about in the darkness. "I have missed something. I have missed something Kate Swift was trying to tell me," he muttered sleepily. Then he slept and in all Winesburg he was the last soul on that winter night to go to sleep.

Loneliness

He was the son of Mrs. Al Robinson who once owned a farm on a side road leading off Trunion Pike, east of Winesburg and two miles beyond the town limits. The farm-house was painted brown and the blinds to all of the windows facing the road were kept closed. In the road before the house a flock of chickens, accompanied by two guinea hens, lay in the deep dust. Enoch lived in the house with his mother in those days and when he was a young boy went to school at the Winesburg High School. Old citizens remembered him as a quiet, smiling youth inclined to silence. He walked in the middle of the road when he came into town and sometimes read a book. Drivers of teams had to shout and swear to make him realize where he was so that he would turn out of the beaten track and let them pass.

When he was twenty-one years old Enoch went to New York City and was a city man for fifteen years. He studied French and went to an art school, hoping to develop a faculty he had for drawing. In his own mind he planned to go to Paris and to finish his art education among the masters there, but that never turned out.

Nothing ever turned out for Enoch Robinson. He could draw well enough and he had many odd delicate thoughts hidden away in his brain that might have expressed themselves through the brush of a painter, but he was always a child and that was a handicap to his worldly development. He never grew up and of course he couldn't understand people and he couldn't make people understand him. The child in him kept bumping against things, against actualities like money and sex and opinions. Once he was hit by a street car and thrown against an iron post. That made him lame. It was one of the many things that kept things from turning out for Enoch Robinson.

In New York City, when he first went there to live and before he became confused and disconcerted by the facts of life, Enoch went about a good deal with young men. He got into a group of other young artists, both men and women, and in the evenings they sometimes came to visit him in his room. Once he got drunk and was taken to a police station where a police magistrate frightened him horribly, and once he tried to have an affair with a woman of the town met on the sidewalk before his lodging house. The woman and Enoch walked together three blocks and then the young man grew afraid and ran away. The woman had been drinking and the incident amused her. She leaned against the wall of a building and laughed so heartily that another man stopped and laughed with her. The two went away together, still laughing, and Enoch crept off to his room trembling and vexed.

The room in which young Robinson lived in New York faced Washington Square[1] and was long and narrow like a hallway. It is important to get that fixed in your mind. The story of Enoch is in fact the story of a room almost more than it is the story of a man.

And so into the room in the evening came young Enoch's friends. There was nothing particularly striking about them except that they were artists of the kind that talk. Everyone knows of the talking artists.

1. Greenwich Village in New York City was in the late nineteenth century becoming a bohemian artistic district, centered around Washington Square.

Throughout all of the known history of the world they have gathered in rooms and talked. They talk of art and are passionately, almost feverishly, in earnest about it. They think it matters much more than it does.

And so these people gathered and smoked cigarettes and talked and Enoch Robinson, the boy from the farm near Winesburg, was there. He stayed in a corner and for the most part said nothing. How his big blue childlike eyes stared about! On the walls were pictures he had made, crude things, half finished. His friends talked of these. Leaning back in their chairs, they talked and talked with their heads rocking from side to side. Words were said about line and values and composition, lots of words, such as are always being said.

Enoch wanted to talk too but he didn't know how. He was too excited to talk coherently. When he tried he sputtered and stammered and his voice sounded strange and squeaky to him. That made him stop talking. He knew what he wanted to say, but he knew also that he could never by any possibility say it. When a picture he had painted was under discussion, he wanted to burst out with something like this: "You don't get the point," he wanted to explain: "the picture you see doesn't consist of the things you see and say words about. There is something else, something you don't see at all, something you aren't intended to see. Look at this one over here, by the door here, where the light from the window falls on it. The dark spot by the road that you might not notice at all is, you see, the beginning of everything. There is a clump of elders there such as used to grow beside the road before our house back in Winesburg, Ohio, and in among the elders there is something hidden. It is a woman, that's what it is. She has been thrown from a horse and the horse has run away out of sight. Do you not see how the old man who drives a cart looks anxiously about? That is Thad Grayback who has a farm up the road. He is taking corn to Winesburg to be ground into meal at Comstock's mill. He knows there is something in the elders, something hidden away, and yet he doesn't quite know.

"It's a woman you see, that's what it is! It's a woman and, oh, she is lovely! She is hurt and is suffering but she makes no sound. Don't you see how it is? She lies quite still, white and still, and the beauty comes out from her and spreads over everything. It is in the sky back there and all around everywhere. I didn't try to paint the woman, of course. She is too beautiful to be painted. How dull to talk of composition and such things! Why do you not look at the sky and then run away as I used to do when I was a boy back there in Winesburg, Ohio?"

That is the kind of thing young Enoch Robinson trembled to say to the guests who came into his room when he was a young fellow in New York City, but he always ended by saying nothing. Then he began to doubt his own mind. He was afraid the things he felt were not getting expressed in the pictures he painted. In a half indignant mood he stopped inviting people into his room and presently got into the habit of locking the door. He began to think that enough people had visited him, that he did not need people any more. With quick imagination he began to invent his own people to whom he could really talk and to whom he explained the things he had been unable to explain to living people. His room began to be inhabited by the spirits of men and women among whom he went, in his turn saying words. It was as though every one Enoch Robinson had ever seen had left with him some essence of himself, something he could mould and change to suit his own fancy, something that understood all about such things as the wounded woman behind the elders in the pictures.

The mild, blue-eyed young Ohio boy was a complete egotist, as all children are egotists. He did not want friends for the quite simple reason that no child wants friends. He wanted most of all the people of his own mind, people with whom he could really talk, people he could harangue and scold by the hour, servants, you see, to his fancy. Among these people he was always self-confident and bold. They might talk, to be sure, and even have opinions of their own, but always he talked last and best. He was like a writer busy among the figures of his brain, a kind of tiny blue-eyed king he was, in a six-dollar room facing Washington Square in the city of New York.

Then Enoch Robinson got married. He began to get lonely and to want to touch actual flesh and bone people with his hands. Days passed when his room seemed empty. Lust visited his body and desire grew in his mind. At night strange fevers, burning within, kept him awake. He married a girl who sat in a chair next to his own in the art school and went to live in an apartment house in Brooklyn. Two children were born to the woman he married, and Enoch got a job in a place where illustrations are made for advertisements.

That began another phase of Enoch's life. He began to play at a new game. For a while he was very proud of himself in the rôle of producing citizen of the world. He dismissed the essence of things and played with realities. In the fall he voted at an election and he had a newspaper thrown on his porch each morning. When in the evening he came home from work he got off a street car and walked sedately along behind some business man, striving to look very substantial and important. As a payer of taxes he thought he should post himself on how things are run. "I'm getting to be of some moment, a real part of things, of the state and the city and all that," he told himself with an amusing miniature air of dignity. Once coming home from Philadelphia, he had a discussion with a man met on a train. Enoch talked about the advisability of the government's owning and operating the railroads and the man gave him a cigar. It was Enoch's notion that such a move on the part of the government would be a good thing, and he grew quite excited as he talked. Later he remembered his own words with pleasure. "I gave him something to think about, that fellow," he muttered to himself as he climbed the stairs to his Brooklyn apartment.

To be sure, Enoch's marriage did not turn out. He himself brought it to an end. He began to feel choked and walled in by the life in the apartment, and to feel toward his wife and even toward his children as he had felt concerning the friends who once came to visit him. He began to tell little lies about business engagements that would give him freedom to walk alone in the street at night and, the chance offering, he secretly re-rented the room facing Washington Square. Then Mrs. Al Robinson died on the farm near Winesburg, and he got eight thousand dollars from the bank that acted as trustee of her estate. That took Enoch out of the world of men altogether. He gave the money to his wife and told her he could not live in the apartment any more. She cried and was angry and threatened, but he only stared at her and went his own way. In reality the wife did not care much. She thought Enoch slightly insane and was a little afraid of him. When it was quite sure that he would never come back, she took the two children and went to a village in Connecticut where she had lived as a girl. In the end she married a man who bought and sold real estate and was contented enough.

And so Enoch Robinson stayed in the New York room among the people of his fancy, playing with them, talking to them, happy as a child is happy. They were an odd lot, Enoch's people. They were made, I suppose, out of real people he had seen and who had for some obscure reason made an appeal to him. There was a woman with a sword in her hand, an old man with a long white beard who went about followed by a dog, a young girl whose stockings were always coming down and hanging over her shoe tops. There must have been two dozen of the shadow people, invented by the child-mind of Enoch Robinson, who lived in the room with him.

And Enoch was happy. Into the room he went and locked the door. With an absurd air of importance he talked aloud, giving instructions, making comments on life. He was happy and satisfied to go on making his living in the advertising place until something happened. Of course something did happen. That is why he went back to live in Winesburg and why we know about him. The thing that happened was a woman. It would be that way. He was too happy. Something had to come into his world. Something had to drive him out of the New York room to live out his life, an obscure, jerky little figure, bobbing up and down on the streets of an Ohio town at evening when the sun was going down behind the roof of Wesley Moyer's livery barn.

About the thing that happened. Enoch told George Willard about it one night. He wanted to talk to someone, and he chose the young newspaper reporter because the two happened to be thrown together at a time when the younger man was in a mood to understand.

Youthful sadness, young man's sadness, the sadness of a growing boy in a village at the year's end opened the lips of the old man. The sadness was in the heart of George Willard and was without meaning, but it appealed to Enoch Robinson.

It rained on the evening when the two met and talked, a drizzly wet October rain. The fruition of the year had come and the night should have been fine with a moon in the sky and the crisp sharp promise of frost in the air, but it wasn't that way. It rained and little puddles of water shone under the street lamps on Main Street. In the woods in the darkness beyond the Fair Ground water dripped from the black trees. Beneath the trees wet leaves were pasted against tree roots that protruded from the ground. In gardens back of houses in Winesburg dry shriveled potato vines lay sprawling on the ground. Men who had finished the evening meal and who had planned to go uptown to talk the evening away with other men at the back of some store changed their minds. George Willard tramped about in the rain and was glad that it rained. He felt that way. He was like Enoch Robinson on the evenings when the old man came down out of his room and wandered alone in the streets. He was like that only that George Willard had become a tall young man and did not think it manly to weep and carry on. For a month his mother had been very ill and that had something to do with his sadness, but not much. He thought about himself and to the young that always brings sadness.

Enoch Robinson and George Willard met beneath a wooden awning that extended out over the sidewalk before Voight's wagon shop on Maumee Street just off the main street of Winesburg. They went together from there through the rain-washed streets to the older man's room on the third floor of the Heffner Block. The young reporter went willingly enough. Enoch Robinson asked him to go after the two had talked for ten minutes. The boy was a little afraid but had never been more curious in his life. A hundred times he had heard the old man spoken of as a little off his head and he thought himself rather brave and manly to go at all. From the very beginning, in the street in the rain, the old man talked in a queer way, trying to tell the story of the room in Washington Square and of his life in the room. "You'll understand if you try hard enough," he said conclusively. "I have looked at you when you went past me on the street and I think you can understand. It isn't hard. All you have to do is to believe what I say, just listen and believe, that's all there is to it."

It was past eleven o'clock that evening when Old Enoch, talking to George Willard in the room in the Heffner Block, came to the vital thing, the story of the woman and of what drove him out of the city to live out his life alone and defeated in Winesburg. He sat on a cot by the window with his head in his hand and George Willard was in a chair by a table. A kerosene lamp sat on the table and the room, although almost bare of furniture, was scrupulously clean. As the man talked George Willard began to feel that he would like to get out of the chair and sit on the cot also. He wanted to put his arms about the little old man. In the half darkness the man talked and the boy listened, filled with sadness.

"She got to coming in there after there hadn't been anyone in the room for years," said Enoch Robinson. "She saw me in the hallway of the house and we got acquainted. I don't know just what she did in her own room. I never went there. I think she was a musician and played a violin. Every now and then she came and knocked at the door and I opened it. In she came and sat down beside me, just sat and looked about and said nothing. Anyway, she said nothing that mattered."

The old man arose from the cot and moved about the room. The overcoat he wore was wet from the rain and drops of water kept falling with a soft little thump on the floor. When he again sat upon the cot George Willard got out of the chair and sat beside him.

"I had a feeling about her. She sat there in the room with me and she was too big for the room. I felt that she was driving everything else away. We just talked of little things, but I couldn't sit still. I wanted to touch her with my fingers and to kiss her. Her hands were so strong and her face was so good and she looked at me all the time."

The trembling voice of the old man became silent and his body shook as from a chill. "I was afraid," he whispered. "I was terribly afraid. I didn't want to let her come in when she knocked at the door but I couldn't sit still. 'No, no,' I said to myself, but I got up and opened the door just the same. She was so grown up, you see. She was a woman. I thought she would be bigger than I was there in that room."

Enoch Robinson stared at George Willard, his childlike blue eyes shining in the lamplight. Again he shivered. "I wanted her and all the time I didn't want her," he explained. "Then I began to tell her about my people, about everything that meant anything to me. I tried to keep quiet, to keep myself to myself, but I couldn't. I felt just as I did about opening the door. Sometimes I ached to have her go away and never come back any more."

The old man sprang to his feet and his voice shook with excitement. "One night something happened. I became mad to make her understand me and to know what a big thing I was in that room. I wanted her to see how important I was. I told her over and over. When she tried to go away, I ran and locked the door. I followed her about. I talked and talked and then all of a sudden things went to smash. A look came into her eyes and I knew she did understand. Maybe she had understood all the time. I was furious. I couldn't stand it. I wanted her to understand but, don't you see, I couldn't let her understand. I felt that then she would know everything, that I would be submerged, drowned out, you see. That's how it is. I don't know why."

The old man dropped into a chair by the lamp and the boy listened, filled with awe. "Go away, boy," said the man. "Don't stay here with me any more. I thought it might be a good thing to tell you but it isn't. I don't want to talk any more. Go away."

George Willard shook his head and a note of command came into his voice. "Don't stop now. Tell me the rest of it," he commanded sharply. "What happened? Tell me the rest of the story."

Enoch Robinson sprang to his feet and ran to the window that looked down into the deserted main street of Winesburg. George Willard followed. By the window the two stood, the tall awkward boy-man and the little wrinkled man-boy. The childish, eager voice carried forward the tale. "I swore at her," he explained. "I said vile words. I ordered her to go away and not to come back. Oh, I said terrible things. At first she pretended not to understand but I kept at it. I screamed and stamped on the floor. I made the house ring with my curses. I didn't want ever to see her again and I knew, after some of the things I said, that I never would see her again."

The old man's voice broke and he shook his head. "Things went to smash," he said quietly and sadly. "Out she went through the door and all the life there had been in the room followed her out. She took all of my people away. They all went out through the door after her. That's the way it was."

George Willard turned and went out of Enoch Robinson's room. In the darkness by the window, as he went through the door, he could hear the thin old voice whimpering and complaining. "I'm alone, all alone here," said the voice. "It was warm and friendly in my room but now I'm all alone."

An Awakening

Belle Carpenter had a dark skin, grey eyes and thick lips. She was tall and strong. When black thoughts visited her she grew angry and wished she were a man and could fight someone with her fists. She worked in the millinery shop kept by Mrs. Nate McHugh and during the day sat trimming hats by a window at the rear of the store. She was the daughter of Henry Carpenter, bookkeeper in the First National Bank of Winesburg, and lived with him in a gloomy old house far out at the end of Buckeye Street. The house was surrounded by pine trees and there was no grass beneath the trees. A rusty tin eaves-trough had slipped from its fastenings at the back of the house and when the wind blew it beat against the roof of a small shed, making a dismal drumming noise that sometimes persisted all through the night.

When she was a young girl Henry Carpenter made life almost unbearable for Belle, but as she emerged from girlhood into womanhood he lost his power over her. The bookkeeper's life was made up of innumerable little pettinesses. When he went to the bank in the morning he stepped into a closet and put on a black alpaca coat that had become shabby with age. At night when he returned to his home he donned another black alpaca coat. Every evening he pressed the clothes worn in the streets. He had invented an arrangement of boards for the purpose. The trousers to his street suit were placed between the boards and the boards were clamped together with heavy screws. In the morning he wiped the boards with a damp cloth and stood them upright behind the dining room door. If they were moved during the day he was speechless with anger and did not recover his equilibrium for a week.

The bank cashier was a little bully and was afraid of his daughter. She, he realized, knew the story of his brutal treatment of her mother and hated him for it. One day she went home at noon and carried a handful of soft mud, taken from the road, into the house. With the mud she smeared the face of the boards used for the pressing of trousers and then went back to her work feeling relieved and happy.

Belle Carpenter occasionally walked out in the evening with George Willard. Secretly she loved another man, but her love affair, about which no one knew, caused her much anxiety. She was in love with Ed Handby, bartender in Ed Griffith's Saloon, and went about with the young reporter as a kind of relief to her feelings. She did not think that her station in life would permit her to be seen in the company of the bartender and walked about under the trees with George Willard and let him kiss her to relieve a longing that was very insistent in her nature. She felt that she could keep the younger man within bounds. About Ed Handby she was somewhat uncertain.

Handby, the bartender, was a tall, broad-shouldered man of thirty who lived in a room upstairs above Griffith's saloon. His fists were large and his eyes unusually small, but his voice, as though striving to conceal the power back of his fists, was soft and quiet.

At twenty-five the bartender had inherited a large farm from an uncle in Indiana. When sold, the farm brought in eight thousand dollars which Ed spent in six months. Going to Sandusky, on Lake Erie, he began an orgy of dissipation, the story of which afterward filled his home town with awe. Here and there he went throwing the money about, driving carriages through the streets, giving wine parties to crowds of men and women, playing cards for high stakes and keeping mistresses whose wardrobes cost him hundreds of dollars. One night at a resort called Cedar Point, he got into a fight and ran amuck like a wild thing. With his fist he broke a large mirror in the wash room of a hotel and later went about smashing windows and breaking chairs in dance halls for the joy of hearing the glass rattle on the floor and seeing the terror in the eyes of clerks who had come from Sandusky to spend the evening at the resort with their sweethearts.

The affair between Ed Handby and Belle Carpenter on the surface amounted to nothing. He had succeeded in spending but one evening in her company. On that evening he hired a horse and buggy at Wesley Moyer's livery barn and took her for a drive. The conviction that she was the woman his nature demanded and that he must get her settled upon him and he told her of his desires. The bartender was ready to marry and to begin trying to earn money for the support of his wife, but so simple was his nature that he found it difficult to explain his intentions. His body ached with physical longing and with his body he expressed himself. Taking the milliner into his arms and holding her tightly in spite of her struggles, he kissed her until she became helpless. Then he brought her back to town and let her out of the buggy. "When I get hold of you again I'll not let you go. You can't play with me," he declared as he turned to drive away. Then, jumping out of the buggy, he gripped her shoulders with his strong hands. "I'll keep you for good the next time," he said. "You might as well make up your mind to that. It's you and me for it and I'm going to have you before I get through."

One night in January when there was a new moon George Willard, who was in Ed Handby's mind the only obstacle to his getting Belle Carpenter, went for a walk. Early that evening George went into Ransom Surbeck's pool room with Seth Richmond and Art Wilson, son of the town butcher. Seth Richmond stood with his back against the wall and remained silent, but George Willard talked. The pool room was filled with Winesburg boys and they talked of women. The young reporter got into that vein. He said that women should look out for themselves, that the fellow who went out with a girl was not responsible for what happened. As he talked he looked about, eager for attention. He held the floor for five minutes and then Art Wilson began to talk. Art was learning the barber's trade in Cal Prouse's shop and already began to consider himself an authority in such matters as baseball, horse racing, drinking, and going about with women. He began to tell of a night when he with two men from Winesburg went into a house of prostitution at the county seat. The butcher's son held a cigar in the side of his mouth and as he talked spat on the floor. "The women in the place couldn't embarrass me although they tried hard enough," he boasted. "One of the girls in the house tried to get fresh, but I fooled her. As soon as she began to talk I went and sat in her lap. Everyone in the room laughed when I kissed her. I taught her to let me alone."

George Willard went out of the pool room and into Main Street. For days the weather had been bitter cold with a high wind blowing down on the town from Lake Erie, eighteen miles to the north, but on that night the wind had died away and a new moon made the night unusually lovely. Without thinking where he was going or what he wanted to do, George went out of Main Street and began walking in dimly lighted streets filled with frame houses.

Out of doors under the black sky filled with stars he forgot his companions of the pool room. Because it was dark and he was alone he began to talk aloud. In a spirit of play he reeled along the street imitating a drunken man and then imagined himself a soldier clad in shining boots that reached to the knees and wearing a sword that jingled as he walked. As a soldier he pictured himself as an inspector, passing before a long line of men who stood at attention. He began to examine the accoutrements of the men. Before a tree he stopped and began to scold. "Your pack is not in order," he said sharply. "How many times will I have to speak of this matter? Everything must be in order here. We have a difficult task before us and no difficult task can be done without order."

Hypnotized by his own words, the young man stumbled along the board sidewalk saying more words. "There is a law for armies and for men too," he muttered, lost in reflection. "The law begins with little things and spreads out until it covers everything. In every little thing there must be order, in the place where men work, in their clothes, in their thoughts. I myself must be orderly. I must learn that law. I must get myself into touch with something orderly and big that swings through the night like a star. In my little way I must begin to learn something, to give and swing and work with life, with the law."

George Willard stopped by a picket fence near a street lamp and his body began to tremble. He had never before thought such thoughts as had just come into his head and he wondered where they had come from. For the moment it seemed to him that some voice outside of himself had been talking as he walked. He was amazed and delighted with his own mind and when he walked on again spoke of the matter with fervor. "To come out of Ransom Surbeck's pool room and think things like that," he whispered. "It is better to be alone. If I talked like Art Wilson the boys would understand me but they wouldn't understand what I've been thinking down here."

In Winesburg, as in all Ohio towns of twenty years ago, there was a section in which lived day laborers. As the time of factories had not yet come, the laborers worked in the fields or were section hands on the railroads. They worked twelve hours a day and received one dollar for the long day of toil. The houses in which they lived were small cheaply constructed wooden affairs with a garden at the back. The more comfortable among them kept cows and perhaps a pig, housed in a little shed at the rear of the garden.

With his head filled with resounding thoughts, George Willard walked into such a street on the clear January night. The street was dimly lighted and in places there was no sidewalk. In the scene that lay about him there was something that excited his already aroused fancy. For a year he had been devoting all of his odd moments to the reading of books and now some tale he had read concerning life in old world towns of the middle ages came sharply back to his mind so that he stumbled forward with the curious feeling of one revisiting a place that had been a part of some former existence. On an impulse he turned out of the street and went into a little dark alleyway behind the sheds in which lived the cows and pigs.

For a half hour he stayed in the alleyway, smelling the strong smell of animals too closely housed and letting his mind play with the strange new thoughts that came to him. The very rankness of the smell of manure in the clear sweet air awoke something heady in his brain. The poor little houses lighted by kerosene lamps, the smoke from the chimneys mounting straight up into the clear air, the grunting of pigs, the women clad in cheap calico dresses and washing dishes in the kitchens, the footsteps of men coming out of the houses and going off to the stores and saloons of Main Street, the dogs barking and the children crying—all of these things made him seem, as he lurked in the darkness, oddly detached and apart from all life.

The excited young man, unable to bear the weight of his own thoughts, began to move cautiously along the alleyway. A dog attacked him and had to be driven away with stones, and a man appeared at the door of one of the houses and swore at the dog. George went into a vacant lot and throwing back his head looked up at the sky. He felt unutterably big and remade by the simple experience through which he had been passing and in a kind of fervor of emotion put up his hands, thrusting them into the darkness above his head and muttering words. The desire to say words overcame him and he said words without meaning, rolling them over on his tongue and saying them because they were brave words, full of meaning. "Death," he muttered, "night, the sea, fear, loveliness."

George Willard came out of the vacant lot and stood again on the sidewalk facing the houses. He felt that all of the people in the little street must be brothers and sisters to him and he wished he had the courage to call them out of their houses and to shake their hands. "If there were only a woman here I would take hold of her hand and we would run until we were both tired out," he thought. "That would make me feel better." With the thought of a woman in his mind he walked out of the street and went toward the house where Belle Carpenter lived. He thought she would understand his mood and that he could achieve in her presence a position he had long been wanting to achieve. In the past when he had been with her and had kissed her lips he had come away filled with anger at himself. He had felt like one being used for some obscure purpose and had not enjoyed the feeling. Now he thought he had suddenly become too big to be used.

When George got to Belle Carpenter's house there had already been a visitor there before him. Ed Handby had come to the door and calling Belle out of the house had tried to talk to her. He had wanted to ask the woman to come away with him and to be his wife, but when she came and stood by the door he lost his self-assurance and became sullen. "You stay away from that kid," he growled, thinking of George Willard, and then, not knowing what else to say, turned to go away. "If I catch you together I will break your bones and his too," he added. The bartender had come to woo, not to threaten, and was angry with himself because of his failure.

When her lover had departed Belle went indoors and ran hurriedly upstairs. From a window at the upper part of the house she saw Ed Handby cross the street and sit down on a horse block[1] before the house of a neighbor. In the dim light the man sat motionless holding his head in his hands. She was made happy by the sight, and when George Willard came to the door she greeted him effusively and hurriedly put on her hat. She thought that, as she walked through the streets with young Willard, Ed Handby would follow and she wanted to make him suffer.

For an hour Belle Carpenter and the young reporter walked about under the trees in the sweet night air. George Willard was full of big words. The sense of power that had come to him during the hour in the darkness in the alleyway remained with him and he talked boldly, swaggering along and swinging his arms about. He wanted to make Belle Carpenter realize that he was aware of his former weakness and that he had changed. "You'll find me different," he declared, thrusting his hands into his pockets and looking boldly into her eyes. "I don't know why but it is so. You've got to take me for a man or let me alone. That's how it is."

Up and down the quiet streets under the new moon went the woman and the boy. When George had finished talking they turned down a side street and went across a bridge into a path that ran up the side of a hill. The hill began at Waterworks Pond and climbed upwards to the Winesburg Fair Grounds. On the hillside grew dense bushes and small trees and among the bushes were little open spaces carpeted with long grass, now stiff and frozen.

As he walked behind the woman up the hill George Willard's heart began to beat rapidly and his shoulders straightened. Suddenly he decided that Belle Carpenter was about to surrender herself to him. The new force that had manifested itself in him had, he felt, been at work upon her and had led to her conquest. The thought made him half drunk with the sense of masculine power. Although he had been annoyed that as they walked about she had not seemed to be listening to his words, the fact that she had accompanied him to this place took all

1. A built-up, stepped platform for mounting and dismounting from a horse.

his doubts away. "It is different. Everything has become different," he thought and taking hold of her shoulder turned her about and stood looking at her, his eyes shining with pride.

Belle Carpenter did not resist. When he kissed her upon the lips she leaned heavily against him and looked over his shoulder into the darkness. In her whole attitude there was a suggestion of waiting. Again, as in the alleyway, George Willard's mind ran off into words and, holding the woman tightly he whispered the words into the still night. "Lust," he whispered, "lust and night and women."

George Willard did not understand what happened to him that night on the hillside. Later, when he got to his own room, he wanted to weep and then grew half insane with anger and hate. He hated Belle Carpenter and was sure that all his life he would continue to hate her. On the hillside he had led the woman to one of the little open spaces among the bushes and had dropped to his knees beside her. As in the vacant lot, by the laborers' houses, he had put up his hands in gratitude for the new power in himself and was waiting for the woman to speak when Ed Handby appeared.

The bartender did not want to beat the boy, who he thought had tried to take his woman away. He knew that beating was unnecessary, that he had power within himself to accomplish his purpose without using his fists. Gripping George by the shoulder and pulling him to his feet, he held him with one hand while he looked at Belle Carpenter seated on the grass. Then with a quick wide movement of his arm he sent the younger man sprawling away into the bushes and began to bully the woman, who had risen to her feet. "You're no good," he said roughly. "I've half a mind not to bother with you. I'd let you alone if I didn't want you so much."

On his hands and knees in the bushes George Willard stared at the scene before him and tried hard to think. He prepared to spring at the man who had humiliated him. To be beaten seemed to be infinitely better than to be thus hurled ignominiously aside.

Three times the young reporter sprang at Ed Handby and each time the bartender, catching him by the shoulder, hurled him back into the bushes. The older man seemed prepared to keep the exercise going indefinitely but George Willard's head struck the root of a tree and he lay still. Then Ed Handby took Belle Carpenter by the arm and marched her away.

George heard the man and woman making their way through the bushes. As he crept down the hillside his heart was sick within him. He hated himself and he hated the fate that had brought about his humiliation. When his mind went back to the hour alone in the alleyway he was puzzled and stopping in the darkness listened, hoping to hear again the voice outside himself that had so short a time before put new courage into his heart. When his way homeward led him again into the street of frame houses he could not bear the sight and began to run, wanting to get quickly out of the neighborhood that now seemed to him utterly squalid and commonplace.

"Queer"

From his seat on a box in the rough board shed that stuck like a burr on the rear of Cowley & Son's store in Winesburg, Elmer Cowley, the junior member of the firm, could see through a dirty window into the printshop of the *Winesburg Eagle*. Elmer was putting new shoelaces in his shoes. They did not go in readily and he had to take the shoes off. With the shoes in his hand he sat looking at a large hole in the heel of one of his stockings. Then looking quickly up he saw George Willard, the only newspaper reporter in Winesburg, standing at the back door of the *Eagle* printshop and staring absent-mindedly about. "Well, well, what next!" exclaimed the young man with the shoes in his hand, jumping to his feet and creeping away from the window.

A flush crept into Elmer Cowley's face and his hands began to tremble. In Cowley & Son's store a Jewish traveling salesman stood by the counter talking to his father. He imagined the reporter could hear what was being said and the thought made him furious. With one of the shoes still held in his hand he stood in a corner of the shed and stamped with a stockinged foot upon the board floor.

Cowley & Son's store did not face the main street of Winesburg. The front was on Maumee Street and beyond it was Voight's wagon shop and a shed for the sheltering of farmers' horses. Beside the store an alleyway ran behind the main street stores and all day drays and delivery wagons, intent on bringing in and taking out goods, passed up and down. The store itself was indescribable. Will Henderson once said of it that it sold everything and nothing. In the window facing Maumee Street stood a chunk of coal as large as an apple barrel, to indicate that orders for coal were taken, and beside the black mass of the coal stood three combs of honey grown brown and dirty in their wooden frames.

The honey had stood in the store window for six months. It was for sale as were also the coat hangers, patent suspender buttons,[1] cans of roof paint, bottles of rheumatism cure and a substitute for coffee that companioned the honey in its patient willingness to serve the public.

Ebenezer Cowley, the man who stood in the store listening to the eager patter of words that fell from the lips of the traveling man, was tall and lean and looked unwashed. On his scrawny neck was a large wen[2]

1. Probably metal clips that held men's trousers up when belts were not in style.
2. A hardened cyst formed beneath the skin.

partially covered by a grey beard. He wore a long Prince Albert coat.[3] The coat had been purchased to serve as a wedding garment. Before he became a merchant Ebenezer was a farmer and after his marriage he wore the Prince Albert coat to church on Sundays and on Saturday afternoons when he came into town to trade. When he sold the farm to become a merchant he wore the coat constantly. It had become brown with age and was covered with grease spots, but in it Ebenezer always felt dressed up and ready for the day in town.

As a merchant Ebenezer was not happily placed in life and he had not been happily placed as a farmer. Still he existed. His family, consisting of a daughter named Mabel and the son, lived with him in rooms above the store and it did not cost them much to live. His troubles were not financial. His unhappiness as a merchant lay in the fact that when a traveling man with wares to be sold came in at the front door he was afraid. Behind the counter he stood shaking his head. He was afraid, first that he would stubbornly refuse to buy and thus lose the opportunity to sell again; second that he would not be stubborn enough and would in a moment of weakness buy what could not be sold.

In the store on the morning when Elmer Cowley saw George Willard standing and apparently listening at the back door of the *Eagle* printshop, a situation had arisen that always stirred the son's wrath. The traveling man talked and Ebenezer listened, his whole figure expressing uncertainty. "You see how quickly it is done," said the traveling man who had for sale a small flat metal substitute for collar buttons. With one hand he quickly unfastened a collar from his shirt and then fastened it on again. He assumed a flattering wheedling tone. "I tell you what, men have come to the end of all this fooling with collar buttons and you are the man to make money out of the change that is coming. I am offering you the exclusive agency for this town. Take twenty dozen of these fasteners and I'll not visit any other store. I'll leave the field to you."

The traveling man leaned over the counter and tapped with his finger on Ebenezer's breast. "It's an opportunity and I want you to take it," he urged. "A friend of mine told me about you. 'See that man Cowley,' he said. 'He's a live one.' "

The traveling man paused and waited. Taking a book from his pocket he began writing out the order. Still holding the shoe in his hand Elmer Cowley went through the store, past the two absorbed men, to a glass show case near the front door. He took a cheap revolver from the case and began to wave it about. "You get out of here!" he shrieked. "We don't want any collar fasteners here." An idea came to him. "Mind, I'm not making any threat," he added. "I don't say I'll shoot. Maybe I just

3. Men's dark-wool dress-coat that was double-breasted and knee-length; popularized by Prince Albert of Saxe-Coburg-Gotha (1819–61), consort to England's Queen Victoria.

took this gun out of the case to look at it. But you better get out. Yes sir, I'll say that. You better grab up your things and get out."

The young storekeeper's voice rose to a scream and going behind the counter he began to advance upon the two men. "We're through being fools here!" he cried. "We ain't going to buy any more stuff until we begin to sell. We ain't going to keep on being queer and have folks staring and listening. You get out of here!"

The traveling man left. Raking the samples of collar fasteners off the counter into a black leather bag, he ran. He was a small man and very bow-legged and he ran awkwardly. The black bag caught against the door and he stumbled and fell. "Crazy, that's what he is—crazy!" he sputtered as he arose from the sidewalk and hurried away.

In the store Elmer Cowley and his father stared at each other. Now that the immediate object of his wrath had fled, the younger man was embarrassed. "Well, I meant it. I think we've been queer long enough," he declared, going to the showcase and replacing the revolver. Sitting on a barrel he pulled on and fastened the shoe he had been holding in his hand. He was waiting for some word of understanding from his father but when Ebenezer spoke his words only served to reawaken the wrath in the son and the young man ran out of the store without replying. Scratching his grey beard with his long dirty fingers, the merchant looked at his son with the same wavering uncertain stare with which he had confronted the traveling man. "I'll be starched," he said softly. "Well, well, I'll be washed and ironed and starched!"

Elmer Cowley went out of Winesburg and along a country road that paralleled the railroad track. He did not know where he was going or what he was going to do. In the shelter of a deep cut where the road, after turning sharply to the right, dipped under the tracks he stopped and the passion that had been the cause of his outburst in the store began to again find expression. "I will not be queer—one to be looked at and listened to," he declared aloud. "I'll be like other people. I'll show that George Willard. He'll find out. I'll show him!"

The distraught young man stood in the middle of the road and glared back at the town. He did not know the reporter George Willard and had no special feeling concerning the tall boy who ran about town gathering the town news. The reporter had merely come, by his presence in the office and in the printshop of the *Winesburg Eagle*, to stand for something in the young merchant's mind. He thought the boy who passed and repassed Cowley & Son's store and who stopped to talk to people in the street must be thinking of him and perhaps laughing at him. George Willard, he felt, belonged to the town, typified the town, represented in his person the spirit of the town. Elmer Cowley could not have believed that George Willard had also his days of unhappiness, that vague hungers and secret unnamable desires visited also his mind. Did he not represent public opinion and had not the public opinion of Winesburg condemned the Cowleys to queerness? Did he not walk whistling and laughing through Main Street? Might not one by striking his person strike also the greater enemy—the thing that smiled and went its own way—the judgment of Winesburg?

Elmer Cowley was extraordinarily tall and his arms were long and powerful. His hair, his eyebrows, and the downy beard that had begun to grow upon his chin, were pale almost to whiteness. His teeth protruded from between his lips and his eyes were blue with the colorless blueness of the marbles called "aggies" that the boys of Winesburg carried in their pockets. Elmer had lived in Winesburg for a year and had made no friends. He was, he felt, one condemned to go through life without friends and he hated the thought.

Sullenly the tall young man tramped along the road with his hands stuffed into his trouser pockets. The day was cold with a raw wind, but presently the sun began to shine and the road became soft and muddy. The tops of the ridges of frozen mud that formed the road began to melt and the mud clung to Elmer's shoes. His feet became cold. When he had gone several miles he turned off the road, crossed a field and entered a wood. In the wood he gathered sticks to build a fire by which he sat trying to warm himself, miserable in body and in mind.

For two hours he sat on the log by the fire and then, arising and creeping cautiously through a mass of underbrush, he went to a fence and looked across fields to a small farmhouse surrounded by low sheds. A smile came to his lips and he began making motions with his long arms to a man who was husking corn in one of the fields.

In his hour of misery the young merchant had returned to the farm where he had lived through boyhood and where there was another human being to whom he felt he could explain himself. The man on the farm was a half-witted old fellow named Mook. He had once been employed by Ebenezer Cowley and had stayed on the farm when it was sold. The old man lived in one of the unpainted sheds back of the farmhouse and puttered about all day in the fields.

Mook the half-wit lived happily. With childlike faith he believed in the intelligence of the animals that lived in the sheds with him, and when he was lonely held long conversations with the cows, the pigs, and even with the chickens that ran about the barnyard. He it was who had put the expression regarding being "laundered" into the mouth of his former employer. When excited or surprised by anything he smiled vaguely and muttered: "I'll be washed and ironed. Well, well, I'll be washed and ironed and starched."

When the half-witted old man left his husking of corn and came into the wood to meet Elmer Cowley, he was neither surprised nor especially interested in the sudden appearance of the young man. His feet also were cold and he sat on the log by the fire, grateful for the warmth and apparently indifferent to what Elmer had to say.

Elmer talked earnestly and with great freedom, walking up and down and waving his arms about. "You don't understand what's the matter with me so of course you don't care," he declared. "With me it's different. Look how it has always been with me. Father is queer and mother was queer, too. Even the clothes mother used to wear were not like other people's clothes, and look at that coat in which father goes about there in town, thinking he's dressed up, too. Why don't he get a new one? It wouldn't cost much. I'll tell you why. Father doesn't know and when mother was alive she didn't know either. Mabel is different. She knows but she won't say anything. I will, though. I'm not going to be stared at any longer. Why look here, Mook, father doesn't know that his store there in town is just a queer jumble, that he'll never sell the stuff he buys. He knows nothing about it. Sometimes he's a little worried that trade doesn't come and then he goes and buys something else. In the evenings he sits by the fire upstairs and says trade will come after a while. He isn't worried. He's queer. He doesn't know enough to be worried."

The excited young man became more excited. "He don't know but I know," he shouted, stopping to gaze down into the dumb, unresponsive face of the half-wit. "I know too well. I can't stand it. When we lived out here it was different. I worked and at night I went to bed and slept. I wasn't always seeing people and thinking as I am now. In the evening, there in town, I go to the post office or to the depot to see the train come in, and no one says anything to me. Everyone stands around and laughs and they talk but they say nothing to me. Then I feel so queer that I can't talk either. I go away. I don't say anything. I can't."

The fury of the young man became uncontrollable. "I won't stand it," he yelled, looking up at the bare branches of the trees. "I'm not made to stand it."

Maddened by the dull face of the man on the log by the fire, Elmer turned and glared at him as he had glared back along the road at the town of Winesburg. "Go on back to work," he screamed. "What good does it do me to talk to you?" A thought came to him and his voice dropped. "I'm a coward too, eh?" he muttered. "Do you know why I came clear out here afoot? I had to tell some one and you were the only one I could tell. I hunted out another queer one, you see. I ran away, that's what I did. I couldn't stand up to some one like that George Willard. I had to come to you. I ought to tell him and I will."

Again his voice arose to a shout and his arms flew about. "I will tell him. I won't be queer. I don't care what they think. I won't stand it."

Elmer Cowley ran out of the woods leaving the half-wit sitting on the log before the fire. Presently the old man arose and climbing over the fence went back to his work in the corn. "I'll be washed and ironed and starched," he declared. "Well, well, I'll be washed and ironed." Mook was interested. He went along a lane to a field where two cows stood nibbling at a straw stack. "Elmer was here," he said to the cows. "Elmer is crazy. You better get behind the stack where he don't see you. He'll hurt someone yet, Elmer will."

At eight o'clock that evening Elmer Cowley put his head in at the front door of the office of the *Winesburg Eagle* where George Willard sat writing. His cap was pulled down over his eyes and a sullen determined look was on his face. "You come on outside with me," he said, stepping in and closing the door. He kept his hand on the knob as though prepared to resist anyone else coming in. "You just come along outside. I want to see you."

George Willard and Elmer Cowley walked through the main street of Winesburg. The night was cold and George Willard had on a new overcoat and looked very spruce and dressed up. He thrust his hands into the overcoat pockets and looked inquiringly at his companion. He had long been wanting to make friends with the young merchant and find out what was in his mind. Now he thought he saw a chance and was delighted. "I wonder what he's up to? Perhaps he thinks he has a piece of news for the paper. It can't be a fire because I haven't heard the fire bell and there isn't anyone running," he thought.

In the main street of Winesburg, on the cold November evening, but few citizens appeared and these hurried along bent on getting to the stove at the back of some store. The windows of the stores were frosted and the wind rattled the tin sign that hung over the entrance to the stairway leading to Doctor Welling's office. Before Hern's Grocery a basket of apples and a rack filled with new brooms stood on the sidewalk. Elmer Cowley stopped and stood facing George Willard. He tried to talk and his arms began to pump up and down. His face worked spasmodically. He seemed about to shout. "Oh, you go on back," he cried. "Don't stay out here with me. I ain't got anything to tell you. I don't want to see you at all."

For three hours the distracted young merchant wandered through the resident streets of Winesburg blind with anger, brought on by his failure to declare his determination not to be queer. Bitterly the sense of defeat settled upon him and he wanted to weep. After the hours of futile sputtering at nothingness that had occupied the afternoon and his failure in the presence of the young reporter, he thought he could see no hope of a future for himself.

And then a new idea dawned for him. In the darkness that surrounded him he began to see a light. Going to the now darkened store, where Cowley & Son had for over a year waited vainly for trade to come, he crept stealthily in and felt about in a barrel that stood by the stove at the rear. In the barrel beneath shavings lay a tin box containing Cowley & Son's cash. Every evening Ebenezer Cowley put the box in the barrel when he closed the store and went upstairs to bed. "They wouldn't never think of a careless place like that," he told himself, thinking of robbers.

Elmer took twenty dollars, two ten dollar bills, from the little roll containing perhaps four hundred dollars, the cash left from the sale of the farm. Then replacing the box beneath the shavings he went quietly out at the front door and walked again in the streets.

The idea that he thought might put an end to all of his unhappiness was very simple. "I will get out of here, run away from home," he told himself. He knew that a local freight train passed through Winesburg at midnight and went on to Cleveland where it arrived at dawn. He would steal a ride on the local and when he got to Cleveland would lose himself in the crowds there. He would get work in some shop and become friends with the other workmen. Gradually he would become like other men and would be indistinguishable. Then he could talk and laugh. He would no longer be queer and would make friends. Life would begin to have warmth and meaning for him as it had for others.

The tall awkward young man, striding through the streets, laughed at himself because he had been angry and had been half afraid of George Willard. He decided he would have his talk with the young reporter before he left town, that he would tell him about things, perhaps challenge him, challenge all of Winesburg through him.

Aglow with new confidence Elmer went to the office of the New Willard House and pounded on the door. A sleep-eyed boy slept on a cot in the office. He received no salary but was fed at the hotel table and bore with pride the title of "night clerk." Before the boy Elmer was bold, insistent. "You wake him up," he commanded. "You tell him to come down by the depot. I got to see him and I'm going away on the local. Tell him to dress and come on down. I ain't got much time."

The midnight local had finished its work in Winesburg and the trainsmen were coupling cars, swinging lanterns and preparing to resume their flight east. George Willard, rubbing his eyes and again wearing the new overcoat, ran down to the station platform afire with curiosity. "Well, here I am. What do you want? You've got something to tell me, eh?" he said.

Elmer tried to explain. He wet his lips with his tongue and looked at the train that had begun to groan and get under way. "Well, you see," he began, and then lost control of his tongue. "I'll be washed and ironed. I'll be washed and ironed and starched," he muttered half incoherently.

Elmer Cowley danced with fury beside the groaning train in the darkness on the station platform. Lights leaped into the air and bobbed up and down before his eyes. Taking the two ten dollar bills from his pocket he thrust them into George Willard's hand. "Take them," he cried. "I don't want them. Give them to father. I stole them." With a snarl of rage he turned and his long arms began to flay the air. Like one struggling for release from hands that held him he struck out, hitting George Willard blow after blow on the breast, the neck, the mouth. The young reporter rolled over on the platform half unconscious, stunned by the terrific force of the blows. Springing aboard the passing train and running over the tops of cars, Elmer sprang down to a flat car and lying on his face looked back, trying to see the fallen man in the darkness. Pride surged up in him. "I showed him," he cried. "I guess I showed him. I ain't so queer. I guess I showed him I ain't so queer."

The Untold Lie

Ray Pearson and Hal Winters were farm hands employed on a farm three miles north of Winesburg. On Saturday afternoons they came into town and wandered about through the streets with other fellows from the country.

Ray was a quiet, rather nervous man of perhaps fifty with a brown beard and shoulders rounded by too much and too hard labor. In his nature he was as unlike Hal Winters as two men can be unlike.

Ray was an altogether serious man and had a little sharp featured wife who had also a sharp voice. The two, with half a dozen thin legged children, lived in a tumble-down frame house beside a creek at the back end of the Wills farm where Ray was employed.

Hal Winters, his fellow employee, was a young fellow. He was not of the Ned Winters family, who were very respectable people in Winesburg, but was one of the three sons of the old man called Windpeter Winters who had a sawmill near Unionville, six miles away, and who was looked upon by everyone in Winesburg as a confirmed old reprobate.

People from the part of Northern Ohio in which Winesburg lies will remember old Windpeter by his unusual and tragic death. He got drunk one evening in town and started to drive home to Unionville along the railroad tracks. Henry Brattenburg, the butcher, who lived out that way, stopped him at the edge of the town and told him he was sure to meet the down train[1] but Windpeter slashed at him with his whip and drove on. When the train struck and killed him and his two horses a farmer and his wife who were driving home along a nearby road saw the accident. They said that old Windpeter stood up on the seat of his wagon, raving and swearing at the onrushing locomotive, and that he fairly screamed with delight when the team, maddened by his incessant slashing at them, rushed straight ahead to certain death. Boys like young George Willard and Seth Richmond will remember the incident quite vividly because, although everyone in our town said that the old man would go straight to hell and that the community was better off without him, they had a secret conviction that he knew what he was doing and admired his foolish courage. Most boys have seasons of wishing they

1. A train that runs from north to south.

could die gloriously instead of just being grocery clerks and going on with their humdrum lives.

But this is not the story of Windpeter Winters nor yet of his son Hal who worked on the Wills farm with Ray Pearson. It is Ray's story. It will, however, be necessary to talk a little of young Hal so that you will get into the spirit of it.

Hal was a bad one. Everyone said that. There were three of the Winters boys in that family, John, Hal, and Edward, all broad shouldered big fellows like old Windpeter himself and all fighters and woman-chasers and generally all-around bad ones.

Hal was the worst of the lot and always up to some devilment. He once stole a load of boards from his father's mill and sold them in Winesburg. With the money he bought himself a suit of cheap, flashy clothes. Then he got drunk and when his father came raving into town to find him, they met and fought with their fists on Main Street and were arrested and put into jail together.

Hal went to work on the Wills farm because there was a country school teacher out that way who had taken his fancy. He was only twenty-two then but had already been in two or three of what were spoken of in Winesburg as "women scrapes." Everyone who heard of his infatuation for the school teacher was sure it would turn out badly. "He'll only get her into trouble, you'll see," was the word that went around.

And so these two men, Ray and Hal, were at work in a field on a day in the late October. They were husking corn and occasionally something was said and they laughed. Then came silence. Ray, who was the more sensitive and always minded things more, had chapped hands and they hurt. He put them into his coat pockets and looked away across the fields. He was in a sad distracted mood and was affected by the beauty of the country. If you knew the Winesburg country in the fall and how the low hills are all splashed with yellows and reds you would understand his feeling. He began to think of the time, long ago when he was a young fellow living with his father, then a baker in Winesburg, and how on such days he had wandered away to the woods to gather nuts, hunt rabbits, or just to loaf about and smoke his pipe. His marriage had come about through one of his days of wandering. He had induced a girl who waited on trade in his father's shop to go with him and something had happened. He was thinking of that afternoon and how it had affected his whole life when a spirit of protest awoke in him. He had forgotten about Hal and muttered words. "Tricked by Gad, that's what I was, tricked by life and made a fool of," he said in a low voice.

As though understanding his thoughts, Hal Winters spoke up. "Well, has it been worth while? What about it, eh? What about marriage and all that?" he asked and then laughed. Hal tried to keep on laughing but he too was in an earnest mood. He began to talk earnestly. "Has a fellow got to do it?" he asked. "Has he got to be harnessed up and driven through life like a horse?"

Hal didn't wait for an answer but sprang to his feet and began to walk back and forth between the corn shocks. He was getting more and more excited. Bending down suddenly he picked up an ear of the yellow corn and threw it at the fence. "I've got Nell Gunther in trouble," he said. "I'm telling you, but you keep your mouth shut."

Ray Pearson arose and stood staring. He was almost a foot shorter than Hal, and when the younger man came and put his two hands on the older man's shoulders they made a picture. There they stood in the big empty field with the quiet corn shocks standing in rows behind them and the red and yellow hills in the distance, and from being just two indifferent workmen they had become all alive to each other. Hal sensed it and because that was his way he laughed. "Well, old daddy," he said awkwardly, "come on, advise me. I've got Nell in trouble. Perhaps you've been in the same fix yourself. I know what every one would say is the right thing to do, but what do you say? Shall I marry and settle down? Shall I put myself into the harness to be worn out like an old horse? You know me, Ray. There can't any one break me but I can break myself. Shall I do it or shall I tell Nell to go to the devil? Come on, you tell me. Whatever you say, Ray, I'll do."

Ray couldn't answer. He shook Hal's hands loose and turning walked straight away toward the barn. He was a sensitive man and there were tears in his eyes. He knew there was only one thing to say to Hal Winters, son of old Windpeter Winters, only one thing that all his own training and all the beliefs of the people he knew would approve, but for his life he couldn't say what he knew he should say.

At half-past four that afternoon Ray was puttering about the barnyard when his wife came up the lane along the creek and called him. After the talk with Hal he hadn't returned to the corn field but worked about the barn. He had already done the evening chores and had seen Hal, dressed and ready for a roistering night in town, come out of the farmhouse and go into the road. Along the path to his own house he trudged behind his wife, looking at the ground and thinking. He couldn't make out what was wrong. Every time he raised his eyes and saw the beauty of the country in the failing light he wanted to do something he had never done before, shout or scream or hit his wife with his fists or something equally unexpected and terrifying. Along the path he went scratching his head and trying to make it out. He looked hard at his wife's back but she seemed all right.

She only wanted him to go into town for groceries and as soon as she had told him what she wanted began to scold. "You're always puttering," she said. "Now I want you to hustle. There isn't anything in the house for supper and you've got to get to town and back in a hurry."

Ray went into his own house and took an overcoat from a hook back of the door. It was torn about the pockets and the collar was shiny. His wife went into the bedroom and presently came out with a soiled cloth in one hand and three silver dollars in the other. Somewhere in the house a child wept bitterly and a dog that had been sleeping by the stove arose and yawned. Again the wife scolded. "The children will cry and cry. Why are you always puttering?" she asked.

Ray went out of the house and climbed the fence into a field. It was just growing dark and the scene that lay before him was lovely. All the low hills were washed with color and even the little clusters of bushes in the corners by the fences were alive with beauty. The whole world seemed to Ray Pearson to have become alive with something just as he and Hal had suddenly become alive when they stood in the corn field staring into each other's eyes.

The beauty of the country about Winesburg was too much for Ray on that fall evening. That is all there was to it. He could not stand it. Of a sudden he forgot all about being a quiet old farm hand and throwing off the torn overcoat began to run across the field. As he ran he shouted a protest against his life, against all life, against everything that makes life ugly. "There was no promise made," he cried into the empty spaces that lay about him. "I didn't promise my Minnie anything and Hal hasn't made any promise to Nell. I know he hasn't. She went into the woods with him because she wanted to go. What he wanted she wanted. Why should I pay? Why should Hal pay? Why should any one pay? I don't want Hal to become old and worn out. I'll tell him. I won't let it go on. I'll catch Hal before he gets to town and I'll tell him."

Ray ran clumsily and once he stumbled and fell down. "I must catch Hal and tell him," he kept thinking and although his breath came in gasps he kept running harder and harder. As he ran he thought of things that hadn't come into his mind for years—how at the time he married he had planned to go west to his uncle in Portland, Oregon—how he hadn't wanted to be a farm hand, but had thought when he got out west he would go to sea and be a sailor or get a job on a ranch and ride a horse into western towns, shouting and laughing and waking the people in the houses with his wild cries. Then as he ran he remembered his children and in fancy felt their hands clutching at him. All of his thoughts of himself were involved with the thoughts of Hal and he thought the children were clutching at the younger man also. "They are the accidents of life, Hal," he cried. "They are not mine or yours. I had nothing to do with them."

Darkness began to spread over the fields as Ray Pearson ran on and on. His breath came in little sobs. When he came to the fence at the edge of the road and confronted Hal Winters, all dressed up and smoking a pipe as he walked jauntily along, he could not have told what he thought or what he wanted.

Ray Pearson lost his nerve and this is really the end of the story of what happened to him. It was almost dark when he got to the fence and he put his hands on the top bar and stood staring. Hal Winters jumped a ditch and coming up close to Ray put his hands into his pockets and laughed. He seemed to have lost his own sense of what had happened in the corn field and when he put up a strong hand and took hold of the lapel of Ray's coat he shook the old man as he might have shaken a dog that had misbehaved.

"You came to tell me, eh?" he said. "Well, never mind telling me anything. I'm not a coward and I've already made up my mind." He laughed again and jumped back across the ditch. "Nell ain't no fool," he said. "She didn't ask me to marry her. I want to marry her. I want to settle down and have kids."

Ray Pearson also laughed. He felt like laughing at himself and all the world.

As the form of Hal Winters disappeared in the dusk that lay over the road that led to Winesburg, he turned and walked slowly back across the fields to where he had left his torn overcoat. As he went some memory of pleasant evenings spent with the thin-legged children in the tumble-down house by the creek must have come into his mind, for he muttered words. "It's just as well. Whatever I told him would have been a lie," he said softly, and then his form also disappeared into the darkness of the fields.

Drink

Tom Foster came to Winesburg from Cincinnati when he was still young and could get many new impressions. His grandmother had been raised on a farm near the town and as a young girl had gone to school there when Winesburg was a village of twelve or fifteen houses clustered about a general store on the Trunion Pike.

What a life the old woman had led since she went away from the frontier settlement and what a strong, capable little old thing she was! She had been in Kansas, in Canada, and in New York City, traveling about with her husband, a mechanic, before he died. Later she went to stay with her daughter who had also married a mechanic and lived in Covington, Kentucky, across the river from Cincinnati.

Then began the hard years for Tom Foster's grandmother. First her son-in-law was killed by a policeman during a strike and then Tom's mother became an invalid and died also. The grandmother had saved a little money, but it was swept away by the illness of the daughter and by the cost of the two funerals. She became a half worn-out old woman worker and lived with the grandson above a junk shop on a side street in Cincinnati. For five years she scrubbed the floors in an office building and then got a place as dish washer in a restaurant. Her hands were all twisted out of shape. When she took hold of a mop or a broom handle the hands looked like the dried stems of an old creeping vine clinging to a tree.

The old woman came back to Winesburg as soon as she got the chance. One evening as she was coming home from work she found a pocket-book containing thirty-seven dollars, and that opened the way. The trip was a great adventure for the boy. It was past seven o'clock at night when the grandmother came home with the pocketbook held tightly in her old hands and she was so excited she could scarcely speak. She insisted on leaving Cincinnati that night, saying that if they stayed until morning the owner of the money would be sure to find them out and make trouble. Tom, who was then sixteen years old, had to go trudging off to the station with the old woman bearing all of their earthly belongings done up in a worn-out blanket and slung across his back. By his side walked the grandmother urging him forward. Her toothless old mouth twitched nervously, and when Tom grew weary and wanted to put the pack down at a street crossing she snatched it up and if he had not prevented would have slung it across her own back. When they got into the train and it had run out of the city she was as delighted as a girl and talked as the boy had never heard her talk before.

All through the night as the train rattled along, the grandmother told Tom tales of Winesburg and of how he would enjoy his life working in the fields and shooting wild things in the wood there. She could not believe that the tiny village of fifty years before had grown into a thriving town in her absence, and in the morning when the train came to Winesburg did not want to get off. "It isn't what I thought. It may be hard for you here," she said, and then the train went on its way and the two stood confused, not knowing where to turn, in the presence of Albert Longworth, the Winesburg baggage master.

But Tom Foster did get along all right. He was one to get along anywhere. Mrs. White, the banker's wife, employed his grandmother to work in the kitchen and he got a place as stable boy in the banker's new brick barn.

In Winesburg servants were hard to get. The woman who wanted help in her housework employed a "hired girl" who insisted on sitting at the table with the family. Mrs. White was sick of hired girls and snatched at the chance to get hold of the old city woman. She furnished a room for the boy Tom upstairs in the barn. "He can mow the lawn and run errands when the horses do not need attention," she explained to her husband.

Tom Foster was rather small for his age and had a large head covered with stiff black hair that stood straight up. The hair emphasized the bigness of his head. His voice was the softest thing imaginable, and he was himself so gentle and quiet that he slipped into the life of the town without attracting the least bit of attention.

One could not help wondering where Tom Foster got his gentleness. In Cincinnati he had lived in a neighborhood where gangs of tough boys prowled through the streets, and all through his early formative years he ran about with tough boys. For a while he was messenger for a telegraph company and delivered messages in a neighborhood sprinkled with houses of prostitution. The women in the houses knew and loved Tom Foster and the tough boys in the gangs loved him also.

He never asserted himself. That was one thing that helped him escape. In an odd way he stood in the shadow of the wall of life, was meant to stand in the shadow. He saw the men and women in the houses of lust, sensed their casual and horrible love affairs, saw boys fighting and listened to their tales of thieving and drunkenness unmoved and strangely unaffected.

Once Tom did steal. That was while he still lived in the city. The grandmother was ill at the time and he himself was out of work. There was nothing to eat in the house, and so he went into a harness shop on a side street and stole a dollar and seventy-five cents out of the cash drawer.

The harness shop was run by an old man with a long mustache. He saw the boy lurking about and thought nothing of it. When he went out into the street to talk to a teamster[1] Tom opened the cash drawer and taking the money walked away. Later he was caught and his grandmother settled the matter by offering to come twice a week for a month and scrub the shop. The boy was ashamed, but he was rather glad, too. "It is all right to be ashamed and makes me understand new things," he said to the grandmother, who didn't know what the boy was talking about but loved him so much that it didn't matter whether she understood or not.

For a year Tom Foster lived in the banker's stable and then lost his place there. He didn't take very good care of the horses and he was a constant source of irritation to the banker's wife. She told him to mow the lawn and he forgot. Then she sent him to the store or to the post office and he did not come back but joined a group of men and boys and spent the whole afternoon with them, standing about, listening and occasionally, when addressed, saying a few words. As in the city in the houses of prostitution and with the rowdy boys running through the streets at night, so in Winesburg among its citizens he had always the power to be a part of and yet distinctly apart from the life about him.

After Tom lost his place at Banker White's he did not live with his grandmother, although often in the evening she came to visit him. He rented a room at the rear of a little frame building belonging to old Rufus Whiting. The building was on Duane Street, just off Main Street, and had been used for years as a law office by the old man who had

1. *Teamsters* drove teams of horses to pull carts or wagons.

become too feeble and forgetful for the practice of his profession but did not realize his inefficiency. He liked Tom and let him have the room for a dollar a month. In the late afternoon when the lawyer had gone home the boy had the place to himself and spent hours lying on the floor by the stove and thinking of things. In the evening the grandmother came and sat in the lawyer's chair to smoke a pipe while Tom remained silent, as he always did in the presence of every one.

Often the old woman talked with great vigor. Sometimes she was angry about some happening at the banker's house and scolded away for hours. Out of her own earnings she bought a mop and regularly scrubbed the lawyer's office. Then when the place was spotlessly clean and smelled clean she lighted her clay pipe and she and Tom had a smoke together. "When you get ready to die then I will die also," she said to the boy lying on the floor beside her chair.

Tom Foster enjoyed life in Winesburg. He did odd jobs, such as cutting wood for kitchen stoves and mowing the grass before houses. In late May and early June he picked strawberries in the fields. He had time to loaf and he enjoyed loafing. Banker White had given him a cast-off coat which was too large for him, but his grandmother cut it down, and he had also an overcoat, got at the same place, that was lined with fur. The fur was worn away in spots, but the coat was warm and in the winter Tom slept in it. He thought his method of getting along good enough and was happy and satisfied with the way life in Winesburg had turned out for him.

The most absurd little things made Tom Foster happy. That, I suppose, was why people loved him. In Hern's grocery they would be roasting coffee on Friday afternoon, preparatory to the Saturday rush of trade, and the rich odor invaded lower Main Street. Tom Foster appeared and sat on a box at the rear of the store. For an hour he did not move but sat perfectly still, filling his being with the spicy odor that made him half drunk with happiness. "I like it," he said gently. "It makes me think of things far away, places and things like that."

One night Tom Foster got drunk. That came about in a curious way. He never had been drunk before, and indeed in all his life had never taken a drink of anything intoxicating, but he felt he needed to be drunk that one time and so went and did it.

In Cincinnati, when he lived there, Tom had found out many things, things about ugliness and crime and lust. Indeed, he knew more of these things than any one else in Winesburg. The matter of sex in particular had presented itself to him in a quite horrible way and had made a deep impression on his mind. He thought, after what he had seen of the women standing before the squalid houses on cold nights and the look he had seen in the eyes of the men who stopped to talk to them, that he would put sex altogether out of his own life. One of the women of the neighborhood tempted him once and he went into a room with her. He never forgot the smell of the room nor the greedy look that came into the eyes of the woman. It sickened him and in a very terrible way left a scar on his soul. He had always before thought of women as quite innocent things, much like his grandmother, but after that one experience in the room he dismissed women from his mind. So gentle was his nature that he could not hate anything and not being able to understand he decided to forget.

And Tom did forget until he came to Winesburg. After he had lived there for two years something began to stir in him. On all sides he saw youth making love and he was himself a youth. Before he knew what had happened he was in love also. He fell in love with Helen White, daughter of the man for whom he had worked, and found himself thinking of her at night.

That was a problem for Tom and he settled it in his own way. He let himself think of Helen White whenever her figure came into his mind and only concerned himself with the manner of his thoughts. He had a fight, a quiet determined little fight of his own, to keep his desires in the channel where he thought they belonged, but on the whole he was victorious.

And then came the spring night when he got drunk. Tom was wild on that night. He was like an innocent young buck of the forest that has eaten of some maddening weed. The thing began, ran its course, and was ended in one night, and you may be sure that no one in Winesburg was any the worse for Tom's outbreak.

In the first place, the night was one to make a sensitive nature drunk. The trees along the residence streets of the town were all newly clothed in soft green leaves, in the gardens behind the houses men were puttering about in vegetable gardens, and in the air there was a hush, a waiting kind of silence very stirring to the blood.

Tom left his room on Duane Street just as the young night began to make itself felt. First he walked through the streets, going softly and quietly along, thinking thoughts that he tried to put into words. He said that Helen White was a flame dancing in the air and that he was a little tree without leaves standing out sharply against the sky. Then he said that she was a wind, a strong terrible wind, coming out of the darkness of a stormy sea and that he was a boat left on the shore of the sea by a fisherman.

That idea pleased the boy and he sauntered along playing with it. He went into Main Street and sat on the curbing before Wacker's tobacco store. For an hour he lingered about listening to the talk of men, but it did not interest him much and he slipped away. Then he decided to get drunk and went into Willy's saloon and bought a bottle of whiskey. Putting the bottle into his pocket, he walked out of town, wanting to be alone to think more thoughts and to drink the whiskey.

Tom got drunk sitting on a bank of new grass beside the road about a mile north of town. Before him was a white road and at his back an apple orchard in full bloom. He took a drink out of the bottle and then lay down on the grass. He thought of mornings in Winesburg and of how the stones in the graveled driveway by Banker White's house were wet with dew and glistened in the morning light. He thought of the nights in the barn when it rained and he lay awake hearing the drumming of the rain drops and smelling the warm smell of horses and of hay. Then he thought of a storm that had gone roaring through Winesburg several days before and, his mind going back, he relived the night he had spent on the train with his grandmother when the two were coming from Cincinnati. Sharply he remembered how strange it had seemed to sit quietly in the coach and to feel the power of the engine hurling the train along through the night.

Tom got drunk in a very short time. He kept taking drinks from the bottle as the thoughts visited him and when his head began to reel got up and walked along the road going away from Winesburg. There was a bridge on the road that ran out of Winesburg north to Lake Erie and the drunken boy made his way along the road to the bridge. There he sat down. He tried to drink again, but when he had taken the cork out of the bottle he became ill and put it quickly back. His head was rocking back and forth and so he sat on the stone approach to the bridge and sighed. His head seemed to be flying about like a pin wheel and then projecting itself off into space and his arms and legs flopped helplessly about.

At eleven o'clock Tom got back into town. George Willard found him wandering about and took him into the *Eagle* printshop. Then he became afraid that the drunken boy would make a mess on the floor and helped him into the alleyway.

The reporter was confused by Tom Foster. The drunken boy talked of Helen White and said he had been with her on the shore of a sea and had made love to her. George had seen Helen White walking in the street with her father during the evening and decided that Tom was out of his head. A sentiment concerning Helen White that lurked in his own heart flamed up and he became angry. "Now you quit that," he said. "I won't let Helen White's name be dragged into this. I won't let that happen." He began shaking Tom's shoulder, trying to make him understand. "You quit it," he said again.

For three hours the two young men, thus strangely thrown together, stayed in the printshop. When he had a little recovered George took Tom for a walk. They went into the country and sat on a log near the edge of a wood. Something in the still night drew them together and when the drunken boy's head began to clear they talked.

"It was good to be drunk," Tom Foster said. "It taught me something.

I won't have to do it again. I will think more clearly after this. You see how it is."

George Willard did not see, but his anger concerning Helen White passed and he felt drawn towards the pale, shaken boy as he had never before been drawn towards any one. With motherly solicitude, he insisted that Tom get to his feet and walk about. Again they went back to the printshop and sat in silence in the darkness.

The reporter could not get the purpose of Tom Foster's action straightened out in his mind. When Tom spoke again of Helen White he again grew angry and began to scold. "You quit that," he said sharply. "You haven't been with her. What makes you say you have? What makes you keep saying such things? Now you quit it, do you hear?"

Tom was hurt. He couldn't quarrel with George Willard because he was incapable of quarreling, so he got up to go away. When George Willard was insistent he put out his hand, laying it on the older boy's arm, and tried to explain.

"Well," he said softly, "I don't know how it was. I was happy. You see how that was. Helen White made me happy and the night did too. I wanted to suffer, to be hurt somehow. I thought that was what I should do. I wanted to suffer, you see, because every one suffers and does wrong. I thought of a lot of things to do, but they wouldn't work. They all hurt some one else."

Tom Foster's voice arose, and for once in his life he became almost excited. "It was like making love, that's what I mean," he explained. "Don't you see how it is? It hurt me to do what I did and made everything strange. That's why I did it. I'm glad, too. It taught me something, that's it, that's what I wanted. Don't you understand? I wanted to learn things, you see. That's why I did it."

Death

The stairway leading up to Dr. Reefy's office, in the Heffner Block above the Paris Dry Goods Store, was but dimly lighted. At the head of the stairway hung a lamp with a dirty chimney that was fastened by a bracket to the wall. The lamp had a tin reflector, brown with rust and covered with dust. The people who went up the stairway followed with their feet the feet of many who had gone before. The soft boards of the stairs had yielded under the pressure of feet and deep hollows marked the way.

At the top of the stairway a turn to the right brought you to the doctor's door. To the left was a dark hallway filled with rubbish. Old chairs, carpenters' horses, step ladders and empty boxes lay in the darkness waiting for shins to be barked. The pile of rubbish belonged to the Paris Dry

Goods Co. When a counter or a row of shelves in the store became useless, clerks carried it up the stairway and threw it on the pile.

Doctor Reefy's office was as large as a barn. A stove with a round paunch sat in the middle of the room. Around its base was piled sawdust, held in place by heavy planks nailed to the floor. By the door stood a huge table that had once been a part of the furniture of Herrick's Clothing Store and that had been used for displaying custom-made clothes. It was covered with books, bottles and surgical instruments. Near the edge of the table lay three or four apples left by John Spaniard, a tree nurseryman who was Doctor Reefy's friend, and who had slipped the apples out of his pocket as he came in at the door.

At middle age Doctor Reefy was tall and awkward. The grey beard he later wore had not yet appeared, but on the upper lip grew a brown mustache. He was not a graceful man, as when he grew older, and was much occupied with the problem of disposing of his hands and feet.

On summer afternoons, when she had been married many years and when her son George was a boy of twelve or fourteen, Elizabeth Willard sometimes went up the worn steps to Doctor Reefy's office. Already the woman's naturally tall figure had begun to droop and to drag itself listlessly about. Ostensibly she went to see the doctor because of her health, but on the half dozen occasions when she had been to see him the outcome of the visits did not primarily concern her health. She and the doctor talked of that but they talked most of her life, of their two lives and of the ideas that had come to them as they lived their lives in Winesburg.

In the big empty office the man and the woman sat looking at each other and they were a good deal alike. Their bodies were different as were also the color of their eyes, the length of their noses and the circumstances of their existence, but something inside them meant the same thing, wanted the same release, would have left the same impression on the memory of an onlooker. Later, and when he grew older and married a young wife, the doctor often talked to her of the hours spent with the sick woman and expressed a good many things he had been unable to express to Elizabeth. He was almost a poet in his old age and his notion of what happened took a poetic turn. "I had come to the time in my life when prayer became necessary and so I invented gods and prayed to them," he said. "I did not say my prayers in words nor did I kneel down but sat perfectly still in my chair. In the late afternoon when it was hot and quiet on Main Street or in the winter when the days were gloomy, the gods came into the office and I thought no one knew about them. Then I found that this woman Elizabeth knew, that she worshipped also the same gods. I have a notion that she came to the office because she thought the gods would be there but she was happy to find herself not alone just the same. It was an experience that cannot be explained, although I suppose it is always happening to men and women in all sorts of places."

. . . .

On the summer afternoons when Elizabeth and the doctor sat in the office and talked of their two lives they talked of other lives also. Sometimes the doctor made philosophic epigrams. Then he chuckled with amusement. Now and then after a period of silence, a word was said or a hint given that strangely illuminated the life of the speaker, a wish became a desire, or a dream, half dead, flared suddenly into life. For the most part the words came from the woman and she said them without looking at the man.

Each time she came to see the doctor the hotel keeper's wife talked a little more freely and after an hour or two in his presence went down the stairway into Main Street feeling renewed and strengthened against the dullness of her days. With something approaching a girlhood swing to her body she walked along, but when she had got back to her chair by the window of her room and when darkness had come on and a girl from the hotel dining room brought her dinner on a tray, she let it grow cold. Her thoughts ran away to her girlhood with its passionate longing for adventure and she remembered the arms of men that had held her when adventure was a possible thing for her. Particularly she remembered one who had for a time been her lover and who in the moment of his passion had cried out to her more than a hundred times, saying the same words madly over and over: "You dear! You dear! You lovely dear!" The words she thought expressed something she would have liked to have achieved in life.

In her room in the shabby old hotel the sick wife of the hotel keeper began to weep and putting her hands to her face rocked back and forth. The words of her one friend, Doctor Reefy, rang in her ears. "Love is like a wind stirring the grass beneath trees on a black night," he had said. "You must not try to make love definite. It is the divine accident of life. If you try to be definite and sure about it and to live beneath the trees, where soft night winds blow, the long hot day of disappointment comes swiftly and the gritty dust from passing wagons gathers upon lips inflamed and made tender by kisses."

Elizabeth Willard could not remember her mother who had died when she was but five years old. Her girlhood had been lived in the most haphazard manner imaginable. Her father was a man who had wanted to be let alone and the affairs of the hotel would not let him alone. He also had lived and died a sick man. Every day he arose with a cheerful face, but by ten o'clock in the morning all the joy had gone out of his heart. When a guest complained of the fare in the hotel dining room or one of the girls who made up the beds got married and went away, he stamped on the floor and swore. At night when he went to bed he thought of his daughter growing up among the stream of people that drifted in and out of the hotel and was overcome with sadness. As the girl grew older and began to walk out in the evening with men he wanted to talk to her, but when he tried was not successful. He always forgot what he wanted to say and spent the time complaining of his own affairs.

In her girlhood and young womanhood Elizabeth had tried to be a real adventurer in life. At eighteen life had so gripped her that she was no longer a virgin but, although she had a half dozen lovers before she married Tom Willard, she had never entered upon an adventure prompted by desire alone. Like all the women in the world, she wanted a real lover. Always there was something she sought blindly, passionately, some hidden wonder in life. The tall beautiful girl with the swinging stride who had walked under the trees with men was forever putting out her hand into the darkness and trying to get hold of some other hand. In all the babble of words that fell from the lips of the men with whom she adventured she was trying to find what would be for her the true word.

Elizabeth had married Tom Willard, a clerk in her father's hotel, because he was at hand and wanted to marry at the time when the determination to marry came to her. For a while, like most young girls, she thought marriage would change the face of life. If there was in her mind a doubt of the outcome of the marriage with Tom she brushed it aside. Her father was ill and near death at the time and she was perplexed because of the meaningless outcome of an affair in which she had just been involved. Other girls of her age in Winesburg were marrying men she had always known, grocery clerks or young farmers. In the evening they walked in Main Street with their husbands and when she passed they smiled happily. She began to think that the fact of marriage might be full of some hidden significance. Young wives with whom she talked spoke softly and shyly. "It changes things to have a man of your own," they said.

On the evening before her marriage the perplexed girl had a talk with her father. Later she wondered if the hours alone with the sick man had not led to her decision to marry. The father talked of his life and advised the daughter to avoid being led into another such muddle. He abused Tom Willard, and that led Elizabeth to come to the clerk's defense. The sick man became excited and tried to get out of bed. When she would not let him walk about he began to complain. "I've never been let alone," he said. "Although I've worked hard I've not made the hotel pay. Even now I owe money at the bank. You'll find that out when I'm gone."

The voice of the sick man became tense with earnestness. Being unable to arise, he put out his hand and pulled the girl's head down beside his own. "There's a way out," he whispered. "Don't marry Tom Willard or any one else here in Winesburg. There is eight hundred dollars in a tin box in my trunk. Take it and go away."

Again the sick man's voice became querulous. "You've got to promise," he declared. "If you won't promise not to marry, give me your word that you'll never tell Tom about the money. It is mine and if I give it to you I've the right to make that demand. Hide it away. It is to make up to you for my failure as a father. Some time it may prove to be a door, a great open door to you. Come now, I tell you I'm about to die, give me your promise."

. . . .

In Doctor Reefy's office, Elizabeth, a tired gaunt old woman at forty-one, sat in a chair near the stove and looked at the floor. By a small desk near the window sat the doctor. His hands played with a lead pencil that lay on the desk. Elizabeth talked of her life as a married woman. She became impersonal and forgot her husband, only using him as a lay figure to give point to her tale. "And then I was married and it did not turn out at all," she said bitterly. "As soon as I had gone into it I began to be afraid. Perhaps I knew too much before and then perhaps I found out too much during my first night with him. I don't remember.

"What a fool I was. When father gave me the money and tried to talk me out of the thought of marriage, I would not listen. I thought of what the girls who were married had said of it and I wanted marriage also. It wasn't Tom I wanted, it was marriage. When father went to sleep I leaned out of the window and thought of the life I had led. I didn't want to be a bad woman. The town was full of stories about me. I even began to be afraid Tom would change his mind."

The woman's voice began to quiver with excitement. To Doctor Reefy, who without realizing what was happening had begun to love her, there came an odd illusion. He thought that as she talked the woman's body was changing, that she was becoming younger, straighter, stronger. When he could not shake off the illusion his mind gave it a professional twist. "It is good for both her body and her mind, this talking," he muttered.

The woman began telling of an incident that had happened one afternoon a few months after her marriage. Her voice became steadier. "In the late afternoon I went for a drive alone," she said. "I had a buggy and a little grey pony I kept in Moyer's Livery. Tom was painting and repapering rooms in the hotel. He wanted money and I was trying to make up my mind to tell him about the eight hundred dollars father had given to me. I couldn't decide to do it. I didn't like him well enough. There was always paint on his hands and face during those days and he smelled of paint. He was trying to fix up the old hotel, make it new and smart."

The excited woman sat up very straight in her chair and made a quick girlish movement with her hand as she told of the drive alone on the spring afternoon. "It was cloudy and a storm threatened," she said.

"Black clouds made the green of the trees and the grass stand out so that the colors hurt my eyes. I went out Trunion Pike a mile or more and then turned into a side road. The little horse went quickly along up hill and down. I was impatient. Thoughts came and I wanted to get away from my thoughts. I began to beat the horse. The black clouds settled down and it began to rain. I wanted to go at a terrible speed, to drive on and on forever. I wanted to get out of town, out of my clothes, out of my marriage, out of my body, out of everything. I almost killed the horse, making him run, and when he could not run any more I got out of the buggy and ran afoot into the darkness until I fell and hurt my side. I wanted to run away from everything but I wanted to run towards something too. Don't you see, dear, how it was?"

Elizabeth sprang out of the chair and began to walk about in the office. She walked as Doctor Reefy thought he had never seen any one walk before. To her whole body there was a swing, a rhythm that intoxicated him. When she came and knelt on the floor beside his chair he took her into his arms and began to kiss her passionately. "I cried all the way home," she said, as she tried to continue the story of her wild ride, but he did not listen. "You dear! You lovely dear! Oh you lovely dear!" he muttered and thought he held in his arms, not the tired out woman of forty-one but a lovely and innocent girl who had been able by some miracle to project herself out of the husk of the body of the tired-out woman.

Doctor Reefy did not see the woman he had held in his arms again until after her death. On the summer afternoon in the office when he was on the point of becoming her lover a half grotesque little incident brought his love-making quickly to an end. As the man and woman held each other tightly heavy feet came tramping up the office stairs. The two sprang to their feet and stood listening and trembling. The noise on the stairs was made by a clerk from the Paris Dry Goods Store Co. With a loud bang he threw an empty box on the pile of rubbish in the hallway and then went heavily down the stairs. Elizabeth followed him almost immediately. The thing that had come to life in her as she talked to her one friend died suddenly. She was hysterical, as was also Doctor Reefy, and did not want to continue the talk. Along the street she went with the blood still singing in her body, but when she turned out of Main Street and saw ahead the lights of the New Willard House, she began to tremble and her knees shook so that for a moment she thought she would fall in the street.

The sick woman spent the last few months of her life hungering for death. Along the road of death she went, seeking, hungering. She personified the figure of death and made him, now a strong black-haired youth running over hills, now a stern quiet man marked and scarred by the business of living. In the darkness of her room she put out her hand, thrusting it from under the covers of her bed, and she thought that death like a living thing put out his hand to her. "Be patient, lover," she whispered. "Keep yourself young and beautiful and be patient."

On the evening when disease laid its heavy hand upon her and defeated her plans for telling her son George of the eight hundred dollars hidden away, she got out of bed and crept half across the room pleading with death for another hour of life. "Wait, dear! The boy! The boy! The boy!" she pleaded as she tried with all of her strength to fight off the arms of the lover she had wanted so earnestly.

• • • • • • •

Elizabeth died one day in March in the year when her son George became eighteen, and the young man had but little sense of the meaning of her death. Only time could give him that. For a month he had seen her lying white and still and speechless in her bed, and then one afternoon the doctor stopped him in the hallway and said a few words.

The young man went into his own room and closed the door. He had a queer empty feeling in the region of his stomach. For a moment he sat staring at the floor and then jumping up went for a walk. Along the station platform he went, and around through residence streets past the high school building, thinking almost entirely of his own affairs. The notion of death could not get hold of him and he was in fact a little annoyed that his mother had died on that day. He had just received a note from Helen White, the daughter of the town banker, in answer to one from him. "Tonight I could have gone to see her and now it will have to be put off," he thought half angrily.

Elizabeth died on a Friday afternoon at three o'clock. It had been cold and rainy in the morning but in the afternoon the sun came out. Before she died she lay paralyzed for six days unable to speak or move and with only her mind and her eyes alive. For three of the six days she struggled, thinking of her boy, trying to say some few words in regard to his future, and in her eyes there was an appeal so touching that all who saw it kept the memory of the dying woman in their minds for years. Even Tom Willard who had always half resented his wife forgot his resentment and the tears ran out of his eyes and lodged in his mustache. The mustache had begun to turn grey and Tom colored it with dye. There was oil in the preparation he used for the purpose and the tears, catching in the mustache and being brushed away by his hand, formed a fine mist-like vapor. In his grief Tom Willard's face looked like the face of a little dog that has been out a long time in bitter weather.

George came home along Main Street at dark on the day of his mother's death and, after going to his own room to brush his hair and clothes, went along the hallway and into the room where the body lay. There was a candle on the dressing table by the door and Doctor Reefy sat in a chair by the bed. The doctor arose and started to go out. He put out his hand as though to greet the younger man and then awkwardly drew it back again. The air of the room was heavy with the presence of the two self-conscious human beings, and the man hurried away.

The dead woman's son sat down in a chair and looked at the floor. He again thought of his own affairs and definitely decided he would make a change in his life, that he would leave Winesburg. "I will go to some city. Perhaps I can get a job on some newspaper," he thought and then his mind turned to the girl with whom he was to have spent this evening and again he was half angry at the turn of events that had prevented his going to her.

In the dimly lighted room with the dead woman the young man began to have thoughts. His mind played with thoughts of life as his mother's mind had played with the thought of death. He closed his eyes and imagined that the red young lips of Helen White touched his own lips. His body trembled and his hands shook. And then something happened. The boy sprang to his feet and stood stiffly. He looked at the figure of the dead woman under the sheets and shame for his thoughts swept over him so that he began to weep. A new notion came into his mind and he turned and looked guiltily about as though afraid he would be observed.

George Willard became possessed of a madness to lift the sheet from the body of his mother and look at her face. The thought that had come into his mind gripped him terribly. He became convinced that not his mother but some one else lay in the bed before him. The conviction was so real that it was almost unbearable. The body under the sheets was long and in death looked young and graceful. To the boy, held by some strange fancy, it was unspeakably lovely. The feeling that the body before him was alive, that in another moment a lovely woman would spring out of the bed and confront him became so over-powering that he could not bear the suspense. Again and again he put out his hand. Once he touched and half lifted the white sheet that covered her, but his courage failed and he, like Doctor Reefy, turned and went out of the room. In the hallway outside the door he stopped and trembled so that he had to put a hand against the wall to support himself. "That's not my mother. That's not my mother in there," he whispered to himself and again his body shook with fright and uncertainty. When Aunt Elizabeth Swift, who had come to watch over the body, came out of an adjoining room he put his hand into hers and began to sob, shaking his head from side to side, half blind with grief. "My mother is dead," he said, and then forgetting the woman he turned and stared at the door through which he had just come. "The dear, the dear, oh the lovely dear," the boy, urged by some impulse outside himself, muttered aloud.

• • • • • • • •

As for the eight hundred dollars, the dead woman had kept hidden so long and that was to give George Willard his start in the city, it lay in the tin box behind the plaster by the foot of his mother's bed. Elizabeth had put it there a week after her marriage, breaking the plaster away with a stick. Then she got one of the workmen her husband was at that time employing about the hotel to mend the wall. "I jammed the corner of the bed against it," she had explained to her husband, unable at the moment to give up her dream of release, the release that after all came to her but twice in her life, in the moments when her lovers Death and Doctor Reefy held her in their arms.

Sophistication

It was early evening of a day in the late fall and the Winesburg County Fair had brought crowds of country people into town. The day had been clear and the night came on warm and pleasant. On the Trunion Pike, where the road after it left town stretched away between berry fields now covered with dry brown leaves, the dust from passing wagons arose in clouds. Children, curled into little balls, slept on the straw scattered on wagon beds. Their hair was full of dust and their fingers black and sticky. The dust rolled away over the fields and the departing sun set it ablaze with colors.

In the main street of Winesburg crowds filled the stores and the sidewalks. Night came on, horses whinnied, the clerks in the stores ran madly about, children became lost and cried lustily, an American town worked terribly at the task of amusing itself.

Pushing his way through the crowds in Main Street, young George Willard concealed himself in the stairway leading to Doctor Reefy's office and looked at the people. With feverish eyes he watched the faces drifting past under the store lights. Thoughts kept coming into his head and he did not want to think. He stamped impatiently on the wooden steps and looked sharply about. "Well, is she going to stay with him all day? Have I done all this waiting for nothing?" he muttered.

George Willard, the Ohio village boy, was fast growing into manhood and new thoughts had been coming into his mind. All that day, amid the jam of people at the Fair, he had gone about feeling lonely. He was about to leave Winesburg to go away to some city where he hoped to get work on a city newspaper and he felt grown up. The mood that had taken possession of him was a thing known to men and unknown to boys. He felt old and a little tired. Memories awoke in him. To his mind his new sense of maturity set him apart, made of him a half-tragic figure. He wanted someone to understand the feeling that had taken possession of him after his mother's death.

There is a time in the life of every boy when he for the first time takes the backward view of life. Perhaps that is the moment when he crosses the line into manhood. The boy is walking through the street of his town. He is thinking of the future and of the figure he will cut in the world. Ambitions and regrets awake within him. Suddenly something happens; he stops under a tree and waits as for a voice calling his name. Ghosts of old things creep into his consciousness; the voices outside of himself whisper a message concerning the limitations of life. From being quite sure of himself and his future he becomes not at all sure. If he be an imaginative boy a door is torn open and for the first time he looks out upon the world, seeing, as though they marched in procession before him, the countless figures of men who before his time have come out of nothingness into the world, lived their lives and again disappeared into nothingness. The sadness of sophistication has come to the boy. With a little gasp he sees himself as merely a leaf blown by the wind through the streets of his village. He knows that in spite of all the stout talk of his fellows he must live and die in uncertainty, a thing blown by the winds, a thing destined like corn to wilt in the sun. He shivers and looks eagerly about. The eighteen years he has lived seem but a moment, a breathing space in the long march of humanity. Already he hears death calling. With all his heart he wants to come close to some other human, touch someone with his hands, be touched by the hand of another. If he prefers that the other be a woman, that is because he believes that a woman will be gentle, that she will understand. He wants, most of all, understanding.

When the moment of sophistication came to George Willard his mind turned to Helen White, the Winesburg banker's daughter. Always he had been conscious of the girl growing into womanhood as he grew into manhood. Once on a summer night when he was eighteen, he had walked with her on a country road and in her presence had given way to an impulse to boast, to make himself appear big and significant in her eyes. Now he wanted to see her for another purpose. He wanted to tell her of the new impulses that had come to him. He had tried to make her think of him as a man when he knew nothing of manhood and now he wanted to be with her and to try to make her feel the change he believed had taken place in his nature.

As for Helen White, she also had come to a period of change. What George felt, she in her young woman's way felt also. She was no longer a girl and hungered to reach into the grace and beauty of womanhood. She had come home from Cleveland, where she was attending college, to spend a day at the Fair. She also had begun to have memories. During the day she sat in the grandstand with a young man, one of the instructors from the college, who was a guest of her mother's. The young man was of a pedantic turn of mind and she felt at once he would not do for her purpose. At the Fair she was glad to be seen in his company as he was well dressed and a stranger. She knew that the fact of his presence would create an impression. During the day she was happy, but when night came on she began to grow restless. She wanted to drive the instructor away, to get out of his presence. While they sat together in the grand-stand and while the eyes of former schoolmates were upon them, she paid so much attention to her escort that he grew interested. "A scholar needs money. I should marry a woman with money," he mused.

Helen White was thinking of George Willard even as he wandered gloomily through the crowds thinking of her. She remembered the summer evening when they had walked together and wanted to walk with him again. She thought that the months she had spent in the city, the going to theatres and the seeing of great crowds wandering in lighted thoroughfares, had changed her profoundly. She wanted him to feel and be conscious of the change in her nature.

The summer evening together that had left its mark on the memory of both the young man and woman had, when looked at quite sensibly, been rather stupidly spent. They had walked out of town along a country road. Then they had stopped by a fence near a field of young corn and George had taken off his coat and let it hang on his arm. "Well, I've stayed here in Winesburg—yes—I've not yet gone away but I'm growing up," he had said. "I've been reading books and I've been thinking. I'm going to try to amount to something in life.

"Well," he explained, "that isn't the point. Perhaps I'd better quit talking."

The confused boy put his hand on the girl's arm. His voice trembled. The two started to walk back along the road toward town. In his desperation George boasted, "I'm going to be a big man, the biggest that ever lived here in Winesburg," he declared. "I want you to do something, I don't know what. Perhaps it is none of my business. I want you to try to be different from other women. You see the point. It's none of my business I tell you. I want you to be a beautiful woman. You see what I want."

The boy's voice failed and in silence the two came back into town and went along the street to Helen White's house. At the gate he tried to say something impressive. Speeches he had thought out came into his head, but they seemed utterly pointless. "I thought—I used to think—I had it in my mind you would marry Seth Richmond. Now I know you won't," was all he could find to say as she went through the gate and toward the door of her house.

On the warm fall evening as he stood in the stairway and looked at the crowd drifting through Main Street, George thought of the talk beside the field of young corn and was ashamed of the figure he had made of himself. In the street the people surged up and down like cattle confined in a pen. Buggies and wagons almost filled the narrow thoroughfare. A band played and small boys raced along the sidewalk, diving between the legs of men. Young men with shining red faces walked awkwardly about with girls on their arms. In a room above one of the stores, where a dance was to be held, the fiddlers tuned their instruments. The broken sounds floated down through an open window and out across the murmur of voices and the loud blare of the horns of the band. The medley of sounds got on young Willard's nerves. Everywhere, on all sides, the sense of crowding, moving life closed in about him. He wanted to run away by himself and think. "If she wants to stay with that fellow she may. Why should I care? What difference does it make to me?" he growled and went along Main Street and through Hern's grocery into a side street.

George felt so utterly lonely and dejected that he wanted to weep but pride made him walk rapidly along, swinging his arms. He came to Wesley Moyer's livery barn and stopped in the shadows to listen to a group of men who talked of a race Wesley's stallion, Tony Tip, had won at the Fair during the afternoon. A crowd had gathered in front of the barn and before the crowd walked Wesley, prancing up and down and boasting. He held a whip in his hand and kept tapping the ground. Little puffs of dust arose in the lamplight. "Hell, quit your talking," Wesley exclaimed. "I wasn't afraid, I knew I had 'em beat all the time. I wasn't afraid."

Ordinarily George Willard would have been intensely interested in the boasting of Moyer, the horseman. Now it made him angry. He turned and hurried away along the street. "Old wind-bag," he sputtered. "Why does he want to be bragging? Why don't he shut up?"

George went into a vacant lot and as he hurried along, fell over a pile of rubbish. A nail protruding from an empty barrel tore his trousers. He sat down on the ground and swore. With a pin he mended the torn place and then arose and went on. "I'll go to Helen White's house, that's what I'll do. I'll walk right in. I'll say that I want to see her. I'll walk right in and sit down, that's what I'll do," he declared, climbing over a fence and beginning to run.

• • • • • • •

On the veranda of Banker White's house Helen was restless and distraught. The instructor sat between the mother and daughter. His talk wearied the girl. Although he had also been raised in an Ohio town, the instructor began to put on the airs of the city. He wanted to appear cosmopolitan. "I like the chance you have given me to study the background out of which most of our girls come," he declared. "It was good of you, Mrs. White, to have me down for the day." He turned to Helen and laughed. "Your life is still bound up with the life of this town?" he asked. "There are people here in whom you are interested?" To the girl his voice sounded pompous and heavy.

Helen arose and went into the house. At the door leading to a garden at the back she stopped and stood listening. Her mother began to talk. "There is no one here fit to associate with a girl of Helen's breeding," she said.

Helen ran down a flight of stairs at the back of the house and into the garden. In the darkness she stopped and stood trembling. It seemed to her that the world was full of meaningless people saying words. Afire with eagerness she ran through a garden gate and turning a corner by the banker's barn, went into a little side street. "George! Where are you, George?" she cried, filled with nervous excitement. She stopped running, and leaned against a tree to laugh hysterically. Along the dark little street came George Willard, still saying words. "I'm going to walk right into her house. I'll go right in and sit down," he declared as he came up to her. He stopped and stared stupidly. "Come on," he said and took hold of her hand. With hanging heads they walked away along the street under the trees. Dry leaves rustled under foot. Now that he had found her George wondered what he had better do and say.

• • • • • • • •

At the upper end of the fair ground, in Winesburg, there is a half decayed old grand-stand. It has never been painted and the boards are all warped out of shape. The fair ground stands on top of a low hill rising out of the valley of Wine Creek and from the grand-stand one can see at night, over a cornfield, the lights of the town reflected against the sky.

George and Helen climbed the hill to the fair ground, coming by the path past Waterworks Pond. The feeling of loneliness and isolation that had come to the young man in the crowded streets of his town was both broken and intensified by the presence of Helen. What he felt was reflected in her.

In youth there are always two forces fighting in people. The warm unthinking little animal struggles against the thing that reflects and remembers, and the older, the more sophisticated thing had possession of George Willard. Sensing his mood, Helen walked beside him filled with respect. When they got to the grand-stand they climbed up under the roof and sat down on one of the long bench-like seats.

There is something memorable in the experience to be had by going into a fair ground that stands at the edge of a Middle Western town on a night after the annual fair has been held. The sensation is one never to be forgotten. On all sides are ghosts, not of the dead, but of living people. Here, during the day just passed, have come the people pouring in from the town and the country around. Farmers with their wives and children and all the people from the hundreds of little frame houses have gathered within these board walls. Young girls have laughed and men with beards have talked of the affairs of their lives. The place has been filled to overflowing with life. It has itched and squirmed with life and now it is night and the life has all gone away. The silence is almost terrifying. One conceals oneself standing silently beside the trunk of a tree and what there is of a reflective tendency in his nature is intensified. One shudders at the thought of the meaninglessness of life while at the same instant, and if the people of the town are his people, one loves life so intensely that tears come into the eyes.

In the darkness under the roof of the grand-stand, George Willard sat beside Helen White and felt very keenly his own insignificance in the scheme of existence. Now that he had come out of town where the presence of the people stirring about, busy with a multitude of affairs, had been so irritating the irritation was all gone. The presence of Helen renewed and refreshed him. It was as though her woman's hand was assisting him to make some minute readjustment of the machinery of his life. He began to think of the people in the town where he had always lived with something like reverence. He had reverence for Helen. He wanted to love and to be loved by her, but he did not want at the moment to be confused by her womanhood. In the darkness he took hold of her hand and when she crept close put a hand on her shoulder. A wind began to blow and he shivered. With all his strength he tried to hold and to understand the mood that had come upon him. In that high place in the darkness the two oddly sensitive human atoms held each other tightly and waited. In the mind of each was the same thought. "I have come to this lonely place and here is this other," was the substance of the thing felt.

In Winesburg the crowded day had run itself out into the long night of the late fall. Farm horses jogged away along lonely country roads pulling their portion of weary people. Clerks began to bring samples of goods in off the sidewalks and lock the doors of stores. In the Opera House a crowd had gathered to see a show and further down Main Street the fiddlers, their instruments tuned, sweated and worked to keep the feet of youth flying over a dance floor.

In the darkness in the grand-stand Helen White and George Willard remained silent. Now and then the spell that held them was broken and they turned and tried in the dim light to see into each other's eyes. They kissed but that impulse did not last. At the upper end of the fair ground a half dozen men worked over horses that had raced during the afternoon. The men had built a fire and were heating kettles of water. Only their legs could be seen as they passed back and forth in the light. When the wind blew the little flames of the fire danced crazily about.

George and Helen arose and walked away into the darkness. They went along a path past a field of corn that had not yet been cut. The wind whispered among the dry corn blades. For a moment during the walk back into town the spell that held them was broken. When they had come to the crest of Waterworks Hill they stopped by a tree and George again put his hands on the girl's shoulders. She embraced him eagerly and then again they drew quickly back from that impulse. They stopped kissing and stood a little apart. Mutual respect grew big in them. They were both embarrassed and to relieve their embarrassment dropped into the animalism of youth. They laughed and began to pull and haul at each other. In some way chastened and purified by the mood they had been in they became, not man and woman, not boy and girl, but excited little animals.

It was so they went down the hill. In the darkness they played like two splendid young things in a young world. Once, running swiftly forward, Helen tripped George and he fell. He squirmed and shouted. Shaking with laughter, he rolled down the hill. Helen ran after him. For just a moment she stopped in the darkness. There is no way of knowing what woman's thoughts went through her mind but, when the bottom of the hill was reached and she came up to the boy, she took his arm and walked beside him in dignified silence. For some reason they could not have explained they had both got from their silent evening together the thing needed. Man or boy, woman or girl, they had for a moment taken hold of the thing that makes the mature life of men and women in the modern world possible.

Departure

Young George Willard got out of bed at four in the morning. It was April and the young tree leaves were just coming out of their buds. The trees along the residence streets in Winesburg are maple and the seeds are winged. When the wind blows they whirl crazily about, filling the air and making a carpet underfoot.

George came down stairs into the hotel office carrying a brown leather bag. His trunk was packed for departure. Since two o'clock he had been awake thinking of the journey he was about to take and wondering what he would find at the end of his journey. The boy who slept in the hotel office lay on a cot by the door. His mouth was open and he snored lustily. George crept past the cot and went out into the silent deserted main street. The east was pink with the dawn and long streaks of light climbed into the sky where a few stars still shone.

Beyond the last house on Trunion Pike in Winesburg there is a great stretch of open fields. The fields are owned by farmers who live in town and drive homeward at evening along Trunion Pike in light creaking wagons. In the fields are planted berries and small fruits. In the late afternoon in the hot summers when the road and the fields are covered with dust, a smoky haze lies over the great flat basin of land. To look across it is like looking out across the sea. In the spring when the land is green the effect is somewhat different. The land becomes a wide green billiard table on which tiny human insects toil up and down.

All through his boyhood and young manhood George Willard had been in the habit of walking on Trunion Pike. He had been in the midst of the great open place on winter nights when it was covered with snow and only the moon looked down at him; he had been there in the fall when bleak winds blew and on summer evenings when the air vibrated with the song of insects. On the April morning he wanted to go there again, to walk again in the silence. He did walk to where the road dipped down by a little stream two miles from town and then turned and walked silently back again. When he got to Main Street clerks were sweeping the sidewalks before the stores. "Hey, you George. How does it feel to be going away?" they asked.

The west bound train leaves Winesburg at seven forty-five in the morning. Tom Little is conductor. His train runs from Cleveland to where it connects with a great trunk line railroad with terminals in Chicago and New York. Tom has what in railroad circles is called an "easy run." Every evening he returned to his family. In the fall and spring he spends his Sundays fishing in Lake Erie. He has a round red face and small blue eyes. He knows the people in the towns along his railroad better than a city man knows the people who live in his apartment building.

George came down the little incline from the New Willard House at seven o'clock. Tom Willard carried his bag. The son had become taller than the father.

On the station platform everyone shook the young man's hand. More than a dozen people waited about. Then they talked of their own affairs. Even Will Henderson, who was lazy and often slept until nine, had got out of bed. George was embarrassed. Gertrude Wilmot, a tall thin woman of fifty who worked in the Winesburg post office, came along the station platform. She had never before paid any attention to George. Now she stopped and put out her hand. In two words she voiced what everyone felt. "Good luck," she said sharply and then turning went on her way.

When the train came into the station George felt relieved. He scampered hurriedly aboard. Helen White came running along Main Street hoping to have a parting word with him, but he had found a seat and did not see her. When the train started Tom Little punched his ticket, grinned and, although he knew George well and knew on what adventure he was just setting out, made no comment. Tom had seen a thousand George Willards go out of their towns to the city. It was a commonplace enough incident with him. In the smoking car there was a man who had just invited Tom to go on a fishing trip to Sandusky Bay. He wanted to accept the invitation and talk over details.

George glanced up and down the car to be sure no one was looking then took out his pocketbook and counted his money. His mind was occupied with a desire not to appear green. Almost the last words his father had said to him concerned the matter of his behavior when he got to the city. "Be a sharp one," Tom Willard had said. "Keep your eyes on your money. Be awake. That's the ticket. Don't let any one think you're a greenhorn."

After George counted his money he looked out of the window and was surprised to see that the train was still in Winesburg.

The young man, going out of his town to meet the adventure of life, began to think but he did not think of anything very big or dramatic. Things like his mother's death, his departure from Winesburg, the uncertainty of his future life in the city, the serious and larger aspects of his life did not come into his mind.

He thought of little things—Turk Smollet wheeling boards through the main street of his town in the morning, a tall woman, beautifully gowned, who had once stayed over night at his father's hotel, Butch Wheeler the lamp lighter of Winesburg hurrying through the streets on a summer evening and holding a torch in his hand, Helen White standing by a window in the Winesburg post office and putting a stamp on an envelope.

The young man's mind was carried away by his growing passion for dreams. One looking at him would not have thought him particularly sharp. With the recollection of little things occupying his mind he closed his eyes and leaned back in the car seat. He stayed that way for a long time and when he aroused himself and again looked out of the car window the town of Winesburg had disappeared and his life there had become but a background on which to paint the dreams of his manhood.

BACKGROUNDS AND CONTEXTS

Letters

To Waldo Frank†

Chicago, November 14, 1916

Mr. Waldo Frank, *Seven Arts* Magazine, New York

My dear Mr. Frank: I sent you a little thing the other day that I believe you will like. Here is a suggestion.

I made last year a series of intensive studies of people of my home town, Clyde, Ohio. In the book I called the town Winesburg, Ohio. Some of the studies you may think pretty raw, and there is a sad note running through them. One or two of them get pretty closely down to ugly things of life. However, I put a good deal into the writing of them, and I believe they, as a whole, come a long step toward achieving what you are asking for in the article you ran in *Seven Arts*.

Some of these things have been used. *Masses* ran a story called "Hands" from this series. Two or three also appeared in a little magazine out here called the *Little Review*. The story called "Queer" you are using in December is one of them.[1]

This thought occurs to me. There are or will be seventeen of these studies. Fifteen are, I believe, completed. If you have the time and the inclination, I might send the lot to you to be looked over.

It is my own idea that when these studies are published in book form, they will suggest the real environment out of which present-day American youth is coming. Very truly yours

† From *Letters of Sherwood Anderson*, eds. Howard Mumford Jones and Walter B. Rideout (Boston: Little, Brown, 1953) 4–5; some notes in this and subsequent letters have been revised. Frank was an editor of *Seven Arts*, which in its first issue (November 1916) carried his admiring review of Anderson's novel *Windy McPherson's Son*, "Emerging Greatness" (73–78). Over the following four years, he and Anderson became good friends and corresponded frequently.

1. "Hands" first appeared in *Masses* 8 (March 1916): 5, 7. The *Little Review* published three Winesburg stories: "The Philosopher," 3 (June–July 1916): 7–9; "The Man of Ideas," 6 (June 1918): 22–28; "An Awakening," 5 (December 1918): 13–21. " 'Queer' " appeared in *Seven Arts* 1 (December 1916): 97–108.

To Waldo Frank†

Chicago, December 14, 1916

Mr. Waldo Frank, *Seven Arts* Magazine, New York

Dear Mr. Frank: I am glad you liked the story "Mother" and that you are going to publish it. Damn it, I wanted you to like the story about Enoch Robinson and the woman who came into his room and was too big for the room.[1]

There is a story every critic is bound to dislike. I can remember reading it to Floyd Dell,[2] and it made him hopping mad. "It's damn rot," says Floyd. "It does not get anywhere."

"It gets there, but you are not at the station," I replied to Floyd, and I think I was right.

Why do I try to convince you of this story? Well, I want it in print in *Seven Arts*. A writer knows when a story is good, and that story is good.

Sometime when I am in New York, I'll bring that story in, and I'll make you see it.

In the meantime, thanks for the check for "Mother." I have another fine story about the same woman's death.[3] Very truly yours

To Arthur H. Smith‡

Marion
June 6, 1932

Dear Arthur H. Smith:

I received your letter with the copy of the little book—HISTORY OF WINESBURG, OHIO. It is very interesting to me. As I have stated before on several occasions, and as publicly as possible, I did not know that there was a real Winesburg, Ohio until at least a year after my book was published.

It was no doubt stupid of me. To make quite sure, I went at the time to consult a list of towns of the state, but I must have got hold of a

† From *Letters*, eds. Jones and Rideout, 5.
1. "Mother" appeared in *Seven Arts* 1 (March 1917): 452–61; Enoch Robinson's story, "Loneliness," was not published prior to its inclusion in *Winesburg*.
2. Novelist, literary editor of the *Chicago Evening Post* (1911–13), and associate editor of the *Masses* (1914–17).
3. "Death" was first published in *Winesburg*.
‡ From *Sherwood Anderson: Centennial Studies*, eds. Hilbert H. Campbell and Charles E. Modlin (Troy, N.Y.: Whitston Publishing Company, 1976) 47–48. Smith was a Methodist minister and author of *An Authentic History of Winesburg, Holmes County, Ohio* (1932?), in which he assured citizens of Winesburg that Anderson was not writing about them. See Ray Lewis White, "Sherwood Anderson and the Real Winesburg, Ohio," *Winesburg Eagle* 12 (April 1987): 1–4.

list giving only those towns that are located on railroads. Imagine their arrogance in making such a list as that.

My dear sir, I do not believe you or any of the real citizens of your real town of Winesburg need feel arrogant toward the citizens of my imaginary WINESBURG and surely I, of all men, do not apologize for them. It is true that none of them were very successful in life. They did not become bankers, or stockbrokers, establish any of our great modern industries or rise to the management of great businesses, but were simple, good people who remained in obscurity in their own little village. Life hurt and twisted them. Lusts came to them. On the whole they remained sweet and good. Do not feel offended if I say that I hope that the real people of the real Winesburg are at bottom as decent and have in them as much inner worth.

As a preacher, you, at least, should know what I mean.

In your book you spoke of my book, concerning the people of my WINESBURG as a "burlesque." I forgive you for that word. I put it down to the fact that you are not familiar with the terms of literature. The book is, of course, in no sense a burlesque, but it is an effort to treat the lives of simple ordinary people in an American middle western town with sympathy and understanding. A great many critics have even said there is a tenderness in it. The book has had an interesting career. When first published, it was almost universally condemned—the average American looked upon it, as I dare say most of the citizens of the real Winesburg would look upon it at the first reading. It was called immoral and ugly. Even the word "filthy" was frequently used.

After a few years however this kind of condemnation of the book passed. I even dare say that people began to love the book. It has been translated since then into almost all the European languages. In Russia, the government had it printed and distributed and here in America, in its various editions, hundreds of thousands of people have bought and read it—I believe with sympathy and understanding.

Referring again to the people of the book—the people of my own WINESBURG—they are people I personally would be glad to spend my life with. Certainly, I did not write to make fun of these people or to make them ridiculous or ugly, but instead to show by their example what happens to simple, ordinary people—particularly the unsuccessful ones—what life does to us here in America in our times—and on the whole how decent and real we nevertheless are.

My dear Reverend Arthur H. Smith, I have enjoyed reading your own book about the real Winesburg but if you ever reprint it in another edition I beg of you to strike out the word "burlesque" in describing my own book about the imaginary people in my own imaginary WINESBURG, OHIO. The word is so very inaccurate.

If there is in the real Winesburg a local weekly paper, it would please me to have you send on to it this letter to be printed in Winesburg.

Also let me convey my greetings to the real Winesburgers. I trust they are all good kind god-fearing people. No doubt, they are.

Sincerely,
Sherwood Anderson

To Arthur Barton†

26 November 1932 [Marion]

Dear Arthur Barton:

I got your letter and the first synopsis of the play *Winesburg* yesterday and have been excited about it ever since. I took a drive in the afternoon and at night went to bed, not to sleep, but to live through possible scenes in the play.

I might as well tell you frankly that I opened the synopsis to read it with fear. Before now attempts have been made to get at plays in some of my stories and novels but always I have found something in the attempts so utterly aside from the spirits of the stories that I felt they were hopeless. On the contrary, my dear Barton, I read your first synopsis, as I have suggested, with a good deal of inner excitement. "It can be done," I found myself saying to myself. Now do not be surprised if I write you two or three letters within the next few days giving you my ideas. I think what I will do is to take your synopsis up, scene by scene, and give you my suggestions and it will take a few days to do this, partly because I want them to develop in my own mind. I have to grow used to the idea of thinking of *Winesburg* as a play.

What I expect you want of me now is a general impression, got from what you have already put down and this is what I will try to give you today.

As to all such matters as the number of scenes in the play, etc., the practical matter of producing it in a theatre—all that I will leave to you.

Now as to the synopsis—pardon me for beginning at the end. You will realize that to make the end effective—the boy leaving the town where he has been raised to go out into the world—we will have to build up this feeling of George's departure to give it significance.

To do that we will have to build all through the play to that one end and this will naturally affect all the characters throughout the play. The feeling will have to be given that George's departure from the town is

† From *Sherwood Anderson: Selected Letters*, ed. Charles E. Modlin (Knoxville: U of Tennessee P, 1984) 152–56. Barton, a New York playwright, had proposed to Anderson that they collaborate on a dramatic adaptation of *Winesburg*. Anderson later became dissatisfied with Barton's contributions and dismissed him. After much rewriting, the play was first performed in 1934 at the Hedgerow Theatre, near Media, Pennsylvania, and published in Anderson's *Plays: Winesburg and Others* (1937).

also a beginning—the beginning of manhood—a thing keenly felt in that way in him at least by the girl Helen.

To do that I believe it will be necessary for you and myself to go over the actual theme of the book which should be the theme of the play.

Now to me it seems that the theme of the *Winesburg* book, the thing that really makes it a book—curiously holding together from story to story as it does—is just that there is a central theme. The theme is the making of a man out of the actual stuff of life.

An American boy as you see growing up in an American village. It is an ordinary American town. There are all sorts of influences playing over him and around him. These influences are presented in the form of characters. playing on his own character, forming it, warning him, educating him. I do not know whether or not you, Barton, were raised in a small town but that does not matter. The same sort of influences would be at work on any boy in American life whether he were raised in a small town or a city. In the midst of the confusion of life the boy is always accepting or rejecting the suggestions thrown out to him by other people, directly and indirectly. In this play we will have to get from the beginning a feeling of growth in the boy.

To go back again for a moment let me tell you something that may amuse you. These stories of the *Winesburg* book were really written in a Chicago tenement, not in a village, and the truth is that I got the substance of every character in the book not from an Ohio village but from other people living around me in the Chicago tenement. I simply transferred them to a small town and gave them small town surroundings.

Now in all my suggestions you must remember, Barton, that I have no experience with the theatre. But this attempt to work with you to make a play and the reading of this synopsis has certainly given me, as I never had it before, a sharp sense of how much we will have to depend upon the players.

Now let me go back a moment to the theme of *Winesburg*. There are these queer, interesting, sometimes essentially fine, often essentially vulgar figures of a town. Think, Barton, what a great percentage of American men and women who come into the theatre were raised either in small towns or on farms. They got their early impressions of life there. Just as our boy George Willard did and then they went away to live in the city as he did. You have heard the saying attributed to the Catholics—"Give me the child until he is ten and you may have him afterwards. I will not lose him." It seems to me that what is notable about *Winesburg* is that it does treat those American villagers, twisted as they may be—"queer hopping figures" a critic once called them—it does treat their lives with respect. That also we will want to do. What the book says to people is this—"Here it is. It is like this. This is what the life in America out of which men and women come is like."

"But out of this life does come real men and women."

That it seems to me is the essence of the theme of the book and the thing we have to put across.

What your first synopsis has suggested to me is the possibilities that lie in four characters of the book. They are

the boy, George Willard
his mother
his father
the girl, Helen White.

These should be the dominant characters in the play because they will all affect most deeply the development of the boy George.

But before discussing them let me discuss also for a minute the young man Seth Richmond. This is what I think about Seth. There is nothing especially evil in him. He is simply a boy who sees life absolutely in terms of himself. He wants the girl Helen White for two reasons. She belongs to a respectable and well-to-do family—is you remember the only daughter of the town banker—and is also to Seth's mind beautiful.

But he will not be thinking of Helen's beauty as a thing worthwhile in itself—aside from himself. He wants to succeed in life, make money, be a big man, and he would like to have Helen to decorate his own successful life.

George Willard

George Willard is not like this. In the first place he is capable of even more brutality than Seth because he is essentially a dreamer. He does not figure out his own acts with the general scheme of his own life in mind. He dreams of becoming a writer but that is only because almost everything in his own life goes wrong and he has a vague feeling that in some novel or story he may write he may be able to build up an ordered fine life. George should be of the rather poetic brooding dreaming type. Always saying things he does not mean and yet in some queer way holding on to some idea of decent manhood and respect for other people and their lives.

The father is a man who began life as a hotel clerk in a shabby hotel in a little village. There was quite a remarkable and spirited girl there, the daughter of the hotel keeper. This could be one of the grand characters of the play and could give some actress a gorgeous opportunity. She is of the kind of girl and woman not so beautiful on the outside but having in her a lot of inner fire. As a young girl living in her father's little shabby hotel she meets all kinds of rather second-rate men, travelling men and others, and goes about with them. Several of them make love to her and she lets them but all the time there is something in her that is seeking a finer type of man who may give her real womanhood. This she never finds and she takes as husband the hotel clerk who becomes ostensibly George Willard's father. As to whether or not he is really the boy's father might very well be false and I have imagined a scene in the play between the husband and wife when she, angered by his attitude toward the boy, tells him, to his teeth, that she doesn't know whether he is the boy's father or not.

Now, Barton, in the book I made this woman a rather drab figure but we will have to be a little careful about her in the play. How about having her a prematurely grey woman of about thirty-five or forty, tall and slight, with tired eyes—rather pale, but still with the same spirit in her that attracted men when she was a girl, when excited or angry her form straightens and she becomes again a living thing capable still of attracting men. And then when the excitement is past swings again into this rather tired defeated woman. I believe there are actresses who could put this across.

I said a moment ago that this woman, when she was a young girl, had a dream of a certain kind of man who might be her lover that she never got. The dream transfers itself to the boy George and she is determined that he shall hang on to some sort of fine manliness she never succeeded in finding in the men who have been her lovers.

The Father

The father, or at least the man who thinks he is George Willard's father, is the typical minded, small town man of the rather mean spirited sort. When he was young he would have been rather good looking. His ambition in life was to be a rich man. He is the boy Seth Richmond beginning to grow old.

Now he is a defeated man and knows he never will be a rich or a big man and like the mother he has transferred his dream of what he would have liked to be to his son but the dream is essentially a cheap dream.

The mother knows this and is afraid of his influence on the boy, thinking that if the boy became what the father wanted, or thought he wanted, he would be a cheap tricky man, at bottom only out after some kind of showy success.

Helen White

I think we should take the girl Helen White as a figure very much like George's mother when she was a young girl.

There is this difference. Helen White belongs to one of the most prosperous families in the town. She is the only daughter. She is not exactly a beauty but is full of fire and spirit. Unlike the mother of George Willard when she was a young girl, Helen White is protected by all the forces of conservative society but like George's mother she is ready to break through conventions whenever she thinks she has found what she wants in a man.

I think of her, Barton, as a pretty shrewd girl really onto Seth Richmond and is in love with George Willard from the beginning but just the same she is not going to take George unless he can make a man of himself.

I've gone into all these details regarding the characters and the theme of the play because I think we should first of all get the various forces around this boy George Willard pulling him this way and that way so that the audience may also have a notion of the forces at work on him and become absorbed in the real theme of the play which is as I see it the simple story of what happens to a boy with these ordinary forces of life playing around him, how he handles them, and what the audience feels he becomes.

I will write you again in a day or two taking up each scene of the play as you have outlined it, suggesting what changes come into my mind and how I think the various forces I have outlined here should find their expression.

In the meantime I will send this letter off to you so that you may be thinking of the play in these terms and also so you may write me and tell me whether or not this general outline will fall in with what you think the play should be. What I think we want to do is to get away from the idea of making the small town ridiculous or too dreary or sentimental—in other words to make people feel that a cross-section taken thus from a life in a small town would not differ from a cross-section of life taken from anywhere and that the forces over this boy George Willard are the same kind of forces that play over all American boys. If we can do that we will have a real play.

Sincerely,
Sherwood Anderson

To George Freitag†

[Troutdale, Virginia] August 27, 1938

Dear George Freitag: It sometimes seems to me that I should prepare a book designed to be read by other and younger writers. This not because of accomplishment on my own part, but because of the experiences, the particular experiences, I have had.

† From *Letters*, eds. Jones and Rideout, 403–7. Freitag, of Canton, Ohio, entered into correspondence with Anderson in the summer of 1938 on problems of the young writer.

It is so difficult for most of us to realize how fully and completely commercialism enters into the arts. For example, how are you to know that really the opinion of the publisher or the magazine editor in regard to your work, what is a story and what isn't, means nothing? Some of my own stories, for example, that have now become almost American classics, that are put before students in our schools and colleges as examples of good storytelling, were, when first written, when submitted to editors, and when seen by some of the so-called outstanding American critics, declared not stories at all.

It is true they were not nice little packages, wrapped and labeled in the O. Henry manner.[1] They were obviously written by one who did not know the answers. They were simple little tales of happenings, things observed and felt. There were no cowboys or daring wild game hunters. None of the people in the tales got lost in burning deserts or went seeking the North Pole. In my stories I simply stayed at home, among my own people, wherever I happened to be, people in my own street. I think I must, very early, have realized that this was my milieu, that is to say, common everyday American lives. The ordinary beliefs of the people about me, that love lasted indefinitely, that success meant happiness, simply did not seem true to me.

Things were always happening. My eyes began to see, my ears to hear. Most of our American storytelling at that time had concerned only the rich and the well-to-do. I was a storyteller but not yet a writer of stories. As I came of a poor family, older men were always repeating to me the old saying.

"Get money. Money makes the mare go."

For a time I was a laborer. As I had a passion for fast trotting and pacing horses, I worked about race tracks. I became a soldier, I got into business.

I knew, often quite intensively, Negro swipes about race tracks, small gamblers, prize fighters, common laboring men and women. There was a violent, dangerous man, said to be a killer. One night he walked and talked to me and became suddenly tender. I was forced to realize that all sorts of emotions went on in all sorts of people. A young man who seemed outwardly a very clod suddenly began to run wildly in the moonlight. Once I was walking in a wood and heard the sound of a man weeping. I stopped, looked, and listened. There was a farmer who, because of ill luck, bad weather, and perhaps even poor management, had lost his farm. He had gone to work in a factory in town, but, having a day off, had returned secretly to the fields he loved. He was on his knees by a low fence, looking across the fields in which he had worked from boybood. He and I were employed at the time in the same factory,

1. That is, the manner of William Sydney Porter (1862–1916), known as O. Henry, prolific author of formulaic stories with "trick" endings. Anderson explains his aversion to them in *A Story Teller's Story* (New York: Huebsch, 1924) 352–63.

and in the factory be was a quiet, smiling man, seemingly satisfied with his lot.

I began to gather these impressions. There was a thing called happiness toward which men were striving. They never got to it. All of life was amazingly accidental. Love, moments of tenderness and despair, came to the poor and the miserable as to the rich and successful.

It began to seem to me that what was most wanted by all people was love, understanding. Our writers, our storytellers, in wrapping life up into neat little packages were only betraying life. It began to seem to me that what I wanted for myself most of all, rather than so-called success, acclaim, to be praised by publishers and editors, was to try to develop, to the top of my bent, my own capacity to feel, see, taste, smell, hear. I wanted, as all men must want, to be a free man, proud of my own manhood, always more and more aware of earth, people, streets, houses, towns, cities. I wanted to take all into myself, digest what I could.

I could not give the answers, and so for a long time when my stories began to appear, at first only in little highbrow magazines, I was almost universally condemned by the critics. My stories, it seemed, had no definite ends. They were not conclusive and did not give the answers, and so I was called vague. "Groping" was a favorite term. It seems I could not get a formula and stick to it. I could not be smart about life.

* * *

And so I had written, let us say, the Winesburg stories. The publisher who had already published two of my early novels refused them, but at last I found a publisher. The stories were called unclean, dirty, filthy, but they did grow into the American consciousness, and presently the same critic who had condemned them began asking why I did not write more Winesburg stories.

I am telling you all of this, I assure you, not out of bitterness. I have had a good life, a full, rich life. I am still having a full, rich life. I tell it only to point out to you, a young writer, filled as I am made aware by your letter to me, of tenderness for life, I tell it simply to suggest to you plainly what you are up against. For ten or fifteen years after I had written and published the Winesburg stories, I was compelled to make my living outside of the field of writing. You will find none of my stories even yet in the great popular magazines that pay high prices to writers.

I do not blame the publishers or the editors. Once I was in the editorial rooms of a great magazine. They had asked me in for an editorial conference.

Would it not be possible for them to begin publishing my stories?

I advised against it. "If I were you, I would let Sherwood Anderson alone."

I had been for a long time an employee of a big advertising agency, I wrote the kind of advertisements on which great magazines live.

But I had no illusions about advertising, could have none. I was an advertising writer too long. The men employed with me, the businessmen, many of them successful and even rich, were like the laborers, gamblers, soldiers, race track swipes I had formerly known. Their guards down, often over drinks, they told me the same stories of tangled, thwarted lives.

How could I throw a glamour over such lives? I couldn't.

* * *

And I am only writing all of this to you to prepare you. In a world controlled by business why should we not expect businessmen to think first of business?

And do bear in mind that publishers of books, of magazines, of newspapers are, first of all, businessmen. They are compelled to be.

And do not blame them when they do not buy your stories. Do not be romantic. There is no golden key that unlocks all doors. There is only the joy of living as richly as you can, always feeling more, absorbing more, and, if you are by nature a teller of tales, the realization that by faking, trying to give people what they think they want, you are in danger of dulling and in the end quite destroying what may be your own road into life.

There will remain for you, to be sure, the matter of making a living, and I am sorry to say to you that in the solution of that problem, for you and other young writers, I am not interested. That, alas, is your own problem. I am interested only in what you may be able to contribute to the advancement of our mutual craft.

But why not call it an art? That is what it is.

Did you ever hear of an artist who had an easy road to travel in life?

Memoirs

SHERWOOD ANDERSON

[The Writing of *Winesburg*] †

When I wrote the stories in the book called *Winesburg, Ohio* I was living in a cheap room in a Chicago rooming house.[1] I dare say that all of the tales in the book came out of some memory or impression got from my boyhood in a small town but, as I had lived in several such towns, I had no one town in mind.

The house in which I had the room was on Chicago's North Side and was occupied by a group of people new to me. They were all either actively in the arts or they aspired to a place in some one of the arts. They were young musicians, young writers, painters, actors, and I found them delightful.

They were always coming into my room and I had many talks with them. For the most part they were what I came afterwards to think of as "Little Children of the Arts." There was a great delicacy in them. They seemed to me to live, most of them, in a little closed-in world of their own. I felt in them little or no lust and it was a strange enough experience to me, coming as I did into that house, out of the world in which my own life was lived and feeling the amazing separation of their lives from the other lives I knew.

I came to them at evening out of an advertising office. A few years before I had been a laborer. I was myself, at that time, filled with all sorts of strange lusts.

I had been sitting with other men at a poker game in a hotel room.

I had been with a woman of the town.

I had become discouraged with life and had been on a drunk.

How strange the house seemed. There was something new to me. It happened that I had come into the house in the later afternoon and there was a young woman crying on the stairs. She had come into

† From *Sherwood Anderson's Memoirs*, ed. Ray Lewis White (Chapel Hill: U of North Carolina P, 1969) 346–50. Some notes have been revised.

1. At 735 Cass (now Wabash) Street.

the house and had put on men's clothes and as she had rather huge breasts the clothes made her look somewhat absurd.

It may be that I had got into talk with that one and that she came with me into my room. She explained to me. She was in love with another young woman in the house and said that the young woman did not love her.

There were these somewhat strange relations going on about me and, coming out of the sort of life I had known, it was all new to me. Whether there was actually any of what is commonly called "perversion" in the house I don't know. I doubt that there was.

The people about me were intent on poetry, on music, on the art of acting. They took all of the arts with a kind of terrible seriousness new to me. They seemed to me always curiously gentle with each other and above all tremendously in earnest.

At the time I lived in this house I had already written and published two or three books.[2] I am quite sure that, up to that time, any writing I had done had been largely influenced by the writings of others. However the critics, suspecting that I had been set off by this or that older writer, never picked the right ones. They were always accusing me of imitating some man I had never read.

I was in this house and it was winter. I began suddenly to write short tales. The tales were all written in a few months, one following the other, a kind of joyous time for me, the words and ideas flowing freely, very little revision to be done. I had set upon an idea and am quite sure the idea had come out of a certain rather fine feeling, toward myself, by the people about me. These rather strange little people (I cannot avoid thinking of them so), so gentle, kindly, so intent upon the arts, seemed always to be paying me a kind of respect that was certainly new to me.

It may be that I had been too much with business men, advertising men, laboring men, men who felt the practise of the arts as in some way unmanly. These new people, in some way a bit hard to explain, emphasized in me, shall I say, my maleness. At least they gave me a new confidence.

The idea I had was to take them, just as they were, as I felt them, and transfer them from the city rooming house to an imagined small town, the physical aspects of the town having, let us say, been picked up from my living in several such towns.

There was a young man, living in the house, who was an actor. He aspired to be an actor. It may be that he was really working in some store, as a clerk. I tried to put him, as I felt him, some inner truth of him, into another.

2. Anderson's chronology is confused. He had not published any books when he lived on Cass Street.

The other might be say the lonely figure of some queer man who lived upstairs over a drug store in a small town.

I changed, you see, every physical fact of my young clerk's life. Had I got him?

As suggested the stories were written, one following rapidly on the heels of another, and, in the house to which I had come, we played a game. I got them all into a room. I read my story aloud.

"Can it be one of you?" I asked.

They looked about, from one to another. They smiled. The test never failed.

"Yes. It is Alfred, or Clara, or James." Not once did they miss.

And so the stories came, in this rather strange way, into existence. I had, in relation to them, a somewhat new feeling. It was as though I had little or nothing to do with the writing. It was as though the people of that house, all of them wanting so much, none of them really equipped to wrestle with life as it was, had, in this odd way, used me as an instrument. They had got, I felt, through me, their stories told, and not in their own persons but, in a much more real and satisfactory way, through the lives of these queer small town people of the book.

So there the book was. It has made for itself a place in the world of books. How much I myself had to do with it I don't know. When it was at last published, having been for a long time peddled about, from publisher to publisher, a few of the stories having got into print in some of the small literary magazines of the times, there was not a single critic who had a good word to say for it.

There was indeed a quite horrible time for us. For weeks, after the book appeared, it was almost universally condemned by those who wrote of it, generally recognized as in some way a powerful book, for weeks my mails were flooded with letters.

Why, I do not mean to say there were not men who recognized the quality of the book. A few did, Mr. Van Wyck Brooks[3] and others. They wrote me letters but did not come to my defense in public.

And these other letters kept coming, for the most part from women. What names I was called. They spat upon me, shouted at me, used the most filthy of words and I remember one letter, in particular, from the wife of a man who had been my friend. She said she had once been seated beside me at a dinner table. "I do not believe that, having been that close to you, I shall ever again feel clean," she wrote.

And so it went on. How strange to think of it now, when the same book is being used as a text book in colleges, a book that was burned on the public square of one New England town, that such critics as Floyd

3. Critic, literary historian and biographer, author of *America's Coming-of-Age* (1915); in 1917–18 he was associate editor of *Seven Arts*.

Dell and Henry Mencken[4] had condemned, not publicly and not, with these men, on moral grounds, but, as they said, because the stories were not stories.

I think that later, a good many years later, both men made claims to having been, more or less, the fathers of the stories. I think that by the time they came to make the claim they had both convinced themselves it was true. I think that it is now generally recognized that the little book did something of importance. It broke the O. Henry grip, de Maupassant grip.[5] It brought the short story in Amcrica into a new relation with life. I myself think that the real fathers and if you please the mothers of the *Winesburg* stories were the people who once lived with me in a Chicago rooming house, the unsuccessful Little Children of the Arts.

SHERWOOD ANDERSON

The Finding†

It is the most difficult moment of all to write of. You are in a room. The particular room in which I sat was in an old house, old as Chicago houses go. Once it had been the house of some fashionable family.

The family had moved into some other, some newly fashionable, section of the city. There had been one of those sudden shifts of the rich and fashionable from one section of the city to another, so characteristic of our American cities. There had been a ballroom on the third floor of the house but now, that whole section of the city having fallen into a place of cheap rooming houses, thin partitions had been put up.

There were many little rooms separated by thin partitions and they were all occupied.

The occupants were all young. They were young musicians, painters, young women who aspired to be actors. I have always wanted to write of the people of that house. They were, for the time, so close to me.

I was no longer young. I was the oldest in that house. At the time the room in which I lived seemed large and later, in my thoughts, it kept growing larger.

I often described it to my wife.

4. H. L. Mencken (1880–1956) was from 1914 to 1923 an editor of the *Smart Set*, which published some of Anderson's early work. Contrary to Anderson's recollections, Mencken was highly complimentary of *Winesburg*; see his review on pp. 162–63, below.
5. Like O. Henry, the French author Guy de Maupassant (1850–1893) was known for his cleverly plotted stories.
† Edited from manuscripts and published with the permission of the Sherwood Anderson Literary Estate Trust. A variant of this text appeared in *Sherwood Anderson's Memoirs*, ed. White, 350–53. Anderson's return with his fourth wife, Eleanor Copenhaver Anderson, to the Cass Street rooming house occurred in the fall of 1933; he wrote "The Finding" on December 31, 1939.

"There was a great desk," I said, "as long as this room in which we now stand." I described for her my bed, the shelves built into the wall. I have always, when at work, loved to walk up and down. I am sure I gave her the impression of myself striding up and down a long room, grown in my imagination into something like a great hall. The council room of a king. Something of that sort.

And then once, years after I had lived there, I made the mistake of taking her to the house.

It was still a cheap rooming house. We drove up in a cab.

Why, how shabby it had grown. There were dirty torn lace curtains at the windows and, as we went into the little hallway on the ground floor, the door being open, we came upon a young couple engaged in a quarrel.

They stood facing us, paying no attention to our entrance. The woman was young. Her hair was in disorder and a cigarette burned between her fingers.

The quarrel was over money. He was accusing her of taking money from his pockets.

"Liar. Liar," she screamed at him.

She ran suddenly up a flight of stairs, the man following, and we heard a door slam.

The landlady appeared. She was a short fat woman of fifty clad in a torn dirty dress.

I wanted to run away. I didn't.

"We are looking for a room," I said and followed her silently up first one and then another flight of stairs. In a room on the second floor, behind a closed door, there was the sound of a woman crying.

"That would be the woman we just saw, quarreling with her man down below," I thought.

We had got to the door of the room. How heavy I felt. My feet were heavy.

"It was in that third room down the hall there that Agnes lived," I thought. Agnes was small and dark. She was a spiritualist and ghosts came into her room at night. She said they came up through the floor and spoke to her but she was not afraid. Once she came clad in a white nightgown into my own room late at night. It was a moonlit night and her eyes shone strangely in the half light. She came to where I lay in the bed and put a hand on my head. "Things will go well with you," she said. "They have told me."

She said the few words and went silently out.

And there was Kate, and William and Lillian and Joe, all younger than myself when I lived in that house. They had come from towns all over the middlewest. They were all poor, all filled with great dreams . . .

Of what they were to do—in painting, in music, in sculpture, on the stage.

What a strange little half world of little children of the arts, ready to sacrifice so much. Why have I never written of my life among them? Where are they now? What has a brutal world done to them?

"This room is unoccupied," the landlady said. Her hand was on the door knob to my old room.

"Don't," I wanted to scream. "Don't open that door.

"Leave me my dream of the room, what it was."

The door opened.

Why, what a shabby little hole. It was all tawdry, the room so small, the wallpaper so dirty.

"We will go there. If the room is unoccupied we will spend a day, a week there," I had said to my wife. I had dreamed of sitting with her at the window that looked down toward the Chicago Loop in the evening, as the day faded, as the lights flashed on in the great buildings of the Loop.

People going along the street below the window, passing under the street light at the nearby corner—shabbily dressed old men, smartly dressed young women, mothers holding young children by the hand, boys playfully pushing each other about filled with young animal life, an occasional prostitute from one of the shabby streets to the west, a policeman strolling, a young student with books under his arm. The house had stood just at the edge of the once fashionable section of the city and then to the west began the streets where the poor lived.

"It was in this room it happened."

What dreams, hopes, ambitions. Sometimes it had seemed to me when, as a young man, I sat at the window of that room, that each person who passed along the street below, under the light, shouted his secret up to me.

I was myself and still I fled out of myself. It seemed to me that I went into the others.

What dreams. What egotism. I had thought then, on such evenings, that I could tell all of the stories of all the people of America. I would get them all down, understand them, get their stories told.

And then came the night when it happened.

But what happened? It is the thing so hard to explain. It is, however, the thing every young man and woman in the world will understand.

I had been working so long, so long. Oh how many thousand, hundreds of thousands, of words put down.

Trying for something.

To escape out of old minds, old thoughts put into my head by others, into my own thoughts, my own feelings.

Out of the others, the many, many others, who had worked in words, to have got so much I wanted but now to be freed from them.

To at last go out of myself truly into those others, the others I met constantly in the streets of the city, in the office where I then worked, the others remembered out of my childhood in an American small town.

To be myself and yet, at the same time, the others.

And then, on a day, late in the afternoon of a day, I had come home to that room. I sat at a desk in a corner of the room. I wrote.

There was a story of another human, quite outside myself, truly told.

The story was one called "Hands." It was about a poor little man beaten, pounded, frightened by the world in which he lived into something oddly beautiful.

The story was written in one sitting. No word of it ever changed.[1] I wrote the story and got up. I walked up and down in that little narrow room. Tears flowed from my eyes.

"It is solid," I said to myself. "It is like a rock. It is there. It is put down."

There was, I'm sure, an upsurge of pride.

"See, at last I have done it.

"It is true. There it is.

"In those words, scrawled on the sheets of the paper, it is accomplished."

I am quite sure that on that night, when it happened in that room, when for the first time I dared whisper to myself that I had found it, my vocation, I knelt in the darkness and muttered words of gratitude to God.

That I had been on the right track, that I dared hope.

Pride, exaltation, all mixed with a new and great humbleness.

"It happened in that room.

"There I found my vocation.

"It is what we all want.

"All of this frantic search for wealth, for fame, position in life. It is all nothing.

"What we want, every one of us, is our own vocation.

"It is the world hunger."

The above words going through my mind as I stood at the door of a shabby room in a shabby rooming house years later with my wife.

Remembering all my failures since that night when I alone there in that room found, for the first time, my own vocation.

Getting for the first time belief in self.

1. Anderson did make numerous revisions of wording on the surviving manuscript of "Hands." See William L. Phillips, "How Sherwood Anderson Wrote *Winesburg, Ohio*," *American Literature* 23 (March 1951): 7–30, a useful source of information on the *Winesburg* manuscript despite its dubious inferences about the order in which the stories were composed.

I must have muttered words to the landlady, taken my wife's arm, hurried out of that house, feeling deeply the shame of my many failures since that, the great moment of my life.

When I found my vocation.

What every man and woman in the world wants.

A vocation.

Reviews

HEYWOOD BROUN

From the *New York Tribune*†

"If you are to become a writer," says Kate Swift in Sherwood Anderson's book [*Winesburg, Ohio*], "you'll have to stop fooling with words."

Some of Anderson's sketches of small town life in Ohio are excellent, but again we find him disregarding Kate Swift's advice.

"Wash Williams, the telegraph operator of Winesburg, was the ugliest thing in town. His girth was immense, his neck thin, his legs feeble. He was dirty. Everything about him was unclean. Even the whites of his eyes looked soiled."

We think that the final sentence of that description is added, not to make us see Wash Williams, but to make us see the literary facility of Sherwood Anderson. It is much too glib for our taste. In school or college we had an English instructor whose favorite model of vivid description was that bit in "David Copperfield" which rounds up with the statement that Uriah Heep looked as if he would bleed white. But we don't favor such models any more. These seem to us pert touches which come between a writer and a character.

It is easier to point out faults in Anderson's book than virtues, although the latter are rather more numerous and substantial. Let it be said, then, immediately that Anderson is a keen observer with a clear insight into character. We are disposed to add that sometimes he sees more than there is to see. We can't believe that even a small town could produce such a large percentage of neurotics as Anderson unearths. We are also inclined to think that the young women of this town were more seduced than usual.

Oftentimes we are not with Anderson. His introductory chapter, "The Book of the Grotesque," meant nothing to us. Later we were puzzled by a passage in the sketch called "Mother." It described various encounters between a baker and a cat and continued: "In the alley the grey cat crouched behind barrels filled with torn paper and broken bottles, above which flew a black swarm of flies. Once when she was alone, and after

† 31 May 1919: 10.

watching a prolonged and ineffectual outburst on the part of the baker, Elizabeth Willard put her head down on her long white hands and wept. ·After that she did not look along the alley-way any more, but tried to forget the contest between the bearded man and the cat. It seemed like a rehearsal of her own life, terrible in its vividness."

We never knew quite why.

The sketch about Louise Bentley, called "Surrender," we found an exceptionally fine piece of work and also the sketch about Kate Swift, called "The Teacher." Anderson has found a great many subjects in his small Ohio town, but he never seems to find any comic ones. The book becomes, therefore, a bit monotonous. It probably owes its existence to "Spoon River Anthology," and is quite in that mood, but these prose tales lack something of the simplicity and directness of Masters.[1]

BURTON RASCOE

From the *Chicago Tribune*†

* * *

These stories [*Winesburg, Ohio*] are practically all concerned chiefly with the sex life of the inhabitants of the Ohio village—of the doctor, the bartender, the school teacher, the young reporter, the hired girl, the bumpkin lad, the village "sport," the woman hater—of every one in this drab community, where there was little incentive to sublimated desire, and where emotion was all the more intense for being defeated and repressed at every turn.

There the rigid old Puritan ethic, to which this country owes at once so much of good and of evil, was an ineradicable and saving instinct and yet an instinct constantly at war with the other instinct for mating; the conflict itself produces drama of an intensely poignant kind, romance of effective and realistic beauty. The awakening of sex in the idealistic youth; the harassing desire for love and companionship that obsessed the lonely school teacher, the simple surrender of the ignorant young girl; all these constantly recurrent incidents of life are told with sympathy, skill, and sincerity.

Mr. Anderson is frequently crude in his employment of English; he has not a nice sense of word values; but he has an intense vision of life; he is a cautious and interpretative observer; and he has recorded here a bit of life which should rank him with the most important contemporary

1. Edgar Lee Masters (1869–1950), author of *Spoon River Anthology* (1915), verse monologues of deceased residents of a small midwestern town, which was generally considered to have influenced Anderson in writing *Winesburg*.

† 7 June 1919: 13.

writers in this country. He may not be, as some one called him, the American Dostoievski,[1] but he is the American Sherwood Anderson.

MAXWELL ANDERSON

A Country Town †

* * *

As a challenge to the snappy short story form, with its planned proportions of flippant philosophy, epigrammatic conversation, and sex danger, nothing better has come out of America than *Winesburg, Ohio.* Because we have little in the field, it is probably easy to over-estimate its excellence. In Chekhov's [1] sketches simplicity is an artistic achievement. With Sherwood Anderson simplicity is both an art and a limitation. But the present book is well within his powers, and he has put into it the observation, the brooding "odds and ends of thoughts," [2] of many years. It was set down by a patient and loving craftsman; it is in a new mood, and one not easily forgotten.

H. L. MENCKEN

[A Book of Uncommon Merit] ‡

It is curious to note that the name of Sherwood Anderson is not in the current "Who's Who in America," dated 1918–19. He printed a very unusual novel, "Windy McPherson's Son," so long ago as 1916, and another of noteworthy quality, "Marching Men," a year later, but his double achievement seems to have escaped the notice of the compilers of the national red book, though they got prompt wind of at least a hundred other new novelists, most of them drivellers and cheesemongers.

1. Fyodor Dostoevsky (1821–1881), Russian author whose novels included *Crime and Punishment* (1866) and *The Brothers Karamazov* (1879–80). Waldo Frank compared Anderson to Dostoevsky in "Emerging Greatness" (*Seven Arts* 1 [November 1916]: 73-78).

† From *The New Republic* 19 (25 June 1919): 257, 260.

1. Anton Chekhov (1860–1904), Russian author of short stories and plays.
2. Quoted from "Paper Pills," p. 16, above.

‡ Source uncertain. Rpt. Ray Lewis White, "Mencken's Lost Review of *Winesburg, Ohio,*" *Notes on Modern American Literature* 2 (Spring 1978): note 11. Mencken wrote another appreciative review of *Winesburg*, "Novels, Chiefly Bad," *Smart Set* 59 (August 1919): 140, 142.

This omission, I dare say, will have to be remedied in the next edition, for Anderson has just printed a fourth book [*Winesburg, Ohio*] (his third, published last year, was a volume of poems, "Mid-American Chants") that embodies some of the most remarkable writing done in America in our time. Here, indeed, is a piece of work that stands out from the common run of fiction like the Alps from the Piedmont plain. Nothing quite like it is to be found in our literature. It lifts the short story, for long a form hardened by trickery and virtuosity, to a higher and more spacious level, and it gets into that form something of the mordant bitterness of tragic drama and something of the reflective detachment of epic poetry. The effect produced is incomparably greater than that one usually encounters. Put beside one of these penetrating sketches of Anderson's, the average magazine story of the O. Henry or Gouverneur Morris type, or even of the Katharine Gerould type, shrinks to the veriest inconsequences and imbecility.

* * *

In brief, a book of uncommon merit—well-ordered, thoughtful, original, alive. And by an author who deserves the utmost hospitality hereafter. He is just beginning to be heard of, but he is by no means a tyro. A man of more than 40 years, he has been writing steadily for half of them—writing and revising, carefully testing and working out his ideas, perfecting his technic, learning his trade. I saw these "Winesburg" stories in manuscript fully four years ago. They then seemed to me to be very remarkable; I was eager to get them into type. But in the interval Anderson has greatly improved them. What was vague in them is now crystal-clear. What was but half thought out is now thought out to the last place of decimals. What was rough is now planed down.

* * *

WILLIAM LYON PHELPS

From *The New York Times Book Review*†

Conceivably these stories [*Winesburg, Ohio*] might have been written before the advent of the new psychology, but if so they would not have been understood. The characters are actuated by motives not exterior; their actions give something of the startling effect of a head and shoulders snapping suddenly out of a hidden trapdoor in an empty room. But Mr. Anderson's expositions make these sudden, infinitesimal, half-mad

† 29 June 1919: 353.

actions as natural to the reader as an excrescence to a physician; both are the result of accumulated secretions. Freud and Jung have taught us how hopes and ideas crammed back into subcellars of consciousness emerge in grotesque masquerade when pressure slackens or becomes too taut; the little tragedies and comedies which take place in Mr. Anderson's town of Winesburg, Ohio, have the support of scientific revelation.

* * *

ANONYMOUS

Sordid Tales†

The reader's first impression is that the "Spoon River Anthology" has been put into prose, and in this there is an abiding truth. The seamy side of a small town's life is exposed in a series of tales of sordid theme [*Winesburg, Ohio*], for the most part grimly ironical in temper. There is no humor, as in many tales of Western and Southwestern small-town life; no fine beauty as in the tales of the New England group; no attempt to bring out provincial quaintness of character. The recurrence of misdemeanors and crimes of sex in the book will be especially irritating to those who, having been reared in a small Middle Western town, know the partial element of truth and the huge element of mendacity in Mr. Anderson's book. The first story relates how a schoolmaster narrowly escaped lynching because he was unjustly suspected of a crime against nature. The second tells how a girl was betrayed and married the doctor who hid her secret. A few pages more and we read a simple sketch of an intrigue between a village girl and a boy. A little further is a nasty story of a forced marriage. A little further still is a story of a minister who would climb to his dark study in the church tower because the little window commanded a view of a young lady's bedroom. One might continue an unedifying list of similar basic ideas for Mr. Anderson's stories, but it is unnecessary to say more than that fully half of the twenty-four bits of fiction are of a character which no man would wish to see in the hands of a daughter or sister.

Apart from the moral objections to the book, and from the distorted, depressing view it gives of life, there is much more to be said of its artistic shortcomings than of its merits. Mr. Anderson showed in that first novel which gained him a reputation that time has not increased a

† From the *New York Evening Post* 19 July 1919: III, 3.

greater ability to devise plot than to draw character. "Windy McPherson's Son" ran near the end into a veritable scenario, a half-clothed skeleton of action. In all these stories there is not a single memorable character and there are only two or three which strike us as true to life. Most of them are puppets with names. Not a single story is a searching or artistic interpretation of life. The book almost totally disregards that kindlier, humaner, cleaner side of small-town life which not only exists but is the larger and dominant side. It has slight claim on the interest of any one who is not in search of sensationalism.

JOHN NICHOLAS BEFFEL

Small Towns and Broken Lives†

This is a testimonial I did not anticipate writing. When I picked up Sherwood Anderson's book of small town tales, "Winesburg, Ohio," I expected the worst. For I had read his novel, "Marching Men," a thoroughly incompetent piece of fiction; a novel to shame both author and publisher, and it was hard to conceive that Anderson could write a creditable book.

But he turned the trick. He has done a daring, relentless thing. Native of a community where everybody calls everybody else by his first name, Anderson has had the fortitude to expose the curtained corners of existence in an American small town.

Let Ohio villages writhe under the glare of the light if they will; this book shows up with equal insistence towns in Illinois, Indiana, New York, and in numberless commonwealths. No sheaf of happy endings, but a social chronicle as pitiless as life itself. Maimed and crippled souls pass by the reader in halting procession. And always the music of the march is in minor key. Passion, loneliness, terrible yearning are in the reeds and the drumbeats.

[The review goes on to quote extensively from the preceding *Evening Post* review and to dispute its claims.]

* * *

But I, too, hail from a small Middle Western town, and I have lived in other American villages, and I know that Anderson has portrayed truth, vividly, as truth is vivid. Admittedly, there is humor in the towns, and beauty, and provincial quaintness of character; but rottenness is

† From the *New York Call* 21 September 1919: 10.

there, selfishness, double dealing by the loudest Amen shouters, terrors which lead to insanity.

* * *

WILLIAM FAULKNER

From the *Dallas Morning News*†

* * *

The simplicity of this title! And the stories are as simply done: short, he tells the story and stops. His very inexperience, his urgent need not to waste time or paper taught him one of the first attributes of genius. As a rule first books show more bravado than anything else, unless it be tediousness. But there is neither of these qualities in "Winesburg."[1] Mr. Anderson is tentative, self-effacing with his George Willards and Wash Williamses and banker White's daughters, as though he were thinking: "Who am I, to pry into the souls of these people who, like myself, sprang from this same soil to suffer the same sorrows as I?" The only indication of the writer's individuality which I find in "Winesburg" is his sympathy for them, a sympathy which, had the book been done as a full-length novel, would have become mawkish. Again the gods looked out for him. These people live and breathe; they are beautiful. There is the man who organized a baseball club, the man with the "speaking" hands, Elizabeth Willard, middle-aged, and the oldish doctor, between whom was a love that Cardinal Bembo[2] might have dreamed. There is a Greek word for a love like theirs which Mr. Anderson probably had never heard. And behind all of them a ground of fecund earth and corn in the green spring and the slow, full hot summer and the rigorous masculine winter that hurts it not, but makes it stronger.

* * *

† 26 April 1925, Part 3, p. 7; rpt. *Princeton University Library Chronicle* 18 (Spring 1957): 89–90. Reprinted by permission of Jill Faulkner Summers. Anderson befriended Faulkner in New Orleans and helped him with the writing and publication of his first novel, *Soldier's Pay* (1926).

1. *Winesburg* was actually Anderson's third published book of fiction, *Windy McPherson's Son* (1916) and *Marching Men* (1917) having preceded it.
2. Pietro Bembo (1470–1547), cardinal of the Roman Catholic Church and influential classical scholar. The concept of platonic love in reference to an unconsummated heterosexual relationship developed from works such as his *Gli Asolani* (1505) rather than from the Greek philosophers.

CRITICISM

WALTER B. RIDEOUT

The Simplicity of *Winesburg, Ohio*†

It is probably impossible, except impressionistically, to isolate the essential quality of any work of art, but Hart Crane may have come close to isolating that of *Winesburg, Ohio* when in another context he wrote of Anderson himself that, "He has a humanity and simplicity that is quite baffling in depth and suggestiveness."[1] Leaving the matter of "humanity" aside, one is indeed struck on first reading the book by its apparent simplicity of language and form. On second or subsequent readings, however, he sees that the hard, plain, concrete diction is much mixed with the abstract, that the sentence cadences come from George Moore[2] and the King James Bible as well as from ordinary speech rhythms, that the seemingly artless, even careless, digressions are rarely artless, careless, or digressive. What had once seemed to have the clarity of water held in the hand begins to take on instead its elusiveness. If this is simplicity, it is simplicity—paradox or not—of a complicated kind. Since *Winesburg* constantly challenges one to define the complications, I should like to examine a few that perhaps lie closest beneath the surface of the book and the life it describes.

It his been often pointed out that the fictitious Winesburg closely resembles Clyde, Ohio, where Anderson lived from the age of seven to the age of nineteen and which became the home town of his memories. Even now the visitor to the two communities can see that Winesburg and Clyde are both "eighteen miles" south of Lake Erie; in both, the central street of the town is named Main, and Buckeye and Duane branch off from it; both have a Heffner Block and a Waterworks Pond; both lie "in the midst of open fields, but beyond the fields are pleasant patches of woodland." As recently as the summer of 1960, the wooden Gothic railroad station, from which Sherwood Anderson and George Willard took the train for the city and the great world, was still standing; and on the hill above Waterworks Pond, where George walked with Helen White on the darkened fair grounds, one can yet see, overgrown with turf, the banked-up west end turns of the race track. Modern Clyde is perhaps half again as large as the town that the future author of *Winesburg* left in 1896, but the growth has shown itself principally in housing development on the periphery. The central village is basically

† From *Shenandoah* 13 (Spring 1962): 20–31. Reprinted from *Shenandoah:* The Washington and Lee University Review, with the permission of the Editor.

1. Poet Hart Crane (1899–1932) made this comment in "Sherwood Anderson," *Double Dealer* 2 (July 1921): 45 [*Editors*].
2. Irish author (1852–1933), best known for his novels, such as *Esther Waters* (1894) and *Evelyn Innes* (1898) [*Editors*].

unchanged, and even now to walk through the quiet old residence streets with their white frame or brick houses and wide lawns shaded by big elms and maples is to walk uncannily through a fictitious scene made suddenly real.

The more one learns of the town as it was in the 1890's, the more he sees the actual Clyde under the imagined Winesburg.[3] Anderson was a story teller, of course, not a historian, and the correspondence of the two communities does not have a one-to-one exactness. Nevertheless the correspondences become striking, particularly as one sees that in many instances Clyde names of persons and places appear only faintly disguised in the pages of *Winesburg*. Anderson wrote about Win Pawsey's shoe store, Surbeck's Pool Room, and Hern's Grocery; in the Clyde of the early 1890's there were Alfred Pawsey's Shoe Store, Surbeck's Cigar Store, and Hurd's Grocery, the last still very much in business. Wine Creek flows through Winesburg instead of the real Raccoon of Clyde, but the former follows the latter's course; and beyond the Wine rises the fictitious Gospel Hill in the same place as the actual Piety Hill, where the Anderson family lived for a time. Sometimes the disguise is somewhat less casual, though it may turn out to be merely a transfer of names. The owner of one of the two livery stables in Clyde was Frank Harvey, but there were Moyers in town, from whom Anderson borrowed half the name of Wesley Moyer for the livery stableman in Winesburg. Clyde personal names, it must be noted, are used almost exclusively for the minor characters, and except for one or two debatable possibilities no character, either major or minor, seems to be recognizably based on an actual resident of the town. The important matter, however, is that the "grotesques" of the several tales exist within a physical and social matrix furnished Anderson by his memories of Clyde.

That he should have visualized the locale of his tales so closely in terms of his home town is not surprising, and the reader may dismiss the matter as merely a frequent practice of realistic writers. Yet Anderson is not a realistic writer in the ordinary sense. With him realism is a means to something else, not an end in itself. To see the difference between his presentation of "reality" and the more traditional kind that gives a detailed picture of appearances, one needs only to compare the drug store on the Main Street of Sinclair Lewis's Gopher Prairie with that on the Main Street of Winesburg. Twice over, once as Carol Kennicott, once as Bea Sorenson sees them, Lewis catalogues the parts of Dave Dyer's soda fountain. Anderson, like his own Enoch Robinson preferring "the essences of things" to the "realities," merely names Sylvester West's Drug Store, letting each reader's imagination do as much or as little with it as he wishes. As with the drug store, so with many other

3. I am grateful to be able to acknowledge publicly my great debt to Mr. Herman Hurd, Anderson's "closest friend" in his Clyde years, and to his son, Mr. Thaddeus Hurd, who have generously shared with me their memories of Sherwood Anderson and of Clyde.

landmarks of Clyde-Winesburg. As he repeats from tale to tale the names of stores and their owners or refers to such elements of town life as the post office, the bank, or the cemetery, there emerges, not a photograph, but at most the barest sketch of the external world of the town. Perhaps even "sketch" implies too great a precision of detail. What Anderson is after is less a representation of conventional "reality" than, to keep the metaphor drawn from art, an abstraction of it.

Realism is for Anderson a means rather than an end, and the highly abstract kind of reality found in Winesburg has its valuable uses. The first of these is best understood in relation to George Willard's occupation on the *Winesburg Eagle*. (Clyde's weekly newspaper was, and still is the *Clyde Enterprise*, but Sherwood Anderson was never its reporter.) It has been suggested that the author may have made his central figure a newspaper reporter in order that he could thus be put most readily in touch with the widest number of people in town and most logically become the recipient of many confidences; yet Anderson's point is that exactly insofar as George remains a newspaper reporter, he is committed to the surface of life, not to its depths. "Like an excited dog," Anderson says in "The Thinker," using a mildly contemptuous comparison, "George Willard ran here and there," writing down all day "little facts" about A. P. Wringlet's recent shipment of straw hats or Uncle Tom Sinnings' new barn on the Valley Road. As reporter, George is concerned with externals, with appearances, with the presumably solid, simple, everyday surface of life. For Anderson the surface is there, of course, as his recurring use of place and personal names indicates; yet conventional "reality" is for him relatively insignificant and is best presented in the form of sketch or abstraction. What is important is "to see beneath the surface of lives," to perceive the intricate mesh of impulses, desires, drives growing down in the dark, unrevealed parts of the personality like the complex mass of roots that, below the surface of the ground, feeds the common grass above in the light.

But if one function of Anderson's peculiar adaptation of realism is, as it were, to depreciate the value of surfaces, a corollary function is constantly to affirm that any surface has its depth. Were we, on the one hand, to observe such tormented people as Alice Hindman and Dr. Parcival and the Reverend Curtis Hartman as briefly and as much from the outside as we view Wesley Moyer or Biff Carter or Butch Wheeler, the lamplighter, they would appear as uncomplicated and commonplace as the latter. Conversely, were we to see the inwardness of Moyer and Carter and Wheeler, their essential lives would provide the basis for three more Winesburg tales. (The real lamplighter of Clyde in the early 1890's was a man named John Becker. It may well have given him the anguish of a "grotesque" that he had an epileptic son, who as a young man died during a seizure while assisting his father in his trade.)

Yet a third function of Anderson's abstract, or shorthand, kind of realism is to help him set the tone of various tales, often a tone of elegiac quietness. Just how this is done will be clearer if one realizes that the real Clyde which underlies Winesburg is the town, not as Anderson left it in 1896, but the town as it was a few years earlier when, as he asserts in "An Awakening," "the time of factories had not yet come." In actual fact the "industrialization" of the small town of Clyde—which, it can be demonstrated, was strongly to condition Anderson's whole attitude toward machine civilization—came in a rush with the installation of electric lights in 1893—"Clyde is now the best lighted town in the state," boasted the *Enterprise* in its September 4th issue—with the paving of Main Street later that year, and with the establishment of a bicycle factory in the late summer of 1894. Subsequently Anderson was to give imaginative embodiment to this development in *Poor White*, but the Winesburg tales he conceived of as for the most part occurring in a preindustrial setting, recalling nostalgically a town already lost before he had left it, giving this vanished era the permanence of pastoral. Here, as always, he avoids the realism of extensive detail and makes only suggestive references, one of the most memorable being the description in "The Thinker" of the lamplighter hurrying along the street before Seth Richmond and Helen White, lighting the lamp in each wooden post "so that their way was half lighted, half darkened, by the lamps and by the deepening shadows cast by the low-branched trees." By a touch like this, drawn from his memory of preindustrial Clyde, Anderson turns the evening walk of his quite ordinary boy and girl into a tiny processional and invests the couple with that delicate splendor which can come to people, "even in Winesburg."

If Anderson's treatment of locale in his tales turns out to be more complex than it seems at first, the same can be said of his methods of giving sufficient unity to his book so that, while maintaining the "looseness" of life as he actually sensed it, the tales would still form a coherent whole. Some of these methods, those that I shall be concerned with, have a point in common: they all involve the use of repeated elements. One such device is that of setting the crisis scenes of all but five of the tales in the evening. In a very large majority of the stories, too, some kind of light partly, but only partly, relieves the darkness. In "Hands," "Mother," and "Loneliness," for example, the light is that of a single lamp; in "The Untold Lie" the concluding scene is faintly lit by the last of twilight; in "Sophistication" George Willard and Helen White look at each other "in the dim light" afforded, apparently, by "the lights of the town reflected against the sky," though at the other end of the fair grounds a few race track men have built a fire that provides a dot of illumination in the darkness. Finally, many of the tales end with the characters in total darkness. Such a device not only links the tales but in itself implies meaning. *Winesburg* is primarily a book about the "night world" of human personality. The dim light equates with, as well as literally illuminates, the limited glimpse into an individual soul that each crisis scene affords, and the briefness of the insight is emphasized by the shutting down of the dark.

Another kind of repeated element throughout the book is the recurrent word. Considering the sense of personal isolation one gets from the atomized lives of the "grotesques," one would expect a frequent use of some such word as "wall," standing for whatever it is that divides each person from all others. Surprisingly that particular word appears only a few times. The one that does occur frequently is "hand," either in the singular or the plural; and very often, as indeed would be expected, it suggests, even symbolizes, the potential or actual communication of one personality with another. The hands of Wing Biddlebaum and Dr. Reefy come immediately to mind; but, to name only a few other instances, George Willard takes hold of Louise Trunnion's "rough" but "delightfully small" hand in anticipation of his sexual initiation, Helen White keeps her hand in Seth Richmond's until Seth breaks the clasp through overconcern with self, in the field where they are working Hal Winters puts "his two hands" on Ray Pearson's shoulders and they "become all alive to each other," Kate Swift puts her hands on George Willard as though about to embrace him in her desire to make him understand what being a writer means. Obviously the physical contact may not produce mutual understanding. The hand may in fact express aggression. One of the men who run Wing Biddlebaum out of the Pennsylvania town at night "had a rope in his hands"; Elizabeth Willard, who as a girl had put her hand on the face of each lover after sexual release, imagines herself stealing toward her husband, "holding the long wicked scissors in her hand"; Elmer Cowley on the station platform strikes George Willard almost unconscious with his fists before leaping onto the departing train. Nevertheless, the possibility of physical touch between two human beings always implies, even if by negative counterpart, at least the possibility of a profounder moment of understanding between them. The intuitive awareness by George Willard and Helen White of each other's "sophistication" is expressed, not through their few kisses, but by Helen's taking George's arm and walking "beside him in dignified silence."

As for George himself, one can make too much of his role as a character designed to link the tales, unify them, and structure them into a loose sort of *bildungsroman* [4]; on the other hand, one can make too little of it. Granted that Anderson tended to view his own life, and that of others, as a succession of moments rather than as a "figure in a carpet," that his imagination worked more successfully in terms of the flash

4. A novel that traces the maturing of a young character [*Editors*].

of insight than of the large design, that his gift was, in short, for the story rather than the novel, still through his treatment of George Willard's development he supplies a pattern for *Winesburg, Ohio* that is as definite as it is unobtrusive. This development has three closely related aspects, and each aspect involves again the repetition of certain elements.

The first aspect is obvious. Whatever the outward difference between created character and creator, George's inward life clearly reflects the conflict Anderson himself had experienced between the world of practical affairs, with its emphasis on the activity of money-making and its definition of success in financial terms, and the world of dreams, with its emphasis on imaginative creativity and its definition of success in terms of the degree of penetration into the buried life of others. The conflict is thematically stated in the first of the tales, "Hands." Wing Biddlebaum's hands are famous in Winesburg for their berry-picking (hence money-making) skill, but the true story of the hands, as told by "a poet," is of course that they can communicate a desire to dream. Wing declares the absolute opposition of the two worlds by telling George that he is destroying himself because " 'you are afraid of dreams. You want to be like others in town here.' " The declaration indicates that George has not yet resolved the conflict, and his irresolution at this point is reinforced by his ambivalent attitude toward Wing's hands. Unlike the other townspeople he is curious to know what lies beneath their outward skill; yet his respect for Wing and his fear of the depths that might be revealed make him put curiosity aside. The conflict between practical affairs and dreams is again made explicit in the third story of the book, "Mother," where it is objectified in the hostility between Tom and Elizabeth Willard and the clash of their influences on their son. *Winesburg* is not a book of suspense, and thus early in the tales the conflict is in effect resolved when George implicitly accepts his mother's, and Wing's, way, the way of dreams. From this point on both the conflict and George's resolution of it are maintained in a formal sense by the opposition between the "daylight world" of the minor characters and the "night world" of the major ones, the grotesques. George continues to run about writing down surface facts for the newspaper, but his essential life consists in his efforts, some successful, some not, to understand the essential lives of others. From these efforts, from the death of his mother, from his achievement of "sophistication" with Helen White, he gains the will to leave Winesburg, committed, as the final paragraph of "Departure" asserts, to the world of dreams.

The second of these closely-related aspects of George's development is his growing desire to be a creative writer and his increasing awareness of the meaning of that vocation. George's interest in writing is not mentioned until the book is half over, when, in "The Thinker," it appears to have been an interest that he had had for some time. He talks "continuously of the matter" to Seth Richmond, and the "idea that George Willard would some day become a writer had given him a place of distinction in Winesburg. . . ." At this point his conception of writing centers on externals, on the opportunities the writer's life offers for personal freedom and for public acclaim. In a remark that suggests a reading of Jack London,[5] George explains to Seth that as a writer he will be his own boss: "Though you are in India or in the South Seas in a boat, you have but to write and there you are." Since writing for George is at this stage mainly a matter of fame and fun, it is not surprising to find him in "The Thinker" deliberately, and naively, planning to fall in love with Helen White in order to write a love story. The absurdity, Anderson suggests, is twofold: falling in love is not something one rationally plans to do, and one does not write thus directly and literally out of experience anyway.

Actually Kate Swift, in "The Teacher," has tried to tell George that the writer's is not "the easiest of all lives to live," but rather one of the most difficult. In one of those scenes where physical touch symbolizes an attempt to create the moment of awareness between two personalities, Kate has tried to explain the demanding principles by which the true writer must live. He must "know life," must "stop fooling with words," must "know what people are thinking about, not what they say"—all three being principles Anderson was to insist on himself as the code of the artist. That George is still immature both as person and as writer is signified at the end of "The Teacher" when he gropes drowsily about in the darkness with a hand and mutters that he has missed something Kate Swift was trying to tell him. This needed maturity comes to him only at the end of *Winesburg*. When, sitting beside the body of his dead mother, he decides to go to "some city" and perhaps "get a job on some newspaper," he is really marked already for the profession of writer, whatever job he may take to support himself, just as Anderson supported himself by composing advertising copy while experimenting with the Winesburg stories. In "Departure" the commitment of George Willard to writing unites with his final commitment to the world of dreams. For both George and his creator the two are indeed identical.

The third aspect of George's development provides another way of charting his inward voyage from innocence to experience, from ignorance to understanding, from apparent reality of the face of things to true reality behind or below. Three stories—"Nobody Knows," "An Awakening," and "Sophistication"—have a special relationship. They all center on George's dealings with a woman, a different one in each case; they contain very similar motifs; they are arranged in an ascending order of progression. The fact that one comes near the beginning of the

5. A popular American author, London (1876–1916) drew upon his own experience as a seaman in works such as his novel *The Sea Wolf* (1904) and *South Sea Tales* (1911) [*Editors*].

book, one about two-thirds of the way through, and one at the end suggests that Anderson was not without his own subtle sense of design.

The first story, "Nobody Knows," is in all ways the simplest. In it George Willard enters traditional manhood by having with Louise Trunnion his first sex experience. In relation to the other two tales in the sequence, the most significant elements of the story, besides the fact of actual sexual conquest, are George's lack of self-assurance at the outset of the affair, his bursting forth with a "flood of words," his consequent aggressiveness and failure to sympathize with his partner, and his action at the end of the story when he stands "perfectly still in the darkness, attentive, listening as though for a voice calling his name." The sexual encounter with Louise has been simply that. It has brought him physical satisfaction and a feeling of entirely self-centered masculine pride. His expectation of hearing a voice, however, would seem to be a projection of guilt feeling at having violated the overt moral code of the community even though "nobody knows."

In the second and third stories these elements, or their opposites, appear in a more complex fashion. In both "An Awakening" and "Sophistication," George's relation with a woman is complicated by the involvement of another man, though, significantly, Ed Handby in the former story is laconic, direct, and highly physical, while the college instructor in the latter is voluble, devious, and pompously intellectual. In both, too, the final scene takes place on the hill leading up to the fair grounds, close, incidentally, to the place where Kate Swift tried to explain to George the difficulties that beset the dedicated writer. Yet the two stories have quite different, if supplementary, conclusions.

As George and Belle Carpenter walk up the hill in the final scene of "An Awakening," he feels no more sympathy for her, has no more understanding of her needs, than he had for Louise Trunnion; but before this last walk he has experienced an exaltation that keeps him from any fear of masculine incompetence. Earlier that January night a kind of mystical revelation has come to him when it seems as though "some voice outside of himself" announced the thoughts in his mind: " 'I must get myself into touch with something orderly and big that swings through the night like a star.' " Unlike the situation at the end of "Nobody Knows," George actually "hears" the external voice, and the voice is now the positive one of inspiration, which has replaced the negative one of conscience. Thereafter he talks volubly to Belle, as he had to Louise; but when in "An Awakening" his "mind runs off into words," he believes that Belle will recognize the new force in him and will at once surrender herself to his masculine power, Now, in actual fact an insistence on the necessity of universal order—" 'There is a law for armies and for men too,' " George asserts—is a characteristic of Anderson's own thinking particularly as expressed in the novel,

Marching Men, which preceded the Winesburg tales in composition, and in the poems, *Mid-American Chants*, which followed; yet George makes this concept ridiculous at the moment because of his intense self-centeredness about his inspiration. As Kate Swift would have said, he is still playing with words, a destructive procedure for the artistic personality as well as for the non-artistic one. Holding the quite uninterested Belle in his arms, he whispers large words into the darkness, until the passionate, non-verbalizing Ed Handby throws him aside, takes Belle by the arm, and marches off. George is left angered, humiliated, and disgustedly disillusioned with his moment of mystic insight when "the voice outside himself . . . had . . . put new courage into his heart."

Where "An Awakening" records a defeat, "Sophistication" records in all ways a triumph. Though Anderson presents the moment in essay rather than dramatic form, there comes to George, as to "every boy," a flash of insight when "he stops under a tree and waits as for a voice calling his name." But this time "the voices outside himself" do not speak of the possibilities of universal order, nor do they speak of guilt. Instead they "whisper a message concerning the limitations of life," the brief light of human existence between two darks. The insight emphasizes the unity of all human beings in their necessary submission to death and their need for communication one with another. It is an insight that produces self-awareness but not self-centeredness, that produces in short, the mature, "sophisticated" person.

The mind of such a person does not "run off into words." Hence Helen White, who has had an intuition similar to George's, runs away from the empty talk of her college instructor and her mother, and finds George, whose first and last words to her in the story, pronounced as they first meet, are "Come on." Together in the dimly-lit fair grounds on the hill overlooking the town of Winesburg, George and Helen share a brief hour of absolute awareness. Whereas his relationship with Belle Carpenter had produced in George self-centeredness, misunderstanding, hate, frustration, humiliation, that with Helen produces quite the opposite feelings. The feeling of oneness spreads outward, furthermore. Through his communication with Helen he begins "to think of the people in the town where he had lived with something like reverence." When he has come to this point, when he loves and respects the inhabitants of Winesburg, the "daylight" people as well as the "night" ones, the way of the artist lies clear before him. George Willard is ready for his "Departure."

Like Hart Crane, other readers will find the simplicity of *Winesburg, Ohio* "baffling"; but it is very probably this paradoxical quality which has attracted and will continue to attract admirers to a book that Anderson himself, with a mixture of amusement, deprecation, defensiveness, and satisfaction, quite accurately termed "a kind of American classic."

SALLY ADAIR RIGSBEE

The Feminine in *Winesburg, Ohio*†

The meaning Sherwood Anderson gives to the characters of women and to the qualities of the feminine is an important source of unity in *Winesburg, Ohio*. Anderson identifies the feminine with a pervasive presence of a fragile, hidden "something" that corresponds both to the lost potential of each of the grotesques and to the secret knowledge that each story is structured to reveal. The themes most frequently identified as the unifying forces of *Winesburg, Ohio*, the failure of communication and the development of the artist, are closely related to Anderson's focus on the meaning of the feminine. In *Winesburg, Ohio* communication is blocked because of the devaluation of the feminine qualities of vulnerability and tenderness even though the artist's creativity springs from deep feelings of vitality which Anderson associates with the feminine.[1]

Through one of Enoch Robinson's paintings in "Loneliness," Anderson creates an image that reveals his vision of a woman's condition in Winesburg and of her potential power. The painting is of a man driving down a road to Winesburg. The look on the man's face indicates that he is vaguely aware of "something hidden" behind "a clump of elders" beside the road. Enoch longs for his critics to see this hidden subject, an essence so beautiful and precious that it could not be rendered directly:

> "It's a woman and, oh, she is lovely! She is hurt and is suffering but she makes no sound. Don't you see how it is? She lies quite still, white and still, and the beauty comes out from her and spreads over everything. It is in the sky back there and all around everywhere. I didn't try to paint the woman, of course. She is too beautiful to be painted."[2] [93]

Enoch's painting portrays precisely the condition of the female characters who inhabit Winesburg. The women are "invisible" because their real identities are eclipsed by their social roles. The relationships between the men and women of Winesburg are corrupted and uncreative, for their acceptance of conventional sexual roles prevents them from experiencing the genuine communication that comes when rela-

† From *Studies in American Fiction* 9 (Fall 1981): 233–44. Reprinted by permission of *Studies in American Fiction* and Northeastern University. Page references in brackets are to this Norton Critical Edition.

1. No study has suggested that the feminine is a major theme of *Winesburg, Ohio*. See, however, the analyses of Anderson's characterization of women by William V. Miller, "Earth-Mothers, Succubi, and Other Ectoplasmic Spirits: The Women in Sherwood Anderson's Short Stories" in *Midamerica*, 1 (1974), 64–81, and by Nancy Bunge, "Women as Social Critics in *Sister Carrie*, *Winesburg, Ohio*, and *Main Street*" in *Midamerica*, 3 (1976), 46–55.
2. Sherwood Anderson, *Winesburg, Ohio* (New York: The Viking Press, 1960), p. 170. All quotations are from this edition.

tionships are equal and reciprocal. The neediness, frustration, and failure that encompass the lives of Louise Bentley, Alice Hindman, Elizabeth Willard, and Kate Swift are the result of the discrepancy between their own capacity for intimacy, affection, and creativity and the inability of others, especially the men in their lives, to "see" or to relate to who they really are. In Enoch's painting, as in Anderson's stories, the beauty and suffering of woman become visible only through art that brings to a level of conscious awareness what is unrecognized by conventional society.

It is in his characterization of Louise Bentley that Anderson shows best the suffering of women that results from the devaluation of feminine needs and aspirations. Louise is completely rejected by her father because, as a female, she is an unacceptable heir. She is ignored and unloved as a child, and her vulnerability is heightened by her instinct to value relationships intensely. As a young girl, Louise has a remarkably intelligent and mature vision of what is necessary for human intimacy. She imagines that Winesburg is a place where relationships are natural, spontaneous, and reciprocal: ". . . Men and women must live happily and freely, giving and taking friendship and affection as one takes the feel of a wind on the cheek" (p. 88) [44]. Louise turns to John Hardy in search of a friend who will understand her dream. She seeks from her husband an intimate exchange of feelings and thoughts. Hardy seems kind and patient; however, his vision of Louise's humanity is limited to his own very inadequate concept of "wife":

> All during the first year Louise tried to make her husband understand the vague and intangible hunger that had led to the writing of the note and that was still unsatisfied. Again and again she crept into his arms and tried to talk of it, but always without success. Filled with his own notions of love between men and women, he did not listen but began to kiss her upon the lips. That confused her so that in the end she did not want to be kissed. She did not know what she wanted (p. 96). [49]

To Hardy, Louise is a sexual object whose human voice he suppresses by kisses which are not a mark of affection but an unconscious means of ignoring and belittling his wife's desperate effort to be her deepest self. Louise's complete defeat in the denial of her personhood by her father and her husband is expressed in her rejection of her child: " 'It is a man child and will get what it wants anyway. . . . Had it been a woman child there is nothing in the world I would not have done for it' " (p. 96) [49]. Anderson's point is that in her surrender to marriage Louise surrenders all hope that her gift for friendship and affection will be realized.

Through the story of Alice Hindman, Anderson shows how the conventional sexual morality of Winesburg works against the fulfillment of women's needs.[3] Alice is clearly morally superior to her lover, Ned Currie, and is capable of a much finer quality of relationship than he is. Just as Ned is contemplating inviting her to become his mistress, Alice proposes that she go to the city to live and work with him until they are sufficiently established to marry. Unable to comprehend the spirit of independence and equality Alice envisions, Ned demands that she wait for him in Winesburg, forcing her into a passive dependency which denies her the sustained relationship she needs. Their brief sexual intimacy is so sacred to Alice that she feels bound to Ned in a spiritual marriage even when years of waiting prove he has abandoned her. Despite her economic and legal independence, Alice Hindman is as much imprisoned by marriage as Louise Bentley is, for she has no understanding of Anderson's concept of "the growing modern idea of a woman's owning herself and giving and taking for her own ends in life" (p. 115) [61].

The tragic loss which characterizes the lives of Louise Bentley and Alice Hindman and the accompanying shriveling of their sexuality and their capacity for affection suggest that Anderson regarded the failure to find fulfillment in love as a crucial issue of female identity. The natural, reciprocal relationships which Louise Bentley and Alice Hindman envision are a reasonable expectation; however, Anderson shows that the patriarchal marriages of Winesburg preclude the possibility of achieving the intimacy of equal relationships. When they are not related to as persons, and no emotional or spiritual dimension emerges in the marriage relationship, all possibility for sexual satisfaction is completely lost to the women. The marriages of Louise Bentley and Elizabeth Willard are in no sense real to them except as a legal duty. Furthermore, the social pressure to limit feelings of intimacy to monogamous marriage denies the women of Winesburg any legitimate way of establishing the kind of relationships they need. When women are subordinates, the institution of marriage becomes a social means of controlling their natural instincts for love and self-actualization.

Similarly, conventional sexual morality does nothing to protect women but actually contributes to their destruction. Alice Hindman's strength of character is undermined when her lover uses social conventions as a rationale for abandoning her and when she succumbs to the pressure to regard her spontaneous expression of love as binding. Anderson makes it clear that conventional sexual mores make no provision for woman's need to judge sexual relationships in terms of spiritual communion. There is no social stigma attached to John Hardy or Tom Willard because they do not love their wives even though the deprivation the women suffer makes them mentally and physically ill. Yet, one of the

3. Two of Anderson's earliest stories, "Sister" and "A Vibrant Life," show his interest in characters who need to break away from the repressions imposed by conventional sexual morality, a theme which is more fully developed in *Many Marriages*.

few moments of genuine intimacy in Winesburg, Elizabeth Willard's self-revelation to Dr. Reefy, is tragically cut short by their fear of being caught in an illicit embrace. As Dr. Reefy knows, "love is like a wind," "a divine accident," which cannot be structured or controlled. The deep, intimate communion which the women of Winesburg are seeking can occur only when traditional role expectations and conventional morality are transcended.

Once the theme of the suffering of women is identified, it becomes obvious that an emphasis on the crippled feminine dimension of life permeates *Winesburg, Ohio*. The image of Elizabeth Willard, "tall and gaunt" with her face "marked with smallpox scars" (p. 39) [16], is repeated in the wounded bodies of other overworked and suffering women who hover in the background: Dr. Parcival's mother with her "red, sad-looking eyes" (p. 53) [24]; Joe Welling's mother, "a grey, silent woman with a peculiar ashy complexion" (p. 103) [53]; Tom Foster's grandmother whose worn hands look like "the dried stems of an old creeping vine" (p. 210) [117]. The general abuse of women is captured most vividly in "Paper Pills" when a young girl is so frightened of the lust of her suitor that she dreams "he had bitten into her body and that his jaws were dripping" (pp. 37-38) [15].

Less immediately apparent, perhaps, is the fact that femininity is the crucial issue in the lives of all of the male grotesques. In *Winesburg, Ohio* mature development depends upon the male's ability to accept affection and passion as natural and valuable aspects of life. As the men struggle to expand their personalities to include these tender feelings, they become obsessed by the figure of a woman upon whom their emotions are projected. Tom Foster finds there is more order in his life after he gets drunk and fantasizes a romantic relationship with Helen White. For Seth Richmond, Helen is the key to freedom from his silence and isolation. Through his intense obsession with Kate Swift, the passion Curtis Hartman needs to renew his religious commitment is born. However, because he does not see Kate as a human being but as the female object of his contemplation, his religion, like Jesse Bentley's, is warped by the split between religious symbols and the meaningful realities of human experience. Each male's grotesqueness is indicated by the gap between his intense need of the feminine and his inability to establish relationships with real women. Enoch Robinson is so open to the power of the feminine that he feels his own identity would be "submerged, drowned out" by any intimate relationship with a real woman. Similarly, Wash Williams struggles to keep the feminine at a distance, first through his idealization of his young wife and then through his obsessive hatred of her.

The male grotesques of Winesburg have not developed the hard masculine persona which would make them immune to femininity. Tom Willard, on the other hand, projects his failures onto the ghostly figure of his wife and falsely views himself as "one of the chief men of the town." Willard warns his son against the introspection that makes him look like "a gawky girl" and tries to force on George his own ambitions for materialistic success, which he defines in terms of masculinity: " 'You're not a fool and you're not a woman. You're Tom Willard's son and you'll wake up' " (p. 44) [19]. The male grotesques who acknowledge their tender feelings are especially vulnerable in a culture in which femininity is not respected. The most striking example of the cruel rejection of the feminine in men is the opening story, "Hands." Anderson shows the foolish and tragic injustice of the devaluation of the feminine when he creates the sharp contrast between society's view of Wing Biddlebaum and Wing's potential identity as a priestly mediator who possesses those secret, holy gifts necessary for spiritual communion: love of truth and affection for mankind. Because the qualities of the feminine are regarded as weaknesses, the most precious human experiences—vulnerability, intimacy, and tenderness—are repressed by those who fear their own deepest mysteries.[4] As a result, marriages fail, and family and community life in Winesburg suffers.

Furthermore, Anderson shows that the qualities of the feminine are intricately related to the powers of creativity and spirituality, and, therefore, the devaluation of the feminine means that these dimensions of human life do not develop in Winesburg. Because characters like Wing Biddlebaum, Elizabeth Willard, and Kate Swift are not nurtured or given the freedom to grow psychologically, their spiritual and artistic gifts are not meaningfully realized. To escape the crippling effects of Winesburg life, George Willard must learn to value the creative, spiritual dimensions of the feminine through the women with whom he is intimate, his mother, Kate Swift, and Helen White.

Through the character of Elizabeth Willard, Anderson shows that the urge for creative self-expression is an extension of the basic feminine instinct for intimacy. Restless and energetic, Elizabeth dreams of becoming an actress in a big city. Her fantasy is a symbolic expression of her need to develop the full range of her personality and to achieve the artistic expression that would bring her into intimate communion with the world. Like Louise Bentley and Alice Hindman, Elizabeth's openness to life makes her open to sexual relationships. Her lovers, the traveling men who stay in her father's hotel, are her only means of

4. Jean Baker Miller, in *Toward a New Psychology of Women* (Boston: Beacon Press, 1976), pp. 29–47, argues that the feminine traits which are often regarded as weaknesses are in fact evidence of superior psychological strength. Women develop a mature sensitivity because they embody for males as well as themselves deep psychological experiences which men tend to fear and repress. *Winesburg, Ohio* illustrates Miller's point well as does the short story "The Man Who Became a Woman," in which the narrator matures as a result of his immersion in his unconscious, which he fantasizes as "becoming a woman." The hero's encounter with irrational male violence, his experience of the vulnerability of being a woman, and his confrontation with his own deepest fears develop in him broader human sympathies which enable him to transcend his adolescent mood and to develop a more balanced personality.

touching the larger and more vital life of the cities. When she turns to marriage as the conventional solution to her restlessness, Elizabeth quickly discovers that the "secret something" growing within her is killed by her insensitive husband. Unable to extend the boundaries of her life, Elizabeth creates dramatic roles for herself in an effort to be the person she can only vaguely imagine. In "Mother," when she is determined to protect the creativity of her son from her husband's materialistic ambitions, Elizabeth uses theatrical make-up to transform herself into the powerful woman who can kill the "evil voice" of Tom Willard.

Just as Elizabeth Willard imagines, women can transform themselves through their own creative powers. In fact, Anderson suggests that the creativity of the feminine is such an energized force in these sensitive women that a moment of crisis can release deep feelings that have been suppressed for years. In these "adventures," the bodies of the women are transformed to reveal their hidden power. When Louise Bentley fears her son is lost, all of her capacities for motherly care flow out to embrace him. To David Hardy, the voice of his mother is "like rain falling on trees," and her face becomes "the most peaceful and lovely thing he had ever seen" (p. 77) [38]. In Alice Hindman's "adventure," the rain releases her suppressed spontaneity; the imagery of falling rain and of leaping and running reveals the potential of Alice's sexual passion and creative vitality. Kate Swift's scarred face is transformed when she walks the winter streets of Winesburg: ". . . Her features were as the features of a tiny goddess on a pedestal in a garden in the dim light of a summer evening" (p. 160) [88]. Elizabeth Willard's wild drive into the country, which she describes to Dr. Reefy in "Death," expresses the mounting tension of her desire to transcend the limitations of her life. The black clouds, the green trees, and the falling rain (symbols of the natural, reproductive processes of the earth) represent the vital, spontaneous, and creative life Elizabeth is seeking but cannot quite comprehend.

The language that describes these "adventures" links the moments of feminine self-actualization to the rich beauty of nature and to the spiritual transformation associated with creative inspiration and mystical religion. The "something" which Elizabeth Willard is seeking is a more humane life in which her sexuality, her need for intimacy, her creativity, and her spirituality, can be fully realized, harmonized, and expressed: a life in which the wholeness of her selfhood, might be recognized and appreciated by some other human being.[5] Years later, in her encounter with Dr. Reefy, Elizabeth glimpses momentarily the magni-

5. See Jarvis A. Thurston, "Anderson and *Winesburg*: Mysticism and Craft," *Accent*, 16 (1956), 107–27. Thurston identifies Elizabeth Willard as one of Winesburg's "frustrated spiritual questers" who seek a "greater union beyond the reciprocal love of man and woman" (p. 113). The point, however, is that Elizabeth Willard and the other grotesques are not experiencing "*reciprocal* love" and are, therefore, driven to self-expression in extreme ways. Mystical feelings are intense because they are a sudden intuition of the discrepancy between ordinary reality and the potential for intimate communion in human experience.

tude and significance of the emotions she has experienced. In the excitement of describing her "adventure" to her friend, she transforms herself into the gifted actress who can miraculously "project herself out of the husk" of an old, tired body into the image of "a lovely and innocent girl" (p. 228) [127]. Dr. Reefy is entranced by the beauty and rhythm of Elizabeth's body, the symbolic expression of her hidden capacity to move with life and to express her creative vitality. This moment of communion in "Death" is the experience of liberating, intimate understanding which all of the Winesburg characters are seeking. The intimacy is achieved because Dr. Reefy possesses the sensitivity and wisdom that enable him to see and appreciate the hidden identity of a woman: " 'You dear! You lovely dear! Oh you lovely dear!' " (p. 227) [127]. When the moment is broken by their fear of an intruder, Elizabeth turns to death as the only lover who can receive her full identity.

Elizabeth Willard hopes that her creative drives will be expressed through her son; however, not until her death does George acquire the quality of feeling necessary for the artist. The progress of his development toward that goal is revealed by the nature of his relationships with women. Early in *Winesburg, Ohio* in "Nobody Knows," George takes advantage of the subordinate position of Louise Trunnion, impersonally using her for sexual adventure. Proud, satisfied, and egotistical, George divorces himself completely from any possible affiliation with Louise, for he sees women only as objects to be used to expand his own sense of personal power. In "The Thinker," a story at the midpoint of the collection, George brags that he plans to fall in love with Helen White to get material for a story. Yet, beneath his nonchalance there is the hint of a deeper self in George which gradually emerges through a series of encounters with Kate Swift, Belle Carpenter, his mother, and Helen White.

Kate Swift is eager to share with George her love of art and her understanding of life. However, George understands Kate's earnest seriousness as evidence that she is in love with him, and his mind becomes filled with "lustful thoughts" about her. Thus, in "Teacher," when Kate comes to him ablaze with the intensity of her desire "to open the door of life," his sexual desire kindles her own, and she loses touch with the intellectual, spiritual, and creative potentials of her emotion.[6] At last, however, George begins to perceive that there is something more to be communicated between men and women than physical encounter; he knows that he is missing something important that Kate Swift is trying to tell him.

6. See Chris Browning, "Kate Swift: Sherwood Anderson's Creative Eros," *TSL*, 13 (1968), 141–48. Browning is mistaken to regard Kate's withdrawal from her physical embrace with George as a deliberate choice. Kate is confused by the intense pressure of her own sexual needs, the cause of her grotesqueness, which Browning tends to ignore.

Gradually his boyish superficiality fades, and in "An Awakening" George consciously begins his search for those truths that will give order and meaning to his life. However, the moment the thrill of a new insight comes to him, he is eager to share it with a woman, not in order to enrich a relationship but to have the pleasure of releasing physically his new surge of energy. George's spiritual experience merely heightens his grandiose egocentricity, and he plans to use his new self-confidence to win sexual mastery over a potent and challenging woman. As George walks with Belle Carpenter, unaware that they are pursued by her lover, he becomes "half drunk with the sense of masculine power" (p. 187) [103]. However, when he is duped by the older couple, George's sudden loss of power becomes precisely the reversal of fortunes his character needs.

Although the Winesburg stories are loosely connected and do not generally follow any logical sequence, the stories that show George Willard's growing understanding of the meaning of the feminine do progress sequentially. In the last third of the collection, George's increasing sensitivity to women is extended through his initiation into suffering. In "An Awakening" George is tricked and humiliated; in the following story, " 'Queer,' " he is knocked "half unconscious" by the force of Elmer Cowley's undirected efforts to express himself. In "Drink" George tries to defend Helen White's good name from Tom Foster's drunken fantasies but, instead, becomes deeply moved by the young man's sincere effort to understand and experience suffering. The story is a humorous, indirect, and understated preparation for "Death."

In "Death" George is still egocentric enough to be "half angry" that his mother's death has interrupted his plan to spend the evening with Helen White. However, when he goes alone to stand by her dead body, George is suddenly overwhelmed by a belief that beneath the still, white sheet, his mother has been transformed into a vitally alive and unspeakably lovely woman. Through this strange, mystical experience, George is miraculously able to see the spiritual essence of his mother's womanhood. His vision of the hidden beauty of his mother is reminiscent of the effect created by Enoch Robinson's painting in which the invisible, suffering woman is a transforming power which permeates the landscape of the artist's canvas. It is a moment of spiritual inspiration for George, for an "impulse outside himself" enables him to speak the same words of full appreciation for his mother's identity that Dr. Reefy has spoken: " 'The dear, the dear, oh the lovely dear' " (p. 232) [129].

The sensitivity that comes to George as a result of his mother's death and his vision of her spiritual beauty prepare him for his experience with Helen White in "Sophistication." "Sophistication" is a very slight story, actually a denouement of the two climactic moments in "Death" when Elizabeth Willard's true identity is recognized. However, the story is profoundly meaningful when it is read with an awareness of the thematic significance of Anderson's portrayal of the devaluation of the feminine throughout *Winesburg, Ohio.* At the end of the story Anderson describes the satisfaction Helen White and George Willard have achieved through their relationship:

> For some reason they could not have explained they had both got from their silent evening together the thing needed. Man or boy, woman or girl, they had for a moment taken hold of the thing that makes the mature life of men and women in the modern world possible (p. 243). [136]

The tone and placement of this passage make it clearly a key thematic statement; yet, there is very little clarity in the passage itself or even in the story about exactly what the "thing" is that Helen and George have experienced. The various interpretations of the passage which focus on the theme of communication are accurate enough,[7] but the episode itself as well as Anderson's emphasis on "the mature life of men and women" certainly indicate that the focus of his concern is not just human relationships generally but the special problems of communication between men and women. It is against the background of Anderson's presentation throughout *Winesburg, Ohio* of the suffering of women and their unfulfilled relationships with men that the encounter of these two young people can best be appreciated.

The positive nature of the experience which George and Helen share is a product of their mutual treasuring of those tender, vital feelings that Anderson associates with the feminine. Both are aware of a fragile, new self that is alive in each of them; their silent communion gives these sensitive feelings the nurturing that is needed. Despite their youth and inexperience, they momentarily share a relationship that is trusting and reciprocal, for in George and Helen, Anderson creates characters who are free of sexual role expectations. It is appropriate that Helen and George should recapture the joyful, natural spirit of childhood when males and females meet in relationships that are equal. Their release of emotions in spontaneous playfulness is integrated with their mature, brooding reflection on the transience of life. George's awareness of the reality of death and of his own finitude is his "sophistication," but he has also learned that he needs to share this new knowledge with a woman, for "he believes that a woman will be gentle, that she will understand" (p. 235) [131]. His acceptance of Helen as a spiritual medi-

7. The "thing" Anderson refers to is defined, for example, by Richard Abcarian in "Innocence and Experience in *Winesburg, Ohio,*" *UR,* 35 (1968), 102, as "the innocence and spontaneity of youth"; by Edwin Fussell in "*Winesburg, Ohio:* Art and Isolation," *MFS,* 6 (1960), 47, as respect for "the essential privacy (or integrity) of human personality"; by Donald Rogers in "The Development of the Artist in *Winesburg, Ohio,*" *STC,* 10 (1972), 95, as "the loving touch of another human being" which can "shatter the walls of isolation."

ator indicates that George's masculinity is balanced by the feminine qualities of tenderness and gentleness, an integration that Anderson suggests is necessary for the artist.

The conclusion of "Sophistication" suggests that *Winesburg, Ohio* is intended to be a prophetic statement about the quality of the relationships of men and women in the modern world. That prophetic tone is even more direct in "Tandy," a story that seems to have been created primarily as an invocation of the woman of the future. The drunken man who defines the meaning of Tandy expresses the view of the feminine that pervades *Winesburg, Ohio:*

> "There is a woman coming. . . . Perhaps of all men I alone understand. . . . I know about her struggles and her defeats. It is because of her defeats that she is to me the lovely one. Out of her defeats has been born a new quality in woman. . . . It is the quality of being strong to be loved. . . . Be brave enough to dare to be loved. Be something more than man or woman. Be Tandy" (p. 145). [79]

The suffering of women, Anderson argues, will lead to the evolution of a new kind of woman who will insist that sexual roles be transcended and that she be loved as a human being, an event that Anderson suggests is as much needed by men as it is by women.[8]

There are clearly two different aspects of the portrayal of the feminine in *Winesburg, Ohio*; Anderson reveals the needs of men and women in a society where the feminine is devalued, and he presents a vision of the feminine as a source of creative inspiration. Anderson's concern for the fulfillment of women as whole persons was, no doubt, inspired in part by the silent, resigned suffering of his own mother, to whom *Winesburg, Ohio* is dedicated. Her stoic endurance, which dominates the opening sections of *A Story Teller's Story,* led Anderson to view women as spiritually superior to men.[9] However, Anderson did not simply idealize woman but recognized in her a maturity that made her a superior human being: "One does so hate to admit that the average woman is kinder, finer, more quick of sympathy and on the whole so much more first class than the average man." [1] Whatever difficulties Anderson had in embracing his own weakness or acknowledging the strength of

8. Donald Rogers' definition of "Tandyism" neglects the central point of Anderson's story, for he makes no reference at all to the story's comment on woman or man's relationship to the feminine.
9. Imagining women gossiping while his mother was giving birth to him, Anderson says: "If the men had to have the babies there would never be more than one child in a family. What do men know about suffering? It's the women who have to do all the suffering in life, I always said—I said a woman feels everything deeper than a man—don't you think so? A woman has intuition, that's what it is." Sherwood Anderson, *A Story Teller's Story* (New York: Scribner's, 1922), p. 105.
1. *A Story Teller's Story*, p. 216.

women,[2] few other modern male writers have been able to convey with such loving sensitivity the hurt women bear or to advocate as openly as Anderson does that the relationships of men and women should be equal. Anderson certainly recognized that those qualities associated with the feminine—vulnerability, tenderness, and the need for intimacy—should be valued and nurtured by society rather than repressed. *Winesburg, Ohio* is one of those "thoughtful books" which Anderson argues must be written if sensitive women are to survive.

In Enoch Robinson's painting the suffering woman brings beauty and unity to the work of art. The theme of the feminine as the source of creative inspiration, which is captured in this image and developed through the growth process of George Willard, is reinforced by Anderson's description of the creative process in "The Book of the Grotesque." The persona of the narrator of *Winesburg, Ohio* is an old writer who compares himself to a pregnant woman. The new life growing within him, however, is not a baby but "a woman, young, and wearing a coat of mail like a knight" (p. 22) [5]. The "young indescribable thing" within the old man inspires the parade of grotesques that becomes the subject of his writing. This creative, feminine power also inspires a youthful vitality which keeps him open to change and prevents his embracing only one truth and becoming a grotesque himself. This image of artistic power as a woman within a woman indicates that Anderson viewed the instinct for growth and creativity in human life as a feminine quality.

Throughout *Winesburg, Ohio* Anderson associates the feminine with a quality of feeling that is delicate and intangible; it is a tender nuance, a transient moment of intimacy, a creative, secret something growing within the self, a slight quiver of insight that seems to hold great promise. Anderson's mode of presentation of the feminine is as appropriate as the invisibility of the woman in Enoch Robinson's painting, for *Winesburg, Ohio* presents a microcosm of the modern world in which the potential of the feminine has not yet been realized.

2. The occasion of Anderson's comment on the superiority of women is an episode in *A Story Teller's Story* when his friend Nora becomes aware of the insecurity beneath his braggadocio. The rest of the quotation is evidence of both Anderson's limits as a male who wants to maintain his superior power and his gift for admitting rather than rationalizing his weakness: "It is a fact perhaps but a fact that I have always thought men should deny with all the strength of our more powerful wills. We men should conquer women. We should not stand in the darkness with our heads on their shoulders, blubbering as I was doing at that moment" (p. 216). Anderson goes on to say, "I was not ready for the Noras. Perhaps I would never be ready for them. Few American men I have ever known have ever shown any signs of being ready for the Noras of the world or of being able really to face them" (p. 217).

JOHN UPDIKE

Twisted Apples†

Sherwood Anderson's *Winesburg, Ohio* is one of those books so well known by title that we imagine we know what is inside it: a sketch of the population, seen more or less in cross section, of a small Midwestern town. It is this as much as Edvard Munch's paintings are portraits of the Norwegian middle class around the turn of the century. The important thing, for Anderson and Munch, is not the costumes and the furniture or even the bodies but the howl they conceal—the psychic pressure and warp underneath the social scene. Matter-of-fact though it sounds, *Winesburg, Ohio* is feverish, phantasmal, dreamlike. Anderson had accurately called this collection of loosely linked short stories *The Book of the Grotesque*; his publisher, B. W. Huebsch, suggested the more appealing title. The book was published in 1919, when Anderson was forty-three; it made his fame and remains his masterpiece.

"The Book of the Grotesque" is the name also of the opening story, which Anderson wrote first and which serves as a prologue. A writer, "an old man with a white mustache . . . who was past sixty," has a dream in which "all the men and women the writer had ever known had become grotesques."

> The grotesques were not all horrible. Some were amusing, some almost beautiful, and one, a woman all drawn out of shape, hurt the old man by her grotesqueness. When she passed he made a noise like a small dog whimpering.

Another writer, an "I" who is presumably Sherwood Anderson, breaks in and explains the old writer's theory of grotesqueness:

> . . . in the beginning when the world was young there were a great many thoughts but no such thing as a truth. Man made the truths himself and each truth was a composite of a great many vague thoughts. . . . It was the truths that made the people grotesques. The old man had quite an elaborate theory concerning the matter. It was his notion that the moment one of the people took one of the truths to himself, called it his truth, and tried to live his life by it, he became a grotesque and the truth he embraced became a falsehood.

Having so strangely doubled authorial personae, Anderson then offers twenty-one tales, one of them in four parts, all "concerning," as the table of contents specifies, one or another citizen of Winesburg; whether

† From *Harper's* 268 (March 1984): 95–97. Reproduced from the March 1984 issue by special permission.

they come from the old writer's book of grotesques or some different set to which the younger author had access is as unclear as their fit within the cranky and fey anthropological-metaphysical framework set forth with such ungainly solemnity.

"Hands," the first tale, "concerning Wing Biddlebaum," introduces not only its hero, a pathetic, shy old man on the edge of town whose hyperactive little white hands had once strayed to the bodies of too many schoolboys in the Pennsylvania town where he had been a teacher, but also George Willard, the eighteen-year-old son of the local hotelkeeper and a reporter for the *Winesburg Eagle*. He seems a young representative of the author. There is also a "poet," suddenly invoked in flighty passages like:

> Let us look briefly into the story of the hands. Perhaps our talking of them will arouse the poet who will tell the hidden wonder story of the influence for which the hands were but fluttering pennants of promise.

A cloud of authorial effort, then, attends the citizens of Winesburg, each of whom walks otherwise isolated toward some inexpressible denouement of private revelation. Inexpressiveness, indeed, is what is above all expressed: the characters, often, talk only to George Willard, and then only once; their attempts to talk with one another tend to culminate in a comedy of tongue-tied silence.

Anderson himself took a long time to express what was in *Winesburg, Ohio*. Raised in the small Ohio town of Clyde, he worked successfully as a Chicago advertising man and an Elyria, Ohio, paint manufacturer, and acquired a wife and three children, but remained restless and, somehow, overwrought. In late 1912, in the kind of spasmodic sleepwalking gesture of protest that overtakes several of the pent-up and unfulfilled souls of Winesburg, he walked away from his paint factory. He was found four days later in Cleveland, suffering from exhaustion and aphasia, and, more gradually than his self-dramatizing memoirs admit, he shifted his life to Chicago and to the literary movement that included Dreiser, Sandburg, Ben Hecht, and Floyd Dell. Already Anderson had produced several long novels, but he later wrote, "They were not really mine." The first Winesburg stories, composed in 1915 as he lived alone in a rooming house in Chicago, were a breakthrough for him, prompted by his reading, earlier that year, of Edgar Lee Masters's *Spoon River Anthology* and Gertrude Stein's *Three Lives*.[1] Masters's poetic inventory of a small Midwestern community stands in clear paternal relation to Anderson's rendering of his memories of Clyde; but perhaps Stein's elevation of humble lives into a curious dignity, along with her remarkably relaxed and idiomatic style, was the more nurturing influence in releas-

1. A collection of short stories about three women (1909). *Spoon River Anthology*: see p. 161, n. 1, above [*Editors*].

ing Anderson into material that he *did* feel was really his and that gave him for the first time, as he later related, the conviction that he was "a real writer."

Both godparents of *Winesburg, Ohio* had a firmness and realism that was not part of Anderson's genius. Masters was a practicing lawyer, and his free-verse epitaphs state each case in almost legal prose; many have the form of arraignments, and a number of criminal incidents are fleshed out as each ghost gives its crisp testimony. Stein, before her confident and impudent mind went slack in its verbal enjoyments, showed an enlivening appetite for the particulars of how things are said and thought, a calm lack of either condescension or squeamishness in her social view, and a superb feel for the nuances of relationships, primarily but not only among women. For Anderson, society scarcely exists in its legal and affective bonds, and dialogue is generally the painful imposition of one monologue upon another. At the climax of the unconsummated love affair between George Willard and Helen White that is one of *Winesburg*'s continuous threads, the two sit together in the deserted fairground grandstand and hold hands:

> In that high place in the darkness the two oddly sensitive human atoms held each other tightly and waited. In the mind of each was the same thought. "I have come to this lonely place and here is this other," was the substance of the thing felt.

They embrace, but then mutual embarrassment overtakes them and like children they race and tumble on the way down to town and part, having "for a moment taken hold of the thing that makes the mature life of men and women in the modern world possible."

The vagueness of "the thing" is chronic, and only the stumbling, shrugging, willful style that Anderson made of Stein's serene run-on tropes affords him half a purchase on his unutterable subject, the "thing" troubling the heart of his characters. Dr. Reefy, who attends and in a sense loves George Willard's dying mother, compulsively writes thoughts on bits of paper. He then crumples them into little balls—"paper pills"—and shoves them into his pocket only to eventually throw them away. "One by one the mind of Dr. Reefy had made the thoughts. Out of many of them he formed a truth that arose gigantic in his mind. The truth clouded the world. It became terrible and then faded away and the little thoughts began again." What the gigantic thought was, we are not told.

Another questing medical man, Dr. Parcival, relates long tales that at times seem to George Willard "a pack of lies" and at others to contain "the very essence of truth." As Thornton Wilder's *Our Town* [2] reminded us, small-town people think a lot about the universe (as opposed to city

2. A play about life in Grover's Corners, New Hampshire, first presented in 1938 [*Editors*].

people, who think about one another). The agonizing philosophical search is inherited from religion; in the four-part story "Godliness," the author, speaking as a print-saturated modern man, says of the world fifty years before: "Men labored too hard and were too tired to read. In them was no desire for words printed upon paper. As they worked in the fields, vague, half-formed thoughts took possession of them. They believed in God and in God's power to control their lives. . . . The figure of God was big in the hearts of men." The rural landscape of the Midwest becomes easily confused in the minds of its pious denizens with that of the Bible, where God manifested himself with signs and spoken words. Jesse Bentley's attempt to emulate Abraham's offered sacrifice of Isaac so terrifies his grandson David that the boy flees the Winesburg region forever. Anderson writes about religious obsession with cold sympathy, as something that truly enters into lives and twists them. To this spiritual hunger sex adds its own; the Reverend Curtis Hartman breaks a small hole in the stained-glass window of his bell-tower study in order to spy on a woman in a house across the street as she lies on her bed and smokes and reads. "He did not want to kiss the shoulders and the throat of Kate Swift and had not allowed his mind to dwell on such thoughts. He did not know what he wanted. 'I am God's child and he must save me from myself,' he cried." One evening he sees her come naked into her room and weep and then pray; with his fist he smashes the window so all of it, with its broken bit of a peephole, will have to be repaired.

There are more naked women in *Winesburg* than one might think. "Adventure" shows Alice Hindman, a twenty-seven-year-old spinster jilted by a lover a decade before, so agitated by "her desire to have something beautiful come into her rather narrow life" that she runs naked into the rain one night and actually accosts a man—a befuddled old deaf man who goes on his way. In the following story, "Respectability," a fanatic and repulsive misogynist, Wash Williams, recalls to George Willard how, many years before, his mother-in-law, hoping to reconcile him with his unfaithful young wife, presented her naked to him in her (Dayton, Ohio) parlor. George Willard, his chaste relation to Helen White aside, suffers no lack of sexual invitation in Winesburg's alleys and surrounding fields. Sherwood Anderson's women are as full of "vague hungers and secret unnamable desires" as his men. The sexual quest and the philosophical quest blend: of George Willard's mother, the most tenderly drawn woman of all, the author says, "Always there was something she sought blindly, passionately, some hidden wonder in life. . . . In all the babble of words that fell from the lips of the men with whom she adventured she was trying to find what would be for her the true word." *Winesburg, Ohio* is dedicated to the memory of Anderson's own mother, "whose keen observations on the life about her first awoke in me the hunger to see beneath the surface of lives."

The author's hunger to see and express is entwined with the common hunger for love and reassurance and gives the book its awkward power and its limiting strangeness. The many characters of *Winesburg*, rather than standing forth as individuals, seem, with their repeating tics and uniform loneliness, aspects of one enveloping personality, an eccentric bundle of stalled impulses and frozen grievances. There is nowhere a citizen who, like Thomas Rhodes of Spoon River, exults in his material triumphs and impenitent rascality, nor any humbler type, like "real black, tall, well built, stupid, childlike, good looking" Rose Johnson of Stein's fictional Bridgepoint, who is happily at home in her skin. Do the Winesburgs of America lack such earthly successes; does the provincial orchard hold only, in Anderson's vivid phrase, "twisted apples"? No, and yet Yes, must be the answer; for the uncanny truth of Anderson's sad and surreal picture must awaken recognition within anyone who, like this reviewer, was born in a small town before highwavs and development filled all the fields and television imposed upon every home a degraded sophistication. The Protestant villages of America, going back to Hawthorne's Salem,[3] leave a spectral impression in literature: vague longing and monotonous, inbred satisfactions are their essence; there is something perilous and maddening in the accommodations such communities extend to human aspiration and appetite. As neighbors watch, and murmur, lives visibly wrap themselves around a missed opportunity, a thwarted passion. The longing may be simply the longing to get out. The healthy, rounded apples, Anderson tells us, are "put in barrels and shipped to the cities where they will be eaten in apartments that are filled with books, magazines, furniture, and people." George Willard gets out in the end, and as soon as Winesburg falls away from the train windows "his life there had become but a background on which to paint the dreams of his manhood."

The small town is generally seen, by the adult writer arrived at his city, as the site of youthful paralysis and dreaming. Certainly Anderson, as Malcolm Cowley has pointed out,[4] wrote in a dreaming way, scrambling the time and logic of events as he hastened toward his epiphanies of helpless awakening, when the citizens of Winesburg break their tongue-tied trance and become momentarily alive to one another. Gertrude Stein's style, so revolutionary and liberating, has the haughtiness and humor of the *faux-naïve* [5]; there is much genuine naïveté in Anderson, which in even his masterwork flirts with absurdity and which elsewhere weakens his work decisively. *Winesburg, Ohio* describes the human condition only insofar as unfulfillment and restlessness—a nagging sense that real life is elsewhere—are intrinsically part of it. Yet the

3. Nathaniel Hawthorne's birthplace, in Massachusetts, and the setting for such works of his as "Young Goodman Brown" (1835) and *The House of the Seven Gables* (1851) [*Editors*].
4. See Cowley's introduction to *Winesburg, Ohio* (New York: Penguin, 1992) 4 [*Editors*].
5. Falsely naive [*Editors*].

wide-eyed eagerness with which Anderson pursued the mystery of the meager lives of Winesburg opened Michigan to Hemingway, and Mississippi to Faulkner; a way had been shown to a new directness and a freedom from contrivance. Though *Winesburg* accumulates external facts—streets, stores, town personalities—as it gropes along, its burden is a spiritual essence, a certain tart sweet taste to life as it passes in America's lonely lamplit homes. A nagging beauty lives amid this tame desolation; Anderson's parade of yearning wraiths constitutes in sum a democratic plea for the failed, the neglected, and the stuck. "On the trees are only a few gnarled apples that the pickers have rejected. . . . One nibbles at them and they are delicious. Into a little round place at the side of the apple has been gathered all of its sweetness." Describing a horse-and-buggy world bygone even in 1919, *Winesburg, Ohio* imparts this penetrating taste—the wine hidden in its title—as freshly today as yesterday.

JOSEPH DEWEY

No God in the Sky and No God in Myself: "Godliness" and Anderson's *Winesburg*†

Of all the wraiths in Winesburg, none seems lonelier than Jesse Bentley. Alone of Anderson's characters, he seems unable to elicit even the sympathy of his creator. Whereas Anderson delicately balances sympathetic amusement with a most profound admiration for his other grotesques, he seems callously unambivalent toward Jesse. In the raging egocentricity of the Ohio landowner who refashions himself into some Old Testament patriarch while shamelessly indulging gross materialism, Anderson seems to express his generation's bitter condemnation of the new age "love of surfaces," the new "religion of getting on" ("To Waldo Frank"). To insert this lengthy lampoon of the Puritan work ethic, Anderson seems to set aside awkwardly not only his artist-hero, George Willard, but also his novel's melancholic ambience, the sense of irresistible yearning for communion that so twists the spirits of his other characters. Examined casually, Jesse does not seem to fit with them. Where they are retiring, he is assertive; where they seem frozen and static, he is a dynamo; where they are lost in self-pity, he crows of his many accomplishments; where they bottle themselves up into tiny chambers, he sees with a vision that encompasses hundreds of acres; where they nurse quiet anxieties to escape Winesburg, he thrusts his roots deeply; where they

† *Modern Fiction Studies* 35 (Summer 1989): 251–59. Reprinted by permission of The Johns Hopkins University Press. Page references in brackets are to this Norton Critical Edition.

seem confused and plagued by doubts, he subscribes to a clear, teleological order; where they seem curiously infertile, he begats with Biblical intensity. Indeed, it would seem appropriate that Jesse lives far outside the corporation limits of Winesburg, a suggestion of how removed he is from Anderson's other grotesques.

Yet Anderson takes Jesse far more seriously than he would some throwaway caricature of feverish pietism. Indeed, the tales of Jesse Bentley are by far the longest in the book. In the description of the impulses that drive Jesse, Anderson points out that Jesse is driven half by greediness and half by fear. To understand Jesse's appropriateness, the reader must explore the complexity of these fears rather than the simplicity of the greed. Refusing the harsh caricature of Puritanism that figures in the work of Anderson's contemporaries, among them Dreiser and Lewis, Anderson offers a sensitive reading of the original Puritan vision that accounts not only for the intensity of Jesse Bentley's campaign to tame the Ohio wilderness but also for his place in the ongoing story of the evolution of George Willard.[1]

I

To understand Jesse Bentley, Anderson cautions early, "we will have to go back to an earlier day" (*Winesburg* 64) [30]. Jesse Bentley reflects Anderson's fascination with the New England consciousness [2]; in journals and letters Anderson assessed the Puritan legacy, joining other early century writers who, uneasy over the loneliness implicit in the human condition unrelieved even by speculation about a possible union with some divinity, reviewed the fervor of the original Puritans and their dream of seeking the transfiguration possible in a union with God.[3]

What those Puritans sought (and what Jesse seeks two hundred years later) was confirmation of the self through communion with some greater whole, an awesome union between creation and creator,

1. Although evidence in Anderson's letters and in his memoirs indicates that the story of Jesse Bentley figured prominently in the creation of the tales, critical reactions to the story have ranged from Irving Howe's early dismissal of it to John A. McAleer's sympathetic defense but apparent inability to "fit" the Bentley story into the scheme of George Willard. Ralph Ciancio suggests that of all the characters Jesse does not seem able to elicit Anderson's sympathy. Rosemary Laughlin's brief explication helps readers understand the story but does not make a place for the tale in Anderson's larger work. Of recent criticism, John O'Neill best treats the subject although he suggests only a unity of tone rather than specific thematic ties between Jesse and the rest of the work. He does make a persuasive argument for the relationship between David and George but does not make any such claims for ties between Jesse and George. Indeed, O'Neill dismisses Jesse's hunger for his God as "fundamentally adolescent" (78).
2. Both Anthony Hilfer and Norman Pearson look at the ties between Anderson and Puritanism. They suggest that Anderson reacted particularly to the writings of Waldo Frank (*Our America*) and of Van Wyck Brooks (*The Wine of the Puritans*), works that treated the influence of the Puritans in harsh, negative terms.
3. Sacvan Bercovicz analyzes the Puritan notions of the self in the American literary tradition. D. Sebastian's unpublished dissertation presents a summary of the Puritan influence at the time of Anderson, a survey that includes Adams, Robinson, Dreiser, London, Crane, Masters, and Lewis.

between the timebound and impotent and the fixed and omnipotent. Yet because the only dignity opened to man was such a restoration of his maimed soul with a divinity that felt no obligation to indicate its attention, the Puritan heritage often reflects anxious lives spent searching for ways to connect with an all-too-distant God, to fight the holy struggle with doubt, despair, and self-insufficiency that often eclipsed the remarkably successful struggle to coax a community from the Massachusetts wastes.

This spiritual hunger felt by Puritans struck Anderson deeply. Although he emphatically rejected the commercial misappropriation of Puritanism and its corruption into the Victorian "virtues" of sexual repression, dry intellectuality, and material acquisition, he did find use for Puritanism in its expressive hunger for communion, a hunger that so many of his Winesburg characters feel. "To the young man a kind of worship of some power outside himself is essential. One has strength and enthusiasm and wants gods to worship" (*A Story Teller's Story* 164).[4] The question that Jesse poses in the novel is one as old as Plymouth Plantation and as immediate as Winesburg itself with its deathly quiet streets: can the imperfect finite earn the infinite, feel the surety of that outside power? In the tradition of Puritan mysticism, Jesse seeks to be blasted by an excess of light. His raging prayers up and down the Wine Creek Valley capture the desperate (and thoroughly) Puritan condition of man never being at home in however splendid a world he finds or builds on earth. Jesse's neat cluster of houses gives ironic testimony to his homelessness; at heart he feels himself an outcast in a Puritan postlapsarian landscape. In an age of exploding capitalism, Jesse resists heroically the purely material. Although tempted by the success of his unending campaign to create a farm non pareil, he finds nevertheless his possessions ultimately unfulfilling. His farm is critical only as a devotion to God. Absurdly he asserts his role as God's chosen; fearfully in the fury of this assertion, he raises traditional questions of Puritan self-insufficiency but to a universe fearfully silent or, worse, fearsomely empty.

The story of Jesse Bentley, then, is not a parable against relentless acquisition or a lampoon of fanatical faith. It is the story of hunger. Jesse's dilemma is not that he is soulless but that his soul is lean and starved. Any satisfaction he may seem to take in his accumulation of land is undercut by this growing desperation for God to assent to its

4. In the letter to Waldo Frank, Anderson writes, "a curious notion came over me. Is it not likely that when the country was new and men were often alone in the fields and forests they got a sense of bigness outside themselves that has now been lost? I don't mean the conventional religious thing . . . the people, I fancy, had a savagery superior to our own. Mystery whispered in the grass." In *A Story Teller's Story* Anderson records a moment of his own experience when such a tie to Otherness was destroyed, leaving him in a paralysis that recalls Jesse: "There was no God in the sky, no God in myself, no conviction in myself that I had the power to believe in God, and so I merely knelt in the dust in the silence and no words came to my lips" (270).

importance. He can dredge a farm from the swamps, drive farmhands relentlessly, work his wife to an early death, even fashion about his own head an unsteady halo—yet without that recognition, without that communion, he is denied peace. As the Puritans discovered, Jesse finds his God incomprehensible, ominously quiet even at times of greatest need. If, as Perry Miller has suggested, the central drama of the Puritan experiment was the relationship between man and his God, it was often a heartcrushingly one-sided communication.

Yet such silence seems profoundly more disturbing for Jesse. In a time when God was big in the hearts of His creation, the Puritans communed with merely a silent God; Jesse communes with an absent God. As Anderson makes clear, Jesse, driven to call on the very God he fears, uses a shofar in the age of the telephone. He is left with the agony of separation. Anderson counsels, nevertheless, a way to resist the implicit threat of being left, as Jesse is, living in a simple material world, a way, in short, to lose God but to keep the faith. When the finite, awash in temporality, find no hope of the sweet union with the infinite promised by religion, Anderson counteroffers a communion by way of art, the articulation of a sympathetic union not of man to God, maimed soul to distant perfection, but rather of man to man or, more exactly, maimed soul to maimed soul. Lovingly, George Willard, gradually educated into this power of communion, will come to gather the fragments of Winesburg's shattered souls and will give compassionate expression to that agony. In such a humane gesture there is a wondrous sort of religion, a healing of souls that offers the bittersweet consolation of human communion to relieve the aching burden of an alienation as wide as the modern cosmos itself.[5] Winesburg, then, must have its failed prophet to underscore the religious dimension of George Willard's commitment to art. In the movement from prophet to artist, in Biblical terms from king to poet, Anderson charts the course in which the art replaced religion. In *A Story Teller's Story* Anderson reveals an emerging artist desperately searching for the security and stability offered by religion. The alternative, a fragmented multiverse or a nothingness too bleak to accept, reduced Anderson to the sort of paralysis that afflicts Jesse by the close of his story. In a novel where any movement has validity, Jesse is a character moving but in all the wrong directions. When Jesse searches the hillsides all about him for validation, George learns to look no further than the nearest human heart; when Jesse looks for peace outside himself, George will learn to look inside; when Jesse looks up in frantic desperation, George will come to look about in gentle compassion.

5. One of the most complete examinations of Anderson's theories of the relationship between religion and art is found in D. Sebastian who makes the points that for Anderson the beauty of art came from humanistic rather than aesthetic impulses and that the finest expression possible for the artist was sympathy.

II

Early on, Jesse Bentley determines that he will not be just another "clod" like those all around him. Such a determination echoes Elizabeth Willard's hopes for her son. "He is not a dull clod, all words and smartness" (*Winesburg* 43) [18]. But the development from Jesse to George is a movement from ego to self. Although Jesse inherits the sense of a driving self-assertion that is so much a part of the American tradition, when his religion fails him so completely, he becomes simply an ego, a forcible will with an unbending purpose. The considerable energy of his self-assertion merely inflates his own character, and therefore he cannot bridge the way toward communion with his God. He is left in the sham resplendence of empty grandeur, alone—as Anderson points out, Jesse is the inventor of a machine that turns wire into fences. In the dazzling spectacle of the Old Testament prophet, Jesse loses the humility necessary not only for the traditional religious experience he seeks but also, as Anderson demonstrates, for an artistic one as well, the sort that George establishes as a man with Helen and as an artist later with the Winesburg citizenry. Jesse's unsympathetic disdain establishes his religion as a self-enclosing impulse, unable to furnish the communion he so desperately seeks. In the relationship with George suggested by Mrs. Willard's hope for her son, Anderson juxtaposes the urgency of Jesse's ego that diminishes the more it asserts itself with the intensity of George Willard's self that expands the more it is asserted.

When Jesse absurdly invokes notions of Puritan typology, he fancies himself the fulfillment of the Old Testament patriarchs, the encroaching neighbors as legions of Philistines, his offspring as potential Davids. He finds not only identity but community as well. When he confronts his bewildered and terrified grandson at the mock-sacrifice, Jesse tries desperately to discover a sympathetic soul who would do what the empty Ohio sky will not—validate what has become for Jesse a mission as burning as the Puritans' mission to erect a City on a Hill. Because Anderson keeps the figure of God so carefully absent, Jesse's entire project threatens to collapse into the absurdity of one man's fanaticism. But clearly Jesse wants to be possessed not so much by God as by significance. He yearns for a sign that what he has created in his hard hunger has validity. His lengthy tale is the difficult story of the insufficiency of what is simply material, coming hard on the story of George Willard's furtive initiation into the mystery of sex with his uninspired coupling with Louise Trunnion. George will find his way finally to the sophisticated touch of Helen White's hand. That Jesse wrings purpose from a religion no longer available drives him more inward than Anderson can allow. Jesse comes to feel the insuperable sense of his farm being simply that. As George moves to tap the tremendous potential of the quotidian, Jesse despairs over it, finally bankrupt. When his God does not touch his fulsome soul, it shrivels into a thin ego. The more he pursues religion, the more he is doomed. He destroys any links with humanity, turns hard eyes away from his wife, his daughter, his grandson, and ends a man alone, far from even the community of Winesburg. Jesse's spirit haunts Anderson's book of spirits. Anderson uses notions of Jesse's farm as a beehive not to suggest that, compared with the other villagers, Jesse is expansive and bustling but to suggest furious kinesis without purpose, relentlessly spent without spiritual invigoration. Ironically, Jesse's soul is finally inert—it cannot expand to the outermost sympathies there to discover the self. In his grandson, he longs to affirm his covenant with his God, his bridge between the finite and the infinite. In the spontaneous prayer session in the woods and later, more dramatically, in the aborted sacrifice of the lamb, Jesse attempts to assert his union. Unable to face the chaos implicit in a godless world, Jesse ends up lost. Anderson hints at Jesse's failings, afflicts him with approaching paralysis and a nervous twitch that marks him in moments of fervent religiosity. Jesse fails to make the transition away from the spent powers of religion toward the potential of art, but the reader can examine what Jesse does accomplish. In the Old Testament tradition that he values, Jesse begats offspring. In the stories of Jesse's daughter and his grandson, tales interwoven with Jesse's, Anderson provides the vital links between Jesse's pathetic deterioration and George Willard's grand maturation.

III

Louise Bentley, Anderson notes, inherited her father's gray eyes. In many disturbing ways, she sees the world much as her father. She longs to be recognized, to be reassured by communion, to be noticed, her significance confirmed. Like her father, she is not happy with the simpler achievements. In her hunger for education, she ransacks the Hardy family library with a spiritual urgency that leads her to feel, like her father, a radical isolation. In her fanaticism, she is abandoned at school and more cruelly by the Hardy daughters, threatened by Louise's obvious achievements. Like her father, the more isolated she feels, the more she ranges about for communion. Unlike her father, she does not look up but rather around her but not gently or lovingly as George Willard will—rather, she looks about like some ravenous animal scouring the landscape for sustenance. She settles on John Hardy for whom she has a vague distaste. When she thinks that the secrets of life are to be possessed, she says quietly to herself what her father says in a rage at the blank skies over the Winesburg countryside. Like her father, she calls "notice me" to a largely indifferent cosmos. Indeed, there are no neater or sadder parallels to Jesse's fist-waving philippics than his daughter's wild carriage ride through the night streets of Winesburg (streets, of course, that are empty) or her setting fire (harmlessly) to the Hardy house, or, finally, her marriage to John Hardy. They are messages unreceived.

Unloved and unloving, Louise is a difficult middle stage between the failing religion of her father and the emerging artistic sense of her son. Of the triptych that Anderson fashions, she fits most closely the profile of Winesburg's citizens. What Jesse seeks in God and what David shows promise of seeking in the imagination, Louise seeks in the sexual act. It is precious tender spent wastefully, like Jesse's heartfelt prayers lost in the distances between stars. Louise finds such simple vitality pitilessly stymied. She marries in desperation, fearing pregnancy; she never connects with her son. Like her father with his fence-making machine, she ends up bitter and walled-in, locked for days in her room. Her story of doorless walls grimly rearing themselves about her soul is the stuff of Anderson's grotesques. Even in her surrender, however, Louise links Jesse to David and by extension to George. In Anderson, the sexual communion is analogous to the act of writing[6]; they are both the spontaneous show of sympathetic sensibility that links souls profoundly. When Louise searches for sexual healing and settles for bloodless coupling with John Hardy, she offers the reader another example of failed communion. Naturally, the title of her story is "Surrender." But she surrenders more than her self, more than her sexuality. She surrenders her son to the care of her father, and in doing so, she initiates the events that will give to Winesburg its first refugee-artist.

Although David Hardy is hardly a conscious artist in the manner of the writer George Willard, he does, nevertheless, in his two stumbling flights from Winesburg foreshadow George's resolution that finally allows him to step beyond Winesburg's city limits. When Jesse's dementia at the mock-sacrifice finally breaks David's "shell of the circumstances of his life" (97) [50], what emerges is at least the embryonic artist, one armed for manhood with both sensitivity and imagination, a concept that shares much with Anderson's notions of the artistic consciousness. From this root Jesse springs forth Anderson's neoredeemer—the prototype artist.

David has brown eyes, a suggestive detail that separates him from the failed version of his mother and his grandfather. Where they are demonstrative and forceful, he is introspective, given to talking to himself. Where Jesse betrays his faith and Louise betrays the sexual impulse, David finds his way to the imagination. As Jesse prepares the lamb for sacrifice, David uses his imagination to invest every action with significance. As Jesse and Louise move into closets of their own fashioning, David, transplanted to the farmhouse, opens up to sounds and sights,

6. The often explicit and somewhat obsessive tie Anderson found between sexual communion and the writing act is summed up in Sebastian, although Benjamin T. Spenser and Maxwell Geismar trace the fascination to parts of Anderson's *Midwestern Chants*.

delighting in the outdoors. Gentle, expansive, imaginative, open—David prefigures Anderson's artist. Like the many citizens of Winesburg who confide in George, Jesse, on a carriage ride about the farm, is struck impulsively to trust the boy to understand the importance of his mission. Clearly, David Hardy, who ponders at odd moments what his life will offer him, is poised on a threshold.

After David strikes out at his grandfather, rejecting outright Jesse's religious enthusiasm, he flees impulsively not only the farm but Winesburg as well. His closing words lend special significance to ties he has with George Willard. "I have killed the man of God and now I will myself be a man and go into the world" (102) [53]. David prefigures George's growth from innocence to experience. He feels strong sympathy for the lamb Jesse chooses for sacrifice and blanches as Jesse approaches with the knife. Far from the "vague and intangible hunger" (96) [49] that finally reduces his mother to bitter surrender, David's terror sparks him to action, although frenzied and unplanned. He forsakes religion, forsakes family, to embrace hesitatingly and fearfully nothing less than the world itself.

David then suggests the function of the lengthy parable of Jesse Bentley. Anderson "slays" the religiosity of Jesse and prepares for the conversion of such destructive energy into the calmer drive of George Willard. David's journey from Winesburg begins, as it must, in fiction. He has only knocked down Jesse; he has not killed him at all. Yet the Jesse he leaves behind is a strangely quieter man. His reaction to his grandson's departure denies Jesse the anagnorisis that would confer on him the dignity of tragedy. Although he does admit he was too greedy, he adds that God has taken his boy. Jesse will not abandon his ego; still he lays claim to a potent God who would speak to him directly if only to admonish him so severely.

IV

It is fitting that a writer so convinced of the religious appointment of the artist in a world reeling from the loss of its God should center his novel on a religious zealot only figuratively slain. Like displaced Puritans, both Jesse and George, finally twin sons of different mothers, seek the reassuring communion with a potent Otherness to rescue them from the legions of the poignant but pathetic, the "clods" of Winesburg. In the passage from Jesse to George, Anderson preserves the sense of religion to define the essence of the artist in the new wasteland in which the springs of religion have dried. The progression from Jesse to David via Louise's failure is a progression from failed religion to art via the thwarting of the sexual communion; it is the triangular relationship that recalls the relationship of the Reverend Hartman, Kate Swift, and George himself. Reverend Hartman, bursting into George's office convinced that the vision of Kate Swift's naked shoulders is a sign from God, recalls Jesse's displaced energy and absurdity in trying to divine the eternal in his farmland. The reader knows that Kate will teach George the basic commandments of Anderson's humane art. Like Louise, she is frustrated sexually, despite her advances to George. She will help nurture the artist-hero by warning George to cease his word-playing and to delve into his humanity.

Finally, to deal with Jesse Bentley solely in terms of acquisition is to deal only with surfaces. His essence connects him with the village ghosts of Winesburg. In Jesse's one-way conversation with the divine, Anderson reenforces the general sense of failed communication chronic in his village. Alone in a cast of inarticulates, however, Jesse can articulate his fears of the atomistic age dawning in America, his ache to be sublime in a cosmos that denies sublimity. More than David, Jesse feels the terror of the closing tale. He tries to pull his grandson into his great arching vision of typological grandeur that could assure him that his life was not splendidly unnecessary. When he is silenced, the book reaches its nadir, a point that only George Willard's gradual ascent can salvage. That he is condemned to search for a God long laid to rest damns him to ineffectuality and prepares the reader for George's eventual assertion of the power of invention rather than invective.

Whereas Jesse prays for God's touch and Louise craves the warming touch of sexual possession, David stumbles toward the new fictive deity. David is, finally, hardier than his family. It is surely no accident that Anderson chooses Jesse as the name for his modern Puritan. Typologically, Jesse corresponds to the Old Testament patriarch, the prosperous sheep-farmer who gives to Israel his son David, the maker of songs, the harper-king. When Jesse confesses that God has taken his boy, he inadvertently suggests what has indeed taken place. But what has taken David is not Jesse's raging omnipotent figure but rather the new god that Anderson offers for the seemingly hopeless disorder of the early century—the god of art. When so much seemed blasted away into a moral wasteland, writers such as Anderson recognized a similar dilemma in the soul-shaking loneliness felt by that generation of Puritans who faced the merciless physical wasteland on a thin strip of land between ocean and wilds. The comfort that those Puritans found in their religion Anderson fuses into his faith in a compassionate art.

To understand the mystery and interiority of George Willard's conversion from hack journalist to artist, one must go by way of Jesse Bentley. George reshapes that feverish frenetic search for spiritual communion to produce his knowing sophistication. For readers who have long puzzled over where George Willard is in the lengthy dissertation on Jesse Bentley, his farm, and his family, the answer can only be suggested. George is present in the rage of Jesse's eyes turned upward toward vacancy; he is in the desperation of Louise's spread fingers grasping the edges of private walls; and, finally, he is in the stumbling resolution of David Hardy's churning feet as he disappears out of the Wine Creek Valley.

WORKS CITED

Anderson, Sherwood. *A Story Teller's Story*. Garden City: Garden City Publishing, 1924.
———. "To Waldo Frank." 27 August 1917. Letter 22. *Letters of Sherwood Anderson*. Eds. Howard Mumford Jones and Walter B. Rideout. Boston: Little, 1953. 23.
———. *Winesburg, Ohio*. 1919. New York: Viking, 1969.
Bercovicz, Sacvan. *The Puritan Origins of the Self*. New Haven: Yale UP, 1975.
Ciancio, Ralph. "The Sweetness of Twisted Apples: The Unity of Vision in *Winesburg, Ohio*." *PMLA* 87 (1972): 994–1006.
Geismar, Maxwell. *The Last of the Provincials: The American Novel from 1915–1925*. Boston: Houghton, 1947. 223–286.
Hilfer, Anthony. *The Revolt from the Village*. Chapel Hill: U of North Carolina P, 1969.
Howe, Irving. *Sherwood Anderson*. New York: Sloane, 1951.
Laughlin, Rosemary. " 'Godliness' and the American Dream in *Winesburg, Ohio*." *Twentieth Century Literature* 13 (1967): 97–103.
McAleer, John A. "Christ Symbolism in *Winesburg, Ohio*." *Discourse* 4 (1961): 168–181.
Miller, Perry. *The New England Mind*. New York: Macmillan, 1939.
O'Neill, John. "Anderson Writ Large: 'Godliness' in *Winesburg, Ohio*." *Twentieth Century Literature* 23 (1977): 67–83.
Pearson, Norman Holmes. "Anderson and the New Puritanism." *Newberry Library Bulletin* 2 (1948): 52–63.
Sebastian, D. "Sherwood Anderson's Theory of Art." Diss. Louisiana State U, 1972.
Spenser, Benjamin T. "Sherwood Anderson: American Mythopoeist." *American Literature* 41 (1969): 1–18.

KIM TOWNSEND

[The Achievement of *Winesburg*] †

* * *

Anderson had written several pages he called "The Book of the Grotesque" [in 1915] just before he wrote "Hands." He thought the piece might provide the title for his collection, but in the event it serves only to introduce the collection very well. The word *grotesque* was in the air. He might have come across it reading Poe, who had titled his satirical stories "Tales of the Grotesque and Arabesque." More immediately, Arthur Davison Ficke had published ten short poems in that first March issue of the *Little Review*, "Ten Grotesques," in which a woman who listened to poetry all night, a disturbed gentleman, the devilish author himself, and others spoke their piece. In November, at Chicago's Little Theatre, Lloyd Head produced *Grotesque: A Decoration in Black and White*, a free-verse play in which marionettes were used to explore levels

† From *Sherwood Anderson* (Boston: Houghton Mifflin, 1987) 110–17. Reprinted by permission of the author. The original form of documentation has been revised for this Norton Critical Edition.

of consciousness.[1] Edgar Lee Masters's *Spoon River Anthology* had been published in April, and in the fall one of the "little children," a musician named Max Wald, lent Anderson his copy, and Anderson stayed up all night reading it. By the next morning, if not before, the idea of bringing together figures who had led buried lives and allowing them their say had certainly crystallized.

Anderson was clear on what made *his* figures "grotesque." "In the beginning when the world was young," he wrote, "there were a great many thoughts but no such thing as a truth." Out of those thoughts, man made his truths, "the truth of virginity and the truth of passion, the truth of wealth and of poverty, of thrift and of profligacy, of carelessness and abandon," and they were all beautiful. But when anyone took one of these truths, took one of them to himself, "called it his truth, and tried to live his life by it, he became a grotesque and the truth he embraced became a falsehood."

In this formulation Anderson placed himself in the tradition of Emerson and Whitman, urging his fellow men to look past the standards, the goals, society seemed to set for them, to recreate themselves in their own language, or to refuse to acknowledge language's limitations altogether—to surpass themselves. "Our friends early appear to us as representations of certain ideas which they never pass or exceed," Emerson had written in "Experience." Before long, we know what they stand for, and what they stand for never changes. By contrast, he proclaimed, "Everything good is on the highway."

It is true of all men and women, for example, that they are drawn, in greatly varying degrees, to members of their own sex. They become grotesque when they or others take attraction to be the truth about them. Wing Biddlebaum is not ugly, but misshapen, without and within, misinformed, his form wrongly taken (and taken in) from those who label him "homosexual." Don't take others' words for anything, he tells George; dream, imagine endlessly for yourself.

At thirty-nine, Sherwood Anderson was still young, practically newborn if we apply the rule he was happy to borrow from Joseph Conrad, "who said that the writer only lived after he began writing."[2] The only truth he clung to was that he was a writer, and that freed him further, for it meant that he could take any form. In "The Book of the Grotesque," he introduces himself as an old man, lying in a bed just like Anderson's, one that has been raised to the level of his window. He is a man who imagines he might die suddenly, unexpectedly, but who takes pleasure in the thought because he has been saved by something young

1. See James Schevill, *Sherwood Anderson: His Life and Work* (Denver: U of Denver P, 1951) 102. See also Marilyn Judith Atlas, "Experimentation in the Chicago Little Theatre: Cloyd Head's *Grotesques*," *Midwestern Miscellany* 7 (1980): 7–19, and Kay Kinsella Rout, "Arthur Davison Ficke's 'Ten Grotesques,' " ibid., 20–27.
2. *Letters of Sherwood Anderson*, eds. Howard Mumford Jones and Walter B. Rideout (Boston: Little, Brown, 1953) 115.

inside himself, not a baby but a youth, not a youth either, but "a woman, young, and wearing a coat of mail like a knight." Not Joan of Arc. The point is not to name: "It is absurd, you see, to try to tell what was inside the old writer as he lay on his high bed and listened to the fluttering of his heart. The thing to get at is what the writer, or the young thing within the writer, was thinking about." One must be true to the variousness of life, to the "long procession of figures" that went before the writer's eyes, "all the men and women the writer had ever known." Anderson was himself both the old writer who was the more alive for contemplating his death and for having the valiant woman/knight within him, and the young reporter who would go on dreaming and someday be a writer. He was the man who might have been "grotesque" at almost forty but for the fact that he had listened to his own advice and had stayed young. He was the man who at midlife found himself just born, come of age, because he was writing well.

Winesburg, Ohio is best known as a book about a small Ohio town during the years just before the coming of industry. It is a town almost entirely without religious or political associations. The minister never meets his congregation; most of his story takes place in a bell tower where he fights the temptations of the flesh that he can see next door through a hole in a stained glass window. George Willard's father is a Democrat whose political hopes vanished when the town went Republican, his one swipe at the "friendship" of McKinley and Hanna being all the talk of politics we hear. There are a few unhappy marriages, entered into as a relief from or atonements for the confusion created by lust, and soon regretted; the relations between parents and children are tenuous at best. The people of Winesburg are almost completely isolated one from another. They talk to no one. If their passions and dreams are not dead, they make one last, startling, pathetic appearance, usually before George Willard. They tell him what has been on their minds and never before expressed. Thus the tales.

After years of waiting for a lover who has no thought of returning, after trying "the devices common to lonely people"—whispered prayers to her lover, attachment to the very furniture of her room, watching the interest in her savings book mount up—one rainy night Alice Hindman runs through the streets of Winesburg without any clothes on, calling out to and for a passer-by, who turns out to be old and deaf. It is the last expression of her loneliness, her last resort, her "Adventure" (as the title has it). Coming to her senses, she crawls through the grass to her home, bolts the door of her room, and begins to try to make herself face the fact (Anderson says, wryly) "that many people must live and die alone, even in Winesburg." Wash Williams foams with misogynistic rage against the wife who betrayed him and the mother-in-law who tried to win him back by having her daughter appear before him naked. "I didn't get the mother killed," Wash tells George. "I struck her once with a chair and then the neighbors came in and took it away. She screamed so loud you see. I won't ever have the chance to kill her now. She died of a fever a month after that happened." One winter night, "The Teacher," Kate Swift, comes to the print shop of the *Eagle*, where George is working late. Thinking she'd seen a spark of genius in the boy, the summer before she had come to counsel him on how to be a writer. This night passion also urges her on, passion for a man, and a passionate desire that this young man know life—and he responds, only to feel her body stiffen, and her "two sharp little fists . . . beat on his face," before she runs away.

At the time, of course, because it insisted on portraying how men and women express their loneliness sexually, or rather, how futile such expression was, *Winesburg, Ohio* was considered unfit for some library shelves. Subsequently, it has been placed among those books debunking small-town life, somewhere between E. W. Howe's *The Story of a Country Town* or Masters's *Spoon River Anthology* and Sinclair Lewis's *Main Street*. But it lives as Anderson's vision—midway through the second decade of the twentieth century, midway through the First World War—of what was happening to the promise of American life. "These studies," he wrote in November 1916, "will suggest the real environment out of which present-day American youth is coming." [3] It had come out of towns like Clyde and emerged, in the present, in cities like Chicago, "a city of the dead," as he described it the same month to a friend, a city given over to the pursuit of money and status. "In the office dead voices discuss dead ideas," he said, as if he were trying to sound like William Blake in London. "I go into the street and long rows of dead faces march past." [4] It was also a city, a culture, trying to drum up enthusiasm for the Allied cause in the Great War—which, after his brief experience of war, made the prospect of the future all the more disheartening for Anderson. While other famous writers-to-be rushed to the Italian front or signed up to drive ambulances, Anderson thought that what was required was "a leader now for America who will have the courage to ask the people to pray and be sad." [5]

By November, having written half of the Winesburg tales, Anderson saw that his own salvation lay in the fancies that he could express, in the "thousand beautiful children [yet] unborn." He imagined that his mission was to keep alive what he called "the very blood and spirit of all this aimlessness" in himself and in the kind of people that he wrote about. There was still "vastness of possibility," he concluded. If nowhere else, one could see it in the land, and "if we can love *that* we can love America. There is only vastness of possibility." [6] His subject was the

3. Ibid., 5.
4. *Letters to Bab: Sherwood Anderson to Marietta D. Finley*, ed. William A. Sutton (Urbana: U of Illinois P, 1985) 15.
5. Ibid., 61.
6. Ibid., 16.

common people of America, his task to give them their voice. "A democratic plea," John Updike has called *Winesburg, Ohio*, "for the failed, the neglected, and the stuck." [7]

There were some in Winesburg who were still alive. There was Doctor Reefy of "Paper Pills," who jotted down thoughts on bits of paper, rolled them up into little balls, and eventually threw them away—"Little pyramids of truth he erected and after erecting knocked them down again that he might have the truths to erect other pyramids." So committed was Anderson himself to this figure of open-mindedness that twelve or thirteen years later, he offered a four-paragraph version of Doctor Reefy as his contribution to *The Bookman*'s series on "Statements of Belief: The 'Credos' of America's Leading Authors." [8] There was Ray Pearson of "The Untold Lie," who, when asked by a young co-worker what to do about the girl he had gotten pregnant, thought of how he himself might have gone to sea or worked out West rather than get married. But he says nothing, knowing that whatever he advised would be a lie, knowing better than to impose his imaginings on another. And there is George Willard himself, lending continuity to the whole, as one "grotesque" after another opens up to him, and as he himself develops into manhood, learning what it takes to be a writer and a lover.

As was true of some of the men at Taylor-Critchfield,[9] George aspires to writing *lasting* prose; as was true of Anderson, his ambition distinguishes him in Winesburg. George is not above fatuousness on that score, telling Seth Richmond it was "the easiest of all lives"; nor is he above the kind of behavior Anderson had paraded before Hecht, planning to fall in love with Helen White and then having Seth tell her in order to "see how she takes it." But he comes to appreciate his teacher's resonant advice: "You must not become a mere peddler of words," Kate Swift had said. "The thing to learn is to know what people are thinking about, not what they say." George is ready to fulfill his mother's dream that he not be "a dull clod, all words and smartness," like his father. At the end of the book, his mother dead, George Willard, age eighteen, boards the train for Chicago. So it had been. Twenty years after Anderson had done the same thing, he dedicated *Winesburg, Ohio* to the memory of his mother. He had done what George Willard had set out to do; he had justified his mother's faith.

Not a novel, not just a collection of stories, *Winesburg, Ohio is* precisely what Anderson called it in a subtitle that many editions omit: "A Group of Tales of Ohio Small Town Life." Though he fell prey to the notion that the final test of literary manhood was the ability to write novels, he was not comfortable in what he said was, by contrast to the tale, "the more compact novel form." "A man keeps thinking of his own

7. John Updike, "Twisted Apples," *Harper's* 268 (March 1984): 97 [see p. 194, above—*Editors*].
8. "Statements of Belief," *The Bookman* 68 (October 1928): 204.
9. The advertising agency in Chicago for which Anderson worked [*Editors*].

life," he said. "But life itself is a loose, flowing thing. There are no plot stories in life." [1] Those who wrapped it up in novels or "short stories" betrayed life. Those, like Dell, who later insisted that a story be "sharply definite," that it must have "a beginning and an end," could not appreciate his effort "to develop, to the top of my bent, my own capacity to feel, see, taste, smell, hear." He wanted, he said, "to be a free man, proud of my own manhood, always more and more aware of earth, people, streets, houses, towns, cities. I wanted to take all into myself, digest what I could." [2]

The sentiments were part Conrad ("My task," he had written in the preface to *The Nigger of the Narcissus*, "is to make you hear, to make you feel—it is, before all, to make you *see!*"), part Whitman ("All this I swallow, it tastes good," he said at the end of one of the longest of his famous catalogues. "I like it well, it becomes mine"). But the idea of collecting the tales and organizing them around a central figure was Anderson's. It was the right form for him, and it was *his* form, his invention, he liked to claim. Though he later read Joyce, he never bothered to compare his own form with the organization of Joyce's *Dubliners*, nor need he have, for the epiphanic moments in Joyce's text do not, and were never intended to, bring a collective people to life. If Anderson knew of what is a closer parallel, Sarah Orne Jewett's *Country of the Pointed Firs*,[3] he never said so. The one precedent he did acknowledge and turn to again and again for encouragement in later years was Ivan Turgenev's *Sportsman's Sketches*, a book of twenty-five pieces that quietly honors rather than makes stories out of the lives of common people. But the sportsman's life does not evolve and so give shape to his sketches. Pressed, Anderson would insist on the uniqueness of his own accomplishment—justifiably. "I can accept no standard I have ever seen as to form," he wrote in 1921; [4] and then in 1938, thinking back on *Winesburg, Ohio* in an effort to regain his writing stride, he added, "It is a form in which I feel at ease. I invented it. It was mine." [5]

Collecting the tales the way he did, he maintained contact with an all but vanished form of social life. It was his way, Antaeus-like, of reestablishing his base, regaining his strength, after too many years of trying to be a financial and social success. Anderson was not writing short stories, "nice little packages, wrapped and labeled in the O. Henry manner," he later said, not writing about or for "the rich and well to do." He was staying "at home, among my own people, people in my own street." [6] He was speaking as one of them, implicitly encouraging them

1. Quoted in Schevill, 96.
2. *Letters of Sherwood Anderson*, eds. Jones and Rideout, 404.
3. A cycle of stories set along the coast of Maine, first published in 1896 [*Editors*].
4. Ibid., 72.
5. Quoted in William Sutton, *The Road to Winesburg* (Metuchen, N.J.: Scarecrow Press, 1972) 434.
6. *Letters of Sherwood Anderson*, eds. Jones and Rideout, 403.

to share one another's lives. After "Tales of Ohio Small Town Life" came other subtitles: "Tales, Long and Short, from American Life" (*Horses and Men*), "A Book of Impressions from American Life in Tales and Poems" (*The Triumph of the Egg*), and "The Tale of an American Writer's Journey" (*A Story Teller's Story*). These were often about life in the Midwest and usually did not succeed as well as *Winesburg, Ohio*, but each one was an attempt to hear and render the voices of "common" people, people who were not usually welcomed into the community of literary figures, people who often had no community themselves.

Winesburg, Ohio, then, is the book in which Anderson came into his own as a writer, the book in which he found his subject and his style, the one inextricably bound up with the other, and it is about that achievement. It is about what he found it took to be a writer. It is the book in which Anderson begins to come to terms with his protean character as a man. What's more, from 1915 on, after "Hands," he considered himself a man insofar as he was satisfied with himself as a writer. More or less explicitly, he had been writing *about* himself from the start, ever since his first contributions to *Agricultural Advertising*. Now his very style would be the measure of himself as a man.

More crudely, "the theme of the book," as he later put it, "the thing that really makes it a book—curiously holding together from story to story as it does," is: "the making of a man out of the actual stuff of life." While planning to convert *Winesburg, Ohio* into a play, he described Seth Richmond as a young man who wanted to make money, "be a big man," and George Willard as a dreamer, wanting to become a writer "because almost everything in his own life goes wrong and he has a vague feeling that in some novel or story . . . he may be able to build up an ordered fine life." It was to be George's life from then on, sometimes a life of which he would be ashamed, the dreamer, Anderson said, being capable of more brutality than the likes of plodding Seth, but a life, on balance, "of decent manhood." [7]

Insofar as the women of Winesburg tend to be sexual dynamos or predators, the men imagine that in order to be men they must subdue and conquer them. Thus, in "Nobody Knows" George convinces himself that he is "wholly male, bold and aggressive," in order to cope with Louise Trunnion; in "An Awakening," he sets out after Belle Carpenter, "half drunk with the sense of masculine power." Anderson never wholly freed himself from the idea that women possessed power over life and death, that they were mysterious, natural forces to be subdued. Nor was he ever fully sure that he was man enough to do it. But at the same time, he was clear about the limits of such thinking. In "Nobody

7. *Sherwood Anderson: Selected Letters*, ed. Charles E. Modlin (Knoxville: U of Tennessee P, 1984) 153–54.

Knows" George wins only a pathetic victory; in "An Awakening" he is summarily defeated, thrust aside by the man Belle really loves. And by the end of the book, George ceases to think like a stereotypical male.

With his mother's death, George "crosses the line into manhood." For the first time, in "Sophistication," he takes "the backward view of life," and he wants to share his understanding with Helen White. For her part, tired of a world "full of meaningless people saying words" (her college instructor is visiting the Whites), she rushes out into the night to meet George. The setting of their meeting—the fairground the night after the annual fair, the fall night cooler and longer, the town almost all closed up for the evening—is frozen in relief:

> In Winesburg the crowded day had run itself out into the long night of the late fall. Farm horses jogged away along lonely country roads pulling their portion of weary people. Clerks began to bring samples of goods in off the sidewalks and lock the doors of stores. In the Opera House a crowd had gathered to see a show and further down Main Street the fiddlers, their instruments tuned, sweated and worked to keep the feet of youth flying over a dance floor.

Together, they do not profess their love, nor is George put to any test: "He wanted to love and be loved by her, but he did not want at the moment to be confused by her womanhood." They kiss—"but that impulse did not last." When they draw apart, it is as if after another kind of conception: "Mutual respect grew big in them." Finally, from such maturity, *in* such maturity, they descend into youth:

> It was so they went down the hill. In the darkness they played like two splendid young things in a young world. Once, running swiftly forward, Helen tripped George and he fell. He squirmed and shouted. Shaking with laughter he rolled down the hill. Helen ran after him.

"For some reason they could not have explained," Anderson says, "they had both got from their silent evening together the thing needed." Maintaining his ability to dream, but no longer brutish, retrieving the innocence of his youth, George enters manhood, ready to go on and become a writer. Appropriately, one of the last strains one hears in the voice of the writer who imagined the making of such a man is that of "Jack and Jill."

DAVID STOUCK

Anderson's Expressionist Art†

In the introductory sketch in *Winesburg, Ohio* the narrator tries to describe what is inside an old writer as he lies on his high bed. Is it a baby, a youth, a young woman wearing a coat of mail like a knight? He cannot say (p. 22) [5]. In the first story, "Hands," the narrator is again reflecting on what is concealed from sight: "Let us look briefly into the story of the hands. Perhaps our talking of them will arouse the poet who will tell the hidden wonder story" (p. 31) [11]. And in the following piece, "Paper Pills," we are told that "Winesburg had forgotten the old man, but in Doctor Reefy there were the seeds of something very fine" (p. 35) [14]. Each passage makes reference to human potential that has not yet been uncovered and released.

In the third story, "Mother," we are introduced to Elizabeth Willard, a woman who is withdrawn and silent, especially in her relation to her husband. But with her son George, a young newspaper reporter, she has established a deep bond of sympathy that centers on her desire that he do something with his life that will justify her unhappy existence. She prays to God, saying she will take any blow he might inflict "if but this my boy be allowed to express something for us both" (p. 40) [17]. She prays, in effect, to be released through her son from her lonely isolation. Elizabeth Willard's prayer is important because it describes the motive behind the Winesburg stories: the artist's desire "to express something" for his characters, to break down barriers and release them from their frustration and loneliness. Equally important is the phrasing of the mother's prayer, "to express something for us both," because it suggests the formal approach Anderson took to his writing, an approach best described by the term "expressionism."

In essays and letters, Anderson stated repeatedly that the goal of his writing was to bring to the surface the hidden depths of thought and feeling in the characters he created, characters representing ordinary humanity in the America of his time. In a particularly vivid statement of these intentions, he wrote to his publisher, Ben Huebsch, that "there is within every human being a deep well of thinking over which a heavy iron lid is kept clamped." The artist's task was to tear that lid away so that "a kind of release takes place" that "cuts sharply across all the machinery of the life about him."[1] His method was to write stories that

† From *New Essays on "Winesburg, Ohio,"* ed. John W. Crowley (Cambridge: Cambridge UP, 1990) 27–51. Reprinted by permission of Cambridge University Press. Page references in brackets are to this Norton Critical Editon.

1. *Sherwood Anderson: Selected Letters*, ed. Charles E. Modlin (Knoxville: University of Tennessee Press, 1984), p. 32.

were almost plotless in the conventional sense, stories that focused instead on an intense moment of feeling. He said in *The "Writer's Book"* that a "short story is the result of a sudden passionate interest," [2] and to Huebsch he wrote that it often would come "all at one sitting, a distillation, an outbreak." [3] That quality of a sudden insight, a revelation, an "outbreak" is what is most indelible in the Winesburg fictions—a repressed woman running naked out onto the lawn in the rain, a minister waving a bloodied fist in the air after breaking the window in the church study. The Winesburg stories accumulate power from those exaggerated, stylized gestures by which a character is revealed or through which a scream of suffering is made to be heard. "Expressionism" is the formal term especially suitable to describing Anderson's art, because in common with the dramatists and painters in that period, Anderson made it his goal to give outward expression to the intense private feelings of both the artist and the characters he created.

1

The link between Anderson and painting is important; he often described himself as a painter using the medium of words. He saw both painter and writer trying, above all else, to express human emotions. Anderson enjoyed a lifelong association with a number of painters. His older brother, Karl, with whom he was always closely associated, made his living as a portrait painter in New York; Karl was involved in bringing a portion of the famous Armory Show [4] to Chicago's Art Institute in 1913. His second wife, Tennessee Mitchell, worked as a sculptor, and Anderson himself turned to the canvas on several occasions to express the essence of what he was experiencing. But probably more important for his writing was his friendship with Alfred Stieglitz, the photographer and art enthusiast, whose gallery "291" introduced Anderson to the best experimental painting being done in America at that time. Anderson was taken to the gallery by Paul Rosenfeld as early as 1917 (he was then writing the later Winesburg stories and had come East to meet the editor of the *Seven Arts* who was publishing them).[5] At the gallery he saw works by Marsden Hartley, John Marin, Arthur Dove, and Georgia O'Keeffe. Through Stieglitz he came to know these artists personally and commented in letters and notebooks on their work. In *A Story*

2. *The "Writer's Book" by Sherwood Anderson: A Critical Edition*, ed. Martha Mulroy Curry (Metuchen, N.J.: Scarecrow Press, 1975), p. 85.
3. Quoted by Martha Mulroy Curry in "Anderson's Theories on Writing Fiction," in *Sherwood Anderson: Dimensions of His Literary Art*, ed. David D. Anderson (East Lansing: Michigan State University Press, 1976), p. 94.
4. A controversial exhibition of modern European art, which had opened earlier in the year at a National Guard armory in New York [*Editors*].
5. Kim Townsend, *Sherwood Anderson* (Boston: Houghton Mifflin, 1987), p. 200.

Teller's Story he states that seeing the work of these modern painters "had given me a new feeling for form and color."[6]

What these painters revealed to Anderson was that representational accuracy conveyed only life's surfaces, that an artist, whether painter or writer, had to alter the perception of surface reality so that "the hidden inner truth" of the subject would emerge. In "A Note on Realism," he refers to Marin's Brooklyn Bridge paintings as examples of art being very different from reality.[7] Marin's paintings of the bridge are not photographic, but transcribe through expressionistic distortions and tiltings the hidden dynamic forces the painter felt present in all things, even man-made engineering structures. Anderson admitted a special preference for the nature paintings of Arthur Dove: "Perhaps at bottom I'm like Dove, a country man. The warm earth feeling gets me hardest." [8] Typically, Dove's paintings render the rural environment, including its flora and fauna, in a stylized way. His country landscapes are not suggestive of a visionary mystery or symbolism, but present nature as vibrantly alive, physically immanent. In his collection of critical essays titled *Port of New York*, which includes an essay on Anderson, Paul Rosenfeld writes of Dove's work in a way that describes Anderson's often stated intentions: Dove's painting of grazing cows "brings the knowledge of someone who has almost gotten into the kine themselves; and felt from within the rich animality of their being . . . and then given it out again in characteristic abstraction." [9]

Through Stieglitz, Anderson also came to know the work of Gertrude Stein. Anderson's first exposure to Stein is presumed to have been the August 1912 copy of Stieglitz's *Camera Work*, which contained Stein's experimental pieces "Henri Matisse" and "Pablo Picasso." [1] It is in the correspondence between Stein and Anderson and in his published writings about her that Anderson most fully discusses his writing in terms of painting. Although the friendship with Stein began after the publication of *Winesburg, Ohio*, his writing about her contains summary opinions held since first reading her work. In *A Story Teller's Story*, dedicated to Stieglitz, he describes his excitement when first reading her purely experimental prose; it reminded him of when he had once been taken into a painter's studio to be shown the painter's colors. In Stein's writing, words were separated from sense: "Here were words laid before me as the painter had laid the color pans on the table in my presence." It struck him then that "words used by the tale teller were as the colors

6. Sherwood Anderson, *A Story Teller's Story: A Critical Text*, ed. Ray Lewis White (Cleveland: Case Western Reserve University Press, 1968), p. 272.
7. *Sherwood Anderson's Notebook* (New York: Boni & Liveright, 1926), p. 72.
8. *Letters of Sherwood Anderson*, ed. Howard Mumford Jones and Walter B. Rideout (Boston: Little, Brown, 1953), p. 247.
9. Paul Rosenfeld, *Port of New York: Essays on Fourteen American Moderns* (New York: Harcourt, Brace, 1924), pp. 171–2.
1. *Sherwood Anderson/Gertrude Stein: Correspondence and Personal Essays*, ed. Ray Lewis White (Chapel Hill: University of North Carolina Press, 1972), p. 7.

used by the painter." [2] In a later piece about Stein, defending her against the charge of automatic writing, he observes that "word is laid against word as carefully and always instinctively as any painter would lay one color against another." [3] In her review of *A Story Teller's Story*, she pays her admirer a compliment by saying that his book does not reflect, describe, embroider, or photograph life, but expresses it "and to express life takes essential intelligence." [4] And after *Sherwood Anderson's Notebook* was published in 1926, with its chapter on the young William Faulkner, she wrote to him suggesting that he should someday "write a novel that is just one portrait," [5] comparing his writing to the work of a painter.

Anderson was complimented indeed by Stein's review of his work, because when she said that he had succeeded in expressing life rather than merely describing it, she was including him with the modern artists whom he so much admired. The verb Stein chose was increasingly being used to describe the artistic goal of the avant-garde. The term "expressionism," however loosely applied, indicated the artist's rejection of a surface realism and the attempt instead to make mainfest the hidden essence of things. It was an attempt, in Freudian terms, to reveal the secret inner life. "What Expressionist art seeks to render visible," writes Ulrich Weisstein, "are soul states and the violent emotions welling up from the innermost recesses of the subconscious." [6] The things that are caught on canvas or on the page are the extreme moods, such as fear, despair, or ecstasy, but it is especially the soul in anguish that the expressionist desires to project—Edvard Munch's painting, *The Scream* being a classic example. Anderson, in a letter to Marietta D. Finley,[7] describes himself working on the Winesburg stories with the same goal: "My mind is tumbling about and trying to fit itself in a mood of sustained work. That will come. You must of course know that the things you want, the warm close thing, is the cry going up out of all hearts." [8]

Critics have acknowledged that the term "realism" does not accurately describe Anderson's writing. Walter B. Rideout has written that "what Anderson is after is less a representation of 'reality' than, to [draw] a metaphor from art, an abstraction of it." He goes on to point out that in Anderson's stories, "what is important is 'to see beneath the surface of lives,' to perceive the intricate mesh of impulses, desires, drives growing down in the dark, unrevealed parts of the personality." [9] Similarly,

2. Anderson, *A Story Teller's Story*, pp. 261–3.
3. White, ed., *Anderson/Stein: Correspondence*, p. 82.
4. Ibid., p. 45.
5. Ibid., p. 56.
6. Ulrich Weisstein, ed., *Expressionism as an International Literary Phenomenon* (Paris: Didier, 1973), p. 23.
7. A long-time friend and correspondent of Anderson's, who lived in Indianapolis [*Editors*].
8. *Letters to Bab: Sherwood Anderson to Marietta D. Finley, 1916–33*, ed. William A. Sutton (Urbana: University of Illinois Press, 1985), p. 85.
9. See Walter B. Rideout, "The Simplicity of *Winesburg, Ohio*," in *Critical Essays on Sherwood Anderson*, ed. David D. Anderson (Boston: G. K. Hall, 1981), p. 148.

Irving Howe observes that "Anderson is not trying to represent . . . the immediate surface of human experience; he is rather drawing the abstract and deliberately distorted paradigm of an extreme situation." [1] Expressionist art cannot, strictly speaking, be designated abstract, because it remains referential, content-oriented, but it does reject the methods of verisimilitude in favor of more stylized techniques—distortions (in both art and literature) of color, shape, syntax, vocabulary, oversimplification of form, exaggeration. The grotesque is often the result of these distortions. Anderson's art in *Winesburg, Ohio* is a particularly striking example of expressionism in literature, where the narrative yields repeatedly to a violent projection outward of "soul states" or, as Howe phrases it, "conditions of psychic deformity." [2]

Short stories are especially congenial to expressionist art, because plot (cause and effect) is pared down to its simplest form. Action in expressionist fiction is always secondary to the transmission of an inner feeling or vision of the world. For example, in *Three Lives*, Stein was concerned to "express" what she referred to as the ground nature of her characters, the essence of the personality, and was not very interested in what happened to them in their daily lives except as it manifested something of the inner life. Similarly, O'Neill's expressionist plays, such as *The Hairy Ape* and *The Emperor Jones*, [3] consist of a few characters and a series of short scenes that dramatize vividly his vision of human nature and society's ills. In longer dramatic narratives, action becomes more important, and fully rounded characters acquire more psychological particularity, which works against the purpose of expressionist art.

But expressionism is more than a style; it is a *Weltanschauung*. [4] Historically it was a reaction in the early twentieth century against the increasing mechanization of society. The impact of the Industrial Revolution in Western civilization was permeating all aspects of living, from the nature of one's work to the forms of one's recreation. In the American Midwest, Sherwood Anderson witnessed the transition of the small town from a rural economy to a factory-based economy. The loss he most lamented was the craftsman's relation to the world, a loss he viewed as both material and aesthetic:

> with the coming into general use of machinery men did lose the grip of what is perhaps the most truly important of man's functions in life . . . the right . . . to stand alone in the presence of his tools and his materials and with those tools and materials to attempt to twist, to bend, to form something that will be expression of his inner hunger for the truth that is his own and that is beauty. [5]

1. See Irving Howe, *Sherwood Anderson* (New York: William Sloane 1951), p. 99.
2. Ibid.
3. Eugene O'Neill's *The Hairy Ape* was first performed in 1922 and *The Emperor Jones* in 1920 [*Editors*].
4. Philosophy of life [*Editors*].
5. *Sherwood Anderson's Notebook*, pp. 153–4.

Anderson had participated in America's industrial "progress" as both an advertising man and a man with his own business. Accordingly, he knew firsthand how individuals are affected by work on an assembly line, how human relations change in a mechanized and commercial world. He told the story of "progress" in the four-part tale "Godliness" in *Winesburg, Ohio* and in *Poor White*, the novel that followed the tales. In both stories the protagonists become slaves of the machinery they use to acquire wealth; they become frustrated and life-destroying figures. Anderson describes men turning to their machines, especially big cars, to compensate for a kind of physical impotence felt when a man no longer works with his hands, no longer expresses himself by crafting things.

To counter humankind's impotence in the age of the machine, the expressionists turned to the cult of primitivism, celebrating generally, as the Fauvists did specifically, the wild beast in man. It was also an acknowledgment of Freud, who was laying bare the phantasms repressed in the depths of the human psyche. For Anderson, the cult of the primitive was a way of rebelling against the repressive work ethic of Puritanism, the specific legacy of American history. In *A Story Teller's Story*, he describes the artist as "a man with a passion" who "wants to dream of color, to lay hold of form, free the sensual in himself, live more freely and fully in his contact with the materials before him than he can possibly live in life." [6] In *Winesburg, Ohio,* this emerges in the descriptions of men who retain something of the child in their characters (figures such as Enoch Robinson), and in *Dark Laughter* (1925) it emerges in the celebration of the American Negro and African-American culture. Releasing "the hidden passion of people" [7] was Anderson's artistic goal as he created the characters in *Winesburg, Ohio*. At the same time, to make visible the inner passionate life was the program central to the expressionist movement in the arts.

2

In a letter to a Russian translator in 1923, Anderson said that the first two novels he published were written under the influence of his reading rather than from his own reactions to life. [8] Looking at *Windy McPherson's Son* (1916) and *Marching Men* (1917), one thinks indeed of realists like Howells and Dreiser, writers committed to recording the changes taking place in society from a journalistic, and in Dreiser's case pseudoscientific, perspective. It was with the Winesburg stories that he felt he "had really begun to write out of the repressed, muddled life about [him]." [9] One might well describe the characters and situations in the

6. Anderson, *A Story Teller's Story*, p. 217.
7. Ibid., p. 237.
8. Jones and Rideout, eds., *Letters of Sherwood Anderson*, p. 92.
9. Ibid., p. 93.

first two novels as repressed and muddled—the words seem appropriate to the content of all of Anderson's work. However, there is a big change between the first two novels and the short fiction, and it is a radical stylistic change, effected in part by the influence of Gertrude Stein. The style in the Winesburg stories is not the realistic, conventional prose style of the period, but rather a vastly simplified kind of writing in which image, rhythm, and what Anderson calls "word color" stand out sharply as the crucial elements in the writing. This is because Anderson has changed his choices of words and the structuring of his sentences.

A passage from *Windy McPherson's Son* beside one from *Winesburg, Ohio* will reveal the change in style. Each passage describes a man living in a town in the Midwest who is remarkable for his unusual appearance. From *Windy McPherson's Son:*

> At the age of forty-five John Telfer was a tall, slender, fine looking man, with black hair and a little black pointed beard, and with something lazy and care-free in his every movement and impulse. Dressed in white flannels, with white shoes, a jaunty cap upon his head, eyeglasses hanging from a gold chain, and a cane lightly swinging from his hand, he made a figure that might have passed unnoticed on the promenade before some fashionable summer hotel, but that seemed a breach of the laws of nature when seen on the streets of a corn-shipping town in Iowa. And Telfer was aware of the extraordinary figure he cut; it was a part of his programme of life. Now as Sam approached he laid a hand on Freedom Smith's shoulder to check the song, and, with his eyes twinkling with good-humour, began thrusting with his cane at the boy's feet.[1]

From "Paper Pills" in *Winesburg, Ohio:*

> He was an old man with a white beard and huge nose and hands. Long before the time during which we will know him, he was a doctor and drove a jaded white horse from house to house through the streets of Winesburg. Later he married a girl who had money. She had been left a large fertile farm when her father died. The girl was quiet, tall, and dark, and to many people she seemed very beautiful. Everyone in Winesburg wondered why she married the doctor. Within a year after the marriage she died.
>
> The knuckles of the doctor's hands were extraordinarily large. When the hands were closed they looked like clusters of unpainted wooden balls as large as walnuts fastened together by steel rods. He smoked a cob pipe and after his wife's death sat all day in his empty office close by a window that was covered with cobwebs. He never opened the window. Once on a hot day in August he tried but found it stuck fast and after that he forgot all about it. (p. 35) [13–14]

1. Sherwood Anderson, *Windy McPherson's Son* (University of Chicago Press, 1965), p. 5.

The differences in these two passages reveal the emergence of Anderson's expressionistic style. The passage from *Windy McPherson's Son* (155 words) consists of four long sentences, three of which are compound-complex in construction. The same number of words from the *Winesburg, Ohio* passage compose ten sentences, four of which are simple, and none of which are compound-complex. The immediate effect of radically simplifying the sentences is to make their content stand out more sharply. Although we are given considerable information about John Telfer in the *McPherson* passage—he is tall, slender, fine-looking, with black hair and pointed beard, and is lazy, carefree, good-humored, and an elegant dresser—the portrait is nonetheless blurred by the arrangement of the details in a series of qualifying phrases. In the second sentence of the *McPherson* passage the details of Telfer's appearance have even less impact because of the delay in identifying the subject ("he") they modify. In the *Winesburg* passage the effect of the shorter sentences with so few subordinate clauses is to render the information about Dr. Reefy with clarity and conciseness. Moreover, there is a rhythm to these short declarative sentences that makes the information solid and incontrovertible, rhetorically unimpeachable statements of fact, not subject to the delays, qualifications, or elaborations in the *McPherson* paragraph.

There is also the difference in point of view. While the *McPherson* passage is propositionally a much denser text, the importance of the information is diminished by being interpreted, evaluated for the reader by an omniscient narrator. We are told that Telfer is fine-looking, but that he appears to be lazy and carefree. We are told that he cuts a strange figure in a corn-shipping town in Iowa. The omniscient narrator also informs us of Telfer's awareness of the impression he creates. The reader is a passive recipient of this information. In the *Winesburg* passage, on the other hand, the lexical items are not interpreted, nor is the staging of the text. The old man (Dr. Reefy) has a white beard, and huge nose and hands, but we are not told if they are attractive or ugly. Nor are we given a source of information for this portrait. The story begins, "He was an old man," presupposing in the use of a pronoun rather than a name that information has preceded. Then the speech situation shifts to "we" and later to "everyone's" point of view. Anderson risks coherence in these shifts in point of view and also in the shifts of subject, from "he" to "she" in the first paragraph to the doctor's hands as subject in paragraph two. This technique foregrounds the art of the story, making us aware of a story being told through many perspectives, rather than a scene being reported as in the *McPherson* passage. It is the difference between a formal, written description of characters and events and oral storytelling.

"How fond we both are of sentences," Stein wrote to Anderson, recommending some of her own in *The Making of Americans.*[2] The sentence was a subject they frequently discussed, and it remained central to their concept of what was new and important in their art. In 1929, Stein tells Anderson, "I am working fairly steadily on the sentence . . . I struggled all last year with grammar, vocabulary is easier, and now I think before more grammar I must find out what is the essence of a sentence."[3] And in his defense of Stein in the *Atlantic Monthly* in 1934, Anderson talks about words and sentences as the materials of the craft and says he has "often heard sentences on the street that glow like jewels." In the same essay he praises Hemingway: "The man can make sentences. He is one of the few American writers who can."[4]

Anderson wrote frequently about the power of sentences to reveal the life within:

> There are sentences written by all writers of note in all countries that have their roots deep down in the life about them. The sentences are like windows looking into houses. Something is suddenly torn aside, all ties, all trickery about life, gone for the moment.[5]

The bedrock of simple sentences in Anderson's prose signals a paring down to the basic experiences and thoughts of the character. The essential facts about Dr. Reefy's life are telescoped into just a few short sentences in the passage cited. The repetitive rhythm of those sentences with their coordinating conjunctions allows Anderson to express an element of fatality to the doctor's life. Repetition was more crucial to Stein's delineation of character *in Three Lives,* but Anderson also uses repetition to get at the essential nature of his character. Here the detail of the doctor's huge hands is repeated and exemplified in a grotesque image of hands like clusters of unpainted wooden balls. The other item repeated is the fact of his wife's death. The old man's strange appearance and his isolation are linked by his repetition, which suggests some inner truth about the character.

Anderson also wrote about the power of individual words to reveal the life within, and once again he credits Gertrude Stein with awakening him to the expressionist power of language. He compares first reading Stein somewhere around 1915 to the excitement of exploring a new and wonderful country, a sort of Lewis and Clark expedition:

> Here were words laid before me as the painter had laid the color pans on the table in my presence. My mind did a kind of jerking flop and after Miss Stein's book had come into my hands I spent days going about with a tablet of paper in my pocket and making new and strange combinations of words. The result was I thought

2. White, ed., *Anderson/Stein: Correspondence,* p. 49.
3. Ibid., p. 68.
4. Ibid., p. 81.
5. Anderson, *A Story Teller's Story,* p. 237.

> a new familiarity with the words of my own vocabulary. . . . Perhaps it was then I really fell in love with words, wanted to give each word I used every chance to show itself at its best.[6]

Anderson was describing the period when he began the Winesburg stories. Stein instilled in Anderson a new respect and love for good solid Anglo-Saxon words from common life. In the preface to *Geography and Plays*, he wrote that "here is one artist who has been able to accept ridicule . . . to go live among the little housekeeping words, the swaggering bullying street-corner words, the honest working, money saving words."[7] And in his essay on Stein in "Four American Impressions" he describes her as a woman in a great kitchen of words, making wonderful preserves from the words of our English speech. In this essay and elsewhere he talks about the sensuality of words. In her kitchen, he writes, Stein "is laying word against word, relating sound to sound, feeling for the taste, the smell, the rhythm of the individual word."[8] It is when words have color and smell, Anderson suggests, that they can convey "the life within."

The paragraphs cited earlier from *Windy McPherson's Son* and *Winesburg, Ohio* again illustrate the way Anderson dramatically sharpened his use of language by the time he wrote the Winesburg tales. Anderson's style was never what might be described as "learned." There is never an abundance of Latinate words in his vocabulary. A marked distinction between the two texts, however, can be seen in the frequent use of vague, unspecific words and phrases in the first passage and uninterpreted, clear, hard, denotative language in the second. Words and phrases like "fine looking," "something lazy and care-free," "might have passed unnoticed," "breach of the laws of nature," and "programme of life" lack specificity. They are suggestive, but not clear or focused in their reference. In the Winesburg passage there are no words or phrases that are comparably vague and suggestive; solid Anglo-Saxon nouns like "horse," "house," "knuckles," and "hands" and adjectives like "huge," "jaded," "large," "tall," "dark," and "empty" are simple and clear in reference. There are no clauses in the conditional mode ("might have passed unnoticed"), no inflated phrases like "a breach of the laws of nature" or "programme of life" that might call for explication. Words that convey simple statements of fact reveal directly the bleak, narrow confines of Dr. Reefy's existence as something innate and inescapable, whereas the unusual character of John Telfer in the first passage is never clearly defined or felt; it is something the reader is told.

"One works with words," wrote Anderson about Stein, "and one would like words that have a perfume to the nostrils, rattling words one can throw into a box and shake, making a sharp, jingling sound, words

6. Ibid., p. 263.
7. White, ed., *Anderson/Stein: Correspondence*, p. 17.
8. Ibid., p. 24.

that, when seen on the printed page, have a distinct arresting effect upon the eye."[9] In the simile describing Dr. Reefy's hands, Anderson releases the physicality of the words used. The doctor's knuckles are like "clusters of unpainted wooden balls as large as walnuts fastened together by steel rods." The words are arresting because of their unusual use in this descriptive context. The words are familiar from farm and workshop ("the little housekeeping words . . . the honest working, money saving words"), but in this context they achieve a curiously poetic quality. The twisted, grotesque character to the doctor's inner life is expressed in a powerfully visible way. As Linda W. Wagner has observed, the emotional life of each character in *Winesburg, Ohio* is presented graphically rather than rhetorically;[1] that is, we are made to see and experience for ourselves the inner life of the character, rather than being told about it.

The result is not realism but expressionism. Reality and art are always separate, Anderson argued, and although realism may be very good journalism, it is always bad art.[2] Anderson was often told that in *Winesburg, Ohio* he had given an exact picture of Ohio village life, but he said that in fact the idea for his characters came from observing his fellow lodgers in a Chicago boardinghouse, not from recalling the villagers of his youth. On other occasions, however, he would credit memories of Clyde, Ohio, as the source of the book. Both statements are probably true and reveal something of his method as an expressionist writer. In his "A Note on Realism" and in his *Memoirs*, Anderson describes his method of creating character. He explains that he would try in his writing to get at "some inner truth" of a character that he had observed, but would then put that character into the physical body of another to see if the essence of the characterization remained intact.[3] Sometimes boardinghouse residents would merge with remembered figures from Clyde. In that way the character would become a denizen of Anderson's imaginative world, no longer an individual realistically observed and drawn "true to life," but a character whose essential being transcended the physical body of the prototype, assuming other external features more expressive of the individual's essential nature.

Another major change in Anderson's writing when he moved from the early novels to the Winesburg stories was a shift away from plot. As an expressionist drama, there is little development of a story line in the Winesburg tales in terms of cause and effect. Typically a story begins with a physical description of the central character, emphasizing some grotesque feature or trait. Then, usually in relation to George Willard as listener, something of the character's past history is revealed (a deser-

9. Ibid., p. 16.
1. Linda W. Wagner, "Sherwood, Stein, The Sentence, and Grape Sugar and Oranges," in Anderson, ed., *Dimensions of His Literary Art*, p. 82.
2. *Sherwood Anderson's Notebook*, p. 76.
3. *Sherwood Anderson's Memoirs: A Critical Edition*, ed. Ray Lewis White (Chapel Hill: University of North Carolina Press, 1969), p. 348.

tion, a death in the family, an unwanted pregnancy). The story usually ends with the character committing a desperate act (getting drunk, shouting in the streets, striking at the newspaper reporter), then fleeing temporarily from the town. By means of distortion and repetition, rather than plot, Anderson is able to reveal something about the hidden inner life of his characters and about the nature of society.

In Anderson's view, the chief obstacle to exploring fully the world of the imagination was the conventional demand for plot. Refusing to acknowledge the importance of plot in fiction became a point of honor with Anderson. Repeatedly in his writings he blames his lack of commercial success on the fact that he would not craft his stories on the formula of de Maupassant or O. Henry, writers whom he considered slick. In *A Story Teller's Story* he writes heatedly on the subject, distinguishing plot from form:

> There was a notion that ran through all story telling in America, that stories must be built about a plot and that absurd Anglo-Saxon notion that they must point a moral, uplift the people, make better citizens, etc., etc. The magazines were filled with these plot stories and most of the plays on our stage were plot plays. "The Poison Plot" I called it in conversation with my friends as the plot notion did seem to me to poison all story telling. What was wanted I thought was form, not plot, an altogether more elusive and difficult thing to come at.[4]

True form, he wrote in his defense of Stein, emerges from words and sentences. Again, drawing an analogy with painting, he wrote that words have color value, and therein lies true form.[5] Writing to Paul Rosenfeld in 1921, he said that he would not be bound by the critic's idea of form, for if he wrapped his packages up more neatly, he would lose the "large, loose sense of life" he was after. In the same letter, he added: "One thing I would like you to know is this: as far as I am concerned, I can accept no standard I have ever seen as to form. What I most want is to be and remain always an experimenter, an adventurer."[6] When he was actually writing the Winesburg stories in 1917, he called them fragments.[7]

This approach is evident in "Tandy," a Winesburg piece with no plot or story line at all. Three characters appear in the sketch: an agnostic widower, his daughter, who is still a child, and a red-haired young man who has come to live in Winesburg and hopes there to overcome his alcoholism. The only character with a name is the widower, Tom Hard. He befriends the young stranger, but the latter does not stop drinking. The only event that takes place is when the drunken stranger one eve-

4. Anderson, *A Story Teller's Story*, p. 255.
5. White, ed., *Anderson/Stein: Correspondence*, pp. 82–3.
6. Jones and Rideout, eds., *Letters of Sherwood Anderson*, p. 72.
7. Ibid., p. 11.

ning drops to the knees and tells the little girl to be "Tandy," the quality in a woman of being "brave enough to dare to be loved" (p. 145)[79]. The point of the sketch is to reveal something that is missing in human relationships—courage for sexual expression in women. It is not the study of an individual—the stranger remains nameless—but of a profound psychological need. Plot is sacrificed to the expressionist's concern to reveal another dimension to a repressive society. Like much expressionist drama, this sketch is pared down to a monologue designed to release the expressionist scream.

3

Anderson's vision of life in *Winesburg, Ohio* is tied directly to the expressionist form of his stories. The narrator in the introductory sketch tells us simply that there is no such thing as truth, but that there are a great many thoughts, that is, many ways of viewing life, all of which are valid. But human beings, he says, have insisted on experiencing life from just one vantage point, which becomes a position of truth. This distorted view of the world in turn distorts the viewer, who becomes a grotesque, a character "all drawn out of shape." That phrase describes the characters remembered by the old writer in the introduction and subsequently the characters in the stories that follow.

Anderson has made each of his characters memorable by means of a bizarre physical trait or a stylized gesture that isolates the individual from society. Dr. Reefy is not the only character with unusual hands. "Hands" is the title of the first story, the tragedy of an effeminate schoolteacher who tries to reach out to others through touch, but whose motives are misunderstood. The narrator says that the constant movement of Wing Biddlebaum's hands is like "the beating of the wings of an imprisoned bird" (p. 28) [10]. In "Respectability," Wash Williams is described as monstrously ugly and dirty like a baboon; even the whites of his eyes look soiled. Yet "he took care of his hands," which are shapely and sensitive (p. 121) [64]. Hands dramatize the individual's deep need for connection to others. Even minor characters are sometimes remarkable for their hands. Tom Willy, the saloon keeper, has a flaming birthmark on his hands. When he becomes excited talking to one of his customers, he rubs his hands together, and the red deepens in color "as though the hands had been dipped in blood" (p. 50) [22]. Other characters, such as Kate Swift, the teacher, and Elmer Cowley, in " 'Queer,' " make their hands into fists and beat at George Willard in a desperate desire to communicate to him some painful truth that they cannot wholly articulate. The Reverend Curtis Hartman puts his fist through the window of the church study. Hands provide a particularly striking aspect of Anderson's expressionist portraits. These hands do not participate in the public handshake or in the caress of lovers, but like the bleeding fist of Reverend Hartman, they signal the pain and the frustrated desire of these characters to make connections to others.

The eyes of the Winesburg characters are also described in a way that reveals something twisted and obsessive in their nature. The soiled whites of Wash Williams's eyes reflect his vision of the foulness of women. The tiny bloodshot eyes of the baker, Abner Groff, convey the scope of his narrow existence as he seeks revenge on a neighborhood alley cat. In the description of Dr. Parcival's eyes, Anderson uses an elaborate simile to render vividly something alien and closeted in this figure. There was something strange about his eyes, says the narrator: "The lid of the left eye twitched; it fell down and snapped up; it was exactly as though the lid of the eye were a window shade and someone stood inside the doctor's head playing with the cord" (p. 49) [22]. Dr. Parcival's refusal of medical assistance when a little girl is thrown from a buggy is like the closing of the window shade. He is left alone with the conviction that someday he will be crucified.

There is a venerable literary tradition of eyes being expressive and central to communication (the poetry of courtly love and Shakespeare's sonnets spring to mind); thus, when a character's eyes are clouded or in any way unusual, interpersonal contact is threatened. On her deathbed, Elizabeth Willard is paralyzed and can no longer speak, but her eyes remain very much alive. She communicates to her son, without the use of words, her desire that he express something for them both: "in her eyes there was an appeal so touching that all who saw it kept the memory of the dying woman in their minds for years" (p. 230) [128]. But the eyes of Jesse Bentley that flame with the passionate burning things in his nature are blind with regard to others, and as he grows older his left eyelid develops an uncontrollable twitch. Similarly, his grandson, David Hardy, has "a habit of looking at things and people a long time without appearing to see what he [is] looking at" (p. 75) [37]. One of the most alien figures in the book, the albino-like Elmer Cowley, has eyes almost bleached of any color: "his eyes were blue with the colorless blueness of the marbles called 'aggies' that the boys of Winesburg carried in their pockets" (p. 194) [108].

The recurring attention to hands and eyes is part of the expressionist method of repetition. Stein explains her use of repetition as a way of approaching the essence of a character, for she argues that people, carefully observed, are seen to repeat themselves, and in so doing they reveal their essential or ground nature. Anderson focuses on the repetitive behavior of his characters—Dr. Reefy writing down his truths on little pieces of paper, Joe Welling talking excitedly about ideas to casual passersby, Alice Hindman taking her lonely walks. But in his larger vision of a repressed society—"everyone in America really hunger[ing] for a more direct and subtle expression of our common lives than we have ever yet had"[8]—he describes many people living in similar circumstances, enacting the same gestures, so that "the almost universal insanity of society"[9] becomes boldly clear. Even family living patterns are stylized by repetition. Boys and young men in the stories live alone with poor old women (mothers, aunts, grandmothers); they live on the margins of the town. Similarly, young women most often live alone with their fathers, or sometimes their brothers. There are no whole families in the book suggesting complete or fulfilled relationships; Anderson's vision is one of repression, loneliness, and the absence of love. As Walter B. Rideout has observed, the setting is one of the repeated elements in the story. In seventeen of the twenty-two stories, the crisis scene takes place in the evening; some kind of light—a lamp, a fire, some lingering light in the sky—partly relieves the gathering dark. Most of the tales end with the characters going off into total darkness.[1]

But even more striking in *Winesburg, Ohio* is the pattern of people in motion who form something like a procession of the living dead. We know that he thought about the frustrated and defeated characters in his early stories as among the living dead, for he described them in a letter to M. D. Finley, 2 December 1916, as building walls of fear around themselves, inside of which they die.[2] In an earlier letter to Finley he used the image of the procession as part of this vision:

> At times there comes over me a terrible conviction that I am living in a city of the dead. In the office dead voices discuss dead ideas. I go into the street and long rows of dead faces march past. Once I got so excited and terrified that I began to run through the streets. I had a mad impulse to shout, to strike people with my fist. I wanted terribly to awaken them.[3]

This was Anderson's vision of Puritan America. In the introductory sketch, "The Book of the Grotesque," the old writer has a waking dream wherein all the people he has known are being driven in a long procession before his eyes. Afterward he creeps out of bed and writes down what he has seen, describing all the people as grotesques because they live by one truth. These are the characters of Anderson's book, originally titled "The Book of the Grotesque" instead of *Winesburg, Ohio*. The image of the procession is evoked in almost every tale by the central character breaking into a run when he or she reaches a point of insupportable frustration.

Kate Swift, the schoolteacher, is a conventional unmarried woman in

8. Anderson, *A Story Teller's Story*, p. 234.
9. Jones and Rideout, eds., *Letters of Sherwood Anderson*, p. 44.
1. See Rideout, "The Simplicity of *Winesburg, Ohio*," p. 149. Other repeated images and motifs in the book are discussed by Monika Fludernik in " 'The Divine Accident of Life': Metaphoric Structure and Meaning in *Winesburg, Ohio*," *Style* 22 (Spring 1988): 116–35.
2. Sutton, ed., *Letters to Bab*, pp. 17–18.
3. Ibid., p. 15.

the eyes of the townspeople, but, within, her passionate nature yearns for companionship and significant achievement. She takes long walks alone at night; one night she walks for six hours. She half loves her former pupil, George Willard, and in her desire to see his talent as a writer flower, she goes to the newspaper office one night to talk to him. But confused by her love for the boy, she cannot express herself adequately and winds up beating him with her fists, then running out into the darkness. That same night, Reverend Hartman, who for weeks has paced the streets at night imploring God to keep him from his sinful habit of peeping into Kate Swift's bedroom window, bursts into the Winesburg *Eagle* office, shaking a bleeding fist, having broken the window of the church study.

Repeatedly, inarticulate characters in a moment of passion wave their hands in the air and burst into a run. Tom Foster, the shy gentle boy in "Drink," falls in love with the banker's daughter, Helen White. The relationship is socially impossible, and one night Tom goes for a long walk and becomes drunk on a bottle of whiskey. He becomes a grotesque figure moving along the road: "His head seemed to be flying about like a pinwheel and then projecting itself off into space and his arms and legs flopped helplessly about" (p. 218) [121]. Jesse Bentley, in "Godliness," who has a vision of being a biblical patriarch, runs through the night begging God to send him a son; years later, when he takes his grandson to sacrifice a lamb, hoping God will finally send a visible sign of his blessing, the scene ends with the flight of the terrified boy from Winesburg. In "Adventure," Alice Hindman, who has been waiting many years for the return of her lover, one night runs out onto the lawn in the rain naked. In the story of the two farmhands, entitled "The Untold Lie," the moment of truth brings Ray Pearson to run across the fields to save his friend, Hal Winters, from marriage.

The most vivid scenes in the book are those of characters in grotesque or violent motion: Elizabeth Willard wearing men's clothes and riding a bicycle through the town's main street; Louise Bentley, the estranged daughter of the biblical patriarch, driving her horse and carriage at breakneck speed through the streets of Winesburg; Jesse Bentley's drunken brothers driving along the road shouting at the stars; Hal Winters's father, Windpeter Winters, drunk and driving his team along the railroad tracks directly into the path of an onrushing locomotive. The repetition of such images expresses powerfully the frustration and despair felt by the characters in the small Ohio town. These gestures are another form of the expressionist scream.

4

Considering *Winesburg, Ohio* as an expressionist work further illuminates its historical significance in American literary history. Anderson has long been recognized as an innovator in style, influenced by the vernacular of Mark Twain and responsive to the prose experiments of Gertrude Stein. What Richard Bridgman sees as innovative in Anderson's style is his ability to write in the American vernacular (and its colloquial rhythms) without the use of a child or fool as first-person narrator. Twain used Huckleberry Finn to write in a uniquely American voice; Ring Lardner used Jack Keefe.[4] Anderson, on the other hand, actually established the simple style and its colloquial rhythms as an independent American prose medium.[5] His attempts to forge this unique American voice are seen to flower in the prose style of Ernest Hemingway. But the extent of that influence goes further than Hemingway, and I shall suggest in conclusion that Anderson's expressionist experiments were bolder than Hemingway's and consequently more far-reaching.

In the mainstream of American writing, Anderson's expressionist style represents a sharp break with both realism (including the writing of the naturalists) and impressionism. The latter term is used to describe the psychological realism of Henry James and those he influenced, that is to say, a style of writing that is always suggestive, ambiguous, and heavily dependent on symbolism. The sentences in an impressionist text are characteristically compound-complex, with many qualifying subordinate clauses, and these sentences are often cast in the conditional mode. At the heart of an impressionist novel or story is an experience, emotion, or idea that cannot be explained, only approached obliquely—in what James called a presentiment or what Willa Cather termed "the thing not named." The impressionists (Conrad and Ford were the most eloquent on the subject) acknowledge the relativity of truth, but it is also an aesthetic of evasion, an art of secrets.

Anderson also acknowledged the relativity of truth. At the center of *Winesburg, Ohio* there is despair over the book's central mission—"to express something" for his characters. The view of art in the book undercuts that goal. The artists in *Winesburg, Ohio,* like the old man in the introductory sketch and like Enoch Robinson, are among the least capable of communicating to others, either in their life gestures or in their art. One of the pivotal insights in the book is the realization that comes to Alice Hindman after her adventure on the front lawn: "that many people must live and die alone, even in Winesburg" (p. 120) [64]. But Anderson does not retreat with this insight to an art of suggestion, of half-guessed truths. He records instead the struggle to communicate, the effort and the frustration of individuals to explain who they really are. The characters in his fiction are grotesque; yet they are rendered whole in their efforts to express themselves.

4. A fictional baseball pitcher who colorfully narrates a series of Lardner's stories, some of which were collected in *You Know Me Al* (1916) and *Treat 'Em Rough* (1918) [*Editors*].
5. Richard Bridgman, *The Colloquial Style in America* (Oxford University Press, 1966), p. 153.

"Loneliness," the story of Enoch Robinson, can be viewed as an allegorical statement about art. Robinson is a painter who is remembered in Winesburg as a quiet, dreamy youth. When he was twenty-one he went to New York City, where he attended art school and studied French, hoping some day to finish his art education in Paris. Robinson does not get to France, but it seems likely that the masters with whom he wanted to study there were from the impressionist school. This is reinforced by the description of one of the paintings he shows to a group of artist friends gathered in his room facing Washington Square. Robinson has painted a scene on a country road near Winesburg. In the picture is a clump of elder bushes, inside of which is the body of a woman thrown from a horse. A farmer passing by is shown looking anxiously about in the picture. The woman who has been hurt is at the center of the painting: "She lies quite still, white and still," thinks Robinson, "and the beauty comes out from her and spreads over everything. It is in the sky back there and all around everywhere." But the woman, in fact, is not shown in the picture at all: "I didn't paint the woman, of course. She is too beautiful to be painted" (p. 170) [93]. Robinson's painting accords with the aesthetic of the impressionist painter and the literary symbolist, where everything depends on the suggestive power of "the thing not named." But what is significant in the story is that Robinson's painting fails to communicate anything to the audience of friends. They talk of line values and composition, but experience nothing of the emotion that went into the picture. The failure of Robinson's impressionist aesthetic is paralleled in his failure to develop as a man—he remains withdrawn and childlike and retreats into the companionship of imagined people whose presences are threatened every time he comes into contact with real flesh-and-blood people. Robinson's aesthetic fails him, and he becomes "an obscure, jerky little figure, bobbing up and down on the streets of an Ohio town," but Anderson's expressionist art of simplifying, distorting, and exaggerating has rendered Enoch Robinson's character vividly. We learn as much as can be known about this character in a third-person narrative.

Sherwood Anderson argued that good writing has the strong color and form of a Cézanne painting.[6] Hemingway also liked to hold up Cézanne as an artistic model and attributed to the painter important influences on his writing. But in fact, the technical features of the Hemingway style—the choice of language, the structuring of the sentences—have their antecedent in Anderson's prose. What Hemingway learned from Anderson was the power of non-literary words, the four-letter Anglo-Saxon words with their direct appeal to the senses and their hard denotative surfaces. He also learned from Anderson that the arranging of these words in short declarative sentences could have enormous power.

6. White, ed., *Anderson/Stein: Correspondence*, p. 83.

> Dick Boulton looked at the doctor. Dick was a big man. He knew how big a man he was. He liked to get into fights. He was happy. Eddy and Billy Tabeshaw leaned on their canthooks and looked at the doctor. The doctor chewed the beard on his lower lip and looked at Dick Boulton. Then he turned away and walked up the hill to the cottage.[7]

In the structuring of sentences, he learned especially how effective conjunctions were instead of subordinate clauses to convey uninterpreted statements of fact. Subordination creates a hierarchical value structure in a sentence, the main clause being of greatest significance, whereas the use of conjunctions (polysyndeton) gives all the clauses equal value. Implicit in this stylistic choice is the intent to describe and the refusal to judge. This technique is fundamental to Hemingway's clear, hard, nonimpressionistic prose.[8]

Throughout his career Anderson saw himself as an experimental writer. He wrote to Van Wyck Brooks in March 1919, saying that "I want constantly to push out into experimental fields. 'What can be done in prose that has not been done?' I keep asking myself."[9] In his novels in the 1920s, he resisted the formal strictures of plot in favor of looser narrative structures that would include, as he said in the same letter to Brooks, "the purely fanciful side of a man's life, the odds and ends of thought, the little pockets of thoughts and emotions that are so seldom touched."[1] In a letter to Alfred Stieglitz, he described *Dark Laughter* as "a 'fantasy' rather than a novel," with "no realism in it."[2] Hemingway, in order to dispel the anxiety of influence he felt in relation to his literary mentor, wrote *The Torrents of Spring* (1926) to expose what he felt were the thematic weaknesses and stylistic mannerisms of Anderson's fiction. But, ironically, those elements of Anderson's prose he highlighted—the dimension of fantasy, the exaggerated comic-book characters, the loose plot structure, and especially the self-reflexive asides between author and reader—have become valued features of contemporary postmodern fiction. *Winesburg, Ohio* is a classic work of fiction about small-town life in the American Midwest, but as an expressionist work it has a further significance in American literary history in that it provides an important link between the modernism of the first quarter of this century and American writing today.

7. Ernest Hemingway, *In Our Time* (New York: Scribner, 1958), p. 28.
8. Paul P. Somers, Jr., "The Mark of Sherwood Anderson on Hemingway: A Look at the Texts," *South Atlantic Quarterly* 73 (Autumn 1972): 487–503, suggests that Anderson's influence on Hemingway was chiefly in the use of colloquial language, that matters of syntax were learned from Gertrude Stein. Although it is not possible to determine this question of influence with certainty, it is clear nonetheless that Anderson demonstrated to Hemingway the usable features of Stein's literary experiments.
9. Jones and Rideout, eds., *Letters of Sherwood Anderson*, p. 46. [For Brooks, see p. 154, n. 3, above—*Editors*.]
1. Ibid.
2. Ibid., p. 129.

Sherwood Anderson: A Chronology

1876	Born Sept. 13 in Camden, Ohio, third of seven children of Irwin M. and Emma Smith Anderson.
1884	Family moves to Clyde, Ohio.
1895	Mother's death.
1896	Moves to Chicago, works as laborer.
1898–99	Serves in U.S. Army during Spanish-American War, stationed in Cuba after war.
1899	Works during summer with threshing crew near Clyde; in fall enrolls in college preparatory program at Wittenberg Academy, Springfield, Ohio.
1900	Completes studies, moves to Chicago, becomes copywriter for advertising firm.
1902	Begins writing a series of essays published over a three-year period in *Agricultural Advertising*.
1904	Marries Cornelia Lane; honeymoon trip to Tennessee and St. Louis World's Fair.
1906	Moves to Cleveland to become head of mail-order business.
1907	Moves to Elyria, Ohio, becomes head of mail-order paint company; birth of first son, Robert Lane Anderson.
1908	Birth of second son, John Sherwood Anderson.
1911	Birth of daughter, Marion Anderson.
1912	Abruptly walks out of office on Nov. 28, shows up three days later in Cleveland in confused mental state.
1913	Returns to Chicago in Feb., lives on South Side near artists' and writers' colony, resumes copywriting; spends winter with his family at cabin in Ozark Mountains in Missouri.
1914	Returns to Chicago and advertising; takes room at 735 Cass St.; publishes first story, "The Rabbit-Pen," in July.
1915	Begins writing *Winesburg* stories in fall.
1916	*Winesburg* stories begin to appear in periodicals; divorced from Cornelia Lane Anderson; spends summer at Upper Lake Chateaugay, N.Y.; marries Tennessee Mitchell there; *Windy McPherson's Son* (novel).

1917	Returns to Upper Lake Chateaugay in summer; *Marching Men* (novel).
1918	Lives in New York City during fall; *Mid-American Chants* (poetry).
1919	*Winesburg, Ohio* published in May.
1920	Spends winter and spring in Mobile and Fairhope, Ala.; in fall moves to Palos Park, near Chicago; *Poor White* (novel).
1921	Visits Europe during summer; *The Triumph of the Egg* (stories).
1922	Lives in New Orleans during winter; moves to New York in August.
1923	Moves to Reno, Nev., in Feb.; *Many Marriages* (novel) and *Horses and Men* (stories).
1924	Divorced from Tennessee Mitchell Anderson; marries Elizabeth Prall; moves to New Orleans in July; lecture tour in fall and winter; *A Story Teller's Story* (memoir).
1925	Spends part of summer in Troutdale, Va.; lecture tour in fall and winter; *Dark Laughter* (novel).
1926	Buys farm near Troutdale, moves there and builds house; leaves for Europe in Dec.; *Sherwood Anderson's Notebook* (essays and notes) and *Tar: A Midwest Childhood* (fictionalized autobiography).
1927	Returns from Europe in March; buys two weekly newspapers at Marion, Va., becomes editor and publisher; *A New Testament* (poetry).
1929	Begins to turn over newspapers to son, Robert; travel to Florida, New York State, and Washington, D.C.; *Hello Towns!* (newspaper selections).
1931	Travel, mostly in the South; *Perhaps Women* (essays).
1932	Lecture tour in spring; divorced from Elizabeth Prall Anderson; to Amsterdam in August to attend peace conference; *Beyond Desire* (novel).
1933	Spends winter in Kansas City; marries Eleanor Copenhaver; to New York City in fall; *Death in the Woods* (stories).
1934	Travel for *Today* magazine; to Media, Pa., in spring to help prepare dramatic version of *Winesburg, Ohio* at Hedgerow Theatre; *No Swank* (essays).
1935	Spends much of winter at Brownsville and Corpus Christi, Tex.; *Puzzled America* (essays).
1936	Trip to Southwest during winter; *Kit Brandon* (novel).
1937	To Corpus Christi in winter; attends writers' conference at Boulder, Colo., in Aug.; *Plays: Winesburg and Others* (plays).
1938	Trip to Southwest and Mexico in winter.

1939 Lectures at Olivet College (Mich.) in Jan. and July; to California in fall.

1940 Lives in New York City much of year; *Home Town* (prose sketches with photographs).

1941 Begins trip to South America Feb. 28; becomes ill on ship, dies of peritonitis, March 8, at Colón, Panama; buried at Marion, Va., on March 26.

Selected Bibliography

LETTERS AND MEMOIRS

Jones, Howard Mumford, and Walter B. Rideout, eds. *Letters of Sherwood Anderson.* Boston: Little, Brown, 1953.

Modlin, Charles E., ed. *Sherwood Anderson's Love Letters to Eleanor Copenhaver Anderson.* Athens: U of Georgia P, 1989.

———, ed. *Sherwood Anderson: Selected Letters.* Knoxville: U of Tennessee P, 1984.

Sutton, William A., ed. *Letters to Bab: Sherwood Anderson to Marietta D. Finley, 1916–33.* Urbana: U of Illinois P, 1985.

White, Ray Lewis, ed. *Sherwood Anderson's Memoirs: A Critical Edition.* Chapel Hill: U of North Carolina P, 1969.

BIBLIOGRAPHIES

Rideout, Walter B. "Sherwood Anderson." In *Sixteen Modern American Authors.* Ed. Jackson R. Bryer. Durham: Duke UP, 1989. Vol. 2, pp. 1–41.

Sheehy, Eugene P., and Kenneth A. Lohf. *Sherwood Anderson: A Bibliography.* Los Gatos, Cal.: Talisman Press, 1960.

White, Ray Lewis. *Sherwood Anderson: A Reference Guide.* Boston: Hall, 1977.

The Winesburg Eagle. Annual Sherwood Anderson checklist.

BIOGRAPHY AND CRITICISM

Anderson, David D., ed. *Critical Essays on Sherwood Anderson.* Boston: Hall, 1981.

———. *Sherwood Anderson: An Introduction and Interpretation.* New York: Holt, Rinehart & Winston, 1967.

———, ed. *Sherwood Anderson: Dimensions of His Literary Art.* East Lansing: Michigan State UP, 1976.

Appel, Paul P., ed. *Homage to Sherwood Anderson: 1876–1941.* Mamaroneck, N.Y.: Paul P. Appel, 1970.

Bredahl, A. Carl. " 'The Young Thing Within': Divided Narrative and Sherwood Anderson's *Winesburg, Ohio.*" *Midwest Quarterly* 27 (1986): 422–37.

Burbank, Rex. *Sherwood Anderson.* New York: Twayne, 1964.

Campbell, Hilbert H., and Charles E. Modlin, eds. *Sherwood Anderson: Centennial Studies.* Troy, N.Y.: Whitston, 1976.

Ciancio, Ralph. "'The Sweetness of the Twisted Apples': Unity of Vision in *Winesburg, Ohio.*" *PMLA* 87 (1972): 994–1006.

Cowley, Malcolm. Introduction. *Winesburg, Ohio.* New York: Viking Press, 1960.

Crowley, John W., ed. *New Essays on "Winesburg, Ohio."* Cambridge: Cambridge UP, 1990.

Ennis, Stephen C. "The Implied Community of *Winesburg, Ohio.*" *The Old Northwest* 11 (1985): 51–60.

Ferres, John H., ed. *"Winesburg, Ohio": Text and Criticism.* New York: Viking Press, 1966.

Fussell, Edwin. "*Winesburg, Ohio:* Art and Isolation." *Modern Fiction Studies* 6 (Summer 1960): 106–14.

Howe, Irving. *Sherwood Anderson.* New York: William Sloan Associates, 1951.

O'Neill, John. "Anderson Writ Large: 'Godliness' in *Winesburg, Ohio.*" *Twentieth Century Literature* 23 (1977): 67–83.

Papinchak, Robert Allen. *Sherwood Anderson: A Study of the Short Fiction.* New York: Twayne, 1992.

Phillips, William L. "How Sherwood Anderson Wrote *Winesburg, Ohio.*" *American Literature* 23 (1951): 7–30.

Rideout, Walter B., ed. *Sherwood Anderson: A Collection of Critical Essays*. Englewood Cliffs, N.J.: Prentice-Hall, 1974.
———. " 'The Tale of Perfect Balance': Sherwood Anderson's 'The Untold Lie.' " *Newberry Library Bulletin* 6 (1971): 243–50.
Schevill, James. *Sherwood Anderson: His Life and Work*. Denver: U of Denver P, 1951.
Small, Judy Jo. A *Reader's Guide to the Short Stories of Sherwood Anderson*. New York: Hall, 1994.
Stouck, David. "*Winesburg, Ohio* and the Failure of Art." *Twentieth Century Literature* 15 (October 1969): 145–51.
———. "*Winesburg, Ohio* as a Dance of Death." *American Literature* 48 (1977): 525–42.
Sutton, William A. *The Road to Winesburg: A Mosaic of the Imaginative Life of Sherwood Anderson*. Metuchen, N.J.: Scarecrow Press, 1972.
Taylor, Welford Dunaway. *Sherwood Anderson*. New York: Ungar, 1977.
Townsend, Kim. *Sherwood Anderson*. Boston: Houghton Mifflin, 1987.
White, Ray Lewis. "The Manuscripts of *Winesburg, Ohio*." *Winesburg Eagle* 11 (1985): 4–10.
———, ed. *The Merrill Studies in Winesburg, Ohio*. Columbus, Ohio: Charles E. Merrill Publishing Co., 1971.
———. "Of Time and *Winesburg, Ohio*: An Experiment in Chronology." *Modern Fiction Studies* 25 (1979–80): 658–66.
———, ed. *Sherwood Anderson: Essays in Criticism*. Chapel Hill: U of North Carolina P, 1966.
———. *"Winesburg, Ohio": An Exploration*. Boston: Twayne, 1990.
———. "*Winesburg, Ohio*: The Story Titles." *Winesburg Eagle* 10 (1984): 6–7.
Williams, Kenny J. A *Storyteller and a City: Sherwood Anderson's Chicago*. DeKalb: Northern Illinois UP, 1988.